Judson
Lavell

Fitch lays on his back facing up toward the jagged ceiling of the mine shaft. The rows of supporting beams overhead. His burning eyes wide open. His chest is void from any breath. His heart is still and silent. Not a single movement. Fitch is cold as a stone from a river. Then from the darkness of the cavern, Fitch begins to hear the heartbeats of a single bat. Then two. Then eight. Then forty. Then one hundred. Then the entire assembly of carnivorous creatures. The heartbeats are nearly deafening.

Thump-thump.

Thump-thump.

Thump-thump.

As swiftly as the racing bat heartbeats had toned into his consciousness, they are gone. Fitch hears the soft imprints of footsteps. Footsteps? Is someone drawing nearer? Is it Doc to come carry him away to his burial place? Has Cougar returned to finish the job? The footsteps continue. Louder and louder.

A desert tarantula slips along the edge of Fitch's boot, up along his pant leg, toward his waist then effortlessly walks along his wounded bat bitten torso. With each step of its eight legs, the sound of the tarantula's footsteps rattle inside of Fitch's head. Louder and louder until suddenly, vanishing. The tarantula slips off of Fitch's shoulder and continues along the rocky mine shaft floor until disappearing from sight into the blinding afternoon's sunlight.

Thump-thump.

Thump-thump.

Thump-thump.

SLINGER
MIDNIGHT RIDER

A NOVEL

BY

JUDSON LOVELL

COVER DESIGN BY
TAMERA LUCAS

SLINGER
MIDNIGHT RIDER

Lizard King Publications
PO Box 1133
Lincoln City, Oregon 97367

Mail Orders Welcome
$17.95
Purchaser Responsible For Own
Applicable Tax
Thank-you For Your Mail Order Purchase
For $17.95, I'll Cover The Shipping And
Handling For Single Edition Orders
USA Only Please…

INTRODUCTION

I began writing screenplays in February 1990. To date, I have written over five-hundred treatments, forty-five screenplays, four-four part television mini series, sixteen outlines for novels, numerous outlines for a series of novels, a spec script for what I felt *should have been* the next "Star Trek" motion picture, "Star Trek X", a pilot spec script for what I felt *should have been and still should be* the next "Star Trek" television series, as well as spec scripts for "Star Trek – Voyager" when it was still on the air. I even went to Paramount and had several pitch meetings for these spec scripts.

To no avail, I failed to play the "Hollywood Game". I have neither sold nor have had anything published. I've gotten close numerous times but have always fallen short. Through the 1990's, I diligently searched and attempted to obtain a Literary Agent. Again, I found myself wanting.

Now, since I have begun this journey of pen and plume at the end of this last century, I have experienced a roller coaster of circumstances which one could simply call, "LIFE". It has taken me longer than I had planned to resume my devotion and dedication to writing. So be it…

I have adapted this novel, "Slinger", from just one of my numerous original screenplays. Although I feel confident with my screenwriting skills and story telling ability, writing a novel is new to me. Please forgive my naïveness in this matter for I am a virgin and this is my first time.

Deepest Regards
Judson Lovell

Dedicated In Loving Memory

To

D. M. K.

CHAPTER I

Smoldering ash lays scattered throughout the high prairie grass covering a sloping lull in the hillside. A light breeze flutters the taller sections of the grass in a soothing and swaying motion as waves would roll over the open sea. A local hometown squad of young and robust firemen mill about the area stomping out flyaway cinders preventing possible flare-ups. The young firemen seem to be wearing a haphazard style of uniforms. Some in jeans and a fireman's jacket. Others wear full fireman gear. As yet others sport jeans, a t-shirt and a fireman's helmet.

An odd stillness has filled the air... deathly quiet. Not even the soothing sounds of the chirping swallows for this time of year. The only sound is the faint breeze rolling off the high prairie grass all around them. With the few remaining trickles of falling ash fluttering downward like a mid-spring snow, the rising sun just beyond the roll of the horizon casts amber and orange hues across the sky. Just a shadow at first, then a silhouette of an abandoned log cabin and decaying lean-to is seen this side of the sparse treeline.

The cabin appears to be in good order with wild grass running ramped all about the wrap-around porch. There are no window coverings or panes of glass to prevent the outer elements from coming inside. A sturdy wooden door hangs on worn leather hinges remains mostly closed left open just a crack to allow smaller critters inside away from the chilly desert nights. Covered with a think layer of cobwebs, a rusting horseshoe dangles directly about the upper frame of the door.

1

The roof is worn from the passing years and constant weather, scattering wooden shingles with sporadic gaps in its aging surface. The once thriving home is now but a shell, a dwelling for an assortment of spiders and other small varmints. Falling ash speckles the extended awning and remaining shingles of the roof. Then, from deep inside of the decaying structure, the faintest of sounds are heard. *Jingle-jingle.*

Although badly outdated, the local fire department's only vehicle, a mint condition 1939 John Deere firetruck is not but more than a few dozen yards from the burned out and charred remains of the main homestead some distance from the abandoned log cabin and swaying lean-to in the background.

Char and ash fill the nostrils of the young firemen as they toil their water hoses around the smoldering remnants of the structure. With the amount of fallen supporting beams, charred framing and an abundance of burned furnishing, the main house looks as if it were a two or three story home before its demise. Mountains of burned lumber and supporting beams lay in haphazard piles throughout the charred remains of chairs, beds, large wooden picture frames, dressers and various other Victorian furniture. All that remains throughout the desolate surroundings is a handful of shotgun and rifle barrels, a charred rocking chair on the porch and the towering chimney and hearth of the fireplace.

Fire Chief Bowman sadly wipes his soot covered brow as he turns and spies something heading their way from the narrow dirt road cutting through a break in the distant treeline. Turning, Bowman remorsefully watches the modern convertible zip along the narrow dirt road heading toward the property leaving billowing clouds of dust in its wake.

As the younger firemen begin rolling up their hoses and stowing their gear back into the classic John Deere firetruck, the convertible rolls to a halt along side of Bowman. The driver's door side of the sleek automobile flings open with a pair of red high heel shoes stepping outward. Nearly three times her age,

Bowman bashfully turns away just as a gust of breeze frills the young woman's short dress.

Sarah Jackson adjusts her dark framed sunglasses with a somber manner as she steps away from her car not bothering to close the door. Sarah moves with a stroll, a glide, more than purposely walking. Looking about herself, Sarah notices the decaying log cabin and rotting lean-to in the distance with the rising sun cresting over the sparsely shingled roof. Shrugging off the log cabin with a mere glance, Sarah begins to move toward the charred remains of the main house.

"We did the best that we could do, Sarah," Bowman replies with almost a whisper. "There was nothing that we could do. We got here as soon as we could." Bowman pauses clearing a knot in his throat. "I'm so sorry," Bowman attempts to be consoling as possible however Sarah's busty figure and continuing fluttering short dress is a constant distraction.

"I'm sure you and your boys did all that you could do," Sarah brushes away a few loose strands of her flowing red hair out from in front of her eyes as she continues to gander about. "Was there anything saved?"

Bowman motions along side of the charred out remains of the main house toward the towering chimney and hearth of the fireplace. "Yeah, we found a couple trinkets, some gun barrels and a pretty burned up hope chest. That's 'bout it."

"That's not what I meant," Sarah replies with a crackle in her voice. A few of the younger firemen, even somewhat attractive under different circumstances, approach Sarah in a consoling manner. A strapping fellow even offers his shoulder for her to cry on. Sarah politely smiles at the young fireman and brushes off the invitation. Bowman tenderly, even fatherly, takes Sarah by the arm leading her up the remains of the charred wrap-around porch.

"Are you ready for this, Sarah?"

"Yes, I think so," Sarah takes a deep breath.

Sarah clutches onto Bowman's thick arm more in need of moral support rather than guidance along the route. Bowman leads Sarah up along the remains of the rickety steps up onto the charred porch. The smell of smoldering cinders and burned timber fills the air. Sarah and Bowman pause a moment where the front door had once stood. The brass swan style door handle lies at her feet in a pile of ash. Taking a remorseful breath, Sarah forces herself inward with Bowman toddling along behind her like a lost puppy.

Sarah carefully steps around the fallen and burned knick-knacks cluttering the floor. A Persian floor rug squishes under her feet, saturated from the firemen's hoses. Bowman continues to follow Sarah through the maze of destruction. Sarah, from the direction that she is taking, seems to need no prompting about the floor plans. She knows her way around with her familiars returning to her.

"How long has it been since you've been to see her?"

"About three years now," Sarah sadly responds. It's funny, she thinks. She and Great Meme lived so close to each other and she never bothered to visit her as much as she used to. Funny... no, not really.

"She missed you," Bowman tries to smile as he takes out his pipe from jacket pocket and begins to clean out the smoked tobacco with his pinky.

"Yeah, I missed her, too."

"You meant a lot to her," Bowman shifts his plump weight from one foot to the other. He fumbles for something else to say while Sarah continues to head in deliberate directions throughout the charred remains of the Victorian furnishings. The Persian rug squishing under her high heels. "Does your mother know yet?"

"Yeah, she and Grandma will be flying in from back East in a few days."

"Well, at least you'll still have the three branches of the family tree."

"Family tree," Sarah almost laughs. "With our family, I wasn't even considered a sapling."

Without any coaxing from Bowman, Sarah stops cold in her tracks. At her feet, an occupied body bag lies on the floor. The only seemingly preserved portion of Great-great-great-great-grandma Clifford is her worn and aged hand extended out from under the edge of the body bag. Her hand appears to be reaching out toward the charred Saratoga chest a few feet from the fireplace and nearest burned handcrafted rocking chair. Sarah lovingly squats down along side of the motionless body bag. She caresses the cold hand, even bringing it to her lips and softly kissing it.

"Sarah, it's time you should be going. The coroner will be here shortly," Bowman whispers from behind. With an uncomfortable pause, Bowman slowly approaches Sarah and tenderly places his callused palm on her frail shoulder. "If there's anything you want, you better take it now."

"I'll take this," Sarah almost smiles as she reaches out and pats the top of the charred Saratoga chest.

Bowman turns and waves toward the nearest pair of younger firemen. The firemen carefully tromp inward so is not to step or damage anything else as they make their way closer. The pair of firemen each chose and end of the charred Saratoga chest, silently nod toward each other, then heave it up and outward. Sarah tenderly places Great Meme's limp hand under the body bag along next to her quiet bones. "I'm so sorry…"

Sarah slowly rises up and looks about the desolate ruins. Wiping away a tear, she turns as if to depart placing her dark sunglasses upon her freckled nose. *Jingle-jingle.*

Sarah whips around and quickly scans the area. Bowman strolls from the outer wrap-around porch, tapping his pipe the opened palm of his other hand, heading toward the rear of the parked John Deere firetruck. The younger pair of firemen continue to tote the charred Saratoga chest toward her convertible. The remaining firemen conclude rolling their hoses and stowing their gear in their proper placing about the firetruck. Sarah slowly pivots from where she stands raising her sunglasses, resting them on the crown of her fiery red head. *Jingle-jingle.*

5

What?

What was that?

Sarah rubs her eyes and stares blankly toward the decaying log cabin and lean-to in the near distance. With the rising sun just beyond, Sarah lifts her hand about her brow and squints. There! Was that movement? Who could it be? A stray fireman or a vagabond lingering and wanting to loot at a later time after everyone has gone? There it was again! Sarah dashes from her position next to the burned hearth and towering chimney toward the far end of the wrap-around porch, not bothering where the back door had once stood.

Sarah trudges through the high wild grass separating the remains of the charred house behind her and the decaying log cabin quickly approaching her from the sloping lull in the hillside. The grass is tall and swaying along the waist of her tiny frame and short dress. The log cabin and lean-to draws nearer. Sarah slows her pace and cautiously steps up onto the rotting wrap-around porch.

Pausing only for a moment Sarah takes note of the clusters of gathered cobwebs covering the horseshoe hanging directly above the front leather hinged front door. The door has a primitive knob with its leather hinges showing the many years of age and weather. Sarah slowly reaches for the brass knob and timidly enters.

"Hello?" Sarah softly replies. Opening the door causes dust to flutter through the air from the sparse furnishings and shelves. The air is stale. Over in one corner, a pot belly stove with a kettle and pan sitting on the rusting surface of the cold burners. In the center of the largest room in the house, a dusty foursome of hand crafted chairs surrounding a sawbuck dinning table with see-saw legs.

The floor is puncheon, made of wooden planks not so uncommon for these parts. The walls of the adjoining corner are cluttered with an assortment of lableless canned goods. Below the canned goods are a meager stack of plates, bowls and coffee cups with even fewer utensils in a small gathering. Off to the far corner, a Boston rocker, covered with a thick layer of dust. The rocker slightly sways back and forth from Sarah's movements throughout the room.

Sarah makes her way down along the makeshift hallway leading toward one of the two doors leading into the rest of the abandoned log cabin. The leather hinged doors, nearly shut allowing the faintest of light escaping through the outer windows of the rooms. The rotting leather hinges are faded and worn almost dangling the doors from their decaying frames.

"Hello, is anyone there?" Sarah tiptoes inward tenderly taking the primitive leather strap of the door handle in hand, pressing the nearest door open. Exactly centered along the nearest wall to her left, a perfectly made brass bed. A few strands of straw protrude from just below the lower supporting frame. Cotton sheets wrap around the bed with handmade comforters covering the upper surface. Feather down pillows at the head of the brass bed are covered with cases matching the sheets. The bed looks inviting and comfy.

Along the adjoining wall stands a dresser covered with a thick layer of dust. Below the only window along the next wall, a maple vanity with a pitcher and wash basin. Sarah hadn't noticed before, the window is lined with lace curtains drawn back to allow the growing sunlight into the quiet room. Sarah comes to the conclusion that a woman had occupied this room, or a husband and wife with the wife having her way on the décor. She begins to stroll across the structure's wooden planked floor approaching the side of the bed. Sarah pats the bed several times causing billowing clouds of gathered dust into the air. *Jingle-jingle.* That came from the other room!

Sarah turns and dashes from the first room, along the makeshift hallway, flinging the similarly constructed door of the second and last room open. "Hello!" Sarah blurts out with more urgency. There is no reply. With less enthusiasm, Sarah enters the smaller room along the back of the log cabin. The feeling is drab and lonely with meager furnishings and assortments. A single low to the wooden plank floor bed stands along the far wall. A single feather down pillow with no outer casing. Straw pokes out from the bed's haphazard bindings to keep the straw in place. A few worn and tattered quilts cover the bed in what looks like an attempt to have it made; very disorganized.

There are no dressers, nor vanities, nor a wash basin and pitcher. A collogue of steamer and shipping trunks line the walls as if the resident had not really lived there or had not planned on staying long. About the only window, gunny sack drapes with moth holes and raged edges. Again, Sarah comes to the conclusion that a man, a single man or widower, must have occupied this room. No woman could've allowed herself to live like this.

Sarah turns and exits the far smaller room slightly closing the door behind herself trying to leave it just how she had found it, then makes her way back along the makeshift hallway. She peers back inside of the first and larger room. It was as she had found it. Sadly, she turns and saunters back into the larger main living area. Sarah pauses a moment wondering how people of that day survived such a hostile and primitive culture. Did this cabin belong to one of her very distance relatives? Why was it so close to Great Meme's Victorian home? "Why am I standing in the middle of a rotting log cabin talking to myself," Sarah says aloud nearly startling herself with her own voice.

"Sarah, are you alright?" Bowman urgently bellows out from the swaying grassy meadow of the high prairie grass.

"Yes, I'm fine!" Sarah reluctantly turns and heads toward the log cabin's main door. Quietly exiting like a school girl sneaking out on a date, Sarah pulls the door closed and steps to the edge of the decaying wrap-around porch. Bowman stands among the swaying tall grass puffing on his pipe.

"The coroner's here. I think it best if you'd be going," Bowman replies out of the side of his mouth.

"Alright," Sarah nods as she steps off the porch of the unkempt steps, creaking under her weight. She turns and takes a final glimpse of the cobweb infested horseshoe hanging atop the now closed main door. Sarah approaches Bowman as he turns and escorts her back along the backside of the charred remains of the main house with billows of pipe smoke lingering behind them.

"Did you find what you were looking for?"

"Just taking a last look around," Sarah responds with a half smile.

The younger firemen sit in a variety of locations on and about the John Deere firetruck, sipping on bottles of water, munching on snacks or pouring coffee into their mugs from their thermos's. Bowman plants himself on the rear bumper of the firetruck continuing to puff on his pipe.

The coroner's hertz stands parked closely to the front of the charred porch of the main house. The Coroner is a tall and lanky fellow looking pale and close to death himself, dressed in an all black suit and southern string tie. He respectfully tips his black wide brimmed hat as he passes Sarah from the distance. Sarah politely nods at the gesture, making her way toward her awaiting convertible.

The pair of strapping firemen stand as bookends along the rear bumper of Sarah's sleek automobile. The charred Saratoga chest sticks partially out of the attempted closed trunk. A trio of bungee cords secure the hood of the trunk down in place holding the Saratoga inside. The pair of firemen gander at Sarah's fluttering short dress as she approaches them. "Thanks for your help," Sarah smiles in an almost flirting manner.

"Our pleasure, miss," the more handsome one of the pair replies. "If you need some help gettin' it out of the trunk, *I'd* be more than happy to oblige."

"*We'd* be more than happy to oblige," snorts the smaller fireman.

"Thank-you boys but I think I can manage," Sarah giggles as she slides in behind the wheel. The more handsome fireman darts about the side of the convertible and closes the door for Sarah, catching a glimpse of her upper thigh as she slides into her seat. Bowman strolls along the opposite side of the convertible, shooing the gawking pair of firemen away. Bowman braces his weight on the passenger side of the rolled down window and leers inside.

"You're all set, Sarah."

"Thanks, Rodger," Sarah whispers with a breath. "Thanks for everything." Sarah slides across the arm rest, pushes herself upward and kisses the stout fire chief on the cheek. Bowman nearly blushes as he raises up with a twinkle in his eye. The pair of gawking firemen muffle their laughter.

"Get back to work!" Bowman bellows out toward them. Still trying to conceal their envious laughter, the pair of younger firemen turn tail and head toward the parked firetruck and other firemen in the near distance. Bowman fatherly smiles at Sarah, turns and heads toward the firetruck himself.

Sarah fires up the convertible then lowers her dark sunglasses onto the bridge of her freckled nose. She revs the engine several times as she looks over her shoulder to see the Coroner hovering over Great Meme's outline concealed under the limp body bag. *Jingle-jingle.*

Sarah focuses in the opposite direction, lingering her attention toward the abandoned log cabin and lean-to along the lull in the hillside in the distance. The sun now fully risen, its rays beam brightly down casting odd shadows atop and throughout the cabin. For the slightest of moments, Sarah *thinks* she sees movement from inside. Then, there is nothing. No, it must have just been the swaying of the tall grass and the flickering sunlight. *Jingle-jingle...*

A smooth and swift moving lizard scurries across the warming pavement of the narrow two-lane highway. Towering cactus dance around the desert floor seemingly reaching out their arms to take in all the growing rays of sunlight. Oceans of rambling tumbleweeds roll across the desert floor in haphazard

directions.   Sparse traffic speeds along the highway in both
directions with inviting day desert life all about.

Sarah's convertible appears along the growing waves of
heat rolling across the highway.   Loud up-beat music fills the air
from Sarah's expensive stereo system. Her red hair wildly flapping
in the wind with her red painted fingernails tapping in time to the
music atop her steering wheel. Glancing about the landscape, less
and less tumbleweeds, plant life and towering cactus are seen
replaced by modern ranches, homesteads and homes. Sarah begins
to ease back on the accelerator and slows her convertible as a sign
appears along the side of the highway.

*"WELCOME   TO   PURGATORY   –   population   3790   –
elevation 1,305 ft. – established
1841 – DRIVE SAFE & COME AGAIN!"*

Sarah slows her sleek convertible to a near crawl entering
the quaint one-horse town. Heading down Main Street, well, for
the most part the only street in town, Sarah passes by numerous
parked cars along the modernized wooden planked boardwalks.
The buildings and businesses seem to have simply stopped in time
and halted their aging in the mid to late 1800's. Except for the
installation of modern lampposts, electricity, pluming, paved
streets and the restored wooden planked boardwalks now
"sidewalks", nothing has changed. The older buildings have been
modernized and refurbished to keep up with the constant flow of
eager tourists but still have kept the simple and quaint feeling of
The Old West.

Just inside of the city limits of Purgatory seems to be the
busiest business of all. Tourists laugh and giggle as they stick their
heads through a large façade of a buxom Madam, a stout bartender
and a sheriff, taking pictures of the humorous sight. A vendor
stands outside of the business, barking out his trade selling
"Purgatory postcards", three for a dollar.

A two story structure stands at the utmost corner of the
modern block taking up nearly an acre. The main entrance is at the
corner with a pair of restored and majestic pair of swinging

11

batwing saloon doors. A wrap-around balcony hangs over the below awning with costumed cowboys and dancehall girls waving to the passing tourists along the street below.

 "HELL'S BELLS – SALOON & SPIRITS". An actress, for lack of a better word, stands at the corner of the entrance of Bell's dressed up in a buxom corset and bustle. She twirls her parasol over her shoulder as she gleefully watches the tourists take their pictures from the façade of "her" likeness. Her hair is up in a wasp's nest with a gleaming smile waving to all that pass. The costumed actress waves to all; locals, tourists, reckon anyone that'll wave back.

From behind the buxom actress seeping outward from the inner walls of the restored two-story saloon, up-beat music. Not of that part of the country, which seems odd, but that of old style New Orleans jazz. A piano, a banjo, a pair of clarinets, a tuba, a trombone, a pair of trumpet players and a percussionist. The music is airy and light although extremely out of place for that era of The Old West.

Scads of tourists mill about and stroll in and out of the wide variety of shops and businesses totting their filled shopping bags with newly acquired trinkets and souvenirs. Mingling along the boardwalks, scores of costumed characters of ole Purgatory greet and meet the onslaught of tourists. Costumed wranglers, ranchers, dancehall girls and even a few gunslingers wave and smile joviantly at the foolish hordes of tourists. The Mayor of Purgatory steps out from City Hall, adjusts his southern string tie and wide brimmed hat and tips it toward Sarah as she slowly inches past him.

Sarah turns down her loud up-beat music of her stereo as she approaches the only four-way stop light in town. It's not a "regulation" stop light just merely the bland red blinking type to caution traffic of an intersection. An older model car turns in her direction with the driver smiling and tossing a wave toward Sarah who politely returns the gesture. She continues through the red blinking red light making her way past a very well kept two story hotel.

Another costumed actress with flaming red hair loose about her shoulders, a hint of a bustle, corset and twirling a parasol along her shoulder. The woman is gleeful and polite, smiling and motioning toward passing tourists. The actress stands at the opened entrance of the freshly painted two-story hotel.

"THE KATHERINE HOTEL," is bright and inviting. An older couple pause a moment, handing their camera to the red headed actress to take a picture of them in front of the lodging place. Thanking the actress, the elderly couple nod with a smile and continue along the well kept wooden planks of the boardwalk. Sarah creeps her convertible along Main Street for a few more moments passing by Wells Fargo Bank, Miss Katy's Boarding House, several other modernized general stores as well and a slew of tourist traps.

Sarah inches along, seemingly slowing to a mere crawl, passing by one of Purgatory's more infamous locations. "That's right everyone, gather 'round real close," the costumed actor barks out toward the forward facing audience of tourists. The actor is dressed in a law enforcement manner. A tall wide brimmed hat, a pair of six-shooters on his hips, a shiny badge pinned to the chest of the leather vest and a pair of silver spurs fastened to the heels of his boots. *Jangle-jangle.* The tourists hang on the actor's every word.

"Now then, folks. In eighteen-sixty-six, the famous "Purgatory Valentine's Day Massacre" took place, right here along Main Street. Sheriff Fitch Woolley was grossly outnumbered; twenty to one. The Cougar Gang had Sheriff Woolley and his faithful dog, Wolfy, surrounded," the actor waves his hands wildly about through the air. "Only by quick thinking, Sheriff Woolley charged an Army wagon nearby and uncovered a Gatling gun. Leaping into the wagon, Sheriff Woolley opened fire upon The Cougar Gang. The Cougar Gang shot back in an onslaught of weapons." Several of the ladies of tourists gasp and cuddle their gawking children closer.

"Sheriff Woolley was shot several times but kept firing the Gatling gun," the costumed actor dramatically takes a deep breath. "When the smoke cleared, all that was standing was Sheriff Fitch Woolley and his loyal dog Wolfy." The audience of tourists cheer and applaud. "Now folks, if you would be so kind as to follow me inside, we can continue our tour," the actor smiles as he leads the breathless group of tourists up on the wooden boardwalk of the sheriff's office and jail near the end of Main Street. As the actor leads the way, his spurs rattle along the boardwalk. *Jangle-jangle.*

The structure is well maintained and well kept. The main door stands in the middle of the forward facing wall with barred windows on opposite sides. The sheriff's office and jail, located along the right side of Main Street just after the billowing smoke of the livery next door. Directly across the street of the sheriff's office and jail stands "THE STARDUST SALOON". A two-story building with a wrap-around balcony forward facing Main Street. The Stardust stands next to the refurbished train depot along the passing railroad tracks.

Sarah slows at the far end of Main Street passing by the sheriff's office and jail to her right, The Stardust and train depot to her left. She crosses over the railroad tracks, turns her signal, making a left hand turn. She continues onward along the narrowing paved side street, now with the railroad tracks to her left. The convertible creeps along entering an endless ocean of neighborhood blocks. Street after street passes by her to the right leading into the residential area of Purgatory. Very few and scattered apartment buildings are seen. Apartments mean transients, people not sticking around too long and Purgatory's just not that kind of town.

The two and three-story homes are well kept and plays along with the motif of The Old West and Purgatory's illustrious history. Lawns are groomed. Shrubs are sculpted. The feeling is quaint and somber. Children play freely from yard to yard with their on-looking parents toiling away at their gardens while other folks sit on the wrap-around porches, rocking back and forth, sipping on lemonade.

Nearing the far end of the last block, Sarah slows her convertible, turns into her driveway and parks in front of the two-car garage. Sarah's home is a two and a half story Victorian style structure. A wrap-around porch complements the first floor Gothic like hand carvings on and along the corners of the supporting beams. Well placed alcoves along the second floor add to the charm and beauty of the dwelling.

Sarah hops out of her convertible and strolls along the well groomed hedging along her cobblestone pathway between the side of the main house and the inner side of the garage. Ivy droops from the above lattice from above creating cool shadows along the narrow pathway. As Sarah rattles her keys in hand, she tosses a glance over her shoulder to the charred Saratoga chest remaining secured in the slightly opened trunk of her parked convertible. Sarah inserts her keys into the lock of the house's utility door leading into the main house with the side door of the garage directly behind herself.

Sarah pauses by the mudroom with the washer and dryer nearby. Mounds of laundry clutter the floor as Sarah trudges her way over them. The walkway opens up through a curved archway in the separating wall leading into the kitchen. The cooking area is bright yet with a warm feeling about it. The counters are covered with copper colored tiles, smooth to the touch. Several potted cactus's have been well placed near the windows soaking in the setting rays of sunlight seeping into the room.

Sarah tosses her keys onto the dinning room table. The surface of the table itself is but a mere round sheet of glass. The lower supporting frame and base is made of an assortment of antlers; elk, antelope, deer and caribou. The four surrounding chairs are constructed in the same manner; a sitting pad and backrest supported by antlers. The aura of the room is western in mood with several Santa Fe style paintings hanging on the walls of the dinning room.

Sarah approaches the phone and message machine resting on the end of the copper tiled counter. There is no blinking light nor new messages. Oh, well. Flinging her purse around a horn of the nearest chair, Sarah begins to undress as she disappears along the curved archway of the adjoining hallway.

From inside, the two-car garage opens with a hum. Sarah makes her way from the side door leading into the cluttered area. Odd up-right standing figures loom in all the corners yet due to the setting sun's rays, unable to clearly make them out right away. For the most part, the garage is dark and shadowed. Sarah adjusts her top of her matching western print sweat suit and nearly skips along in her moccasins. She makes her way into the amber rays of the setting sun and approaches the trunk of her convertible. With little effort, Sarah unfastens the bungee cords securing the burned Saratoga chest. With all her might, she heaves the chest up and outward.

K-THUD!

Sarah crouches over and strains to push the Saratoga chest along the driveway. Nope, that won't work. She bounds around the opposite end of the charred chest and takes a hold of the surprisingly intact leather side handle. The chest scrapes along the driveway and moves wildly from side to side as Sarah drags it into the darkness of the garage. She and the Saratoga chest vanish from sight in the depths of the garage. Sarah reappears for a moment only to close the convertible's trunk. She turns and disappears for the last time with the garage door humming to a close.

As the garage door seals, the fading amber colors of the setting sun fade. The soothing overhead light settles to a comfortable level. Sarah's eyes adjust to her surroundings as she pulls the charred Saratoga chest toward the center of the room.

The walls are crammed with filled book shelves of every shape and size of book. The shadowed images before now come into focus. Movie mogul cardboard figures linger in and about the area; John Wayne, The Lone Ranger, Mae West, Roy Rodgers, Dale Evans, Buffalo Bill, Jesse James, Billy the Kid, Doc Holiday, Wyatt Erpp, The Long Riders and several of Clint Eastwood posing in his spaghetti westerns. The few remaining sections of wall space not consumed with book shelves are filled with western film posters and theater marquees. Sarah, a true western film buff.

Along the opposite wall of the now closed garage door along the next wall of the side door looming under a haphazard bookshelf, a complete office area; cluttered desk, computer and monitor, and stacks of unorganized papers. Atop one stack of papers, an opened magazine. The upward facing article, "CHUCK WAGON COOKING – WRITTEN BY SARAH JACKSON." Scattered among the over hanging shelves, volumes upon volumes of the same magazine.

The center of the garage is actually homey and comfortable looking. A complete set matching leather bound couches form a somewhat square design. In the center of the pair of couches stands an old stagecoach wagon wheel transformed into a glass covered coffee table directly in the center of the garage. Below the wagon wheel coffee table lays a sprawling Native American print floor rug.

Sarah gracefully moves her way in and around the leather couches and approaches the charred Saratoga chest at the end several yards in from the closed garage door. Giving the chest one final tug inward, Sarah maneuvers it around facing the opened corner of the pair of couches. Squatting along side of the wagon wheel coffee table, Sarah begins to carefully examine the charred chest.

"What's inside of you? Secrets? Love letters?" Sarah pauses, "What's inside..." she whispers with a curious tone. She moves her hands across the charred surface sliding her fingers along the melted iron clasps. Sarah struggles for several moments, attempting to open the Saratoga chest's secrets.

RING-RING.

Sarah's hand slips on one of the melted iron clasps breaking one of her red painted fingernails. "Blast it!" Sarah exclaims.

RING-RING.

Sarah glances down at her broken fingernail as she quickly stands and approaches her phone and message machine resting on the cluttered corner of her office and work area. Sarah quickly answers the phone. "Hello? Yes, Mr. Douglas. Yes, I know," Sarah slightly pulls the receiver away from her ear as her scolding continues for several moments. The "blah-blah-blah" can be clearly heard from the far other end of the phone. "Yes, Mr. Douglas. The article *will* be done by deadline. Thank-you. Yes. Thank-you," Sarah nearly slams down the phone. "Putz!"

Sarah turns and makes her way back toward the charred Saratoga chest. She stands there with crossed arms for a long moment, simply staring down at it. Over her shoulder, she glances in disgust at her quiet and blank computer monitor. "Yeah, I really need to finish that article," Sarah thinks aloud. Looking down at the Saratoga chest then back toward the empty monitor of the computer screen, "Blast it!" Sarah angrily storms toward the side door leading out of the garage and disappears under the drooping ivy leaves leaving the charred Saratoga chest unattended. *Jingle-jingle.*

Sarah takes an unwilling sip of her coffee mug remaining seated facing the empty monitor of her computer. The only company she has is the small and annoying blinking cursor at the top of the screen.

Blink-blink.

Blink-blink.

Pausing a moment, she tosses a look over her shoulder toward the beckoning Saratoga chest. "I'm sorry, I'll have to get to you tomorrow," Sarah says with a sigh. Frustrated, Sarah returns to her computer and begins her furious typing.

The garage door has been opened. Sarah stands just outside allowing the cooling breeze of the evening sky to flow freely through her loose red locks dangling about her shoulders. She has graduated from her coffee mug to a Tequila Sunrise. Sarah sips on the drink while behind herself, the computer continues to produce a low hum, downloading her completed article to her editor, Mr. Douglas' office.

RING-RING.

"Now what!" Sarah murmurs to herself.

RING-RING.

Sarah reluctantly makes her way past the quiet and awaiting charred Saratoga chest, weaves her way around the leather couches and stagecoach wagon wheel coffee table, toward her desk and office area. Defiantly, Sarah punches the phone's intercom function. "Hello?"

"What do you call this *crap*? I thought you were a journalist!"

"I'm sorry, Mr. Douglas."

"I've read some real *crappy* articles in my day but I think this one is the worse one I've forced my aging eyes to endure!"

"Mr. Douglas, there's only *so* much someone can write about "the many uses of maize.""

"I don't care! You better have an article on my desk by deadline or you're through!"

CLICK.

"Yeah, well I've heard *that* before!" Sarah snaps at the phone, Mr. Douglas having already hung-up. Sarah rubs her hands over her eyes through her loose hair. Ever so slowly, she takes her "maize" article in hand and flips through the pages. Making her way around the side of the wagon wheel coffee table, Sarah plops down on one of the leather couches, "He's right. This is *crap!*"

Sarah sits motionless for several moments reliving Mr. Douglas' "blah-blah-blah" speech. She tosses the article onto the coffee table. Taking a deep breath, Sarah rises and approaches her office area. Finding the mouse, Sarah clicks on "DELETE

FILE?". Sarah clicks "YES". The computer asks, "ARE YOU SURE – YES/NO". Sarah again clicks "YES". The monitor screen wipes away Sarah's entire "maize" article; one line at a time. She watches as the screen quickly is erased and becomes blank. The only item that remains is the small annoying blinking cursor at the top of the screen.

Blink-blink.

Blink-blink.

Sarah reaches up and turns off the computer and monitor. Leaning over, she flicks off the table lamp and stands. Shaking her head at the piles upon piles of research papers and cluttered mayhem, Sarah takes a deep breath and puffs out her cheeks exhaling. Making her way to the side door, she presses the garage door opener.

The garage door lowers into place with a low hum. Flicking off the above soft lights, Sarah exits through the side door, locking the door behind herself leaving the charred Saratoga chest abandoned and forgotten in the darkness. *Jingle-jingle.*

The abrupt sound of a screaming lawnmower outside causes Sarah to bolt awake. Sitting up in bed, she looks about her surroundings. The South Western print bed spread covers her lower half, wearing a child-like Cowboy and Indian print set of pajamas. Sarah's bedroom is similar to the rest of the house; western and rustic. A replica old style kerosene lantern chandelier hangs from the ceiling in the middle of the room with new, but purposely "aged" dressers and chests about the inner walls. A gunny-sack looking set of drapes hangs about the two windows of the alcoves outside. Sarah stretches and yawns, tossing the western bed spread off of herself. She scratches her thigh, stumbling toward the opened bedroom door.

"Good-morning, Pedro," Sarah sparks with a twinkle in her eye. She motherly pours a sparse amount of water onto one of the potted cactus's sleeping on the copper tile counter of the kitchen. Sarah moves about the cooking area, watering Pedro's remaining potted companions. The smell of fresh coffee fills the air. The coffee maker percolates as Sarah takes a mug from the cupboard. She pours herself a large cup of the steaming beverage, scratches her thigh again, then heads for the mudroom.

The garage is dark and lifeless. Sarah enters, flicking on the light as she goes. She fumbles her way toward the office area and desk. Reluctantly turning on the computer and monitor, Sarah plops down in her western style chair and faces the blank screen. In a matter of moments, the annoying cursor appears in the corner of the monitor.

Blink-blink.

Blink-blink.

"Use me! Write something, will ya!" the cursor in the corner of the monitor demands. Sarah takes a sip of her steaming coffee and slouches down in her chair. *Jingle-jingle.*

Quickly turning, Sarah stares for a long moment at the charred Saratoga chest sitting on the floor adjacent to the stagecoach wheel wagon coffee table and nearly meeting corners of the pair of leather couches. Sarah slowly, even timidly, stands and approaches the burned chest. Setting her coffee mug down onto the wagon wheel coffee table, Sarah sits, staring at the upward looking melted iron clasps of the Saratoga chest. "Fine, then. Let's see what secrets you're holding."

Sarah slides off of the leather couch and settles onto the Native American print floor rug. She takes a quick glance at her broken fingernail, yet deliberately and purposely reaches for the melted iron clasps. An odd feeling overwhelms her. With a playful smirk, she takes the pair of melted iron clasps into her fingers.

CLICK-CLICK.

The melted clasps of the charred Saratoga chest open. Sarah nervously lifts the lid of the chest to its fullest extent. Like an eager child looking into a fish bowl for the first time, Sarah peers inward. Her eyes widen. Her jaw drops. "Oh my goodness,"

Sarah whispers to herself. "What have I found!?" She carefully reaches inside.

A wooden Mahogany handmade music box rests on top of stacks of outdated and oddly enough, current local and national newspapers, several no more than a few years old. Sarah takes the music box in hand and tenderly opens it. Light melodic music fills the air with a tiny ballerina slowly twirling around. The contents of the music box appear tarnished and faded. Rings and broaches of little or no value flop around its velvet lining as Sarah places the music box next to her coffee mug on the coffee table. The fleeting music of the music box fades as she reaches into the opened Saratoga chest a second time.

Grabbing a random pile of newspapers, Sarah takes note of the front pages and concurring dates; *January 12th 1998, March 2nd 1996, June 3rd 1991, October 13th 1986, April 30th 1979.* Sarah sets the first stack of newspapers aside next to the music box then flips through another random stack of fading newspapers. *December 22nd 1906, May 6th 1901, August 19th 1897, February 26th 1874, July 11th 1859,* and what appears to be the first collected newspaper on the bottom of the stack, *March 17th 1852.*

Eighteen-fifty two? Sarah flips through the random stacks of current and historical newspapers. *March 17th 1852*, yep that's the first newspaper collected. "Wonder why," Sarah mumbles to herself. She sets the stacks of newspapers atop the coffee table next to the music box. Taking a sip of her cooling coffee mug, she reaches back into the charred Saratoga chest retrieving a small stack of faded fliers or wanted posters. The fliers have the likenesses of a variety of bandits, ruffians and outlaws. The most of which belong to "THE COUGAR GANG – WANTED DEAD OR ALIVE - $500.00 REWARD – WANTED FOR BANK ROBBERY & MURDER." A few of the fliers appear charred and burned around the edges.

Sarah flips through the remaining fliers then sets them down on top of the nearest stack of fading newspapers on the coffee table. Looking deep into the Saratoga chest, hers eyes widen. A classic and forgotten art; a daguerreotype or tin type. For that era, very rare and expensive. Sarah gazes upon the tin type.

A handsome young man sporting a grey wide brimmed hat, a pair of ivory handled Colt revolvers hanging low at his hips, a sparkling badge pinned to his chest and a pair of silver spurs clung to the heels of his worn boots. Standing closely next to the handsome young man, almost arm in arm, a fiery redhead with her wavy locks hanging loosely about her shoulders. The young woman wears a hint of a bustle and corset. She is well fitted in her full length light blue Victorian style dress with lace costumed around the cuffs and free flowing edges. The couple look very happy and very much in love, standing in front of a motionless railroad boxcar.

Sarah sets the tin type down next to the charred edged wanted fliers on the coffee table and reaches into the Saratoga chest a third time. She retrieves a second tin type. This one, a few years more modern than the last one with a different young man and redheaded young woman. A buxom, more than middle aged woman, wearing the flowing dress and garb of a Madam of the Night, her cleavage thrusting out for all to admire, totting a parasol over her shoulder, hair up in a bee hive bun. The sturdy woman stands next to a stout man wearing a soiled apron, a Southern string bowtie, a dark vest, white shirt with a garter around both upper arms.

Oddly enough, the younger red headed woman is in the same picture. The younger woman looks older now, worn and tired with a bundled infant in her arms. Standing next to her on one side, the different man dressed in a wide brimmed hat, a pair of six-shooters at his hips and a badge pinned to his chest. On the opposite side of the red headed woman trying to fake a smile for the photographer, a round colored woman dressed in a plain and drab dress stands close. The colored woman resembles a favorite aunt one might have, smiling and cheerful.

All about the foreground, immigrant workers pause their labors, crouch down and pose for the photographer. Lingering piles of tools, shingles and timber clutter around their worn boots. The buxom Madam, the stout bartender, the worn redhead clutching onto her infant, the lawman and colored woman pose in front of the newly rebuilt establishment, "THE KATHERINE HOTEL". Freshly painted and newly reopened for business.

Sarah sets the second tin type down onto the growing piles of antiquities on the coffee table and reaches into the charred Saratoga chest again. She pauses a moment. Resting on top of a large bundle below, a layer of dime novels, very popular for that time. The covers of the thin books look quite humorous and even unbelievable. Outlaws and lawmen battling it out along the main street of a nameless town. The hero swooping up the damsel in distress. One particular dime novel cover catches Sarah's eye, a lone sheriff standing in the back of a cargo wagon firing a Gatlin gun toward a small army of outlaws.

As Sarah places the dime novels onto the cluttering coffee table, an object falls from the thin books onto the floor. She reaches down and takes a blood stained deputy's badge in hand. Its luster has faded. The smeared blood stained on the tarnished surface forever. She runs her broken fingernail across its surface. Tenderly placing the deputy's badge onto the coffee table next to the music box, Sarah turns her attention back toward the Saratoga chest.

Sarah retrieves several handfuls of hand written letters secured together in small bundles by thin leather straps. The outer handwriting is faded and smeared, unreadable. The edges are tattered, worn from age. The letters are just that, letters. No envelopes for the day in age. Simple sheets of worn paper each folded several times to conceal their inner most secrets. Sarah places the handfuls of letters onto the top of the wagon wheeled coffee table then reaches into the charred Saratoga chest again.

Sarah retrieves a tightly bundled package. The outer coverings are of gunny sack several layers thick. Sarah quickly unties the gunny sack bundle and to her amazement, the full length light blue colored Victorian dress. Sarah stands, holding the lacy dress in front of herself. She twirls and dances in circles to the unheard music of the wooden music box resting on the coffee table. The dress is simply lovely. Sarah carefully drapes the nineteenth century light blue dress over the back of the nearest leather couch then returns to the awaiting Saratoga chest. She gazes inside. Her face turns pale with near fright.

Sarah's hands tremble as she reverently dips her hands inside of the chest and removes a large stack of faded onion papers. Some of the edges of the papers have been scorched and charred, not from Great Meme's flames, but burned from a blaze long ago.

Sarah rests down the first stack of onion papers and reaches inside of the chest to retrieve yet another stack, then another stack. There must be nearly twenty years of journals! Sarah takes the last of the stacks of onion papers in hand and rests them on the coffee table then notices the top page of onion papers… a family tree? Who's? Ours? Mine? "Oh my goodness," Sarah exclaims. "Yes. Yes it *is* our family tree!"

At the utmost top of the faded onion paper family tree, Elizabeth O'Donnell. The branches fan out toward the next name, Sarah Elizabeth O'Donnell. Under the second entry, an additional name has been added, Sarah Elizabeth O'Donnell marries and becomes Sarah Elizabeth Clifford. Great-great-great-great-grandma Meme! Grandma Sarah Clifford! The numerous added names flow with the sprawling branches of the family tree; Stephanie Evans, Madelyn Buffet, Caroline Moores and then Sarah Elizabeth Jackson.

"Hey, that's me!" Sarah exclaims. She follows her broken fingernail through the various branches of the family tree; born and died dates appearing after most. Great Meme, Sarah's grandmother Buffet, her mother Caroline and Sarah herself all have born dates but no dates of death. Sarah sadly realizes that there is no one to write in Great Meme's day of death.

Sarah's finger follows the branches of the family tree. Odd, the accounting of the family is all in a woman's perspective. Only a few men are mentioned and represented. In a shaky handwritten fashion, the man's name Morris Allen is seen close to Elizabeth O'Donnell and Sarah Elizabeth's name. Sarah follows the dates until coming across an uncompleted entry; Sheriff Fitch Woolley – born May 6th 1840... the next entry is blank. No date of death. "Someone just forgot to write it in," Sarah thinks aloud.

Sarah sets down the onion paper family tree next to the wooden music box, the stacks of current and outdated newspapers, the scattered dime novels, the blood stained deputy's badge and the smaller stack of wanted fliers. She stares blankly at the stacks of onion paper entries, probably spanning nearly over two decades.

Taking a sip of her cold coffee, Sarah reaches forward to the stacks of onion papers, now noticing dates in the corners of about every other page. She scans, mumbling the dates in her head. As she flips through them, the dates are oddly in the concise order. Back... back... back even further to what appears to be the first entry. This journal, this diary of sorts. But who's? Sarah settles back into one of the leather couches with a large stack of the onion papers in her lap. Sarah begins to read the first entry...

"It seems that I have known Fitch for my whole life. For the most part, that is true. It is only now upon my birthday, has it occurred to me to account for my life, my departed parents and my growing concern of never being wed. Yes, Elizabeth O'Donnell, you may just end up and Ole Maid."

"The trip from New York was a difficult one. My father, Daniel O'Donnell and mother Katherine, had joined up with a wagon train headed out West. Unknown to my father at the time, my mother was with

child, me.   Through the weather conditions, Indian attacks and numerous encounters with outlaws and road bandits, although they were <u>less</u> than outlaws, all they took was supplies and some grub, we arrived in the New Mexico Territory in June 1842."

"My father's plan was to continue West to the Silver Mine's Rush but my mother had other words to say about that. I was born shortly afterwards and mother was in no condition to travel any further. So, against his better judgment, my father decided that The O'Donnell Family would settle in Purgatory, New Mexico Territory. Father, with the reminder of our funds, purchased a battered down hotel in town. My mother was livid! We lived in one of the better suites of the hotel while father hired some local boys for free room and board to help fix the place up."

"I don't recall Doctor "Doc" Herring upon my arrival into this world, but he has become a good friend and confidant over the years. Doc was tearful when he told me some years later that my mother's death was, in an around and about way, caused by my birth. Mother fought to stay with us for nearly a week then slipped away into the night with my father at her side. It was up to my father alone to raise me. Not an easy task for a business owner and widower in 1842."

"As I grew in years, I helped out as much as I was able about the hotel my father named after my mother,

"The Katherine." From my earliest recollections, Sheriff Theodore "Theo" Woolley was a kind and warm soul. There wasn't much trubble in Purgatory in those years. Everyone was headed for the Silver Mines. Theo and father had gotten to know each other plainly for they had something in common, raising a young'un on their own."

"Theo's son and daughter-in-law had died some years earlier due to a bad case of the pox, leaving a ten year old boy to fend for himself. I had seen Fitch from time to time when father and Theo were discussing local politics and such. But I really never paid much attention to the lanky and annoying boy."

"Doc was at my side when father was bed ridden with the fever. Father was delirious with his ramblings about the voyage from New York, my mother and even apologetic to my mother in his fever, for dragging her out to this God forsaken country, for if he hadn't, she'd still be alive."

"Doc was kind to me after father had passed, taking me in under his wing. Doc introduced me to Bell, a helluva business woman. Bell taught me how to run the hotel, manage the books, hire and handle the help and taught me how the West was Won. It wasn't with a Colt revolver… women conquered and tamed it!"

"For the next few years, I saw Fitch and Sheriff Theo at social gatherings, New Year's Eve, The Forth of July and such. I think The Almighty had plans for us even back then. It wasn't till 1852 that I remember noticing Fitch. Not acknow-ledging him as the stringy and odd moving boy I had once known. A boy turning into a young man. Though I was only ten years of age and Fitch was merely twelve, I remember the day when I felt the warm and frilly feeling in my belly."

"I recall the day I fell in love with Fitch and knew one day, we would be together as husband and wife, raising fine children of our own. The winter rains still lingered. The grazing cattle of the nearby ranches roamed freely about the high desert prairies. Along the tops of the nearby mountains, soft spatterings of snow clung to the peaks for as long as they could before the spring weather melted them away."

"Yes, I remember the day vividly. I was ten years old. I remember it as if it were yesterday. I was ten and Fitch was a mere two years older than I was when I fell in love with him. That was March 1852..."

CHAPTER II

The vast oceans of sand and rolling tumbleweeds span out for as far as the eye can see. Clusters of amber and tan boulders protrude from the area like the haphazard spots on a dairy cow. Gatherings of Joshua Trees provide the only shade for wayward high desert critters trying to escape the rising sun of the New Mexico Territory. Off in the distance, a range of rolling hills with a deep valley carving its way toward the north. The Woolley Ranch is not a sprawling homestead but a mere residence away from Purgatory. A simple and quiet life. Hard at times, yet satisfactory for those seeking a challenge.

The main ranch house is located in the center area of the homestead. A one floor structure solidly built. A primitive yet sturdy wrap-around porch with a swaying rocking chair near the cracked open front door. The roof's shingles are well placed keeping out the rain and snow of the harsher months. Nothing fancy about the home, just the essentials.

A two story barn stands off to the side of the main house thirty or so yards away. The upper hay loft of the barn is opened to the elements with its leather hinged doors slightly swinging to the cool high desert breeze. Mounds of hay freely flow outward from the opening with clucking chickens, milling about below the forward opened main doors of the barn.

Three sets of corrals consume the three remaining perimeters of the barn. The planked log containments house nearly a dozen horses. Some for riding with most for working about the high desert ranch. A pair of stallions snort and glare toward each other in a challenging manner, not quite sure as to the other's intentions of a full on brawl.

The corral along the backside of the barn is the largest of the three. Beef cattle and a trio of dairy cows bask in the warming rays of the morning sun. The nearest corral to the ranch house is blessed with four mares and two colts. One colt in particular stands out with a bluish-grey or smoky color to him. The grulla colored colt sports a white streak from below the eyes all the way down to his curious muzzle. The colt twitches his eyes as he senses someone approaching.

Theodore "Theo" Woolley stumbles his way through the wayward roaming chickens throughout of the inner shadows of the opened barn doors. Plainly dressed as a common high desert rancher would, wearing a sweat stained hat, Theo totes in each hand a pail of barley and oats. Theo is along in years yet well built and taller than most. Below his bushy mustache, a half grin or smirk is detected. Yes, Theo has got plenty of rowdy years left in him.

Theo empties the pails into the troughs of the mares and colts. The bluish-grey colt frolics over and quickly begins to devour the meal. "That a boy, Blaze," Theo replies to the colt as he reaches down to stroke the bluish-grey mane. Clunking footsteps from the main house draw Theo's attention.

"Grandpa?" the nearing voice beckons.

Theo strokes the colt's bluish mane and pats him on the muzzle as the hoofed creature continues to feed, pressing his way into the troughs preventing the mares and other colt to feed. Turning with a devilish grin, Theo strolls away from the corrals to be met by a strapping young boy.

Fitch Woolley shows signs of nearing manhood. Strong shoulders and a wide chest. Sandy locks sway with his movements, more of a stride. Fitch dons his nightshirt tucked into his plain britches with his work boots tromping along. In his hands, a double holster gunbelt with a pair of ivory handled Colt model revolvers.

"Grandpa?" Fitch eagerly approaches and motions the gunbelt toward Theo.

31

"Yes, Fitch?"

"Can we practice now?"

"Are all of your chores done?"

"Well," Fitch pauses. "Most of 'em."

Theo twists one end of his graying mustache with a disappointed expression. "I reckon you'cn finish up afore lunch," Theo replies with a fatherly tone. "Go'n set 'em up." Theo takes the gunbelt in hand as Fitch turns and dashes away heading toward the nearest cluster of amber and tan boulders. Theo strolls behind after the twelve year old youth, fastening the gunbelt low on his hips as he goes.

Fitch skids to a halt at the base of the cluster of boulders. He quickly lunges to the ground taking several rusting coffee cans in hand. The cans are riddled with bullet holes and tears in the tin. Fitch places the twelve cans along the ridges in no particular arrangement or manner. Nearly a dozen other rusting coffee cans with similar bullets holes still remain at Fitch's feet. Theo approaches and halts a mere twenty or so yards away facing the amber boulders and bullet ridden coffee cans. Fitch turns tails from the cans and dashes to his Grandpa's side.

"Always be calm," Theo whispers. "It's better to be slower and accurate than faster and miss. With practice and time, you'll learn to be fast *and* accurate." Theo wiggles his hips a moment then settles his boots into the sand and dirt. Taking a slight breath, Theo pauses and focuses on the coffee cans in the distance.

As Theo draws his left Colt revolver from his hip, he cocks back the hammer with his thumb. Theo quickly aims and fires at the rusting cans with deliberance and moderate speed, cocking back the hammer with his thumb after every shot.

BLAM. BLAM. BLAM.

The three coffee cans Theo had aimed for flop along the ridges of the boulders then topple to the sandy ground. Theo holsters the revolver and remains focused on the remaining coffee cans sprawled out across the facing boulders. "Now, pay attention," Theo instructs without looking down toward Fitch.

Theo draws his right Colt revolver with lightening speed, quickly cocking back the hammer with his thumb after every deadly shot. BLAM. BLAM. BLAM. BLAM. BLAM.

All five of the rusting coffee cans in which Theo had aimed for flip-flop across the ridges of the boulders then sputter to the ground below. Theo twirls the revolver about his forefinger then neatly stuffs it back into its holster at his hip. He unfastens the gunbelt and swings it over toward Fitch, "Reload."

Fitch takes the gunbelt in hand and swiftly wraps it around his narrow waist. He has to cinch the gunbelt up to the last eye hole. The gunbelt is loose fitting and dangles about his growing hips but yet still secure enough not to drop to his knees.

Fitch draws the right revolver from its holster. He pulls back the loading lever from under the barrel, releasing the empty cylinder. Fitch removes the empty cylinder from the revolver with one hand as he takes a preloaded six shot cylinder from its leather snap case along the side front of the gunbelt. He slides the empty cylinder into the worn leather case and secures the brass snap.

Fitch loads the cylinder into the Colt revolver, secures it in place then pulls the loading lever back into position. Slightly glancing up toward Grandpa Theo in the near distance, Fitch quickly draws the left Colt revolver from his hip and begins to reload it as he had done to the first revolver.

Theo sets up the rusting coffee cans along the ridges of the amber and tan boulders, turns and shoots a wink and a smile at Fitch. The young man quickly finishes reloading the second Colt revolver, then slides it into its loose fitting holster at his hip.

Theo approaches Fitch and stands along side of him as one of the distant mares bellows out a concerned whiney. Theo raises and cups his hand over is eyes to the nearby narrow dirt road leading to The Woolley Ranch. A carriage leaves a wake of dust behind itself as it rolls along drawing nearer. It will still be some time before the visitors arrive. Theo turns toward Fitch, tenderly placing his gruff hand on the young man's shoulder. "Be calm," Theo grumbles. "Focus, then draw." Fitch takes a deep breath and stares blankly at the rusting coffee cans scattered about the forward facing boulders. Fitch has had to adapt with shooting skills. With his smaller hands and thumbs, he is unable to pull back the hammer and fire with a single hand. Fitch swiftly draws the left Colt revolver and brings his right palm over the hammer, fanning and cocking it back after every accurate shot.

BLAM-BLAM. BLAM-BLAM. BLAM. BLAM.

Fitch holsters the Colt revolver. The six cans spin for a moment along the ridges of the boulders then topple to the sand and dirt below. "Again! Faster!" Grandpa Theo commands. Fitch draws the right Colt revolver from his hip and fans his left opened palm over the hammer as he fires.

BLAM-BLAM. BLAM. BLAM-BLAM- BLAM.

The six rusting coffee cans wildly flip-flop through the air then splatter to the sand and dirt below. Fitch holsters the ivory handled Colt revolver, turns and looks up toward Theo for approval. "Good, much better than the last time," Theo compliments. "Go'n set 'em again."

Theo pats Fitch on the shoulder then turns toward the ranch house, the visitors continue to draw nearer. Fitch fumbles for the coffee cans and hurriedly sets them up along the ridges of the boulders. He saunters back to his marksman spot, beginning to reload each chamber of the empty cylinders of the Colt revolvers with fresh black powder from his flask, a wad and a perfectly shaped round.

"Mornin', Doc," Theo bellows out as he steps up onto the side of the wrap-around porch, making his way toward the front of the house. Doctor "Doc" Herring eases back of the reigns of his single horse drawn chaise. The accordion-style hood fully extended to shade the pair of occupants from the growing heat of the desert sun.

"Morning, Theodore."

"Mornin', Elizabeth," Theo smiles as he raises his hat up and over his brow.

"Good morning, Sheriff," a squeaky voice echo's from under the raised chaise's hood.

Doc struggles down from the carriage and lumbers up onto the wrap-around porch. Theo and Doc politely shake hands in greeting. Doc is a lanky fellow dressed in a black jacket and trousers, white shirt and a southern-style string tie, totting his filled black medical bag at his thigh. Doc's gruff facial features are mostly hidden by his wiry grey whiskers concealing his true age. "What brings you out, Doc?" Theo asks slightly leaning against one of the upper supporting beams of the porch.

"We had to check in on Mrs. Turnsul and the little one," Doc replies as he steps up onto the lower step. "We're on our way back to town and thought I'd look'n on you."

"Nothin' ailing me, Doc."

"How's that stomach of yours?"

"Fine, since I've been takin' that jungle-juice you give me."

"Well then, while I'm here I might's well give you a look over."

"Can I offer you a spot?" Theo stands upright away from the upper supporting beam.

"Well," Doc looks upward toward the continuing raising desert sun, "It's after breakfast. A spot sounds dandy." Theo extends his arm outward motioning Doc into the house. The pair of aging coots disappear inside followed by manly laughter. The chaise is shadowed and quiet. The squeaky voice from inside… all but forgotten. The carriage slightly rocks from side to side as the petite side passenger flings herself from the padded seat out on the dusty ground.

Elizabeth "Beth" O'Donnell puffs out her cheeks with a deep sigh. A light colored bonnet covers her flowing red locks of hair dangling over her shoulders. A frilly Sunday dress with ruffles and lace down to her knees. Light colored stockings and front laced boots concludes her attire. Beth glances about the empty porch, hearing Theo and Doc exchange their banter from inside.

BLAM. BLAM-BLAM. BLAM. BLAM-BLAM.

Beth cocks her head with an odd smile, making her way around the lower sections of the wrap-around porch, toward the far side of the ranch. Fitch stands steadfast at his marksman position. He twirls the left Colt revolver recklessly around his forefinger. Without looking over his shoulder, he smells the soft fragrance of lilacs. Fitch smirks to himself as he holsters the Colt revolver and adjusts the loose fitting gunbelt around his waist.

"How have you been, Fitch?" Beth playfully smiles at the young man in a flirting manner.

"Fine'n you, Beth?" Fitch responds as if he were bluffing at a high stakes poker game. Beth stands along side of Fitch as they each give the other the "one-two" look over. "You're fillin' out, Beth."

Beth is frightfully embarrassed, trying to maneuver herself in a manner so is not to attract anymore attention to her developing ten year old body. However, Fitch *did* and *does* notice. Fitch begins to sweat. Jeepers, *that* was the wrong thing to say. Fitch attempts to quickly change the subject. "Watch this, Beth!"

Fitch faces the forward facing nine coffee cans resting on the various ridges of the amber boulders. Taking a slight deep breath, Fitch draws the right Colt revolver with lightening speed, fanning his opened left palm over the hammer before every shot. BLAM-BLAM. BLAM-BLAM. BLAM-BLAM.

Smoke spits out from the end of the barrel of the Colt revolver. Fitch strains a moment to see clearly through the haze of smoke as Beth politely covers her mouth, giggling. "Watch what, Fitch? The cans rusting?" In his eagerness to impress Beth, Fitch has missed all of the coffee cans he was aiming for.

"It was the wind," Fitch abruptly responds. Beth covers her eyes and lifts her pointing forefinger into the air, checking for the wind and surrounding landscapes. With a mischievous smile, Beth uncovers her eyes and lowers her forefinger, staring at Fitch with a twinkle in her eye... there is no wind. Fitch cowardly holsters the Colt revolver and turns to head back toward the ranch. "I've got chores to 'tend to," Fitch humbly replies. He sulks away, dragging his worn work boots away from Beth.

"It was good to see you, Fitch!" Beth eagerly waves after Fitch's turned back. Fitch gives a half-ass acknowledgement with a less than enthusiastic wave continuing toward the two-story barn and corrals. Alone again, Beth stands there for a moment allowing the warming rays of sun to beat down upon her bonnet. Kicking the sand, Beth makes her way back toward the front of the house and Doc's awaiting chaise.

Fitch rounds the corrals making his way toward the bluish-grey colt, "Morning, Blaze." He leans over the second highest corral board and looks inward. The grulla colored colt frolics about with the other colt, the mares and Blaze's mother looking oddly at the overactive galloping colt. "Women," Fitch mumbles to himself. "Can't live with 'em, 'n'ya can't shoot 'em." Fitch shuffles his feet as he makes his way around the outer corrals heading into the dark shadows of the opened front barn doors.

Beth sits alone on Theo's front porch with her laced boots resting on the top step. In her lap, a hand carved wooden Mahogany music box. Light music fills the air as the pink and frilly ballerina slowly spins in small circles. Beth watches the ballerina, cocking her head from side to side. The music is soothing to her young soul.

Boisterous laughter seeps outward from inside the ranch house behind her. Theo and Doc nearly crash through the front door stepping out onto the wrap-around porch. The laughter dies. Doc mournfully glances down at Beth's back turned to him as the music box continues to tinker out the melodic melody. "Are you ready, Elizabeth?" Doc fatherly asks.

Without a word, Beth closes the Mahogany music box, tucks it under her arm and slithers toward the passenger's side of Doc's chaise. She hobbles herself upward and disappears back into the shadows of the drawn hood of the carriage. "Reckon so," Doc turns toward Theo with an odd glance.

"Doc."

"Theodore," Doc responds as he and Theo firmly shake hands.

"Take care of this ole coot, Elizabeth."

"I will, Sheriff," Beth echo's out from under the raised hood of the chaise. Doc rambles toward the carriage and lumbers inward sitting next to Beth, waiting in silence. Taking the reigns, Doc clicks his mouth. The horse slightly bolts a moment then begins to trot forward with fluid movement. Doc waves over his shoulder from under the chaise's drawn hood, turning the carriage away, heading along a different path in the narrow dirt road in which they had arrived. Theo stands along the top step of the porch for a long moment following Doc's chaise with his eyes. Turning, Theo scans the ranch for any traces of Fitch... there are none.

Hearing the departing chaise, Fitch charges through the mounds of loose hay in the loft of the barn. Theo's loose gunbelt flapping wildly at his hips. He nearly slams himself against the boards of the supporting wall, peering through a knot hole in the wood. Fitch sees Doc's single horse drawn chaise rolling along the narrow roadway heading back into town. There is no sign of Beth poking her red locks of hair outward and behind for a final farewell.

Dust billows behind the carriage as it swiftly continues to move along and away from The Woolley Ranch. Fitch raises his head from the knot hole and freely falls backward into a large pile of gathered hay. He stares blankly up at the wooden rafters of the barn, releasing a deep sign, "It was good to see you too, Beth..."

Theo slowly rocks back and forth, cockeyed from the warming flames of the fireplace. A thick beam spans above the crackling flames below the hearth with a double barreled shotgun hanging from the log planked wall. Theo puffs on his pipe as he gazes into the flames of the burning cinders.

Seated at the well built rectangular dinner table, Fitch appears intensely focused on his task. A primitive kerosene lantern lights the area with the flicker light of a single candle within arms reach. The gunbelt lays off to the side of the worn dinner table with a single reloaded Colt revolver next to it. The pair of reloaded backup cylinders stand upright on the dinner table next to the empty leather snap cases along opposite side of the side front of the gunbelt. Wearing his fading nightshirt, the young man continues to reload the empty chambers of the Colt's cylinders in his hands.

Fitch carefully pours in the proper amount of black powder into the chamber, stuffs in a small wad then slides the perfectly formed bullet into place. With all the chambers of the cylinder loaded, Fitch takes the flickering candle, slightly upends it and drips a few drops of melting wax onto each of the bullets, securing them in place. "While Doc was lookin' me over t'day, I saw you practicin'" Theo nearly grumbles.

"Yes, Grandpa," Fitch humbly replies.

"Never showboat or at least *try* to showboat. That's what gets people kilt. Never draw out of anger or drunkenness. Always keep focused and in control. Chances are, whoever you'r confronted with is's scarred out of their wits as you'r. Knowin' this and keepin' your wits about you, you'll live a might longer time'n I have."

"Yes, Grandpa," Theo obediently replies.

Theo looks over his shoulder and tosses Fitch a smile. "Now then, 'tend to the dishes and kitchen." Fitch humbly nods and raises up from the dinner table. He slides each of the reloaded Colt revolvers into their proper holsters. Fitch takes the reloaded backup cylinders and secures them inside of the leather snap cases along the gunbelt. Taking the gunbelt in hand, Fitch hangs it over the backrest of one of the dinner table chairs. He turns and scurries along the puncheon floor toward the copper wash basin and soiled dinnerware and plates along the far wall.

Theo sits across from Fitch at the dinner table as he continues to sew a torn shirt sleeve, at least attempting to sew. His glasses rest low on the bridge of his nose as the dim kerosene lantern offers little light for the needle and thread. Fitch remains affixed at his meager pile of books. Fitch reaches up and adjusts his flickering student lamp, drawing it closer to himself.

"...and said to the mountains and rocks," Fitch continues reading aloud. "Fall on us and hide us from the face of Him who sits on the throne and from the wrath of the Lamb! For the Great Day of His wrath has come, and who is able to stand?"

"That's fine, now onto your history lesson," Theo replies, still attempting to thread that blasted needle! Fitch closes up the worn leather bound Bible and retrieves his thin history book from the meager pile of school books and lessons. "Ha!" Theo exclaims startling Fitch. Success! The thread is drawn into the needle.

Triumphant on his simpleton's task, Theo ties the thread and knots the far end. Sliding the needle into the torn shirt sleeve, Theo begins to mend the damage. Fitch's lips murmur together as he continues to read to himself. Unaware of his Grandpa, an odd sound catches Theo's ear causing him to look up and blankly stare straight ahead to the closed front door of the ranch house. Theo waits a long moment before tossing the torn garment onto the dinner table then suddenly bolts for the crackling fireplace and hearth.

"What is it, Grandpa?" Fitch looks up from his history lesson with a puzzled look.

"Be still," Theo nearly scolds. He takes the double barreled shotgun from the wall and releases its open bellied stock to confirm the weapon is loaded. Snapping the shotgun to its firing position, Theo storms to the front door and flings it open. Nearly frightened, Fitch scampers close behind. With legs spread apart and boots firmly placed on the top step of the porch, Theo squints through the darkness of night for any signs of approaching intruders. Fitch cowers behind the opened door, just able to peer around the corner.

"Sheriff! Sheriff!" the voice beckons out.

"Ivan? Ivan, is that you?" Theo answers. The winded deputy gallops out from the darkness and skids his mount to a halt along the front porch with Theo standing facing him. Deputy Ivan McClaine wears a common hat, leather vest with a deputy's badge pinned to his chest, wrangler trousers and worn boots. Ivan looks more like the runt of the liter than a deputy. "What's this all about, Ivan?" Theo asks as he lowers the cocked double barreled shotgun.

"Sheriff, Cougar 'n'is boys'r'n town raisin' a ruckus over at Bell's!" Ivan tries to blurt out while catching his breath.

"Where's'r men?"

"They're all'n town waitin' fer you."

"I'll be there directly. Go'n without me. Tell'em to wait 'till I get there," Theo orders.

"Right, Sheriff," Ivan pulls back hard on the reigns of his horse, turns the beast and thunders out into the darkness headed back to Purgatory. Theo whips his shotgun over his shoulder and pauses a moment. Shaking his head, he turns and enters his home through the opened front door. Fitch timidly backs away from his concealed location from behind the door, tip-toeing his way after his Grandpa. Theo replaces the shotgun over the crackling fireplace, pausing a moment to take a deep breath. Without a word, Fitch understands the events and consequences of the last several minutes.

Theo stands in the middle of the central dinning area, wrapping his gunbelt about his waist. The pair of Colt model ivory handled revolvers, hang snug about his hips. After fastening the buckle of the gunbelt, Theo takes his gray wide brimmed Stetson hat from Fitch, placing it firmly upon his head. Fitch is obedient, handing his Grandpa his silver spurs. Theo cocks up each of his boots sliding the silver spurs onto each of his heels. With each foot placed onto the puncheon floor, Theo's boots make a distinctive sound. *Jingle-jingle.*

Lastly, Fitch humbly hands Theo his sheriff's badge. Theo pins it to his leather vest then reaches up to slightly adjust his grey

Stetson. He sways his shoulders, lowering his palms to settle in the pair of ivory handled Colt revolvers at his hips so is not to poke or prod himself. Theo slightly smugs as he reaches down to mess up Fitch's hair. Fitch looks up at his Grandpa as Theo gives the young man a loving and fatherly wink. "Finish up your studies'n don't stay up too late," Theo smiles.

"Yes, Grandpa," Fitch respectfully replies as Theo messes up Fitch's hair for the second time. Sheriff Theo Woolley turns then heads toward the cocked open front door. Without looking back toward the impressionable youth, Theo slightly glances over his shoulder as he steps off the porch leading out toward the corrals.

"I'll be back afore 'ya know it." Then, Theo vanishes into the darkness. Fitch strains his eyes for a moment before turning tail back into the dinning area. Taking his student lamp in hand, Fitch bounds back through the opened front door and raises the lamp out into the darkness.

Several longing minutes pass as Fitch knows Grandpa is saddling his horse inside of the furthest corral. Then, the thundering of a galloping beast cuts through the pitch black of night. Fitch sees the fading image of Grandpa slipping out into the darkness. Taking his student lamp in hand, Fitch turns and enters the ranch house, closing the front door behind himself; feeling alone and forgotten for the second time in his life.

The soft pattering hooves of Theo's horse slow from a trot to a mere walk. Mounted upon his faithful steed, Deputy Teddy Blackston awaits the approaching sheriff by the town's welcoming sign, "WELCOME TO PURGATORY – POPULATION 457 – ELEVATION 1,305 FT. – ESTABLISHED 1841."

Teddy is a plain looking man with crow's feet about his eyes and brow. More than likely recruited from the long and hot days of farming and tending crops to the field of law enforcement. "Sheriff," Teddy calls out as Theo continues to slowly approach.

"Deputy."

"There all still inside of Bell's. The rest of our boys'r scattered 'bout waitin' on yer word," Teddy responds with a nervous tone.

"Then lets not keep'em waitin'," Theo snaps the reigns of his horse causing the steed to slowly move forward. Teddy follows close behind along his raggedy horse, swiftly catching up to his sheriff. The pair enter the far end of Purgatory passing along the train depot to one side and the sheriff's office and jail to the opposite side of Main Street. Theo and Teddy slow their horses in front of the quiet livery next to the far side of the sheriff's office. They dismount and loosely tie the reigns to the worn hitching post.

As Theo and Teddy stroll along the wooden planked boardwalk, a pair of young men hobble along their attached slits, adding small bundles of wood and kindling to the cracking and bright flames of the lit lampposts at the corners of Main street. Theo and Teddy quietly make their way across the street. One of Theo's deputies slightly tips his hat, leaning at first against one of the upward supporting beams. The deputy turns and begins following Theo and Teddy, yet remaining along the far side of the street.

Continuing to pass by the closed general stores and dry good suppliers, Theo and Teddy pass by the Katherine Hotel. The brightly light lobby is a welcoming sight. Theo nods and tips his hat toward Cleo, the night shift clerk. Cleo is a colored woman in her middle years. She has a round and pleasant face with a motherly warm smile. Plain dress and apron with a large wrap about her head. Cleo smiles up from behind the lobby's front desk counter and returns Theo's smile then resumes her attention on the guest registrar and small piles of paperwork.

The Bank of Purgatory stands near the center of town with a few general stores scattered in between it and City Hall. From down the street, up-beat ragtime music begins to fill the air growing louder as Theo and Teddy step off the wooden planked boardwalk, crossing the only cross side street of Purgatory.

Stepping up onto the continuing boardwalk, Theo and Teddy are met by another pair of deputies each toting a cocked and loaded double barrel shotgun. Without a word, Theo leads the trio along the boardwalk with the four other deputies crossing Main Street to join them.

Very few local townspeople are seen along the boardwalks. At first, they smile and nod toward the sheriff and deputies, then sense something is amiss. Sheriff Theo Woolley hardly ever comes to town at night let alone with his deputies in tow. The upbeat ragtime music grows louder, the unseen piano player banging and hammering away at the black and white keys. Theo leads Teddy and the other deputies across the last opened section of dirt, stepping up onto the last establishment on this side of town, "BELL'S SALOON – SPIRITS & GAMING".

The large, two-story building takes up nearly one city block resting on the direct end corner of Main Street. The upper balcony is cluttered with dancehall girls dressed in lavish lace and full length dresses. Powered rouge covers their cheeks as the ladies continue to flirt and "entertain" their various cowboys and ranchers. Bell's main entrance is seen at the direct corner of the building and Main Street with a pair of handsome swinging batwing doors inviting all inward. Its wooden plank boardwalk stretches out in opposite directions along the lower floor of the building.

Theo leads his deputies along Bell's boardwalk meeting up with Ivan leaning up against an upward supporting beam. The hitching posts along the street are filled with an assortment of saddled horses. "Sheriff," Ivan nods.

"Ivan, they still in there?" Theo asks.

"Yep. They've settled down a bit but the place's still a wreck," Ivan approaches Theo. From inside, the ragtime music continues to fill the air muddled with laughter and the sounds of various conversations. There's no shooting nor sounds of arguments. All appears as it should be. Theo peers around the corner and takes a peek over the top of the batwing doors. Pausing a moment, Theo turns toward Ivan and the other deputies. "Wait out here for a spell."

"Whatta you gonna do, Sheriff?" Teddy asks.

"I'm gonna go wet my whistle," Theo glances over his shoulder with a playful wink. Theo adjusts his Colt revolvers at his hips, reaches out and pushes open the batwing doors entering the smoky drinking establishment. Ivan fidgets for several moments, nervously looking about Main Street. The young lamplighters continue to hobble along on their slits, loading the cracking lampposts with additional wood and kindling. Teddy and the other deputies begin to fidget as well.

"Why'd'e go in all by his self?" one of the deputies ask.

"He knows what'es donin'," Ivan replies with an uncertain tone. "Jest said to wait'n that's what were gonna do," Ivan looks over the other deputies with the pair of them clutching onto their cocked and loaded double barrel shotguns.

Sheriff Theo Woolley allows the batwing doors to swing closed behind himself as he pauses and surveys the situation. In the nearest far right corner, a pitcher tosses out a trio of dice with a handful of ragged cowboys betting on the game of chuck-a-luck. Along the next right wall, three billiard tables span out filling most of the remaining wall. Plainly dressed businessmen politely discuss politics, exchanging shots with their cues. At the third and last billiard table, a five-some of roughnecks, that must be them. Just beyond the third billiard table, an elderly colored man hammers away at the black and white keys of his piano just at the foot of a duel staircase leading up to the second floor mezzanine into the upper hallways of "guest bedrooms".

The far back wall is consumed with an extended saloon style bar. Filling the twirling leather padded stools, cluttered ranchers and wranglers tear over their drinks chit-chattin' among themselves. Behind the bar, rows of glasses, whiskey and tequila bottles and an assortment of other intoxicants.

Robert appears from the nearly hidden hallway along and under the dual staircase leading out from the pair of owner's suites and storage rooms. He totes several filled whiskey bottles under his arms as he scurries behind the bar, setting down the bottles in front of various forward facing patrons. Robert is a stout man, broad shoulders and a curved barber's mustache. His soiled white shirt with garters about his upper arms, a vest and a stained apron tied about his thick waist. Robert glances up from pouring several shots of whiskey to see Theo quietly making his entrance, approaching the far end of the bar along the left side of the saloon.

The remaining and largest area of Bell's is filled with gaming and poker tables. Gamblers, ranchers and probably even a few outlaws continue their hands of poker as Theo meanders along the far left wall through the maze of filled tables. Over a dozen scadly dressed dancehall girls swoon over the winning poker players coaxing their "hosts" to keep buying rounds of whiskey and tequila. Odd though, a saloon with dancehall girls but no dance hall nor burlesque stage. Theo nods and slightly smiles down at the poker players keeping quiet and to himself. Seeing the sheriff's badge upon Theo's chest, a few of the poker players quickly fold, gather their meager winnings and make a quick exit; probably a few of the outlaws.

Six chairs lay in shattered pieces throughout the central walkway of Bell's. The vacant area between the poker and drinking tables and the billiard tables along the far side of the saloon. Among the debris of chairs, a pair of poker tables lay in ruin with broken whiskey bottles and shattered glasses about the wooden planked floor. From the backroom and storage area from under the nearly hidden hallway under the staircases, a pair of dancehall girls quickly make their way toward the destroyed chairs and tables beginning to clean and sweep up the broken glasses and bottles.

Outside along the boardwalk, Ivan peers inside through the last street facing window to see Theo approaching the far left end of the bar. Ivan paces back and forth until shuffling his way back toward the batwing doors which suddenly burst open with the few poker players scurrying toward the hitched horses. Teddy and the other deputies appear more calm than Ivan, leaning against the upward supporting beams, yawing, growing bored and restless.

Theo finds a vacant stool at the far end of the extended bar with the last outside window to his left. Robert slides down the bar and faces Theo. "Sheriff," Robert nods as he wipes away a puddle of left behind ale.

"Robert. Heard you had a scuffle in here earlier," Theo replies.

"That's them over there," Robert whispers. Robert cocks his eyes to his immediate forward left over Theo's right shoulder. Pauses his sight, then motions toward the third billiard table closest to the bottom of the dual staircase and colored piano player. Robert pours Theo a shot of whiskey then turns and attends the rest of his patrons along the bar. Taking a sip of the whiskey, Theo slightly turns to his right looking over his shoulder, keeping to himself, not calling attention to his actions.

From under the hidden hallway under the dual staircases, Bell makes her appearance. A buxom woman in her late thirties or early forties, sandy-blonde long hair curled and weaved in a wasp's nest atop her head. Although in no need of one to show off her attributes, Bell wears a corset, thrusting her well endowed curves for all to see. With no bustle, her French style dress flows freely behind herself in a swaying manner.

Pleasant face and round cheeks with no signs of painted makeup or rouge, unlike her employed troop of dancehall girls. Bell catches a glimpse of Theo at the far end of the bar yet continues her steadfast course behind the pair of dancehall girls cleaning up the broken chairs, tables and shattered bottles. Bell approaches them, taking the remains of a broken table in hand, dragging it back toward the storage area.

The pair of dancehall girls take their filled dustpans and empty them along the waste container at the near end of the bar. Theo finishes his shot of whiskey as Robert approaches and pours the sheriff another. Bell returns to the central area collecting a pair of broken chairs, likewise dragging them toward the back storage area as the dancehall girls take one final sweep of the floor, turning and dumping the dustpans into the waste container. Tucking the brooms and dustpans behind the bar, the pair of dancehall girls return to the poker and gaming tables trying to rustle up some "business" for themselves. From the third billiard table across the saloon, a single shot glass it tossed into the air.

BLAM. BLAM.

The shots thunder through the air. The surrounding poker players, wranglers, businessmen and dancehall girls shutter from the shots but say nothing and continue with their own business. The shot glass rains down onto the wooden planked floor as the shootist lunges forward, wrapping his arms about Bell's curved waist, "How 'bout 'nother round over here, Bell!" Cougar exclaims. He spins Bell around and releases her causing her to nearly topple over the railing and bottom step of the dual staircases. Robert fumes, making his way from behind the bar, assisting Bell to her feet, quickly checking for any injuries.

Cougar, now there's an interesting fellow. Leader of the pack of four lowlife scoundrels. Claimed to have robbed more stages than any man alive. An almost handsome fellow wearing nearly all grey attire. A pair of broken-in revolvers holstered low at his hips. A silk bandana tied loosely around his neck with a wide brimmed sombrero looking hat. Not more than sixteen or seventeen years of age. His ragged "associates", not much older, hinting at Latino origins. Darker in skin color and dressed accordingly with an assortment of pistols and weapons about their gunbelts.

Cougar returns to his billiard table taking a cue from one of his partners. He leans over to take a shot when a nearby businessman at the next billiard table swings around and accidentally knocks into Cougar causing him to miss his shot. The businessman swiftly whips around with a humbled look on his face. "I-I'm sorry, mister," the business man trembles.

Without a word nor a single thought, Cougar takes the butt of his billiard cue stick and smashes it across the businessman's head. The man drops to the floor with a loud thud. Cougar's posse laughs out loud and pats Cougar and each other on the back. All around, the gamblers, wranglers and dancehall girls and even the colored piano player not missing a note, say nothing and keep to themselves, continuing to attend to their own activities.

The fellow businessman's friends quickly collect him up off of the floor, support him under his arms and swiftly exit through the swinging batwing doors. Not giving the incident a second thought, Cougar turns from the third billiard table and bellows out toward the bar, " 'Ow 'bout that drink, Ole Man!"

Robert slightly turns toward Theo who gives his long time friend a subtle nod. Cougar notices the gesture and cocks his head to the side, still saying nothing more. Robert takes a bottle of tequila and pours five shots for Cougar and his gang. Bell saunters along the bar as Robert places the tequila shots onto a tray. Theo smiles and nods at Bell who nervously takes the tray in hand. "Hey!" Cougar barks out. "Who the hell'r you sayin' we'cn drink'er not?"

Theo keeps to himself remaining seated forward at the bar sipping on his second shot of whiskey. "I'm talkin' to you, mister!" Cougar determinedly walks away from the third billiard table, crosses the opened central area of the saloon and approaches the near end of the bar. "Hey, mister!" The colored piano player eases off the keys, then turns to watch. The scattered poker games and chuck-a-luck game in the corner cease. The dancehall girls seem to scatter from the poker tables. Cougar's pack fans out behind him as Cougar slides his hand across the bar's surface, continuing to slowly approach Theo. As he passes, the few remaining patrons sitting at the bar quickly get up and dash to the opposite sides of the saloon. Cougar pauses merely five or so yards away from Theo. "Well mister. Who'd you think you'r? You think I don'ave enough money'ta pay for my own drinks?" Cougar demands.

"Your money's no good here, Cougar," Theo responds in a low growl.

"You know me, mister? I don' know you," Cougar cautiously steps away from the bar a few feet carefully placing his right palm on the handle of his holstered revolver. Theo slams the last of his shot of whiskey down his throat then stands defiantly to his feet. His boots land hard onto the wooden planked floor. *Jingle-jingle.*

"I reckon I know you. Last spring you robbed my bank."

"*Your* bank? Sounds'ta me like you think this's *your* town," Cougar laughs with his posse closing in behind him along the bar. Slightly cocked to the side, Theo fully turns to face Cougar, his sheriff's badge glimmering in Cougar's face. "I'll be skinned! This's *your* town, "Sheriff"," Cougar replies with a chuckle. His low laughter fades with an evil and stern glare crossing his face. "But not fer long…"

At that instant, gunfire explodes throughout the saloon. Cougar ducks and covers as Theo draws his pair of ivory handled Colt revolvers returning fire. Cougar's pack fans out wildly firing their drawn weapons at Theo. Ivan and Teddy charge into the saloon leading the other deputies inward, firing upon Cougar and his gang. Billows of smoke fill the room.

Bell and Robert cower in each others arms crouched down behind the bar. The dancehall girls scream as they frantically dash up the staircase. The colored piano player dives from his stool under the hidden shadowed area under the staircase. The dealers, gamblers, ranchers and businessmen dive for cover, turning and flipping the scattered poker tables up onto their sides creating as much cover as possible. Gatherings of townspeople carefully approach Bell's along Main Street. The young lamplighters quickly hobble along their stilts wanting to catch a glimpse of a gun battle. Blazing gunfire continues for several moments from inside of Bell's. Then a moment of deathly silence…

BLAM-BLAM.

All becomes still. The townspeople creep closer. The young lamplighters quickly rest themselves onto Bell's boardwalk, swiftly removing their stilts. With full force, Cougar thunders out through the batwing doors with a smoking revolver in each hand. His grey shirt and trousers seeping with blood. Cougar's left eye severely damaged nearly dangling out of its socket. He holsters his left revolver, reaches up and tears off his silk bandana from around his neck. Cougar scoops up his damaged eye trying to keep it in place; blood continues to gush from the wound.

Cougar violently waves his drawn right revolver in all directions toward the frightened townspeople, waiting for another challenge. There are no other challenges. Cougar swiftly unties his mount at the hitching post, leaps up into the stolen saddle and charges up Main Street. The gawking townspeople watch as Cougar disappears into the darkness at a full gallop beyond the train depot to one side and the sheriff's office and jail to the other. Then, the faint sounds of sobbing echo out onto the street from inside of Bell's.

Wearing his nightshirt, the Mayor bounds out from the front door of City Hall from across the street. An odd sight, an overweight man, wearing a nightshirt, boots and a stove pipe hat, looking like a dressed chicken. "What's happened here!" the Mayor shouts having heard the gun battle and seeing the gathered townspeople.

The Mayor gently presses the swinging batwing doors open and enters Bell's. The lingering smoke of the blazing gun battle causes the Mayor's eyes to slightly water. At the far corner of the saloon, the colored piano player creeps out from under the hidden area under the dual staircases. Scattered dancehall girls are comforted by the cowardice gamblers and few remaining business men. Ivan lays flat on his back on the bar as Robert attends to his badly wounded left arm. Blood flows from the injury at the elbow. Ivan cries out in pain as Robert tightens a belt above the wound attempting to stop the blood.

The Mayor tiptoes in further followed by a few curious townspeople. Tables and chairs are smashed up and tossed to their sides with countless bullet holes riddling their flat surfaces. The rectangular mirror hanging behind the bar, shattered. Teddy and

51

the rest of the slain deputies lay scattered in growing pools of blood soaking into the wooden planks of the floor. The Mayor and growing number of townspeople inch their way closer to the bar. The Mayor nearly stops cold in his tracks.

Bell kneels down onto the floor along the tossed aside bar stools. Theo, cradled in her arms with two bullet wounds through the back. Bell sobs with rivers of Theo's blood covering her hands and the front of her frilly dress. Tearful, Bell looks up to the approaching Mayor who lowers his head and respectfully removes his stove pipe hat. "Hell's bells," Bell tearfully whispers.

Robert and the Mayor crash through the front door of Doc Herring's office. Slung under their arms supporting his weight, Ivan moans as he continues to bleed all over them. Ivan is in terrible pain fading in and out of consciousness. The room is dark and bland with four chairs along the wall of the lobby for awaiting patience. "Doc! Doc, wake up!" Robert shouts. A lantern is lit from inside the next room. Robert and the Mayor drag Ivan down the short and narrow hallway toward the far back room.

Dressed in a worn nightshirt and boots, Doc stumbles out from one of the first rooms, down the short hallway and enters the back room… the dreaded operating room. "What in tar nation happened?"

"Big shoot out at Bell's. Nearly kilt everyone," the Mayor fumbles for a response.

"Git'im up on the table!" Doc orders. Robert and the Mayor strain to heave Ivan up onto the cold steel surface of the table. Ivan lets out a girlish whimper. From the shadows of the short hallway, a door opens from a side door. Beth peeks her head outward, gazing at the activity and carnage. There is blood everywhere! Beth keeps her distance in her doorway, ever so closely watching. "I'm sorry, Ivan. There's nothin' I can do." Doc pauses a moment, "That arm'll have to come off!"

"No, Doc! Anythin' but that!" Ivan screams.

"I'm sorry, lad," Doc turns and takes a blood stained saw from one up the upper counter tops cluttered with an assortment of soiled medical tools and devices. Doc clutches onto the blood stained saw, giving Robert and the Mayor a stern and remorseful glare. "Hold'im tight!"

Using his stout weight, Robert nearly sits on Ivan's chest. Doc extends out a narrow metallic plank from below the operating table. He stretches out Ivan's wounded arm and straps it onto the metallic plank both at the wrist and about the wounded elbow. The Mayor stands on the opposite side of the table, pressing down with all his might on Ivan's right arm and shoulder keeping the injured deputy pinned to the table. Doc takes a bottle of whiskey from the cluttered counter top and nearly pours all of the alcohol down Ivan's throat. Ivan chokes and coughs yet manages to swallow most of it.

Doc takes the whiskey bottle and guzzles a throat full for himself. Wiping his mouth with the sleeve of his nightshirt, Doc pours the rest of the whiskey onto Ivan's wounded arm. "This may hurt abit..." Doc sighs clutching tightly onto the blood stained saw. From down the narrow and dark hallway, Beth's eyes widen as Ivan lets out a blood curdling scream.

Bell stands along the boardwalk of her saloon just outside of the closed batwing doors. Her hands and the front of her frilly dress, covered with Theo's blood. A handful of the town's men carry each of Cougar's slain companions outward and toss them in a row facing upward along the front boardwalk facing Main Street. Laying next to the pile of dead outlaws, a slain gambler, a wrangler and businessman more respectfully placed facing upward.

The businessman's grieving wife weeps over her bullet riddled husband merely at the wrong place at the wrong time. The gambler and wrangler have no one to morn for them. A trio of Bell's dancehall girls hover over the two attempting to be as mournful and saddened as possible. The sounds of heavy footsteps draw nearer from inside of the saloon. Bell turns to see eight men of Purgatory respectfully carry Sheriff Theo Woolley's slain body out through the swinging batwing doors.

53

The thinning crowd of the townspeople make a path for the eight men as they step off the boardwalk, making their way toward the center of Main Street and continue to carry Theo's stiffening body toward the sheriff's office and jail at the far end of town. The townspeople lower their heads and quietly shuffle off into the night. From the pitch of darkness, an ear piercing scream cuts through the air.

Bell cocks her head and listens to the terror for a second time. Ivan's terrifying screams flood out onto Main Street. Bell sadly lowers and shakes her head, "Hell's bells, Doc." Bell reaches up and unfastens the wasp's bun in her head allowing her golden locks to flow down over her shoulders. She turns and saunters in through the batwing doors. From inside, the colored piano player begins to play a slow and hypnotizing melody. Not a tune of cheer, but one of remorse and solitude, drowning out the fading screams of Ivan's agony.

Melting blankets of springtime snow dance across the surrounding mountain tops. Oceans of high desert wasteland spans the valley below with clusters of amber and tan boulders slightly accented with sparse Joshua Trees. The rising sun is low off the horizon casting its welcoming rays through the cloudless sky. Yet, the ominous feeling of thunder and lightening, a spring storm looms overhead in the distance.

From the narrowing road leading in from town, a silhouette of images are faintly made out. The images somberly draw nearer with the clanking of the gear and the bridles of the pair of horses towing the flat cargo wagon. Human figures are finally made out sitting about the padded seats of the wagon but are still too far away to clearly see their features. A foursome of saddled riders slowly ride up along the rear of the rolling wagon with the convoy drawing nearer to the main house of The Woolley Ranch.

Wiping the sleep from his eyes, young Fitch steps out from the front door out onto the wrap-around porch. Fitch senses something is the matter, watching the wagon and foursome drawing nearer. Fitch steps off of the porch in a slow manner, then darts to a gallop toward the approaching visitors.

A surviving gambler and wrangler maneuver their mounts along the far sides of the flat cargo wagon. A businessman and the Mayor trot along completing the saddened caravan. The expressions are solemn with their faces concealed by the wide brims of their lowered hats. Still covered with Ivan's blood, Robert clutches onto the reigns of the pair of horses leading the cargo wagon with Bell seated next to him along the padded seat. Theo's blood is stained to the front of her frilly dress. There are no passengers to be seen from the cargo area of the rolling wagon.

Fitch slows to a halt in front of, yet along side of the wagon. Robert pulls back on the reigns, steps down onto the side brake, then secures the reigns to the padded seat. Not waiting for any assistance from Robert, Bell bounds out from the passenger's seat and engulfs Fitch into her motherly arms. Bell embraces Fitch, holding him close to her bosom, "Fitch, darling."

"Bell? Where's Grandpa?" Fitch whispers. Bell clutches onto Fitch holding him ever so closely. Robert makes his way from around the cargo wagon, pauses a step along side of Bell and Fitch, resting his hand tenderly upon Fitch's shoulder. Without a word, Robert motions Fitch toward the rear of the cargo wagon. The gambler, wrangler, businessman and the Mayor sit quietly in their saddles as Fitch approaches the opened tailgate of the wagon.

Fitch stares blankly at the tarp covered figure laying in the back of the cargo wagon. The top of the tarp seeping with drying blood. The gambler, wrangler, businessman and the Mayor respectfully remove their hats and lower their heads. Bell reaches out standing behind Fitch, placing both of her motherly hands upon his shoulders. Wiping a single tear from his eye, Fitch reaches up and pulls away the lower section of the tarp. Grandpa's boots and silver spurs stick out from the bloody image. Fitch forces himself to identify the boots and silver spurs. Reaching up, Fitch flicks his finger at the nearest spur. *Jingle-jingle...*

Main Street, Purgatory. Not a soul to be seen. A deathly stillness has fallen over the high desert community. A light high desert breeze rustles along causing slightly opened shutters to tremble and sway. The batwing doors of Bell's saloon swing freely to a fro. An occasional dust devil twirls behind the backsides of the facing buildings and general stores.

City Hall, Bank of Purgatory and the majority of the dry goods and general stores; closed for the day. Bell's at the far end of town as well as The Katherine Hotel are open for the day however stand still and lifeless. The ever so faintest commotion is detected from around the far corner of Bell's saloon. The sounds of footsteps and slow trotting hooves. The rattling of bridles and wagon gear. Then, the soothing voices of men and women singing a remorseful, "Amazing Grace".

Doc is the first to appear from around the far corner of Bell's. Doc wears a black derby and black Sunday-meetin' clothes. He clutches onto the reigns of his black pair of horses pulling a grim looking wagon. In the other hand, Doc clutches onto Beth wearing a light colored dress, lace up the front boots and a bonnet. The hearse, slowly towed behind. Upright glass partitions surround the wagon allowing access only from the closed tailgate. Inside for all to see, slain Sheriff Theodore Woolley lays flat on his back.

Theo has been cleaned and tended to and has been dressed in his best Sunday-meetin' suit. His face is cold and somber, yet with a devilish smirk about his lips. The hearse bares enough room for two, however Theo has been placed in the direct center. The pair of Doc's black horses continue to pull the hearse as more and more of the townspeople begin to make their way from around the far corner of Bell's continuing to mournfully sing, "Amazing Grace."

The Mayor is next to appear following close behind Doc and Beth followed by the entire compliment of Purgatory all dressed in their finest Sunday-meetin' attire. Along the precession, scattered flat bed cargo wagons house the rest of Theo's deputies;

Teddy and the other four… well, the other four which most of the people of Purgatory can't even recall their names. Ivan, Purgatory's newly appointed sheriff, rounds the corner next with his left arm severed and bandaged about the elbow. Theo's sheriff's badge pinned to his leather vest.

Lastly along the precession, Bell and Robert walk along on opposite sides of Fitch, leading the last gatherings of townspeople. Fitch wears Theo's oversized wide brimmed Stetson hat, Sunday-meetin' best, the pair of ivory handled Colt revolvers hanging loose and low about his hips and Grandpa's silver spurs at the heels of his boots. *Jingle-jingle.*

Robert wears no soiled apron but an odd print suit jacket, off colored trousers and a southern style string tie looking very badly mismatched. Oh well, he tried. Bell rests a parasol on her shoulder with her golden hair flowing freely about her shoulders. A French dress drapes behind herself with no need of a bustle or corset.

A slew of dancehall girls follows behind making do with what presentable dresses they could muster. No face paint or frillies, looking as respectfully as possible. Bringing up the furthest tail-end of the precession, Bell's colored piano player and Cleo, late night clerk and maid of The Katherine Hotel. Both welcomed to the precession, but not openly. The caravan of mourners continue along Main Street passing by the silenced dry goods and general stores, The Katherine Hotel, City Hall, The Bank of Purgatory, the livery, then finally the sheriff's office and jail at the end of town. One by one, each man, woman, child and wagon continue outward past the train depot, heading for a slight upward lull in the distance speckled with meager gatherings of Joshua Trees.

"What can I say about this man? Sheriff Theodore Woolley was a man of the people. A man of trust and dignity. A man to turn to in an hour of need. Sheriff Theodore Woolley was… was my friend," Doc speaks aloud. The townspeople surround a freshly dug opened grave. Theo rests atop of a pair of planks supporting him as he remains facing upward on his back. Doc chokes back the tears. "Let us pray. Our Father..." The assembly of townspeople repeat and follow Doc's lead.

"Our Father..."

"Who art in Heaven..."

"Who art in Heaven..." the townspeople of Purgatory continue to follow Doc's fellowship as Fitch angrily recites the prayer from memory. Having spent many nights with his studies and Grandpa's teaching of The Good Book, Fitch knows the prayer well... well enough to know it didn't do any good for his Grandfather this time...

Doc remains steadfast at the head of the fresh grave continuing to lead the gathered mourners in the prayer. The Mayor, Robert, the shoot out's surviving gambler and wrangler, Bell's colored piano player and Ivan, lower the ropes that support Theo's body. They slowly begin to lower him to his final resting place. Tears flow from the cheeks of the women and children. Towering men conceal their sorrow. Bell has gathered up Beth, clutching her close to herself with young Fitch staring blankly at Grandpa's grave on the opposite side of her.

Reaching out in front of Bell's dress, Beth tenderly takes a hold of Fitch's hand and lovingly squeezes it. In a stone cold glaze, Fitch remains focused on Grandpa being lowered into the grave. Tossing the ropes aside, the Mayor, Robert, gambler, wrangler, Bell's piano player and Ivan take their shovels and begin tossing the mounds of dirt into the grave. Ivan, struggles with his good arm, yet manages to keep up with the others. Beth leans over across Bell and kisses Fitch on the cheek.

"A-men," Doc concludes.

"A-men," the community responds.

Beth pauses a moment, turns and follows behind Doc gathering up the reigns of his pair of black horses still harnessed to the hearse. Not struck until now, Fitch reaches up and tenderly touches his cheek where Beth had kissed him. Fitch turns to see

Doc and Beth leading the hearse away with the majority of Purgatory's population following close behind. The Mayor, Robert, gambler, wrangler, piano player and Ivan continue to fill Theo's grave. "Come along now, dear," Bell motherly beckons toward Fitch.

"I'll be awhile, Bell," Fitch whispers.

"All right, then. Come along when you're ready," Bell attempts a motherly tone. As he continues to shovel earth into Theo's grave, Robert looks up and tosses Bell an understanding wink. Bell smiles back, collects up the remaining dancehall girls and begins to stroll back into town. As Robert and Ivan toil, they glace up from time to time, seeing the young man, standing steadfast at his Grandpa's grave. They grey wide brimmed Stetson hat upon his smaller head, the oversized gunbelt with the holstered pair of ivory handled Colt revolvers and the silver spurs at the heels of his boots. Fitch continues to stare downward into the grave. Grandpa Theo growing deeper and deeper into the dirt. Fitch shifts his weight from one foot to the other. *Jingle-jingle.*

"I remember that day as if it were yesterday. Fitch's broken heart. Grandpa Theo raised him as his own son after his parents died. Grandpa was all he had. Fitch sulked around for a couple of years. Doing odds and ends. Trying to make his mark on the world. He even worked for Ole Man Gentry in the livery for a spell. Fitch didn't take to that to well. Cleaning stables, shoeing horses and such. Fitch ran fliers for the Mayor during his reelection campaign but that only lasted 'till fall."

"Fitch spent nearly three months with Doc Herring trying to study to be a doctor. Those were glorious

months. Fitch was at Doc's office and operating room nearly everyday. Don't think he noticed me too much, though but I'd like to think he did. He didn't have the stomach for all that blood and guts. One afternoon, Mr. Spencer came in with a boil on his... on his backside. Doc had to lance the boil and asked Fitch to assist him. Sakes-alive! I nearly wet myself! Doc cut into Mr. Spencer's hide and this... stuff came pouring out. Fitch lost all control, bolted to the door and lost his breakfast in the nearest watering trough. Doc and Mr. Spencer got the biggest hoot out of that. They didn't stop laughing for nearly an hour."

"With no other family, Purgatory, well, Ma Bell kinda took Fitch in. Funny thing about Bell, took me in, too. She's gotta thing about strays and orphans. Robert and Bell gathered up all the town together to figure out what to do with Fitch. He had become taxingly restless. Purgatory all pulled together and collected up a purse, like an offering in church. Robert recalled Grandpa Theo's ramblings that he wanted to send Fitch off to school to learn himself about the law. On Grandpa's wages, that just couldn't've been done. On Fitch's sixtieth birthday, Bell and Robert gave Fitch the purse to go off to Philadelphia to learn the law. That was the saddest day of my life."

"Was Fitch ever gonna come back? Would he meet a young filly out there in the big city? If he did come back, would he even remember me? God Almighty! I didn't want him to leave… ever."

"Four years and some time had passed since Grandpa Theo had been shot. It was a gala event to see Fitch bound up into the wagon hitched up to a pair of stallions. Robert figured Fitch could sell 'im if he had to. He had tied off the younger stallion to the end of the wagon. Fitch had a thing for that grulla colored horse. Fitch didn't wanna wear him out during the long trip but didn't wanna leave him behind. Who know's how long he'd be gone."

"The entire town of Purgatory was there. Ivan, still the sheriff, waved his wooden arm Doc had special ordered him from New York. Besides myself, I gather Bell and Robert, mostly Robert, was the saddest to see Fitch go. Kinda a kinship Robert and Fitch had made but one couldn't place your finger on it. The whole town looked in and took care of Fitch after Grandpa was kilt."

"Then that's when it happened! Fitch had said all of his good-byes, waving like a full-on loon. He took up the reigns of his wagon, clicked his mouth and moved the pair of stallions no more than a few yards. The Mayor and townspeople had already begun to leave, continuing about their daily business. Robert and Bell had waved, turned and disappeared inside of the saloon and Ivan was making his way back to the sheriff's office and jail. No one saw what happened next."

"Fitch tied off the reigns, lumbered off the wagon and darted toward me. Standing there, dumb struck, I thought he was going to say his final-final farewells never to return, or that he'd miss me, somethin' poetic. Fitch planted the softest and wettest kiss on my lips I had ever known! I'd seen kisses like that afore but had never had one."

"My belly tossed. My thoughts and head became light. My eyes closed. I felt the warmth on his gentle grasp on my shoulders. Fitch didn't say a word. Afore I knew it, my eyes opened. He was already back in the wagon galloping away. My cloud filled eyes followed to see if Fitch looked back. With a wink, he did."

"I swear, if I had died that day, I wouldn't have died unhappy. That was the most loving and tender kiss a young woman could have ever asked for. The warmest kiss I had ever known... until James Williams came to Purgatory..."

CHAPTER III

The high desert wasteland is endless. Mere clutters of gathered amber and tan boulders are the only landscape's décor. Withering Joshua Trees cower under the blazing sun of the New Mexico Territory. The range of rolling hills are sprinkled with a dusting of the early December snow, now slowly melting into the deep cutting valley below. Drawing nearer, The Woolley Ranch in a decaying and forgotten state.

The main ranch house is covered with the summer's onslaught of blowing high desert sand and past dust-devils. Tumbleweeds run ramped throughout the once thriving homestead. Dozens of shingles are missing from the roof of both the main ranch house and the nearby two story barn. There hasn't been any fresh hay in the barn's loft in over a decade. The rocking chair sways lightly along the unkempt and rattling wrap-around porch.

Along the three sides of the rotting barn, the remains of the three corrals. Several cross beams lay cockeyed from one side to the other. In another section of the corrals, entire sections of planked fencing are gone. No cattle, no stallions, no mares, no livestock of any kind. The Woolley Ranch is dead. Then, the faintest pair of boot prints appear from the mixture of sand and dirt about the main ranch house. Someone *has* been here.

Thundering hooves roar along Main Street. Purgatory has come a long way in the past several years. As usual, Bell's Saloon & Gaming is bursting at the seams with business. Wranglers and businessmen nod and greet each other as they enter, passing through the swinging batwing doors on the corner of the two-story building and corner of the street.

Loud up-beat New Orleans style music bursts outward onto Main Street. Odd type of music for these parts. Stagecoaches rumble through town with a wide assortment of cargo wagons, cowboys and pedestrians scurrying about from one side of the wooden planked boardwalk to the other. Dry goods and general stores expand along opposite sides of Main Street followed by City hall and the Mayor's office kitty corner and across the street from Bell's.

A make-shift cross-street now cuts in the middle of Purgatory allowing stagecoaches and wagons to move freely from one side of town to the other. The barber shop stands directly across from Wells Fargo Bank, once The Bank of Purgatory. Next to the barber shop is tucked in nicely along side of the Katherine Hotel with couples of well dressed folks exiting and entering the lodging place. Several other thriving dry goods and general stores have been erected filling in the gaps along both sides of the street.

A few years back, Miss Katy's Boarding House came to town. It seemed there wasn't enough "room" at The Katherine for the ruffians and deadbeats drifting for work to be housed at the well established hotel. Katy's Boarding House stays full alright. There never seems a lack of supply of drifters through Purgatory.

Main Street is filled with small armies of townspeople dashing about, dodging the rambling stagecoaches and cargo wagons. The locals are gleeful as they continue to hang banners, flags and an assortment of festive red, white and blue decorations making Purgatory look more like the town is about to celebrate The Forth of July rather than New Year's Day.

At the far end of Main Street, newly repaired railroad tracks lay across the ground cutting along the high desert sand in spanning opposite directions. The train depot remains with a narrow alley way next to the Stardust Saloon built just a few years ago. The Stardust stands two stories with a railing along its upper balcony. Dancehall girls stroll along the upper balcony, waving and attempting to draw in any more "business" for themselves and away from Bell's down the street.

Rowdy music from the piano player echo's out from within cluttered with boisterous laughter and the clanking of beer mugs.

The owners of the general store and next door dry goods, which once had stood in the Stardust's location, took a bath on the deal. Word has it Ned, the owner of the Stardust, only paid a fraction for the land then turned around and tore down the struggling businesses.

Across the street from the Stardust Saloon, the sheriff's office and jail with a narrow alleyway separating it and the next door livery. Billows of smoke pour out from the livery with the constant hammering of the anvil deep and dark inside. Leaning up against an upward supporting beam of the sheriff's office and jail, Deputy Cory Edwards looks out toward the chaos and activity of the townspeople continuing to decorate for the oncoming celebration.

Cory is a lanky fellow with a kind of dusty way about him. A pair of six-shooters holstered at his hips and a dim deputy's badge pinned to his leathery vest upon his chest. Yet, Cory seems polite with a good manner about him. Glancing to one side, Cory spies an out-of-towner leading his saddled horse toward the opened doors of the livery. The well dressed man's horse slightly limps from a tossed shoe.

Looking across the street, Cory gazes upon the dozens of crates, Saratoga chests, steamer trunks, mounds of luggage and even a few stallions prepared to be loaded up onto the next arriving train. Beyond the spanning railroad tracks, a large work area has been set up. With the Civil War over now, color seems not to bother most people in Purgatory… most people. It appears that the "cause" and "sensible reasoning" of the Civil War hadn't quite made it this far West… yet.

The mixture of laborers work like an assembly line, sawing and hammering at the eight-foot logs in a see-saw manner creating a portable barrier resembling more of a movable "X" hitching post. There are rows upon rows of the constructed barriers as the laborers continue to build even more of the odd looking things.

Yes, Purgatory has grown. The feeling is light and carefree. Prosperity flows from every established business and newly arrived venue. As the laborers continue to saw and hammer at the see-saw barricades, the soot covered blacksmith barters with the tourist needing his horse shoed.

Cory looks out from under the awning of the sheriff's office and jail, watching the townspeople continue the festive decorating of banner and flags under the haphazard supervision of the aging Mayor; stove pipe hat and all. The competing piano music from the Stardust across the street and the New Orleans Jazz from Bell's at the far end of town are muffled by the hooves of the arriving stagecoaches and rumbling cargo wagons. Suddenly, Cory feels a sudden chill. He steps off the boardwalk and strolls onto Main Street at a safe distance from the incoming and outgoing traffic. Looking up into the sky, he sees, no… feels a dark cloud slowly moving in on the growing carefree town…

Purgatory Cemetery. A dim and lonesome place. A few scattered Joshua Trees provide meager shelter from the burning rays of the afternoon sun. Headstones and plots cover the seldomly visited location. A poorly painted white cast iron fence boarders the plots and graves showing signs of rust and decay. A low breeze blows across the lull in the slopping hillside. Less than a half mile below, the town of Purgatory. *Jingle-jingle.*

Deputy Fitch Woolley remains motionless as if he were a gargoyle looking over the headstones of the dead. Fitch stands tall with broad shoulders. Grandpa Theo's oversized gray wide brimmed Stetson hat shields and even shadows his piercingly dark and handsome eyes. Pinned to his leather vest, a worn and fading deputy's badge. Fastened around his waist, the gunbelt and pair of ivory handled Colt revolvers looking as new as the day Captain Theodore Woolley received them for a courageous triumph during his many campaigns of the Indian Wars. After years of waiting, the gunbelt now fits perfectly around his hips. Fitch removes his Stetson hat and rests it across his chest as he kicks a mound of dirt. *Jingle-jingle.* The pair of silver spurs rattle, fastened tightly to the heels of his boots.

"What am I doing here? I know, I know. I made a promise to you, Grandpa. I said, "When I grow up, I wanna be jest like you." Well, here I am, "jest like you." Now, what do I do? I'm second fiddle sheriff to Ivan. Don't get me wrong, he's a fine sheriff and a good man. But, I feel my life's no longer here... without you...ma...pa..."

Fitch slightly turns his head and gazes down at a single headstone along side of Theo's headstone. The years of weather and beating sun has faded the grave. All that remains are, "IN LOVING MEMORY – FATHER AND MOTHER WOOLLEY". Fitch reaches down and brushes away a few gatherings of fallen Joshua Tree branches from the top of his parents headstone. Fitch squats, turning back toward Theo's headstone, staring blankly toward it.

"I should be in Boston where I was offered that job practicin' law. Not totting your pair of hog-legs around half the New Mexico Territory. Grandpa, your silver spurs are hard to fill, Lord knows I'm tryin'. This badge has lost its romantic appeal. Law and order and all that. And Grandpa, your hat. Well, your hat needs reblocking."

Fitch fiddles with the gray Stetson a moment then places it back upon his head and tries to adjust it. Nope, it really doesn't fit that well.

"What in tar nation am I doing here? My life was supposed to lead me down a different path. I know I made a promise, Grandpa. I just don't know if I want to be a lawman like you were." Fitch whispers aloud, "A promise is a promise." From the near distance, a low snort is heard.

Fitch quickly turns his head and seems to confront himself out loud to the wind. "What am I doing here!?" he barks as he kicks the toe of his boot into the sand. *Jingle-jingle.*

Blaze snorts a second time and tosses his thick gray mane from side to side. Fitch approaches his faithful mount, running his hand down along his powerful neck. Blaze is an astonishing animal. His bluish-gray coat glimmers and shines. Powerful legs

67

and strong shoulders. A sunburst of white from between his ears all the way down to his muzzle to the base of his nose. A magnificent creature.

Fitch pats Blaze on the muzzle as he looks over his shoulder at Grandpa Theo's weathered headstone. He catches the approaching sounds of thundering hooves from behind. Turning, Fitch sees Deputy James "Jay" Williams galloping toward him. Jay skids his sturdy stallion, Diamond, to a halt just outside of the poorly painted cast iron fence surrounding the cemetery.

Jay is a fine looking man. Strong jaw and facial features with almost shoulder length sandy blonde hair. Wide brimmed hat similar to Fitch's however Jay's fits properly upon his head. A dim deputy's badge is seen pinned to his vest. Jay only wears a single revolver at his right hip. A fast draw rig. "Fitch," Jay struggles out of breath. "Fitch!"

"What is it, Jay?"

"It's Doc! He's corned again and he's…" Jay can't finish his sentence, attempting to contain his laughter.

"…and he's buck-naked *again*, isn't he?" Fitch responds with a smirk.

"Yeah, he is."

"Where's the Sheriff?"

"Doc won't talk to'im. Sheriff's across the street, Cory's at City Hall, 'n Luke's over at the bank. We're all waitin' fer you. Seems you'r the only one Doc'll talk to lately."

"I'll be there directly."

"I'll tell the Sheriff you'r comin'," Jay spins Diamond about and thunders back down the slopping lull back toward Purgatory. Readjusting the oversized Stetson upon his head, Fitch gives Theo's headstone a tender pat.

"See what you got me into, Grandpa?" Fitch turns and effortlessly bounds up into his saddle. Taking the reigns in hand, he coaxes his faithful stallion forward, "Come on, Blaze. "To serve and protect"…"

Fitch and Blaze slip into town along the backside of the sheriff's office and jail passing by the cowering laborers ducking for cover behind the growing rows of see-saw barricades. Fitch slides out of the saddle and hands the reigns to the soot covered blacksmith standing in the opened pair of doors at the rear entrance. The blacksmith chuckles to himself with a shake of his head. "I know," Fitch grins. "It's Doc... *again.*"

The blacksmith leads Blaze inward, tucking him into the cleanest and largest stable. Fitch passes a primitive eating and sleeping area then continues past the smoldering flames and worn anvil as the blacksmith begins to unsaddle Blaze. Fitch takes a deep breath as he heads for the forward facing livery doors leading out onto Main Street. In the near distance, a pair of gun shots thunder through the air followed by a woman's brief terrified scream.

Main Street has been cleared. Mothers cover their children's eyes, scuffling them into the nearest dry goods or general stores. Wranglers and cowboys keep close to their hitched horses, milling about opposite facing boardwalks keeping off the street. No stages nor wagons rumble through. Not even a single pedestrian.

Doc Herring, along in years now, sports a raggedy gray beard and unkept barber's mustache. He wears his worn and faded stovepipe hat, an empty gunbelt, a pair of smoking peacemaker pistols in each hand and his black boots; that's it!

BLAM. BLAM.

As Doc fires wildly into the air, the Mayor cowers from one of the front windows of City Hall. Cory stands with his shotgun cocked and ready along the wooden boardwalk with the Mayor peering out from window just behind. Across the street, Deputy Luke Mayers places his palms upon the holstered revolvers hanging low at his hips.

BLAM. BLAM.

Doc fires another pair of rounds wildly into the air. Standing under the wrap-around awning of the Katherine Hotel,

Ivan, still the sheriff of Purgatory, leans against the nearest upward supporting beam. His left arm replaced at the elbow with a wooden prosthetic limb, mostly covered by the sleeve of his shirt. Theo's sheriff's badge upon his leather vest appears faded and dimmer from the passing years.

Appearing from the opened lobby doors of the Katherine Hotel, Cleo dares to venture outward onto the boardwalk. Cleo has aged very little keeping her pleasant round cheeks, motherly manner about her, wearing the plain and drab attire and tied mop about her graying head. Cleo steps out further, coming along side of Ivan continuing to watch Doc's antics. "It's alright, miss," Cleo slightly turns and beckons over her shoulder.

Elizabeth "Beth" O'Donnell tiptoes out from the inner shadows to the Katherine's lobby. Beth has blossomed into a fine young woman. A flowing full length dresses dusts the wooden boardwalk as she moves. Her fiery red hair hangs loose in long curls about her shoulders. The snug fitting corset shows off her curves and busty figure. The slight hint of a bustle lights her backside but not to the extent of appearing "large".

The lightly painted freckles of Beth's younger years have now but all disappeared with a light yet not pale complexion. Beth and Cleo stand slightly hovering in the opened doorway of the Katherine with Ivan in front of them continuing to keep an eye on Doc, staggering in the center of Main Street.

From directly across the street, Jay looks protectively on with subtle and affectionate glances toward Beth. A lingering look most people would not notice, but Cleo clearly sees Jay's attraction toward Beth, but keeps her thoughts and smile to herself.

BLAM. BLAM.

"That's not a real sound way to keep faith in the community, Doc," Fitch's voice echo's out from behind. Doc Herring whips around with his pair of peacemakers waving about.

BLAM. BLAM.

Doc hits nothing. Fitch has mysteriously made his way along the backsides and alleyways of Purgatory. As if the deputy hadn't a care in the world, Fitch leans up against an upward supporting beam of a general store next to Wells Fargo Bank directly across the street from the Katherine Hotel. Fitch slightly smiles and tips his Stetson to Beth as he nonchalantly continues to lean against the supporting beam watching Doc Herring running buck-naked through Main Street firing his peacemaker revolvers like this was a usual occurrence... well, it is.

"Fitch? Fitch Woolley, is that you? You blasted whippersnapper! What in tar nation are you doin' there?" Doc bellows out.

"Well, Doc. I heard that you were shootin' off again and wanted to stop by to see what I could do. Seein' that you won't talk to the sheriff'n all," Fitch replies as he calmly remains resting against the upward supporting beam. "I can't have you scarrin' off the business this week. The Mayor and Bell'll have my hide if I allow that to happen." Fitch pauses a moment, "Doc, I need your guns."

"Blast it all! I nearly raised you myself!" Doc waves his peacemakers in wild directions. "Lickey-split, I nearly raised *most* of you all!" Doc's tone changes abruptly. He stares blankly, buck-naked, in the middle of Main Street directly at Fitch. "You want my guns, you welp... come get'em..." Fitch calmly steps off of the wooden boardwalk. *Jingle-jingle.*

BLAM.

Doc fires wildly at Fitch who doesn't waver, continuing to approach Doc.

BLAM.

Doc's round skids along the outer shoulder of Fitch's arm. Slight traces of blood begin to seep outward from the wound running down his arm. Yet, Fitch continues forward. Doc raises both his peacemakers and aims with drunken accuracy.

CLICK-CLICK.

"You're empty, Doc," Fitch continues forward. Defeated, Doc lowers his peacemakers and holsters them at his bare hips. Fitch slows his pace and halts, facing Doc with a forlorn look.

"One of these days you're gonna be wrong, Woolley," Doc slurs with a mumble.

"Maybe Doc, but not today," Fitch reaches up and brotherly squeezes Doc's naked shoulder, "...not today."

Ivan scurries from the Katherine Hotel carrying a blanket. The sheriff quickly wraps the blanket around Doc and escorts him back toward the Katherine. Over his shoulder, Ivan gives Fitch an envious glare. In a matter of moments, Main Street comes to life. Stagecoaches return to their schedules. Cargo wagons resume and thunder along. Local townspeople as well as folks passing through return to their conversations and shopping. Fitch strolls across the street as Cleo turns and enters the opened doors of the Katherine. Beth dashes toward Fitch taking notice of his seeping bullet wound. "Better come inside," Beth motherly whispers. "I'll get you all cleaned up."

From across the street, Jay watches as Beth coddles Fitch as she leads him up the wooden steps leading up into the Katherine. Jay removes his wide brimmed hat and slaps it against his thigh. Replacing the hat upon his head, Jay attempts to be polite and reassuring as he walks along the boardwalk, smiling and tipping his hat to the swarms of out-of-towners and local townspeople. Jay's cheerful façade fools the tourists but not the locals... they know better. Jay wears his feelings for Beth on his sleeve. A blind man could see it. But then again, Fitch isn't blind... is he?

Beth leads Fitch into the waiting parlor off and next to the lobby of the Katherine. Cleo manns the front desk counter checking in a well-to-do couple looking as if they were from back East. Well dressed suit and top hat for the man with a flowing Victorian style light colored dress with lace at the cuffs and edges, corset, bustle and matching parasol for the well-aging woman. Beth gazes at the dress for a long moment before returning her attention to Fitch. "Finely done, Sheriff," the well dressed man calls out to Fitch.

"Oh, he's *not* the Sheriff," Beth blurts out without thinking first. She quickly turns toward Fitch. Too late. Her words had hurt him. Beth tries to fumble for something to say as she rolls up Fitch's bloody sleeve revealing Doc's gunshot wound. Fitch nearly chuckles, attempting to shrug off Beth's spiteful comment.

"It's funny," Fitch smiles.

"That you got shot?"

"This isn't being shot. This's just a scratch," Fitch pauses a moment. "It's funny that Grandpa left me with our family business and your father left you with yours." Beth darts behind the front desk counter nearly pushing Cleo aside and retrieves a bottle of iodine, a cleaning rag and a wrap of bandage. Beth quickly returns to Fitch and begins cleaning Doc's bullet wound seeing that in fact, the bullet only grazed his shoulder.

"What's so amusing about that?" Beth wipes away the last of the blood.

"Don't' know. I've just been thinkin' lately. Maybe the law business isn't for me. I've got a little saved up. Maybe I could fix up the ranch and buy some cattle. Become a cattle rancher. I'd need a lot of help, though," Fitch sighs as Beth dabs some of the iodine onto his wound. "I think it's about time I settled down."

"Really!?" Beth responds with a twinkle in her eye. Fitch looks down at the bullet wound as Beth begins to wrap the bandage around his arm.

"Naw, not really. I just wanted to see how you'd react," Fitch replies with a devilish grin. Beth purposely digs her thumb into Fitch's wound as she secures the wrapped bandage. "Ow!"

"Sorry, Fitch," Beth sarcastically responds. With the bullet wound cleaned and wrapped, Beth stands back a bit as Fitch rolls down his blood stained sleeve. Heavy footsteps rattle the staircase with Ivan rambling down from the second floor of guest rooms.

"Doc'll be alright in the morning," Ivan snorts.

"That's fine, Sheriff," Fitch nods. Without another word, Ivan gathers up himself and moseys outside. Fitch buttons the bloody sleeve and raises up facing Beth. Fitch and Beth's lips are but a mere breath away from each other. "Let Doc sleep it off. The county'll pay for the room."

"...as usual."

"You don't *like* our arrangement?" With a wink and a slight smile, Fitch collects his grey Stetson, turns and exits through the opened front door.

"No, not really," Beth whispers. She gathers up the bloody cleaning rags and iodine, replacing the bottle back behind the front desk counter. Tossing the bloody rags into the laundry pile behind the front desk counter, Beth shuffles upstairs to check in on Doc. Keeping to herself behind the front desk counter, Cleo smirks as she watches Beth climb the stairs; the oddities of youthful frustration.

Fitch strolls down Main Street heading toward the sheriff's office and jail. *"That was the wrong thing to say,"* Fitch thinks. He attempts to be polite, tipping his wide brimmed Stetson hat with a smile at the passing townspeople and tourists. Fitch wishes he could've taken that back. He'll just have to try and make it up somehow.

Ivan shuffles a small stack of papers along the worn desk with his good arm. About the far wall stands a row of rifles and shotguns in an opened faced wooden case. Three vacant cells appear along the back wall with their barred doors open and inviting any wayward strangers inward. Fitch enters the sheriff's office and jail with little more than a mumble. "What was that, Fitch?" Ivan asks resting back in his wheeled desk chair.

"I was just thinking what're all those criss-cross things at the end of town?"

"Mayor's havin'em built," Ivan replies. "Kinda like moveable corrals to keep the visitin' folks kinda pinned in'ta Main Street. Keepin' the shops open later so's folks can buy more."

"Our Mayor, quite the entrepreneur."

"Naw, don't think it has any'thn to do with cattle," Ivan answers. Fitch looks over toward Ivan with a puzzled expression as he hangs his hat on a hook along the wall next to the filled gun rack.

"What, Sheriff?"

"Yeah, don't think the Mayor's gonna let cattle run 'round Purgatory," Ivan settles back in his chair. ""On-tra-pa-nuer". Ya' know, manure. Spread it around." Fitch chuckles to himself. "What? What'd I say?" Ivan becomes defensive.

""En-tre-pre-neur." It's one who undertakes to start and conduct an enterprise or business. "Entrepreneur"," Fitch retorts.

"Well, *pardon me*, "Mister I Can Read and Write". I thought "on-tra-pa-nuer" meant a whole lotta crap!" Ivan stands and scuffles across the planked floor.

"Ivan, I apologize. I didn't meant it like that it's just I've got a lot on my mind." Ivan reaches out and pats Fitch on the shoulder.

"I understand, Deputy. Love'cn do that to a man." Before Fitch can even respond, Ivan chuckles as he heads out the door. Cocking his head, Fitch sits in the wheeled chair behind the worn and cluttered desk. He props his boots up onto the edge of the desk. *Jingle-jingle.* Cupping his hands behind his head, Fitch looks blankly at the beams in the ceiling. ""Love'cn do that to a man." Ha!"

"Fitch is different somehow. He's been back over three months now and has only been to court me twice. Is there something wrong with me? Am I still the young girl he fell in love with so many years ago? Did Fitch ever love me? If he did, has he fallen out of love with me? God Almighty! This could drive one to drink... or at least run buck-naked through the street blazing away."

"I've kept all the letters that Fitch wrote and sent me while he was in Philadelphia. He kept expressing to

me how much he missed me as I sensed there was something more than that. He couldn't wait to see me again. Six years was a long time to wait for the one you love. Fitch's words were loving and gentle, not the words of the foolish boy I once knew. He had turned into a fine young man."

"Fitch sent me all sorts of things from all over his travels. Trinkets from Kansas City. Dime novels from New York. He's always been here with me... but not really. Jay has always been here... for me. Since he and his family moved to Purgatory nearly five years ago, Jay and I have been almost inseparable. Jay and I spent our teen years together, that's something Fitch and I will never have. Jay... James is a good man but Fitch is the one I love... or so I had thought."

"At any rate, Fitch has returned to Purgatory, he seems a changed man. Odd in a way. Knowing of his return and duty or even guilt of obligation to Grandpa Theo to carry on his name and work. Far too much responsibility in such a sort time. I feel a part of Fitch no longer wishes to be here in Purgatory. I feel a part of Fitch no longer wishes to be with me."

"How I long for the young man who wrote me those letters from the far away places from not so long ago. Where is he? Where is the boy, the man I feel in love with? I do so miss him..."

"Howdy, Beth," Jay charges into the Katherine's lobby unannounced... as usual. He makes his way to the forward facing area of the front desk counter. Beth frantically gathers her stack of freshly written onion papers she had sent away for from New York and stuffs them under the counter. "What's the matter? You look flushed."

"Nothing, Jay," Beth brushes a few of her red strands of hair away from her face. "Was there something I can do for you?"

"Wanna list?" Jay replies with a cocky manner. Seeing that Beth is not responding to his playful advances, Jay leans over the front desk counter with a confident smile. "Just here to check in on Doc."

"He's doing just fine."

"So," Jay fidgets a moment. "What're writin'?"

"Just some notes. Here and there. So on and so forth."

"Anything 'bout me?"

"You are as bold as you are mistaken," Beth scolds.

"Just askin'," Jay fiddles with his deputy's badge pinned to his chest followed by an awkward moment. "So's I hear, someone has a birthday 'round the corner." Beth's eyes light up. "No, Beth. I didn't forget." Jay arrogantly tips his hat, turns and heads for the opened door. He glances over his shoulder with a glimmer of envy, "But I'll wager I know who did..." With that, Jay leaves. Furious, Beth reaches under the front desk counter and takes a hold of the growing stacks of onions papers. Taking a plume in hand, Beth feverishly begins to write...

"Blast you, Fitch Woolley! You DID forget my birthday, didn't you!?"

Beth tosses the writing object and onion papers down below the front desk counter and storms off down along the nearest hallway leading toward the suites. Moments pass before Cleo appears at the top of the staircase, creeping her way quietly downward totting a pail and cleaning cloth. Cleo sets the pail down along side the baseboards of the front desk counter, glancing down the hallway with a quirky smile about her round cheeks.

Cleo saunters around the end of the front desk counter, pausing a moment, smiling down the nearest hallway. She can hear the most polite swearing she has ever heard. A grumbling of ramblings from Beth as she continues to angrily murmur to herself. Cleo turns and strolls out through the opened front door. Stepping out onto the wooden boardwalk, Cleo hears the lively up-beat New Orleans jazz echoing down along Main Street. She smiles as she begins tapping her worn sole to the music, nodding her head in time with the beat.

Bell's Saloon & Gaming is bursting with activity. Scads of cowboys, professional gamblers dressed to the hilt, wranglers and even a handful of local businessmen crowd the main lower room. Entering Bell's from the corner main entrance through the swinging batwing doors, to the far right in front of the piano along side the dual staircase and third billiard table, a New Orleans jazz quintet blasts their music.

A handful of wranglers and cowboys exchange their cues taking turns at their billiard shots with the pitcher of the chuck-a-luck table tossing out the three die for gambling ranchers. Above the second floor mezzanine, dancehall girls laugh and giggle, pretending their "escorts" wit and joke telling is actually humorous. Below along the main floor, the extended saloon bar filled with nearly twenty men of different walks of life, fill the spinning bar stools.

Robert, wearing his soiled apron atop his dark vest, white shirt, southern style string bowtie and a garter around each upper arm, shuffles back and forth attending to his patrons. Robert has aged well, even having lost a tad of his girth. "'Nother round?" Robert belts out toward the end of the bar.

"Sounds fine, Robert," Mr. Fuller replies. "Just one more snort then I'd better get my hide home," the well dressed president of Purgatory's Wells Fargo Bank replies. He pulls his gold watch from his vest pocket to check the time then tucks it back into the pocket of his well tailored suit next to his dangling lavender velvet purse tucked into his belt. Robert returns to Mr. Fuller with a shot of whiskey and a glass of warm beer.

"Not playing the tables t'night?"

"Not tonight. I can't spend all the bank's money all at once," Mr. Fuller laughs. "'Sides, I'm saving up for New Year's. I hear there's a lot of players comin' to town."

"I reckon. If ya' need anything else, just give a whistle," Robert turns and begins to tend to his other patrons along the forward facing bar. Catching the corner of his eye, an out of place youth darts from one of the filled poker tables wiping away spilled beer and whiskey. The stringy young man shuffles through the maze of gamblers collecting empty beer and shot glasses.

Trigger is a mere fifteen years old, swanks rather than walks. Baggy britches, suspenders and an oversized shirt looking as if it had once belonged to the stout Robert. If Trigger weren't employed by Bell, one would think he's be a street rat or beggar. "Trigger!" Robert bellows out from behind the bar. Taking a set of soiled glasses from a currently vacant poker table, Trigger dashes to the near end of the bar leading back into the storage room and private living quarters.

"Yeah, pa?"

"Stage came in yesterday," Robert replies over the New Orleans jazz quintet's lively music and the rumblings of the saloon. Trigger sets down the empty glasses onto the bar as Robert reaches under the lower backside of the whiskey and tequila bottles retrieving a worn leather satchel. Robert hands the satchel to Trigger. "Thought you'd like these. Straight from Boston." Trigger unfastens the leather tie and opens the satchel. Inside, a thick stack of handwritten copied music... classical music. Trigger's eyes well up with delight.

"Thanks, pa," Trigger gleefully sputters. Trigger lunges around the end of the bar and gives Robert a half hug. Robert, unused to youthful affection, pats Trigger on the shoulder and swiftly pulls him away to the odd looks of the bar's patrons.

"You can practice later," Robert sternly replies. "Now, back to work." Trigger tucks the leather satchel under his arm and dashes around the bottom of the dual staircase leading into the narrow dark hallway leading into the storage room and private quarters of the saloon.

Trigger enters his drab living quarters. The room is but a mere broom closet cleared out to house the young man. A meager dresser with a single kerosene lantern on its splintery surface. Trigger slides across his straw mattress and tenderly tucks the leather satchel under his worn down pillow. Patting the pillow making sure that the leather satchel is tucked in for the night, Trigger stands and darts back into the noisy saloon to resume his chores and duties.

The poker tables are filling up with more and more wranglers, local businessmen and newly arrived professional gamblers in town for New Year's. Nearly at each arm, a frilly and painted dancehall girl swoons over the poker players waiting for their chance to invite the winners upstairs to the "entertaining" rooms. Trigger appears from the back private living quarters and quickly begins collecting empty beer and shot glasses. "Trigger," a motherly voice beckons. Trigger turns and shuffles to a gathering of filled poker tables along the left side of the saloon.

Bell is as cheerful and attractive as she ever was. A French corset accents her buxom figure and curves. Still, with no need of bustle, her backside is round, tossing lacings of her flowing dress in hypnotic circles. Bell's long flowing hair is wound and tied up upon her head is a wasp's nest. The years have been kind. No signs of crow's feet with only a few signs of aging wrinkles around her pouting lips. "Trigger, you speak with Robert this evenin'?"

"Yes, ma," Trigger replies with a grin. "Thank-you."

"No need thankin' me. Robert thought you'd like 'em," Bell pauses with a playful wink. "Now, back to work." Trigger takes his handful of empty beer mugs and shot glasses toward the end of the bar as Bell watches the young man eagerly continue his tasks.

Mr. Fuller wobbles from the opposite end of the bar beginning to weave his way through the maze of gambler filled poker tables. "G'night, Bell," Mr. Fuller spats out while attempting to tip his hat.

"G'night, Lewis. See you t'morrow night," Bell waves with a smile. Mr. Fuller staggers along the opened central area of the saloon before nearly toppling out through the swinging batwing doors. The New Orleans jazz quintet concludes their up-beat tune with scattered patrons tossing coins at their feet. The quintet nods in thanks, tucking the coins into their raggedy pockets, turns toward each other with a nod and begins playing yet another up-beat ragtime jazz melody. The lively music continues to slither out onto Main Street with the inner activity of Bell's creeping into the early morning hours.

"'Nother cup of coffee," Ivan calls out.

"Sounds fine, Sheriff," Jay replies as he continues to lean up against an upward supporting beam along the boardwalk of the sheriff's office and jail. "'Evenin', Mr. Fuller," Jay tips his hat. Mr. Fuller strains to keep saddled on his horse. The banker sways from side to side as he passes in front of the sheriff's office and jail heading out of town. Mr. Fuller blurts out a farewell, yet unable for Jay to clearly understand.

Ivan hunches over the warm pot belly stove in the corner with the front hatch opened. The sheriff reaches into the opened hatch with a poker to stoke the dwindling flames. Closing the hatch with his other hand, Ivan takes a cup of coffee toward the opened front door. Ivan hands the tempered cup of coffee to his deputy leaning up against the upward supporting beam. Jay takes the coffee and sips on it, continuing to look out along the sparse traffic of Main Street. "Sheriff…"

"Yeah, Jay?"

"You're hand's on fire, again."

Ivan quickly looks down at his left artificial limb. The fingertips are smoldering with a few traces of burning plastic and timber. Ivan panics, nearly tossing himself from the edge of the wooden planked boardwalk, dashing to the nearest horse trough. He plunges his smoldering limb into the stale water. Smoke and steam billows upward from the watering trough. Several hitched horses look oddly up at him. With a sign of relief, like he could actually feel the burning pain subsiding, Ivan turns. "Thanks, Jay," Ivan humbly replies.

"Anytime, Sheriff," Jay smiles taking a sip of his coffee. Disinterested in Ivan's smoldering limb, Jay scans Main Street looking out in a distant trance. "Got a lot of work'ta do in the next few days." Scattered well dressed couples linger along the opposite sides of the boardwalks gazing to the windows of the closed dry goods and general stores. Fancy dresses. Top hats. A souvenir of the "Wild West" to take back home to the East Coast. Main Street is nearly complete with hanging banners, flags and welcoming posters. An ocean of red, white and blue. It will be a grand New Year's Eve celebration. Jay quietly chuckles to himself as he turns and follows Ivan back into the sheriff's office and jail.

Fitch stands quietly in the dark, clutching onto Blaze's reigns in one hand, staring blankly forward. The Woolley Ranch is deathly still. Not even the cool high desert breeze offers any comfort. Fitch leads Blaze toward the decaying and unattended two-story barn. Pinning his faithful stallion inside of the last remaining stall, Fitch begins to unsaddle his mount. Resting the horse blanket and saddle onto the side pen, Fitch reaches up and runs his hand down along the white strip along Blaze's muzzle, "G'night, boy."

Blaze lets out a snort. Fitch loosely closes the gate of the stable allowing Blaze to roam free if he wishes to. He looks about the rotting barn remembering the days when he used to play inside of these walls... so long ago it seems. Taking a glance back at Blaze beginning to feed on his ration of barley and oats, Fitch exits through the opened front barn doors. Without a lit lantern or candle, Fitch quietly slips out into the darkness...

"Morning, Luke," Fitch makes his way inside of the sheriff's office and jail. *Jingle-jingle.*

"Mornin', Fitch," Luke answers as he sets down his steaming cup off coffee onto the edge of the cluttered central desk.

"Where's everyone?" Fitch asks as he makes his way around the backside of the desk switching places with Luke.

"Sheriff's talkin' with the Mayor, Cory's over at Bell's, guess they already had a brawl over there this mornin'" Luke replies as he collects his hat, making his way toward the opened front door.

"And Jay?" Fitch mumbles as he sits down in the wheeled chair behind the desk.

"Don't know where Jay's at," Luke steps out onto the wooden planked boardwalk. "The shop's all yers. See'ya t'morrow," Luke places his hat upon his head as he shuffles out into the bustling morning sunlight.

"Yeah," Fitch grumbles to himself. Luke's heavy boots clunks down along the boardwalk for a moment before fading under the rolling wheels of passing stagecoaches and cargo wagons. Fitch eases back into the chair for a moment glancing over at the filled gun rack then tosses a look into the three empty jail cells.

Fitch raises up and strolls across the puncheon floor, leaning up against the upward supporting beam of the front door jam. Looking out onto Main Street, Luke leads his horse out from the next door livery, bounds up into the worn saddle and rides out of town crossing over the railroad tracks and passing the laborers continuing to set up the rows of see-saw "X" barricades.

Fitch remains in the doorway watching the stagecoaches and cargo wagons cluttering the street. A wide assortment of pedestrians mill to and fro, in and out of the dry goods and general stores totting their purchased trinkets and souvenirs. Directly in front of Fitch across the street, the Stardust Saloon is already busy with cowboys, ranchers and well dressed gamblers entering and exiting through the forward facing swinging batwing doors.

The hitching posts out front are lined with saddled horses waiting the return of either their penniless or fortunate owners. Kitty corner across the street, Fitch focuses on the Katherine Hotel. Taking a deep breath, he moves to the edge of the boardwalk and bounds onto the dusty ground heading for the livery next door. *Jingle-jingle.*

The blacksmith nods with a smile of his soot covered cheeks as Fitch enters and makes his way toward his saddle bags draped over the top railing of Blaze's stable. Blaze lets out a low snort then returns to his trough of oats. In the next stable, Diamond looks about, seeing the deputy flip open the forward facing flap of his saddle bag.

Fitch retrieves an oddly wrapped package nearly two feet across, one foot wide and a half a foot deep. The wrapping is that of a newspaper although unclear from what city, state, or territory. Fitch reaches down and adjusts and frills the light blue ribbon keeping the package held together. *"Frilling a ribbon?"* Fitch thinks to himself. The blacksmith and Blaze toss Fitch an uncertain look. Shrugging off the glance, Fitch tucks the newspaper wrapped package under his arm and heads for the opened main livery doors leading out onto Main Street. *Jingle-jingle.*

"Thank-you, folks," Beth smiles. "Trigger'll show you to your room," Beth hands the well dressed man his room key. With his wife in tow, the gentleman follows Trigger up the staircase leading up toward the forward facing second floor rooms. Trigger struggles to carry all the luggage himself, yearning for at least a meager gratuity. Beth files the visiting couple's paperwork into the ledger when she notices a shadow standing in the opened front door of the lobby. With a triumphant grin, Jay saunters toward her, facing Beth from the opposite side of the front desk counter. "Do'ya know what t'day is?"

"Yes, it's Thursday," Beth replies as she slides the guest book across the top of the counter.

"No," Jay replies reaching into his front trouser pocket. He removes a small velvet box and hands it to Beth. "Happy Birthday, Elizabeth."

"Oh, James," Beth gleefully takes the velvet box from Jay and opens it. Inside, a beautiful gold locket and matching gold chain. She takes it from the velvet box and holds it out and away from herself to admire the craftsmanship. "It's wonderful! Will you help me put it on?" Beth giggles.

Jay makes his way around the near end of the front desk counter as Beth unclasps the chain and hands it to him. She turns her back to him as Jay loops the gold locket and matching chain up and over her head.

Fitch pauses a moment crossing Main Street allowing a stagecoach and cargo wagon to pass in front of him heading in opposite directions. As he is about to step up onto the boardwalk heading toward the far end of the forward facing windows of the Katherine Hotel, Fitch stops cold in his tracks. Unsure of what he sees, Fitch ducks out of the line of sight, attempting to conceal his presence between the separating partitions of the front windows. Fitch leers forward, looking in through the nearest front window.

Standing behind Beth, Jay fastens the gold locket and matching chain along the back of Beth's neck. She remains facing away from Jay, looking down at the locket to admire how the sparkling gift looks hanging just above her cleavage. Beth spins around, wraps her arms about his shoulders and plants a long and wet kiss on Jay's wanting lips. "Oh, thank-you, James," Beth whispers. Jay wells up with passion, leaning inward to return the kiss.

"You're welcome, Elizabeth," Jay embraces Beth for the longest of moments. The sounds of footsteps rattle along the upper mezzanine of the second floor.

"Last of the beds'r made, miss," Cleo announces. She stomps down the staircase and bounds to the lower floor with a bucket of water and a drying rag in hand. Beth and Jay quickly separate like nothing had just happened between them. Like charging horses, Trigger thunders down the staircase with several shiny coins in his hand.

"Thanks, Beth!" Trigger waves his handful of coins bounding through the opened front lobby door. Before Beth can even respond, Trigger has left the building. As Cleo approaches the far end of the front desk counter, Jay slithers from around the back of it, standing across from Beth at a safe distance.

Tossing Jay a disapproving look, Cleo marches toward the inside forward facing windows of the parlor and begins washing away smudges and fingerprints on the glass. There, nearly face to face only separated by the panes of glass, Fitch and Cleo stare at each other. The older colored woman can see the hurt in Fitch's eyes, clutching onto the newspaper wrapped package under his arm. Turning away, Fitch steps off the end of the wooden boardwalk, disappearing into the crowded activity of Main Street. Saying nothing, Cleo returns to her window washing.

"Well, if'ya need anything, I'll be right around the corner," Jay announces for all to hear.

"Thank-you, Deputy," Beth replies in a loud manner trying to conceal her conflicting feelings.

"My pleasure," Jay reaches the opened front lobby door. "Cleo," Jay tips his hat toward Cleo seeing the deputy through the wall of inner windows separating the lobby from the parlor. Jay's boots are heavy along the wooden planks of the boardwalk, then stepping out onto Main Street, he resumes his patrols of the bustling town. Beth gazes down at her gold locket and matching chain, touching it and gently running her finger over its smooth surface.

"You'r ridin' da' fence, miss," Cleo exits the parlor with her water bucket and drying rag in hand. Cleo almost timidly approaches the front desk counter facing Beth.

"What was that, Cleo?"

"Said, you'r ridin' da' fence. I 'ad me a beau once. Two of'em, in fact. The pappy of my young'us one 'n my massa afore I was free. I was beddin' bof of'em at da' same time. Kinda jest

86

worked out that way. I'd be called t'the massa's room jest afta I'd bedded my man," Cleo recalls as she turns and begins washing the inner windows of the parlor, with her back turned toward Beth, not seeing her employer's blank expression.

"Go on, Cleo," Beth whispers.

"Ya see, The War took my beau. Funny thin' way my massa want'd to marry me. In the South no less! Kin you believe it? Once word got out that my massa want'd't be hitched to a colored woman, people's didn' take kindly to it. They strung'im up on 'is own land for all t'see. Never did find out it was me, though. I was shuffled off'n sold t'another massa," Cleo pauses. "Your' ridin' da' fence, miss. Careful, you could lose'em bof."

"Thank-you, Cleo," Beth humbly replies. "Best be off and get some rest." Cleo tosses the damp drying rag into the soiled bucket of water. Without another word, Cleo turns and makes her way along the far lower floor hallway leading to her private living quarters. Beth looks down at her gold locket and matching chain for a long moment. The shiny gift is hypnotizing. Sparkling. Beth stares blankly at it for a moment when she is struck out of her daze by the blowing of the incoming train.

There are no passengers nor any kind of luggage along the platform of the railroad depot. The day clerk stands along the platform watching an extended locomotive and boxcars roll to a halt several dozen yards away from the edge of town just beyond the last row of see-saw "X" barricades. A hulking figure lumbers off the slowing locomotive and switches the railroad tracks. The locomotive and boxcars pause along the main railroad tracks then slowly begin to reverse and back up along the turn-around section of tracks; a section of track that run for nearly two hundred yards then ends, leading to nowhere.

The locomotive and boxcars hiss to a halt along the furthest point of the turn-around railroad tracks. The locomotive's engineer waves from the train's engine. The hulking figure switches back the railroad tracks allowing any arriving or departing locomotives access to the main tracks. Steam pours out from under the locomotive's under carriage, then falls deathly still. From the train depot's platform, the day clerk sees the big and bright painted letters on the forward facing panels of the boxcars. The day clerk smiles to himself, "The Carny's come to town!"

"G'night, miss," Cleo calls out from behind the Katherine Hotel's front desk counter. Beth turns at the opened lobby door.

"Good night, Cleo," Beth smiles. Turning, Beth exits the lobby out into the night, softly walking along the wooden boardwalk. Making her way along the narrow alleyway between the Katherine and the general store next door, Beth runs her hand along the mane of her waiting stallion harnessed to her chaise. Climbing up onto the padded duel seat, Beth clutches onto the reigns, clicks her mouth and coaxes her horse and buggy forward.

The narrow dirt road is dark and bleak. Faint rays of moonlight beam downward showing her the way. A nasty place to be if road agents were to appear. Beth begins to hum to herself attempting to draw her mind and thoughts elsewhere. The pale moonlight reflects and sparkles down onto her gold locket and matching chain.

Beth unfastens her horse from the harnesses of the chaise, corralling the stallion under the well built lean-to. Straining her eyes through the darkness, Beth makes her way around the far side of the wrap-around porch of her log home. The light is dim. No features are clearly made out. She stumbles up onto the porch and approaches the front.

What?

What was that?

Beth slightly kicks a shadowy object at her feet. Leaning downward, Beth picks up a crinkly item. Taking it in hand, she enters her home, passing under the hanging horseshoe above the door jam, then closes the door behind herself. Beth places the shadowed object onto the central see-saw legged table with four hand carved chairs about it. Lighting a kerosene lantern, Beth sets the crinkly object on the table top as the flickering light begins to fill the room. Beth studies the oddly wrapped package. It's a newspaper! Turning the package about on all sides she discovers what appears to be the top with the blue ribbon neatly tied.

The newspaper's headlines scream, "THE BOSTON HERALD – MAY 12TH, 1865". "This is over six months old," Beth thinks aloud to herself. The blue ribbon twirls through her fingers as Beth quickly begins to unwrap the package. "Oh, it's beautiful!" Beth exclaims. She holds the baby-blue, Victorian full length dress up in front of herself. She spins around allowing the dress to frill and flow about. Lavish dressings and lace accent the collar, cuffs and lower seemed edging. A slightly off-color of baby-blue wrap-around is lined with lace used for a sash-like accessory matching the ribbon that the package was wrapped in. Beth tenderly places the dress over her shoulder, reaching down toward the crumpled newspaper carefully spreading out atop the table. "THE BOSTON HERALD – MAY 12TH, 1865." "Oh, Fitch you rascal. You didn't forget my birthday…"

Purgatory Cemetery as quiet. An odd stillness looms over the rows of gravesites and headstones. The morning sun rises over the horizon casting eerie shadows. The poorly painted cast iron fence creeks and rattles with the few clusters of Joshua Trees rustling in the light breeze. Faint footsteps tiptoe through the winding pathways between the headstones yet, there is no one to be seen.

Main Street's morning traffic is light allowing Ivan and Fitch to politely maneuver and coax an arriving and departing stagecoach toward the far end of town. Handfuls of pedestrians gaze at their efforts, clearing the entire street. At the far end of Main Street, the laborers set in place the last of the "X" see-saw barricades just that side of the railroad tracks adjacent to the train depot on one side and the livery to the other. A wide central pathway separates opposite sides of the rows of barricades creating what looks like a modern day parking lot.

Main Street is, for lack of a better phrase, "boxed in". Pedestrians mill freely from side to side gawking at the shops opening early to capture all business possible. Ivan and Fitch lead a stagecoach through the far central pathway of see-saw barricades separating Bell's at one corner and the under-construction hotel across the street. As Fitch leads the stagecoach outward, a trio of wranglers ride up and gaze at the well placed barricades. "Morning, boys," Fitch blurts out.

"What's gonin' on, Deputy?" one wrangler replies.

"We're getting ready for t'morrow's celebration. It's New Years Day Eve t'morrow."

"We know," answers the second wrangler as he slides off his horse. "That's why we're 'ere."

"Thought we'd visit Bell's, 'ave a few drinks and try'r "gaming"'", laughs the third. "Gotta start the New Year with a bang, if ya'know what I mean, Deputy!" The three wranglers laugh.

"Go ahead and string up here, boys," Fitch attempts a chuckle as he motions them to the see-saw barricades. "Have a good time and try to stay out of trouble."

"Sure thing, Deputy," the first wrangler tips his hat. The trio of wranglers mosey their way through the central pathway of the barricades and take a sharp right hand turn, momentarily disappearing through the swinging batwing doors of Bell's. Ivan and Fitch turn about surveying the barricades.

"Sheriff."

Ivan glances down Main Street to see Luke and Cory approaching. "Yes," Ivan replies.

"The other end of town and the cross street 're all finished," Cory explains. "Only way in'r out's through the alleys and these there gaps at both ends," Luke motions toward the central pathway between the barricade.

"What's Jay up to," Ivan asks the group of deputies.

"He's over at the Carnie checkin' in on 'em," Luke replies.

"Fine then, boys. Looks like we're all set fer t'morrow. Let's go have a drink," Ivan smiles. Fitch looks up into the sky. It's a little early to be wetting your whistle. As Ivan leads Cory and Luke toward Bell's, Fitch heads up the street.

"I'll go check on the Stardust," Fitch says over his shoulder.

"Sure you will," Cory whispers to Ivan under his breath.

Fitch can hear the slight chuckles of Ivan, Cory and Luke as they step up onto the boardwalk outside of Bell's. As they enter, the soothing and melodic sounds a gentle piano playing is hear. Not that of ragtime or a slow jazz tune but that of classical. Handel or possibly even Chopin. The sheriff and deputies aren't quite sure.

As Fitch strolls down the center of Main Street, he smiles and tips his gray Stetson hat still too big for his head, at passing by locals and tourists. Fitch slows his pace and nearly pauses walking past the Katherine Hotel. Glancing through the front windows, he sees Cleo manning the front desk. Beth hasn't arrived yet. Fitch tips his hat toward Cleo who returns the gesture with a motherly wink.

Reaching the far end of town, Fitch steps up onto the wooden boardwalk just outside of the Stardust. Light up-beat piano playing seeps outside to invite all comers in for a drink. Fitch peers over the batwing doors to see that the Stardust Saloon holds only a handful of gamblers at their tables as well as a quartette of worn looking dancehall girls. The Stardust Saloon, no match for Bell's at the other end of town. Fitch continues onward for a spell until reaching the backside of the train depot.

Looking outward across the street, the sheriff's office and jail, next to the livery at the end of town. Rows of see-saw barricades line up in a similar manner along this end of town. A half dozen saddled horses, a stagecoach and a pair of cargo wagons stand in organized rows along the opposite side of the railroad tracks. Nearly one hundred yards out, the carnival train has parked along the turn-around. The boxcars opened with ramps leading from their doors to the ground allowing soon-to-be visitors access inward.

Several wooden rings have been placed some distance away from the row of boxcars and locomotive. A gathering on colorful tents have been erected on the outskirts of the wooden rings. The carnival shows brisk activity with carnie workers securing tent lines, clearing away any loose tumbleweeds and debris. What appears to be the Ringmaster or leader of this ragged bunch of gypsies, appears from a rear passenger car. The lumbering man wears his top hat, boots, long tail jacket and his full set of long-johns. An odd sight Fitch thinks. The Ringmaster waves out a good morning to Fitch who returns with a tip of his hat. "Yeah, it's gonna be a peculiar couple of days," Fitch thinks aloud.

"Why's that, Fitch?" a voice echo's outward from inside the Stardust Saloon. Fitch turns to see Jay exiting through the swinging batwing doors. "Why's that?" Jay asks again as Fitch motions toward the carnival. "Yep, they *are* an odd bunch," Jay grins.

"Everything alright in there?"

"Yep, looks like were set."

Fitch fiddles with his Stetson for a moment. "Jay, I've been meanin' to talk with you for a spell now," Fitch replies unsure of himself.

"'Bout what?"

"Well, it's just that-"

"Deputy Woolley!" the Mayor blurts out from across the street. The Mayor swiftly approaches Fitch and Jay, wildly waving his hands in the air. "Deputy Woolley! Someone has stolen "the key to the city!"" the Mayor cries out.

"The Sheriff's over at Bell's."

"I know, he sent me looking for you," the Mayor replies. "I want *everyone* questioned!"

"*Everyone*, Mayor?"

"Yes, *everyone!*" the Mayor exclaims.

"I'll catch up with you later, Fitch," Jay turns with a grin. Boy, Fitch has his hands full with the Mayor. As the Mayor continues his rantings, Fitch phases out this round man's rambling words. Where is Jay heading? He's not crossing the street. Is he off to see Beth? No. Cleo is still there. But what if he had missed Beth coming into town using the back way with all the barricades in the way. What in blazes is the Mayor babbling about? Where is Jay going!?

"Deputy! Deputy, did you hear what I said?" the Mayor balks out. Fitch snaps to his senses turning toward the Mayor.

"Let's check out your office first. Maybe you just missed placed it," Fitch nods.

"I haven't lost it in the last fifteen years. I'm not gonna start now!"

"Fine then, let's still go take a look," Fitch takes the Mayor by the arm and leads him down the boardwalk along the same route Jay had taken. But, there is no sign of Jay as they continue along the wooden planks. Passing by the Katherine Hotel, Fitch peers in through the now opened main door. There is no one manning the front desk. No Cleo. No Beth. And… no Jay. Fitch and the Mayor continue along the boardwalk heading toward City Hall. Main Street is beginning to fill up with clusters of pedestrians milling about, bidding each other a good morning and gazing at the magnificent red, white and blue decorations and banners fluttering in the light breeze.

It's midmorning before Ivan finally steps out from the shadows of Bell's. The music inside has changed. An up-beat ragtime tune tinkles outward spilling out onto Main Street. Ivan takes a few moments to adjust his sights to the blinding sun hanging low in the sky. The muffled sounds of approaching horses draws Ivan's attention to the make-shift parking lot at the end of town. A stagecoach rumbles to a halt along the outer most part of the rows of barricades. The stagecoach door flings open with a pair of hulking "escorts". The mass of weight of the pair of men must cover five hundred pounds. They are each dressed in a matching manner. Black suits, black derbies, a pair of six-shooters at each of their hips, white shirts and black batwing ties.

The stagecoach driver bounds atop the stage and unfastens several lavish pieces of luggage tossing them down to the pair of identical men. The men take the luggage in hand and what seems to be standing at attention on opposite sides of the opened stagecoach door. A hulking figure steps outward and plants his feet solidly on the ground. Bryson Rockefeller looks like a peacock! A crush blue velvet long coat, black top hat, tailor made britches, riding boots up to his knees, a frilly French shirt, barber shop style mustache and odd spectacles of a dark nature shielding his eyes from the sun.

Bryson tosses the stagecoach driver a few coins and without a word, trudges forward. The pair of escorts, twin brothers, Moe and Joe, follow behind with luggage in tow. Bryson pauses a moment at the foot of the boardwalk directly in front of Ivan standing outside of Bell's. "Morning, Sheriff."

"G'morning, Sir," Ivan responds.

"I am Bryson Rockefeller and these are my "associates", Moe and Joe."

"Sheriff Ivan McClaine. Pleasure to meet you."

"Likewise, Sir," Bryson pauses a moment. "Can you tell me where the best game in town is?"

"Why, that'd be here at Bell's," Ivan replies.

"Very good. Thank-you for your time," Bryson nearly dismisses Ivan. Bryson continues forward leading Moe and Joe up Main Street heading for the Katherine Hotel. Ivan shakes his head following his eyes along after Bryson and the massive twin brothers disappearing into the growing crowds of locals, wranglers and scampering tourists.

"Oh, the dress is lovely. More than I had ever hoped for. It fits perfectly like Fitch had known all

along what my size was and my favorite color to boot. Yet, Jay's gift is as lovely as Fitch's. I know on Jay's salary, he must have saved for a long time. But, Fitch was selling dime novels and newspapers in Philadelphia. He must have saved just as long."

"What am I to do? Was Cleo right? Am I ridin' the fence? Who should I chose? I've loved Fitch for nearly all my life. They say that absence makes the heart grow fonder. But how much absence can the heart take? Jay has always been there for me while Fitch was away. I knew this day would come. My heart aches. My mind is in a whirlwind. What if I make the wrong choice? I'll hurt one and not the other. Yet doing so, I'll loose the friendship of the other."

"Blast-it! It would've been easier if Fitch had never returned. It would've been easier if Jay and his family had never moved to Purgatory. But, he did and they did. Men! They're just like horses. Either they're a stallion or they're lame. I've got two stallions on my hands... Am I the lame one? God, I wish Father were here. He could tell me ."

Beth looks up to see Fitch and Trigger playfully making their way down Main Street. Trigger looks happy as he dances around Fitch in a "tag – your it" manner. Beth smiles to herself, toying with the edges of the onion paper in front of herself on the front desk counter top.

"Fitch would make a good father. But, being a good father doesn't mean he would make a good husband.

"Husband". A law man for a husband. Being woken up at all hours of the night with some terrific tradady, some awful crime being committed, leaving me in darkness with a posse for days and even weeks at a time never knowing if he'll return. Then what of Jay? He too is a law man but his family owns a cattle ranch out of town. Maybe Jay would return to his cattle and give up this heroic occupation."

"Fitch could return to the law but in a judicial position. A judge never gets shot at. Well, hardly ever. "Judge Fitch Woolley and Mrs. Elizabeth Woolley". That has a nice ring to it. However, Jay would make a good rancher. But what does a bunch of cows have to do with being a good husband? Nothing. Not a thing! God Almighty! A woman could drive herself to drink with all this nonsense! I wish... I wish that..."

The sounds of heavy footsteps thunder up the boardwalk and tromp inside. Beth looks up from her small stack of onion papers to see Bryson, Moe and Joe standing in front of herself. "Morning, miss."

"G'morning, sir. May I help you?"

"I hope so. This the Katherine Hotel, isn't it?"

"Yes, sir. It is."

"I am Bryson Rockefeller. I wired you a reservation some months ago."

Beth quickly tosses the onion papers below the counter and fumbles with a stack of ragged slips. Quickly finding the correct one, Beth returns to Bryson's attention. "Yes, sir. Right here. A pair of downstairs adjoining rooms. If you'd just sign here please,"

Slinger: Midnight Rider

Beth nearly trembles as she hands him the room key. "How long will you be staying, Mr. Rockefeller?"

"Oh, till about the second or third."

"Very good, sir. Shall I show you to your room?"

"Do you come with it?" Bryson leers.

"Ah… no sir," Beth sputters out.

"Well then, I think we can manage, miss," Bryson winks. Moe and Joe tote the luggage down the nearest hallway following close behind Bryson. Beth peers around the corner to see the trio disappear around the far corner. Beth sighs. Tucking the reservation slip into a stack, Beth retrieves her stack of onion papers and sets them on the front desk counter top. She stares blankly downward, looking at her words. Beth is becoming more and more confused as the days go by.

Scattered spectators gaze at the wonderment of the carnival. Well dressed folk gather shade under the colorful tents in awe at the trinkets and souvenirs. The carnival is not in full swing yet has erected enough attractions to draw attention to itself. The row of boxcars appear along the turn-around with inviting ramps downward.

Haphazard fire eaters and jugglers roam freely with gawking locals and tourists amazed at their odd feats. Fitch and Trigger appear among the crowds weaving their way in and out of the spectacles. Suddenly, Trigger stops cold in his tracks pointing toward the nearest opened boxcar and wooden ring on the ground. "Hell's bells, Fitch! Look it!"

An oddly dressed carnival wrangler leads six zebras from the ramp of the opened boxcar. A crowd quickly gathers around the wooden ring as the wrangler takes the reigns of the lead zebra into the ring. Strung together, the half dozen zebras gallop around the inner ring stretching their legs. "Those's the oddest hosses I'd ever seen!" exclaims Trigger.

"Those aren't horses, Trigger. Those are zebras. From Africa," Fitch fatherly responds.

97

"Zebras? What'r they?"

"Well," Fitch fumbles. "They're kinda like horses. Cousins to a mule and a..."

"You don' know, do ya?" Trigger smirks.

"No, not really. I've seen afore though."

"Yeah? Where?"

"Well ah... in books."

"That's what I thought," Trigger slugs Fitch in the arm. Fitch playfully shoves Trigger to the side. Fitch and Trigger continue through the growing maze of couples, families and awestruck wranglers and cowboys.

"Have you been practicing?"

"When I git the time. "Ma" 'n "pa" got me runnin' 'bout like a chicken. It really swartz me at times."

"Don't be to tough on 'em. They love you an' are just trying to teach some things."

"Like what?"

"Well, you an' those hands of yours. *I* could never do what you do on that piano. You should be proud of yourself."

"When'r you gonna teach me how to draw 'n shoot?"

"Trigger, I think you're missin' what I'm sayin'. You don't *need* to learn how to draw and shoot. That's something my Grandpa taught me. "Use your hands to create, not to destroy." You make mighty fine music with those hands of yours. You don't need to pick up a gun. Keep practicin' the music Robert gives ya. Understand?"

"Kinda," Trigger pauses seeing that this conversation is not going the way he had planned. "I'd best be gittin' back. I'll see'ya later, Fitch." Trigger troddles off into the crowds leaving Fitch seemingly standing alone. In fact, he is. Feeling a strange sensation overwhelm him, Fitch spins in all directions looking for a friendly face. He sees none, only out-of-towners, a handful of unfamiliar wranglers and cowboys, a few scattered business men and ladies... no one he recognizes. Just like his first day in Philadelphia. Fitch becomes anxious and nervous. His surroundings closing in on himself. *"I've gotta git outta here,"* Fitch thinks.

Fitch nearly pushes and shoves his way through the growing crowds. Making his way beyond the carnival, over the railroad tracks, toward the livery, Fitch disappears inside. Blaze muffles out a series of snorts in confusion.

From the opened back doors of the livery, Blaze thunders outward. Fitch clings onto the reigns with full grasp as Blaze picks up more and more speed. Blaze and Fitch rocket away from Purgatory leaving a wake of sand and dust behind themselves. High above, the lingering clouds collect and begin to dim, fading to a darker expression. There *is* a storm coming...

The evening suns dips beyond the horizon. The distant carnival has reached full operation. The sights and sounds seep into the far end of Main Street. Flashing blasts of torch-lit jugglers and fire eaters roam along the outskirts of the three wooden rings on the ground. Tourists, locals and wranglers weave their gazing eyes in and out of the open ramped boxcars along the turn-around. The Ringmaster, in full costume, barks out his trade, making his way throughout the growing crowds, greeting people as he goes.

A pair of lamplighters, balance their way from lamp post to lamppost along Main Street, alighting the well placed wooden torches at the cross street corners as well as along the boardwalks. The flickering flames of the lampposts light up Main Street crating a calm and soothing feeling. Townspeople, out-laying farmers and ranchers, families, as well as gamblers and cowboys cheerfully take in the sights. Greeting each other and wishing passersby's a "Happy New Year". Fitch tips his hat to a passing couple, continuing to make his way for the Katherine. Fitch takes a deep breath before stepping up onto the wooden boardwalk. Adjusting his ivory handled Colt revolvers about his hips, Fitch enters the propped open main door. *Jingle-jingle.*

Cleo hovers around the front desk counter. Beth shuffles a stack of papers and the registrar in front of her. "Now, Cleo. If you need anything, anything at'll, have the sheriff send out one of the deputies. I'll be here directly."

"I'll be fine, miss," Cleo smiles. "'Ave a g'night."

"You too, Cleo," Beth replies with a nervous tone. As Beth turns and rounds the end of the front desk counter, she finds herself face to face with Fitch. He pleasantly looks down upon her soft face and warming locks of hair. "Fitch."

"Beth."

Footsteps pound downward from the second floor. Fitch and Beth pull away from each other with Cleo gleaming in the background. Trask makes his way to the foot of the staircase, pausing between Fitch and Beth. Trask Bailey is, or at least was, a handsome man. Standing at an average height as most men, striking jaw line and tender looking eyes. Trask dresses in a common manner yet better than most appearing clean and tidy. "Mr. Bailey. When did you arrive?" Beth asks.

"Last evening. I'm sorry I missed you. How have you been?"

"Fine, thank-you. And yourself?"

"Fine. Just in town a few days to pick up a few things and enjoy the New Year's celebration."

"It was good to see you, Mr. Bailey."

"As you, Elizabeth," Trask slightly turns toward Fitch, glances at his badge upon his chest and merely tips his hat. Trask swaggers through the opened door out into the night leaving Cleo behind the front desk trying to look busy and not paying attention to Fitch and Beth.

"I'll walk you out," Fitch finally says under his breath. "G'night, Cleo."

"'Night, sir," Cleo attempts to conceal her smile.

"Remember, if there's any trouble, send one of the deputies to come fetch me," Beth reminds Cleo over her shoulder as she exits with Fitch attached to her arm.

"Yes, miss," Cleo whispers. "But which Deputy?..." she smiles to herself.

Fitch escorts Beth to her stallion hitched up to her buggy along side of the Katherine Hotel along the narrow alleyway. Beth takes Fitch's hand as he helps her up into the two passenger seat. Beth takes the reigns in hand waiting for Fitch to say something. Fitch fiddles with his oversized hat. "I'll pick you up in the morning, then?"

"That sounds wonderful, Fitch."

"Well then, g'night, Beth."

"Good night, Fitch." Beth rattles the reigns maneuvering her horse to the end of the alleyway. Beth cocks back on the reigns just as she is to round the backside of the row of buildings. "Fitch!" He turns about to face her. "Thank-you for the dress. It's lovely. Good-night." Beth clicks her mouth coaxing the horse forward quickly disappearing behind the backside of the buildings.

"Guess that's a good sign. She liked the dress," Fitch mumbles to himself, making his way back toward Main Street and the growing crowds milling about the boardwalks.

BLAM-BLAM. BLAM. BLAM-BLAM-BLAM.

Fitch dashes from the shadows of the alleyway onto Main Street. Scanning the area, he sees scads of people ducking for cover. In the center of attention, a pair of drunken cowboys stagger to keep the other upright. Their pistols high in the air with lingering smoke seeping from their barrels. Fitch cautiously places his hands on the ivory handles of his Colt revolvers as he approaches them. "Howdy, fellers." The drunken cowboys spin about nearly collapsing on each other.

"Howdy, Sheriff!" one cowboy exclaims.

"I'm *not* the Sherr- " Fitch stops himself. "Whatta you boys up too?"

"Jest bringin' in the New Year," the other blurts out.

"Well boys, there's to be no firin' of side arms until New Year's Eve."

"Sorry, Sheriff."

"Would they stop calling me that!" Fitch thinks. "I'm gonna ask you boys you put those hoglegs away 'till t'morrow."

"Sure shootin', Sheriff!" one of the cowboys strains to holster his pistol. Arm in arm, the drunken cowboys stagger across the street toward Miss Katy's Boarding House. They erupt in laughter, toppling over each other, trying to even make it onto the wooden boardwalk.

" "Sheriff", I don't think I'll ever get used to that," Fitch thinks, turning down Main Street. From one end of Purgatory, a ragtime tune is accompanied by a pair of banjos. The lively music pours out from the Stardust Saloon. Fitch stands in the middle of Main Street wondering what direction to go. The New Orleans jazz music is more to his liking coming from Bell's at the other end of the street. Tourists oddly look upon Fitch, awkwardly standing there with a blank and confused look upon his face. Not knowing where to go... not knowing what to do...

The New Orleans music is nearly deafening. Every poker table is filled. Billiard players hover around their tables studying their opponents next move. Dancehall girls scurry about from table to table trying to secure their next "host". At one table, Moe and Joe stand opposite to Bryson seated at the table. The chairs are full with gamblers. The dealer spits out the cards to the players continuing a Southern version of poker. Resting on the table in front of Bryson, the tables largest pile of coins and paper money.

Bell makes her way through the tables, patting various players on the shoulders, making sure the dancehall girls are satisfying their customers and generally overseeing the operation. Bell comes to a table with a particular player having his back toward her. Bell tenderly pats the player on the shoulder. "Hey there, fella. Havin' a good time?" The player folds his cards, turns and looks up toward Bell.

"I'm having a fine time, Bell. How have you been?" Trask asks. Bell is stunned at first, quickly turning toward the filled saloon bar across the room. Robert scampers back and forth behind the bar continuing to serve his forward facing patrons. Robert hasn't seen, nor acknowledged Trask's presence yet. Bell turns quickly toward Trask.

"I'm well, thank-you. What are you doing here?" Bell exclaims under her breath.

"I'm in town to pick up a few things. Thought I'd stop by and say "hello"".

""Hello". I'd appreciate if you take yourself down the street to the Stardust if you want a game of cards or a drink. No tellin' what Robert would do if he sees you here."

"Are you in, sir," the dealer motions toward Trask.

"No, deal me out," Trask replies finishing his drink. Trask stands, takes his hat and politely nods toward Bell. "Ma'am." Without another word, Trask makes his way though the central pathway between the edge of poker tables and the billiard tables. Trask slip out through the batwing doors into the darkness. Robert scowls for a long moment with Bell's longing eyes at the swinging doors. Just as Bell turns, Robert quickly returns to his patrons as if he had seen nothing. Seeing that Robert is unaware, Bell continues her rounds through the gamblers and dancehall girls. Her eye is caught on Trigger, eagerly sitting in a chair mere inches away from the New Orleans jazz quintet.

Trigger carefully watches each of the cord progressions and changes, taking it all in. Memorizing each note. Each bridge. Each melody. "Yeah!" a voice exclaims from the other side of the room, a winning poker hand. Trigger quickly looks up to see Bell scoldingly motioning toward him, "back to work." Trigger scampers from the quintet and begins wiping tables and removing empty glasses. The commotion came from Bryson's table. Bryson gloats as he swoops his winnings closer to himself. Two of the players stands and leave the table. Another pair of dancehall girls join the pair already at Bryson's beck-and-call. Bell approaches Bryson. "Good for you, mister. If there's anything I can get you, let me know." Bryson looks over Bell's curvy figure.

"That, ma'am, sure will do," Bryson leers. His mound of coins and paper money growing by each hand. Moe and Joe lingering in the background facing Bryson from a near distance across the room. Oddly, with the other players back's toward them...

"Alright, boys, t'morrow's the day. New Year's Eve Day. Lotta people in town," Ivan stands behind his sheriff's office desk like it were a preacher's pulpit. Fitch, Jay, Cory and Luke surround Ivan in a half circle. The vacant jail cells directly behind himself. "Fitch'll take the first watch t'night. Seems he wants to spend some time with the O'Donnell lass." Muffled laughter comes from the deputies. All but Fitch and Jay who exchange almost glaring looks. "I got us a few rooms at Katy's Boarding house if you need anything," Ivan turns toward Fitch.

One by one, Ivan and the deputies file out of the office onto the boardwalk. Jay pauses a moment, then continues onward, disappearing out into the night. Fitch follows behind, leaning on the supporting door jam. Ivan, Cory, Luke and Jay cross the street in a kitty-corner fashion heading for Katy's. Fitch stands there for a long moment, watching to see if Jay turns about to look over his shoulder. He does with a modest scowl. Jay faces forward and follows Ivan and the other deputies into Katy's.

Taking a deep breath, Fitch removes a chair from just inside the sheriff's office and settles in, carefully watching Main Street for any signs of trouble, propping his chair halfway inside the doorway, but just enough inside not to see the entire street. The quieting carnival to one side, the slowing activity of the Stardust Saloon and the quiet cross street separating the middle of town. The other half of Purgatory is blind to him... even the Katherine is unseen from where he sits.

Main Street is quiet. Only a handful of stragglers stumble and topple their way toward the Katherine Hotel, either of the boarding houses, or even the few remaining locals attempting to get to their horses or wagons to make the journey home. Fitch nods off in his chair right outside of the sheriff's office and jail.

He catches himself and is startled awake. Fitch quickly looks over the street, nothing to concern him.

PLUNK-PLUNK-PLUNK. KER-PLUNK. PLUNK-PLUNK. PLUNK.

Fitch raises up and makes his way off of the boardwalk. He strolls along Main Street taking note of the filled sew-saw barricades at the far end of town. The under construction hotel looms quietly in the darkness.

PLUNK-PLUNK. KER-PLUNK. PLUNK-PLUNK.

"Hells bells, Trigger, are you gonna play that thing'r what?" Bell snaps. Fitch continues onward until reaching the boardwalk of Bell's. A stillness follows. Fitch carefully swings the batwing doors opens and enters.

Bryson, two other gamblers and the dealer sit at the far table. No other tables are occupied. A pair of straggly dancehall girls slouch in nearby chairs with Moe and Joe alert off to the corners facing Bryson yet behind the dealer and pair of players. "I'm out, mister," one player tosses in his cards. "You're got one helluva time'o luck."

"Thank-you, sir," Bryson smirks. Fitch passes the card player on his way out. He makes his way to the end of the bar and takes a stool. Robert slowly makes his way down and pours Fitch a shot of whiskey. Robert returns to his glasses, wiping each clean. Bell remains behind the bar and cash register counting out the day's returns. Fitch playfully turns away from the bar.

"Hell bells, Trigger. Are you gonna play that thing or what?" Fitch sarcastically mimics Bell who shoots him a playful glare. Robert glances up at Trigger who sits at the piano flipping through the pages of music from the leather satchel. Trigger spreads out several pages across the top of the music stand of the piano.

PLUNK-PLUNK. KER-PLUNK. PLUNK-PLUNK.

Trigger studies the music for a moment. His fingers then gracefully begin to flow across the black and white keys. Symphonic and harmonious music fills the saloon. Trigger reads the sheets of music as he plays. The tempos and crescendos change but the melody remains the same; Mozart's "*Ah! Vous dirai-je, Maman*" in twelve variations. One version is slow and hypnotizing. Another, bluesy and sorrowful. Yet, another brisk and light. Trigger seems at ease playing all versions. Then with a final crescendo, the piece is finished. Trigger sits there a moment staring blankly at the pages of music.

CLANK. TINKLE. CLANK-CLANK.

Trigger turns around along his piano bench to see Bryson, the gambler, dealer, Fitch, Robert and Bell tossing coins at his feet. Trigger gleefully bounds from his piano bench and collects up the tossed coins. "Oh no, you're not done yet, Trigger," Fitch winks. "Practice!"

Trigger stuffs the coins into his pockets, turns and replaces the sheets of music back into the leather satchel. He quickly flips through the contents before removing another piece of music. Trigger spreads out the piece out in front of himself and studies it for a long moment. Robert returns to his glasses. Bell to her counting of money. Fitch sits at the end of the bar sipping his whiskey. At the sole table, the dealer tosses out cards to Bryson and the lowly gambler trying to win back some of his lost money.

There is no one on the street to take notice of the five shadowy figures ridding into town. The images slow and halt their horses beyond Main Street, tying them to the see-saw barricades just outside of Bell's on the corner. The figures move in and out of the darkened shadows of the lit lamp posts on the street corners, seeming to stay out of the light. Yet, the apparent "leader" fans out and takes point. In a "V" shaped formation as a flock of migrating fowl, the five shadowed images walk down Main Street; unchallenged and undetected.

Trigger's soothing piano playing causes the five images to slow and take in the music… just for a moment. The leader motions the group onward past Bell's and along the street. The leader nods with the other four obedient to his unsaid command.

106

One by one, they cross the center of the street and head for the finest accommodations in town; The Katherine Hotel.

Cleo lays slouched over the front desk counter. Her head laying on her crossed arms. Cleo's light snoring causes her not to be able to hear the footsteps approaching her from the opened door. "I'd like two rooms please," the dark and low voice declares.

Cleo starts awake quickly rubbing her eyes, "I'm so sorry, sa'. What kin I git for you's."

"I'd like two rooms," the leader tosses a filled leather poke on the counter. Cleo nervously looks each man up and down. The first from the left end, a scraggly fellow in dire need of a bath. Spider sports a bull whip at his hip, covered with a layer of dust, ragged hat, a plain six-shooter tucked in his belt and missing several teeth. Next to him is Dandy, a colored fellow with broad shoulders and finely dressed. A suave smile and gleam almost in a flirting manner toward Cleo. Tall and handsome. Dressed just like direct off the afternoon stage from Kansas City. A gambler for sure with a Henry rifle propped over his shoulder with his gloved hand stuck in the trigger and lever action.

At the far right end, Jesse, a slim and trim man. Rugged jeans and worn boots. A single Colt model revolver hangs holstered at his hip. Charming in a boyish kind of way. Jesse tips his hat as he seems over shadowed by the Indian, Chote' who stands nearly a foot and a half over Jesse.

Chote's long black hair flows freely over his shoulders. Leather jacket and knives. Yes, the knives. Too many for Cleo to count tucked into his belt. One in particular, a James Bowie knife, shiny and intimidating.

The fifth man, much different than the others; the leader of the pack. Knee high cavalry boots with the lower pants leg of his trousers tucked into the tops in an almost safari outfit manner. A sash about his waist his a pair of Colt revolvers holstered along his of his Civil War saber in its sheath. A faded white shirt under his half-coat bolero. Wide shoulders and a strong face. A modified

Civil War officer's wide brimmed hat with no sign of rank or insignia. The oddest thing about the fifth man, he wears a black patch over his left eye. "I'd like to have two rooms, please," Cougar reminds Cleo...

CHAPTER IV

"If I knew what was good for me, I'd turn tail and head back north to Boston. What in tar nation am I doing here? I should be practin' law in a nice comfy office with a French secretary," Fitch thinks to himself. *"Not out here. Not back to Purgatory. What's in Purgatory for me now?"* Fitch pauses a moment. *"Elizabeth."*

Fitch rides Blaze through the widening trail heading out to a large clearing. The rising sun is warm, yet not to late in the morning to cause drastic heat. A cool breeze blows across the tall wild grass roaming free. The rolling prairie appears somewhat out of place. The surrounding areas are mostly desolate and barren. Fitch and Blaze cut their way from the makeshift roadway from a sprawling treeline off to the west. A ravine cuts along the trees with a trickling brook providing water for the nearby homestead.

There are no fences nor corrals. Not even a barn. The log cabin is a single story structure with an enclosed lean-to several yards off in the distance. A single stallion shades its self under the lean-to with a two seated chaise between it and the main house. The wrap-around porch beckons to all visitors with a pair of rocking chairs slightly swaying to the breeze on opposite sides of the leather hinged main door.

"Mr. Daniel O'Donnell, you sure picked out a spread when you chose this place. Looks like God himself stepped onto the New Mexico Territory and left this behind. Beautiful. A glorious place to raise a family... A family. What am I talking about? I don't want a family! I don't even want to be a law man. What am I doing here!?" At that moment, Beth opens the main door of her home and stands in the doorway with the hanging

horseshoe directly above her head. *"Oh, that's what I'm doing here."*

Beth is simply radiant. Her flowing baby-blue dress fits to the tee. Her red locks of hair slightly flowing loosely about her shoulders with the off blue ribbon tying back several large strands. The lace about her neck, cuffs, and waist frilly with the cooling breeze. Beth's cheeks, warm and glowing. Giggling, Beth twirls, and spins around showing off her dress. Simply radiant. "Do you like it, Mr. Woolley?"

"Yes, Miss O'Donnell. I most certainly do," Fitch replies with a sinking feeling in his stomach. *"What was I thinking about?"* Fitch dismounts and strings Blazes reigns to the nearest supporting beam of the porch.

"Sorry, Fitch."

"For what, Beth?"

"I lost track of time. I was meaning to hitch up the buggy but I was getting dressed."

"Time well spent, Beth," Fitch playfully smiles at her. Beth nearly blushes as she closes the door behind herself and walks along the edge of the wrap-around porch. Fitch makes his way under the lean-to and collects Beth's horse. Leading the horse to the buggy, he fastens the straps and secures the lines. Turning toward the edge of the porch, Fitch extends out his hand, "Miss, your carriage awaits."

"Thank-you, kind sir," Beth steps off the porch with a spring in her step. Taking Fitch by the hand, Beth steps up into the chaise and slides over.

The ride into Purgatory is a quiet one. The flirtations and quip remarks have faded. Fitch and Beth ride along in the chaise with the hood drawn over to shield them from the growing heat of the sun. Blaze trails behind tied off to the chaise's rear end. Fitch and Beth politely smile, searching for something to say. Thus far, the trip has been uneventful. "Fitch," Beth finally blurts out.

"Yes."

"I've been meaning to ask you, why did you wear your guns and badge today? I thought Ivan gave you the day off."

"He did."

"Then why the guns and badge?"

"'Cause bad guys *don't* take the day off."

"Do you except any trouble?"

"Not to worry," Fitch replies in a soothing manner, "Everything'll be just fine."

"One more thing, Fitch."

"Yes, Beth?"

"Why'd you bring Blaze? You could've left him at my spread."

Fitch chuckles a moment before slightly turning toward Beth with a playing leer, "A good horse is like a good woman. You never leave one behind." Beth grins from ear to ear with a glimmering twinkle in her eye. *"Boy! That was the wrong thing to say,"* Fitch thinks to himself as he politely smiles at Beth with his boot in his mouth…

Purgatory, New Mexico Territory
New Years Eve Day, 1865

Fitch and Beth ride along with the smells and sounds of joyous celebration filling the air. At the far end of town, rows upon rows of the see-saw barricades are filled with hitched horses, parked cargo wagons and stagecoaches. More and more wrangles hitch up and dash down Main Street. Fitch steers the chaise along the backside of the far row of buildings passing Bell's at the corner first. Loud up-beat New Orleans jazz echo's outward followed by the sounds of laughter and horseplay.

Back doors and window coverings line the structures and businesses as Fitch and Beth catch glimpses of activity filling Main Street. Locals and tourists alike frolic to and fro dancing and tossing each other about. Fitch steers the chaise along passing the cross street barricaded by the see-saws. Wells Fargo Bank – Purgatory, is next to their left continuing along the backside of the buildings. Passing several general stores, Katy's Boarding house, then the sheriff's office and jail. Fitch slows the chaise, turning it inward between the jail and livery. Fitch turns to Beth with an uncertain grin, "Shall we?"

Taking Fitch by the arm, Beth proudly makes her entrance onto Main Street with her man. Main Street is a maze of chaos resembling a swarm of ants scurrying to get out of the rain. Every boardwalk is filled with tourists, gamblers, business men and wranglers. Fitch can hardly recognize the locals, there are so many people. Slightly down the street, the Stardust Saloon is consumed with patrons entering and exiting. A ragtime piano plays along with a trio of banjo players. The music is light and airy.

"What would you like to do first, Beth?" Fitch replies.

"No matter. I have all I want right here," Beth whispers.

"That was really the wrong thing to say, Woolley," Fitch thinks. "Alright then, let's do some shopping." Fitch leads Beth across the street to the finest dry goods store. As they disappear into the crowds filling Main Street, Jay steps out of the shadows from Katy's Boarding House. He enviously watches Beth playfully tug at Fitch's arm as they step up onto the far boardwalk and disappear inside the dry goods store. Jay slaps his hat on his thigh, sighs and strolls down the boardwalk looking for at least one drunkard to rustle up and toss in jail.

Beth gazes as she runs her fingers over the shelved bottles of Italian soaps, French perfumes and Oriental sticks of incense. Fitch could care less about shopping, dragging his silver spurs behind himself. *Jingle-jingle.* He smiles and nods with every treasure Beth finds along the dusty shelves.

BLAM-BLAM. BLAM-BALM. BLAM-BLAM.

Beth leaps into Fitch's arms. Well dressed women cower in their less-than-protective husbands chests. "Blast it! What was that, Fitch?"

"Nothin' to worry 'bout, Beth. The Mayor thought it'd be a good idea to have a few contests out back. There's a quick-draw, a sharp-shootin' and a few others. Oh, and at noon there's gonna be a big race for a five-hundred dollar purse Mr. Fuller's putting up the money for. Kinda like an adversment for the bank."

"A quick-draw? Why don't you enter?"

"Beth, you know I only draw when I have to," Fitch pauses. "See sump'thn you like?"

"Oh, there are so many things here. I can't decide."

"Who says you have to? But, Beth. This is our first stop. Don't you wanna look around a bit more?"

"I reckon you're right," Beth smiles. She extends out her hand leading Fitch toward the door. "Shall we?" Fitch smiles.

BLAM-BLAM. BLAM-BLAM. BLAM-BLAM.

"Four out of six!" shouts the Mayor along the backside of the row of business and structures. A gathered crowd applauds for the cowboy reloading his revolver then holstering it. "Any other contenders!?" the Mayor bellows out. A slick dude steps forward with glimmering six-shooters hanging low at his hips, dark leathery attire and polished boots; a professional gunfighter. "Fifty dollars to the winner. Would you like to take a chance, mister?" The Mayor asks. The gunfighter nods without a word.

The Mayor stands ready as the gunfighter calmly places his palm on his holstered Colt model revolver at his hip. The Mayor takes six coins in hand and turns toward the gunfighter, "Ready?" The Mayor tosses the six coins into the air far and out away from the crowd. The gunfighter draws his right revolver and fans his opened left palm over the hammer, cocking it back after each accurate shot.

BLAM-BLAM. BLAM-BLAM. BLAM-BLAM.

The crowd cheers and applauds. "Five out of six! The winner!" the Mayor yells. The crowd pats the gunfighter on the shoulders as he moves in toward the Mayor to collect his prize.

"That was pretty nifty," a low voice responds. The crowd falls still as they turn to see Jesse roll the cylinder of his Colt revolver checking the ammo, "But kin he do it with'is left hand?" Jesse challenges. The gunfighter seems uneasy but nods. The crowd backs away as the gunfighter and Jesse stand shoulder to shoulder. The gunfighter places his left palm of the handle of his revolver. The Mayor takes six coins in hand and tosses them into the air far and away from the crowd. The gunfighter draws his left holstered revolver.

BLAM-BLAM. BLAM-BLAM. BLAM-BLAM.

The coins fall to the sand. "Four out of six," the Mayor declares taking six more coins from his pocket. Jesse winks at the gunfighter and crosses his arms in front of his chest. The Mayor tosses the six coins into the air far and away from the crowd with Jesse still gawking at the gunfighter. The six coins continue upward for a moment, pause then begin their descent. With lightening speed, Jesse draws his left revolver from its holster and fans the hammer with his opened right palm.

BLAM-BLAM. BLAM-BLAM. BLAM-BLAM.

The coins fall to the sand. "Six out of six! The winner!" the Mayor declares. The crowd cheers and applauds swarming Jesse with hand shakes and pats on the shoulder. The gunfighter is not pleased as he secures the loading lever back into place. Both of his reloaded revolvers holstered low at his hips. The Mayor hands Jesse five-ten dollar coins. The gunfighter turns and slinks away. "Hey, mister!" Jesse bellows out toward the gunfighter. "You should see me shoot with my right hand!" Jesse gloats. The gunfighter is steamed.

"Fine then. Let's see how good you are, boy," the gunfighter draws both revolvers on Jesse even before Jesse can turn to face him.

KA-BLAM. KA-BLAM.

Two shots explode in the sand between the gunfighter's boots. The crowd spreads like a parting sea. From the distance, Dandy walks with a strut, with his Henry rifle leveled at the gunfighter. The barrel of the Henry rifle now mere inches away from the gunfighter's head. "Mister, I don't know you but I've been ridding with him for nearly three years now. I know he doesn't want to kill you and you don't wanna to be dead," Dandy lowers the Henry rifle. "Let it go, mister."

Ashamed and outmatched, the gunfighter holsters his revolvers, shoves his way through the crowds and disappears through an alleyway onto Main Street. Jesse takes the coins from the Mayor, "Pleasure doin' business wit' you," Jesse smirks. The crowd fans out making their way along the backsides of the structures and businesses. Dandy and Jesse bring up the rear. "I could'a takin' 'im, Dandy."

"I know, kid. But now's not the time or place," Dandy answers. "Come on, Jess. Let's go check out the half breed," Dandy checks the lever action of his Henry rifle.

"Is it gettin' dark out here or is it just me?" Dandy asks with a playful meaner. Jesse slaps Dandy on the arm as they stand off in the background of the gathered crowd. Toward the forefront of the makeshift area, three bow and arrow like targets have been erected. Standing just over ten yards in front of the targets, a hulking Mexican and Chote'. Most of the crowd is Mexican creating a mixed complexion of spectators.

"Come on, "greaser"," Jesse shouts out to Chote'. The Apache Indian sneers at Jesse and Dandy.

"I'm no "greaser", white man," Chote' barks out. "I'll scalp your hide before you hit the ground!" The crowd murmurs in concern as Luke steps forward.

"This is the last round, "gentlemen"," Luke orders. "Three blades nearest to the bulls eye wins fifty dollars courtesy of Mr. Fuller and Wells Fargo Bank." The massive Mexican steps forward and draws three large blades from his sash.

THA-WHAP. THA-WHAP. THA-WHAP.

Two of the blades stuck in the bulls eye with the third just outside the bulls eye. The crowd reluctantly applauds as the Mexican retrieves his blades. Chote' steps forward to face the same target. The Mexican stands next to Chote' nearly a foot and a half over his size. The Mexican tucks his blades into his sash glaring down at the little Indian man. Chote' sneers up at the immigrant. With lightening speed, Chote' snaps the Mexican's own pair of blades from his sash and hurls them at the target. Chote' draws his Bowie knife from his own sash and likewise hurls it at the target.

THA-WHAP. THA-WHAP. THA-WHAP.

The Mexican's blades impact directly in the center of the bulls eye. Chote's Bowie knife hits with full force splitting one of the Mexican's blades down the handle in two. All three inside the bulls eyes. The crowd is reluctant to applaud, quickly making their way toward the nearest alleyway. Looking about to see the event is quickly over, Luke hands the five-ten dollar coins to Chote'. "Congratulations," Luke nervously forces himself to say. Luke darts away following the last group of pale complected people. The Mexican spectators hover around the hulking Mexican attempting to console him.

Chote', Dandy and Jesse stand at ease with their collected one hundred dollars tinkling in Dandy's hand. "Is that 'nuff, Dandy," Jesse asks.

"Yeah, that'll get me in the game."

"You better be off then," Chote' chimes in.

"Good luck," Jesse adds.

"Thanks, boys," Dandy tucks the coins into his French vest pocket as the trio turns and heads down the nearest alleyway.

"Fitch! Fitch, we've got trouble!" Ivan bellows out as he charges toward Fitch and Beth along the boardwalk.

"What is it, Sheriff?"

"Come quick! Hurry!" Ivan shouts. Ivan tugs at Fitch's arm pulling him away from Beth who stumbles to keep up. Ivan drags Fitch through the mazes of locals and tourists filling Main Street.

"What's this about?" Fitch blurts.

"Come on!" Ivan yanks at Fitch.

116

The far end of Main Street is consumed with gathered people. Seeing Ivan dragging Fitch along, the locals smile and part, making a pathway for Ivan, Fitch and Beth. Ivan leads Fitch through the parted crowd where Blaze stands saddled and lined up with over three dozen other riders and horses. "What's goin' on, Ivan," Fitch demands.

"The race! There's been a lawman runnin' in this race since afore yer grandpa Theo. I'm getting' too old fer it. You ride!"

"No! Let Cory or Luke or even Jay ride n'stead. No, Ivan."

"Come on, boy! You'n Blaze'r unbeatable," Ivan pauses. "Five hundred dollars kin' go along way to fixin' up the Woolley Ranch."

"You can do it, Fitch," Beth whispers.

Fitch shakes his head and pauses a moment. Taking the reigns from the blacksmith, Fitch leaps up and mounts Blaze. Cheers and applauds fill the air. The dozens of riders are suddenly nervous. From the rear of the pack, a striking whinny is heard. A burst of confusion erupts with a lone rider charging forward. Cougar and his mount gallop into view and stomp along side of Fitch and Blaze. Cougar tips his hat to Beth, maneuvering his horse into place.

"*Cougar! You sonuva-bitch! I hoped you'd been killed by now!*" Fitch is outraged. Fitch remembers clearly when Robert and Bell came to The Woolley Ranch with Grandpa slain in the back of the wagon. Cougar and his bandits shot him dead. "*If I wasn't wearin' a badge right now, I'd shoot you dead where your sat.*"

"Riders, take your mark!" Ivan yells as he draws his revolver from its holster. "Set…"

BLAM!

The riders thunder forward. Fitch and Cougar bolt their mounts taking up the middle of the pack. Cheers and applauds fill the air as the crowd closes the gap from the riders starting line. "Go, boy! Go!" Ivan yells out waiving about his wooden arm.

"Be careful, Fitch," Beth whispers.

117

"He'll be alright," a familiar voice is heard behind Beth. Turning, Jay stands facing her with a wanting look on his face. "He'll be just fine."

"I hope so, Jay," Beth replies unconvinced.

Most of the galloping herd has fallen back. Only a dozen riders remain. Fitch and Cougar are nearing the forward middle. Thundering hooves. Wild dust clouds in their wake. There! A few more riders fall out of the race. Fitch and Cougar are neck and neck. Blaze at full speed. Heaving forward. Fitch looks ahead to see the finish line. A span of cargo wagons on opposites sides with cheering locals and tourists. Fitch and Cougar charge onward.

One…

Three…

Six…

Nine riders fall back. It's only Fitch, Cougar and one last rider. The finish line draws nearer. The gathered crowd cheers. Fitch and Cougar exchange determined looks. The last rider can't make it as he slows his horse to a panting gallop. All that remains is Fitch and Cougar. Cougar and Fitch. Fitch and Cougar. Cougar and Fitch… the finish line! A Tie!

The crowd cheers and applauds turning to see the pair of horsemen slow their mounts, return to the finish line and split the prize money… but they do not. Fitch and Cougar thunder forward out into the desert. Fitch leads for a spell then Cougar catches up. Neck and neck. Shoulder to shoulder. Neither man giving up.

"You robbed our bank! Killed my Grandpa and left me all alone! You took everything that meant anything to me, you sonuva-bitch! I didn't _want_ to go to law school!" Rage wells up deep inside of Fitch. With that, shoulder to shoulder, at a full run, Fitch heaves himself from the saddle and powerfully collides into Cougar.

Fitch and Cougar topple to the sand leaving their horses galloping out into the desert. Fitch and Cougar tussle for a moment. Fitch is the first to his feet as Cougar staggers to get his balance. Fitch delivers a blow across Cougar's jaw sending him

118

reeling. Wobbly only for a moment, Cougar charges Fitch and counters with three devastating blows, knocking Fitch from his feet. Fitch struggles to draw one of his Colt revolvers from Grandpa's holsters.

"Not so fast, Johnny Law," Cougar snarls. Cougar has already drawn one of his revolvers and has it dead to rights aimed at Fitch's head. "What's with you, lawman? I've been out-range a long time. I'll I wanted was a few days in town fer me'n the fellas'. No need fer all this ruckus," Cougar slowly holsters his revolver. His horse trots over to him. Cougar leaps up into the saddle and tips his hat in a sarcastic manner, ""Sheriff"." Motioning his horse away, Cougar gallops off back into town. Snort! Fitch turns and looks up at Blaze looking oddly down at his dusty master.

"What?"

Blaze snorts again, lowering his head, nudging his muzzle against Fitch's back. "Alright, alright!" Fitch struggles to his feet and brushes himself off. Blaze strolls a few feet away and collects the gray Stetson at his feet. Blaze hands the wide brimmed hat to Fitch who reluctantly places it upon his head. "It still needs blocking..."

The starting line is vacant. Cougar has collected his five-hundred dollar prize. The cargo wagons and crowds have gone. Beth and Jay stand alone at the outskirts of town awaiting Fitch's return. It is late in the afternoon. The setting sun castes amber and orange colors across the sky. The lively ragtime music from the Stardust Saloon echo's in the distance. "You said he'd be alright," Beth scolds.

Jay looks out toward the horizon, trying to look concerned. Well, in a way he is. Fitch *is* his friend but he's wanted Beth for as long as he can remember. Jay hopes, wishes, even prays that Fitch will not return and if he does... just go away.

"There!" Beth exclaims pointing out to the horizon. Jay shields his eyes from the setting sun. Yep! There he is.

"I told you he'd be alright," Jay mumbles in defeat.

Without a second thought or a word of thanks for staying with her, Beth bolts forward, leaving Jay standing there with his "gun" in his hand. "You'r welcome." Jay turns and sulks back into town past the filled rows of hitched horses along the rows of see-saw barricades, cargo wagons and stagecoaches. Over the horizon, Fitch dismounts Blaze and leads him toward Beth. The setting sun behind them accents their quick embrace and kiss on the cheek. Side by side, Fitch and Beth lead Blaze closer to the far end of Main Street.

"He's not doin' what he's been told," Cougar snaps. Dandy, Chote' and Jesse hover around Cougar as they stand at the far end of the saloon bar. Every poker and billiard table is filled at Bell's. The New Orleans quintet continues to play their up-beat music off in the corner. Trigger dashes from table to table collecting empty glasses and wiping away spilled ale and beer. Dancehalls girls flock around the poker tables looking for their next "heist." Cougar slams his shot of whisky down his throat and motions his posse to follow. Cougar glares down at the poker table as he passes then exits.

Spider sits at the poker table with Mr. Fuller, Bryson, one other gambler and the dealer. "Your call, mister," the dealer motions toward Spider.

"I fold. I'll have to wait for another table. Good luck, sirs," Mr. Fuller raises up, tips his hat and exits the table.

"I'm out, too. Too rich for my blood," the last gambler replies taking his half glass of ale with him leaving Spider, Bryson and the dealer.

"I'll raise three hundred," Spider sneers. Several dancehall girls swarm about with nearly one thousand dollars in the pot. Bryson slightly glances upward with Moe and Joe standing in the shadows behind Spider.

"I'll raise and call three hundred dollars," Bryson grins.

"That's three hundred dollars to you, sir," the dealer turns to Spider who carefully looks down at his cards. Two down and two up with one card to go. Spider's up cards are a king of diamonds and a queen of hearts. Looking at his hole cards, a king of clubs and a king of spades.

"I'll call," Spider tosses in his three hundred dollars. Spider glances over to Bryson's up cards. An ace of hearts and a jack of clubs. Bryson carefully looks at his hole cards, an ace of spades and a jack of hearts; two pair does not beat three of a kind. Bryson and Spider pause for the dealer to toss them their last cards. To Spider, the king of hearts! Four of a kind. Bryson is dealt the ace of diamonds; three aces don't beat four kings.

"How 'bout we make this interesting, " Bryson oddly gloats. "All in! What'cha got, mister?" Spider surveys his situation. He *knows* he's got Bryson beat. What's he up to?

"How 'bout a new deck, mister?"

"What?

"How 'bout a new deck? Seein' how your boys behind me bin' callin' the shots all night. Tellin' you what I got in my hand," Spider pauses. "I *know* I got you beat!"

"You callin' me a cheat, mister?"

"I'm callin' it like I see's it. And don't call me "mister"".
Spider lunges forward and tears Bryson's cards from the table; four aces and one jack! The unseen slight of hand that had pulled the ace from his sleeve.

"Gentlemen, I think Mr. Spider needs a lesson on manners," Bryson beckons out toward Moe and Joe. Spider spins around drawing his bull whip a moment to late. Moe and Joe tackle Spider and powerfully thrust him to the floor.

"Not in here!" Robert pleads. "Take it outside!"

Moe and Joe forcefully take Spider by the arms and drag him outside with Bryson grinning as he stands at the table. "Watch the funds, my dear good man. This won't but take a minute," Bryson orders the dealer.

121

Moe and Joe pound Spider into the dirt along Min Street. Fists fly. Kicking and stomping. Bryson appears at the edge of Bell's watching Moe and Joe pulverize Spider. Where's there a lawman when you need one? The gawking crowd cheer and shout both for Spider to get up and fight back as others want Moe and Joe to send Spider to an early grave.

Spider is hammered to the ground, waits a moment, then spins and rolls on his back, springing up to his feet. Taking his bull whip in hand, Spider whips it about at Moe and Joe. Blood pours from Joe's cheek. Spider snaps the whip again causing Moe to drop to his knee. Among the gathered crowd, Cougar, Dandy, Jesse and Chote' look onward. Spider lunges toward Moe and powerfully kicks him in the groin sending Moe screaming to the ground. Spider clutches his fist and pounds at Joe's already broken nose. Joe falls in a lump along Main Street. With a snap of his wrist, Spider snags the tip of his bull whip around Bryson's neck. Bryson is violently pulled from the boardwalk and topples to the street.

Spider quickly lifts up Bryson's right sleeve to reveal four additional aces, three kings, three queens and a pair of jacks. The crowd murmurs. Spider unravels his whip from around Bryson's throat and begins to whip him. His suit jacket frays. His expensive trousers cut and replaced by bloody wounds. The gathered crowd can take no more of the abuse. They quickly disperse into the street covering their mouths or holding their stomachs in disgust.

Spider continues to choke Bryson with the far end of his bull whip wrapped several times around the gambler's throat. Bryson is within an inch of his life. Cougar and his gang are about ready to jump in when Cory and Fitch appear and surround Spider at a too-near of distance for Spider to use the whip. Dandy lunges forward to save Spider from arrest.

"No!" Cougar orders as he holds Dandy back.

"But we need 'im."

122

"He's on his own. We'll just have ta' do without 'im," Cougar whispers leading his gang away from the departing crowd and newly arrived lawmen. Better later than never.

"That man's a cheat!" Spider protests.

"That doesn't give you the right to choke 'im to death," Cory barks. Cory fastens the handcuffs behind Spider's back and begins to lead him to the sheriff's office and jail. Fitch crouches down and loosens the bull whip from around Bryson's throat.

"Thank-you! Thank-you," Bryson gasps.

"Don't thank me, yet. Cheatin' is cheatin'. You're lucky I didn't let him choke you to death. I want you out of town... t'night!"

"But..." Bryson protests.

""But" is the back end of a mule. I want you gone t'night or you'll be spending it with him "at my place"."

"Yes, Sheriff," Bryson reluctantly agrees as he is helped to his feet by Fitch.

"I'm *not* the Sherr-," Fitch cuts response short. *""Sheriff", I'll never get used to that,"* Fitch thinks.

"Fitch?" a soft voice beckons. Fitch turns to see Beth waiting in the near distance. Collecting his hat, Fitch saunters over toward Beth. "Are you finished playing with the boys, yet?"

"Yes, ma'am," Fitch humbly replies.

"Then take me to the carnival, sir."

"My pleasure," Fitch proudly states with a sigh of relief. Beth takes up Fitch's arm as he leads her to the far end of Main Street toward the smells and sounds of the odd colored tents and opened box cars of the train. Lurking in the shadows, Cougar hangs back in the darkness. It's good to know who the lawman has taking a liking too...

A roving band of musicians dressed in an Arabian fashion play their lutes and horns along the outskirts of the laid three rings. The Ringmaster tips his hat and smiles to the local townspeople and tourists taking in the oddities around them. In one circle, the trainer leads the zebras around the inner area. Maneuvering a zebra one at a time, they perform jumping tricks and balancing acts.

Arm in arm, Fitch and Beth stroll away from the first ring and pause at the second. Another trainer holds the reigns of a camel while four monkeys flip and perform tricks along the camel's pair of humps. Off to the side, the third ring houses an elephant along side of a platform. The third trainer leads gleeful children atop the custom saddle of the elephant. The trainer leads the elephant and children around the inner area of the third ring three times. The children's parents smile and wave at their offspring from the outer area of the ring, Fitch motions toward Beth. "Wanna go for a ride?"

"Gracious, no! I'm not getting up on that beast!" Beth protests. Almost holding her hand, Fitch leads Beth away from the three rings toward the nearest opened boxcar with locals and tourists able to enter it by way of the extended ramp.

A carnie worker sits at his stool with the inner areas of the adjoined boxcars shielded by a positional barrier, "Three bits a piece, folks." Fitch reaches into his trousers and hands the worker six bits. "Thank-you, folks. Enjoy!" Fitch and Beth move to the side making their way into the first compartment as a visiting well dressed couple files in behind them. "Three bits a piece, folks."

Beth nearly looses her breath. The "wolf boy" is the first attraction, sitting in his "cage", "growling" at passing on-lookers. Next to him, the obese bearded lady weighing in at nearly eight hundred pounds. Her full length beard and mustache covers her entire face, covers her massive chest and stomach, drooping down to where Fitch thinks her knees should be.

The next attraction are the Siamese Twin brothers connected at the midriff. They share the same heart, lungs and liver. Each brother has one arm having to work as a team, as a single unit. Oddly, the brothers have three legs making it assuredly difficult to get around.

Fitch and Beth follow the forward patrons through the opened end of the boxcar, over a placed ramp between cars, into the next attractions. A thin tattooed man with bulging eyes, swoops his sword in wild directions. Cocking his head back, the tattooed man lifts the sword and swallows it whole. Retracting the sword, he appears fine and repeats the stunt for the preceding visitors. The boxcar is becoming unusually warm as Fitch and Beth round the next corner.

The light of a hundred lit lanterns is almost blinding keeping the compartment very warm. Sitting in the center of the area of a lavish throne, The Lizard King. Half man half lizard. He appears to have the shape and form of a man yet covered with scales from head to toe. No sexual organs and no body hair whatsoever. The Lizard King flicks out his forked tongue and blinks several times with his glazed and pale reptilian eyes.

Exiting the warm area, Fitch and Beth find themselves in a darkened compartment. A large tank filled with water houses a live mermaid. That *can't* be real! Her flowing hair shadows her bare breasts as she swims above the surface of the water to take a few gasps of air, Plunging downward, her singular fin paddles back and forth, using her human arms and hands for balance and control. The mermaid winks at Fitch hovering down around the bottom of the tank. Beth playfully slaps Fitch in the arm. "What? She's not my type."

"Am *I* your type, Fitch?" Beth asks.

"Don't know," Fitch pauses then motions his head a few attractions back. "I think that bearded lady is more to my liking." Beth giggles, pressing Fitch's arm tightly against herself, squeezing him as close as she can. Fitch leans his head over touching his cheek to her flowing red locks. As subtly as he can, Fitch inhales Beth fragrant hair... lilacs and lavender.

Entering the last opened boxcar, Fitch and Beth stroll along the narrow far side of the car. Filling the opposite side, a row of cages. A pair of female lions in one cage next to a single male lion in a cage by himself. The next cage has a pair of tigers followed by a cage within a cage with a massive boa constrictor inside. The boa is in the middle of feeding time with its unlocked jaws wrapped around a good sized goat. Fitch watches in fascination as the boa consumes the goat. Beth has had enough the oddities, turning her head away. Smiling, Fitch takes a final gander at the boa as he leads Beth toward the opened far door of the boxcar.

"Sump'thn you don' see everyday, eh folks?" the photographer barks out at the end of the exiting ramp of the boxcar. "Would's ya' like 't 'ave your picture takin?" the photographer shuffles in closer to Fitch and Beth.

"Oh, Fitch. Could we?"

"Cost'a dollar," the photographer grins. Fitch reaches into his pocket and tosses the lanky man a silver dollar. "Jest stan' o'r there, please." Fitch and Beth position themselves with a boxcar behind. The photographer hustles over behind the photography unit standing up on a tripod. The man tosses the dark cloth covering over his head, looking through the lens. With one hand, he cups the forward lens cover in his palm. With his other hand, still looking into the lens, he lights the "flash" with sulfur, lifts it over his head and… "Smile!"

FLASH!

The man lowers the flask, poking his head out from under the covering. "Won' but be'a minute, folks," the man slides a small thin metal sheet into the forward slot of the camera.

"Fitch! Fitch!" a young voice bellows out from the crowds. Turning, Fitch and Beth see Trigger galloping toward them.

"What's the matter, Trigger?"

"Nothin'. Bell sent me 't come fetch you," nodding to Beth, "'N' you too."

"'Ere ya go, folks," the photographer hands Beth the tin type. Looking down at the photo, Beth sees herself and Fitch standing very close together, arm in arm, in front of the boxcar. "Thank'e, folks," the man smiles then quickly spies a well dressed couple exiting the ramp of the last opened boxcar. "Sump'thn you don' see everyday, eh folks?"

Main Street is filled to the brim with locals, tourists, out-laying ranchers and wranglers. Bell and her dancehall girls as well as the Stardust Saloon dancehall girls linger around, milling with the single cowboys, wranglers and gamblers come into town. The young lamplighters hobble along on their stilts lighting the well placed lampposts at the street corners of town.

The Mayor stands along side of Bell about her boardwalk just outside her swinging batwing doors. The New Orleans jazz quintet sets their instruments up facing Main Street. "Hells bells, Trigger! Took you long enough," Bell snaps.

Trigger leads Fitch and Beth to the foot of the boardwalk with Bell hovering over like a concerned hen. "What's gonin' on, Bell?" Fitch asks.

"Well, you've been away for all those years. Purgatory's got this dance we hold every New Year's. Thought you'd wanna be a part of it," Bell turns toward the quintet. "Boys, sump'thn lively, eh!" The quintet bursts into tune with an up-beat melody more suited for these parts, not the New Orleans jazz Bell hired them for.

Main Street comes alive! Husbands and wives dance and twirl each other about. Dancehall girls toss their frilly dresses in the air accompanying wranglers and cowboys. Doc Herring free hoofs it to the up-beat music, twirling about. Fitch tosses Doc a glance, *"Doc better not get buck-naked, again,"* Beth smiles, taking Fitch by the hand and waist. "Beth," Fitch nervously whispers.

"Yes, Fitch."

"I can't dance."

"You can't dance?" Beth giggles.

"No. Not a step."

"All that time in Philly and you never learned how to dance?"

"Never needed to."

"Well then it's 'bout time you learned." Beth is patient, taking Fitch's hand in hers, wrapping her other hand about his waist. Step by step, Fitch fumbles not to trample on Beth's feet. All around them, couples jig to the music. A handful of stag wranglers have formed a circle of their own not being able to find a female partner. The wranglers jive and wiggle to the music in a hoe-down. Bell claps her hands to the music, beaming outward from the boardwalk. "Ma," Trigger tugs on Bell's dress coats.

"Yes, Trigger?"

"May I 'ave this dance?"

"Why, certainly."

The young gentleman that his, Trigger escorts Bell off the boardwalk and joins the gleeful crowd frolicking along Main Street. From behind, Fitch feels a tap on his shoulder. "May I cut in?" Jay nervously asks. Fitch and Beth slightly part. Fitch and Jay awkwardly look each other over.

"I reckon, Jay. I'm not gettin' the hang of this." Fitch tosses Beth a defeated glance, turns and sulks away. Jay takes up Beth's hand and wraps his other arm around her waist.

"Just like last Forth of July, eh Beth?" Jay asks. Beth looks over Jay's shoulder to see Fitch slightly turn back to see her and Jay beginning to dance with each other.

"Yeah, Jay," Beth responds with an uncertain tone, "Just like the Forth of July…"

"Alright everyone, settle down!" the Mayor orders. Main Street falls still and silent with only a few traces of murmurs and whispers. The Mayor looks down at his gold pocket watch strung to his gold chain. Crowds of people anxiously await the New Year. Husbands and wives cling to each others arms. Dancehall girls hover about with eager wranglers and cowboys waiting for probably their only kiss of the year.

Among the mass assembly, Dandy, Chote', Jesse and Cougar appear around a gathering of Stardust Saloon dancehall girls. Oddly close to Dandy, Mr. Fuller and his wife. Bell, Robert and Trigger huddle close together at the foot of the steps leading up into Bell's with Doc bracing himself on an upward supporting beam. Ivan, Cory and Luke linger in the distance. In the center of Main Street, Fitch and Beth stand ever so close. An attractive dancehall girl clings to Jay's disinterested arm. "Five... four... three... two... one! Happy New Year!" the Mayor exclaims.

BLAM-BLAM. BLAM. BLAM. BLAM. BLAM-BLAM.

Husband and wives embrace and kiss. The wild gun fire of peacemakers, revolvers, Henry rifles and shotguns thunder into the smoky air. Handheld sparklers are lit casting festive glows and sparkling light in all directions. Ivan clutches onto a sparkler as he receives several kisses from local women.

"Sheriff!" Luke barks out as Ivan continues to receive kisses.

"Yes?"

"Sheriff, your hand's on fire again," Luke replies. Ivan quickly turns away from a young lady to see that the lit sparkler has lit his wooded hand on fire. Jumping about, Ivan dashes to the nearest water trough and shoves in his hand. Slight chuckles and murmured laughter is heard.

"Thanks, Luke."

"Anytime, Sheriff," Luke turns and finds himself a young lady who hasn't been kissed by him yet.

Strangers embrace and kiss one another. Chote' seems out of place. No sane woman would want to kiss a savage. Dandy plants a wet kiss on at least three nearby dancehall girls. Finding himself momentarily alone, Dandy glances over toward Chote'... kissless. "Don't look at me!" Dandy snorts. Chote' and Dandy smile and shake each other's hand.

Robert kisses Bell. Bell kisses Trigger. Trigger and Robert shake hands. Bell and Robert kiss again. Alone in the shadows, Trask looks on, tips his hat toward Bell over Robert's shoulder and slips away into the crowds.

"Happy New Year, Beth."

"Happy New Year, Fitch." Beth and Fitch tenderly embrace, exchanging a long and loving kiss.

"Come 'ere, boy!" Bell shouts out whipping Fitch around. Bell lands a big kiss on Fitch's lips. "Been waitin' fer that fer years!" Bell exclaims. Robert kisses Beth on the forehead then turns to gather affections from nearby dancehall girls. A strong grasp takes Beth by the arm from behind. Jay spins Beth around and plants a long and wanting kiss on her lips. The kiss is warm. Beth's belly twists. Jay tightly embraces Beth then tenderly pushes her away, still remaining face to face.

"Happy New Year, Elizabeth."

"Happy New Year, James…"

BLAM-BLAM. BLAM. BLAM. BLAM. BLAM-BLAM.

Gunfire continues for several more moments. Smoke from the countless gun barrels fills the air. Cowboys, wranglers and ranchers fire their weapons in all directions. Reluctant, Fitch raises his right Colt revolver into the air, slightly backing upward as he goes. Suddenly, Fitch is bumped into. He spins around with his revolver drawn to find himself face to face with Cougar, also with his revolver drawn. The two stare each other down for a long moment. Slowly, Cougar holsters his revolver and tips his wide brimmed Civil War hat. "Happy New Year, lawman."

"Happy New Year," Fitch struggles to politely reply. Cougar turns and rejoins Jesse and Chote'. The trio head down Main Street following a group of dancehall girls and gamblers toward the Stardust Saloon. Dandy and Mr. Fuller turn toward each other with arrogant grins.

"Shall we continue," Mr. Fuller asks.

"After you, Mr. Fuller," Dandy replies. Mr. Fuller and Dandy file suit into Bell's with Robert, Bell and the dancehall girls leading the way. Trigger assists the quintet inside, totting what instruments he can. Main Street suddenly seems barren. Couples return to the carnival at the end of town as others file their way into the Stardust Saloon or Bell's. Within a matter of moments, the New Orleans quintet kicks in, filling Bell's with lively jazz music.

"I'd best go check in on Cleo," Beth squeezes on Fitch's arm.

"I'll collect you at the Katherine," Fitch responds with a hopeful smile. Beth frills her dress, turning away from Fitch. He ponders a moment before turning and heading toward the sheriff's office and jail down the street. Beth quickly enters the Katherine Hotel where Cleo stands post behind the front desk counter.

Coming down the staircase with luggage in hand, Trask approaches the front desk. "Is something the matter with your room, Mr. Bailey," Beth asks.

"No, dear," Trask replies with a sorrowful tone. "Didn't find what I was lookin' for."

Beth sadly nods her head. "Sorry, Mr. Bailey." Beth pauses a moment looking over the ledger resting on the top of the front desk counter. "T'night's on me. No charge."

"It was good to see you again, Beth. And you too, Cleo."

"Sa'," Cleo attempts a smile. Trask collects his bags, turns and disappears out into the night. "Miss."

"Yes, Cleo."

"I needs's 't use the ladies room 'for you be head'n off."

"By all means."

As Cleo darts down the hallway to relieve herself, Beth retrieves her stack of onion papers, taking her plume in hand.

"Poor, Mr. Bailey. A run of bad luck his way. Back in '47, he and one of Bell's girls had a fling. From what I hear tell it wasn't one of Bell's girls it was Bell herself. That wasn't so bad if he'd not been married. What made it worse is that he was a school teacher at the time. Knowing how small towns are, they found out about the affair. Mr. Bailey's wife left him with the kids. Went to Kansas is what I heard. Mr. Bailey was "asked" to leave Purgatory. More run out of town was more like it."

"Mr. Bailey roamed around for a spell, teaching and tutoring well off kids in the gold mining towns of California. Then it happened. He found God or at least

God found him. He found the error of his ways and took up preaching. Odd thing. A teacher and a preacher. Kinda' the same thing if you ask me."

"He came back to Purgatory a few years back. Keeps pretty much to himself living beyond the dunes. Teaching and preaching to folk who can't make it into town on a regular basis. Poor Mr. Bailey. I hope he finds what he's looking for one day. Sure can't have Bell. She's Robert's woman. I do wonder sometimes how that would've turned out if Mr. Bailey and Bell got hitched."

"Beth? Are you ready to go?" Fitch calls out from the chaise directly out front.

"Just a moment, Fitch. I'm waiting on Cleo."

"I'm 'ere, miss," Cleo appears from the hallway.

"If you need anything, send one of the deputies to fetch me."

"I will, miss," Cleo pauses as Beth makes her way from around the front desk counter. "Calvin!"

"What was that, Cleo?"

"Calvin, miss," Cleo smirks.

"Who's Calvin?"

"He was my ol'est boy."

"That's fine to know, Cleo. Why are you telling me?"

"Miss, I fig'urd that you'll be needin' a chil's name af't t'night," Cleo winks as she motions her head toward Fitch waiting in the chaise.

"Oh, Cleo! Good-night!" Beth scolds.

"G'night, miss," Cleo smiles.

Beth makes her way to the chaise and bounces in. Blaze appears strung out behind the buggy. Fitch turns toward with a curious look. "What was that all about?"

"Cleo was wishing me a Happy New Year. You as well."

"Oh," Fitch takes the reigns in hand. Clicking his mouth, Fitch coaxes Beth's horse onward with Blaze following behind. Passing by the sheriff's office and jail, Jay stands post, leaning up against a supporting beam. Jay seems to glare at Fitch, ridding along with Beth, heading out of town toward her spread. Fitch and Beth ridding along, pass through the filled see-saw barricades, beyond the quieting carnival, vanishing into the darkness.

"You want anything?" Jay calls out into the sheriff's office.

"Naw, I'm fine," Cody responds. "Go 'head. I got it here. Go git some sleep."

"I'm gonna go git drunk!" Jay snarls. Cory shakes his head, settling into a long night. Spider lays on his primitive cot in his cell looking up at the stone ceiling. The cell next to him is occupied with a trio of drunken wranglers sleeping it off. The third cell oddly is vacant. It has been a slow night for New Year's Eve in Purgatory.

Cougar, Jesse and Chote' hover around the far billiard table taking turns. The pitcher of chuck-a-luck has retired for the night. Three worn gamblers sit at one table with the dealer tossing them their cards. Trigger sits at his piano playing a melodic slow ragtime tune he had memorized from the jazz quintet. Robert continues to clean his glasses at the far end of the saloon bar with Ivan sitting at the stool facing him. Ivan is sloshed. Bell has her back turned counting out the day's returns.

Sitting at a poker table near the center of the room, the dealer faces Dandy to one side and Mr. Fuller to his other. The dealer tosses Mr. Fuller and Dandy their third up card continuing the variation of five card poker. "It's to you, mister," the dealer replies to Dandy. In the center of the table, a large pile of gold and silver coins mixed in with haphazard paper money.

"Don't wanna keep you up too late," Dandy smirks toward Mr. Fuller. "Sure you gotta get up in the morning to get to work."

133

"Don't you fret about that. T'morrow's a holiday. I'll be in about nine to finish up the year. That means I get to sleep in a bit."

"Well, then. Let's play some cards," Dandy smiles. Slightly looking upward, Dandy gives Cougar a slight wink. Chote' takes his turn at billiards, handing the cue to Jesse.

"Could we 'ave 'nother round over here?" Cougar bellows out.

"Be just a sec', mister," Robert motions to Cougar, beginning to pour three shots of whiskey. The last remaining dancehall girl quickly takes the shots, places them on a trey and scurries over toward the billiard tables.

"Gad dimn, mish-ma-lulla-ruble-ra-ta-blah-muma…" Ivan mumbles at the end of the bar.

"Quiet it down, Sheriff," Robert whispers. "You'r in no condition to take those boys on."

"What boys, Robert?" Jay replies as he enters the saloon. "How's it gonin', Sheriff?" Jay pats Ivan on the shoulder. Jay sits down next to Ivan who sways from side to side trying to keep his balance on the bar stool.

"Those boys over there. You weren't here then."

"They haven't done nothin' wrong-"

"T'night!" Ivan yells.

"Simmer down, Ivan," Robert encourages Ivan.

"What's this all 'bout?" Jay asks. Bell turns with a stack of paper money in her hand and faces Jay. Trigger continues to play the melodic tune, slightly drowning out Bell's voice.

"Some years back, Cougar and his boys, not these boys, other ones, came to town and robbed the bank. Kilt Sheriff Woolley-"

"My bess frien'" Ivan blurts.

"Anyhow, kilt Sheriff Woolley, Fitch's grandpa-" Cougar's ears perk up.

"'N got outta town," Bell concludes.

"Why can't you do anything 'bout it?" Jay tries to pry the story out of Ivan.

"Stature of mimitations."

"You mean "statue of limitations"."

"Yeah, that!" Ivan slurs. "Can' touch 'em. Bin over seven years!" Ivan pauses a moment then slams his shot of whiskey down his throat. "'T-blazes with that!" Ivan moves in violent and sudden movements. He draws his revolver and staggers from the bar stool. "You'r all under arrest," Ivan waves his guns at Cougar, Jesse and Chote'. Cougar calmly raises his hand in the air.

"Don' want no trouble wit' you , Sheriff."

"Come on, Ivan. Sit down," Jay coaxes Ivan, taking him by the shoulders.

"Ma'am," Cougar politely tips his hat as he motions Jesse and Chote' to follow. "We were jest leavin'. 'Night."

"Gad dimn, mish, a-must, do-ra-plat-ma-crap!" Ivan mumbles. Jay leads Ivan to the end of the bar setting him down on a bar stool. With his back half turned to the row of windows along the near wall, Jay stares down Cougar as he, Chote' and Jesse make their way through the central walkway. Cougar gives Dandy a slight nod walking behind Mr. Fuller. Dandy slightly nods back.

Cougar, Jesse and Chote' swing their way through the batwing doors, step off the boardwalk and out into the quiet street. "We keep to the plan," Cougar whispers. "Come on." Cougar leads his boys along Main Street with the lit lampposts flickering their soft glow across the facades of the town.

Fitch pulls back on the reigns halting Beth's chaise along side of the lean-to. Without a word, Beth hops out of the buggy with no assistance from Fitch. Beth shuffles along the wrap-around porch and disappears inside of her quaint home.

That was it? No "good-night"? No kiss? Nothin'?" Fitch pauses a moment then climbs out of the chaise himself. Taking the harness and reigns of Beth's horse, he leads the beast under the lean-to and closes the makeshift corral fence. "Just you and me, Blaze," Fitch whispers leading Blaze to the front porch.

Fitch stands there a long moment in the darkness. Looking in through the front door left cracked open, Fitch sees the faint glow of a lit kerosene lantern. "Beth?" There is no reply. Fitch loosely hitches Blaze to the cross beam of the porch and steps upward, slowly pressing the front door open. "Beth, are you alright?" The hanging horseshoe overhead catches Fitch's eye as he enters.

The single lantern rests in the center of the kitchen table. There is no other movement of any kind. "Fitch?" Beth beckons from the nearest room.

"Yes, Beth?"

"Close the door."

Fitch turns his body half way around, closing and fastening the front door. Taking the lantern from the kitchen table, Fitch softly walks through the main portion of the house, approaching the first door down the narrow hallway. "Beth?" Fitch tenderly presses the door open. Beth stands across the room with her back toward Fitch. She sets another lit kerosene lantern on the far dresser by the window and turns to face him.

"My God, you're beautiful!" Fitch thinks. Beth has loosened her fiery red locks allowing them to hang freely along her back and shoulders. The thin cotton night shirt leaves little to the imagination. The flickering glow of the lantern directly behind herself reveals every inch, every curve of her supple figure. The lower edging hangs above her knees trimmed with lace. Cuffs and plunging neck line sport lace as well. *"My God, the neck line."* The deep "V" stops shy of Beth's naval with her parted breasts and stomach revealed. *"Oh, Jay's locket he gave her for her birthday…"*

"Fitch, close the door," Beth commands in a sultry voice. Fitch softly closes the door behind himself, setting his lantern on the top of the Saratoga chest at the side of the bed. Beth slightly turns and blows out her lantern then tiptoes toward Fitch. She tenderly kisses Fitch on the cheek. "Coming to bed?"

"Hell yes!" Fitch watches as Beth makes her way around the far side of the bed and crawls in under the handmade comforters. She lays there on her side facing Fitch on the opposite side of the bed near the door. He takes off his gray Stetson hat, placing it on top of the Saratoga trunk. Fitch slowly leans over and blows out the last kerosene lantern…

"'Ow 'bout 'nother roun'," Jay slurs trying to hold himself up on the saloon bar. Slouching next to him, Ivan is done for the night, drooling all over the mahogany wood surface.

"I think you both 'ave had enough," Robert finishes cleaning his last glass.

"Jest one mor'."

"<u>One</u> more," Bell calls out from the cash register with several stacks of counted money in her hand. "Robert, I'm puttin' this away." Bell slips out from behind the saloon style bar to the pair of living quarters beyond the left hand side of the staircase. Robert nods as he scans the saloon for intruders or would-be robbers. All Robert sees is Jay and Ivan, skunked, at one end of the bar, Trigger gracefully playing a soft classical melody at the piano near the foot of the staircase and the dealer, Mr. Fuller and Dandy remaining at the last occupied poker table.

"Sorry, gentlemen. It's time to close up for the night," Robert declares.

"Last hand," the dealer states as he looks upon the cards on the table. The pot is enormous, nearly five thousand dollars.

"No matter how this turns out, Dandy," Mr. Fuller replies, "It's been a pleasure playing cards with you."

"You too, Mr. Fuller," Dandy replies looking down at his pair of up cards. A three of clubs and an ace of diamonds. Merely peeking, Dandy looks at his hole cards. A three of diamonds and a three of hearts. So far, three threes… a fair hand. Mr. Fuller looks at his up cards. A jack of clubs and an ace of diamonds. Cocking his head, Mr. Fuller looks at his hole cards. A queen of clubs and a queen of spades. A possible three of a kind of queens... It all depends on the last up cards. The dealer tosses Dandy and Mr. Fuller their last card. Dandy, an ace of clubs, two pair. Mr. Fuller, a king of hearts, leaving him only a pair of queens.

"I'll bet a thousand and call," Mr. Fuller declares, trying to bluff. Knowing he has the better hand, Dandy decides not play it out.

"Too rich for me, Mr. Fuller. I fold."

"Ye-haw!" Mr. Fuller exclaims pulling all his coins and paper money toward himself.

"Nice game," Dandy pauses, "I wanna let you know... I'll be gettin' that back."

"Maybe so, but not t'night," Mr. Fuller grins. Dandy raises, tips his hat and saunters toward the swinging batwing doors as Mr. Fuller removes a lavender crush velvet poke with a gold-like string from the inside of his jacket pocket. Slightly turning, Dandy tosses the dealer a twenty dollar gold coin then disappears out into the night. Mr. Fuller stuffs his winnings of coins and paper money into the lavender poke. Finding it full, he draws the gold tie, then stuffs it into the inside pocket of his jacket. Mr. Fuller tosses the dealer a five dollar silver coin, gloats a moment then shuffles toward the batwing doors.

"Have a good-night, Mr. Fuller," Robert bellows out.

"Thank-you, Robert. Seems my luck's changing. G'night."

"Trigger," Robert turns.

"Yeah, Pa?"

"Time to turn in. Close up for me, will'ya?"

"Sure thing," Trigger obeys. Trigger tucks his sheet music under his arm, makes his way toward the batwing doors and slides the solid doors into place, lightly fastening the right side.

"Hells bells fella's, time for you to go," Bell orders, making her way to the far end of the bar. There is no hope for Ivan. He's been passed out for nearly an hour. Jay is still somewhat sober... somewhat sober.

"Let 'im sleep it off. I'll collect 'im 'n the mornin'," Jay struggles with the words from his lips.

"You'll be alright, Jay?" Bell motherly asks.

"Fine. Be right's rain by mornin'," Jay stumbles past Trigger. As Jay leaves, Trigger slides closed the left solid door and locks it. Making his way around the saloon, Trigger blows out all the lanterns and candles. Robert and Bell scoop Ivan up on opposite sides, dragging him up the staircase. Bell grunts.

"I think Ivan's put some weight on since the last time we had to do this."

"I reckon you're right, sweetie," Robert replies.

With the lower floor of the saloon drawing dim and dark, Trigger takes a final glimpse of his piano, his home then turns and disappears under the passageway under the dual staircase.

Jay staggers along Main Street. The young lamplighters, tromp along their stilts, adding wood to the dimming flames. Jay manages to make his way to the hitching posts outside of the sheriff's office and jail. He has to strain to focus, seeing the colorful tents and boxcars packing up in the middle of the night. Why not? New Year's Eve is over.

Jay crashes into the sheriff's office causing Cory, asleep in the chair, to topple to the floor. Cory draws his pistol with Jay slamming into him. "Your' drunk, Jay!"

"And then some…" Jay staggers toward the far opened jail cell. In the first cell, Spider and the trio of drunkards toss a turn on the meager cots provided for them. The second cell is occupied by a pair of wranglers too rowdy for the New Year's celebration. Jay braces himself along the opened cell door, pauses then thrusts himself inward plopping face down on the last cot of the vacant cell.

"Happy New Year, Jay," Cory whispers. There is no reply.

"Happy New Year, Deputy," Spider sneers from the shadows.

"Shut-up!"

139

The morning's sun crests over the horizon. Fully dressed, Fitch steps out onto the wrap-around porch of Beth's home. He notices that Beth's horse and chaise are not there. Blaze, still hitched to the cross support beam of the porch, gives Fitch a "good-morning" snort. "You, too, Blaze." Fitch unfastens Blaze's reigns, leaps up into the saddle and coaxes his best friend forward.

"Good-morning, Cleo," Beth cheerfully bubbles as she enters the Katherine Hotel. Cleo, in a motherly way, smiles to herself.

"'Guess it 'tis, miss," Cleo rounds the front desk counter. "Every'thin' is's it should. I'll be seein' ya t'night."

"Thank-you, Cleo," Beth grins from ear to ear. Cleo collects her bag and heads down the hallway to her private sleeping quarters, "and, Cleo."

"Yes, miss?"

"Happy New Year."

"Thank'e, miss 'n you too," Cleo slips further into the dimming shadows to the hallway. Beth reaches down for her stack of onion papers and takes a pen in hand. Beth is glowing with a spring in her step. A joyous glimmer upon her cheeks.

"So much has happened in the past couple of days. Where do I start?..."

"Blast it, Woolley, what were you thinkin'? Why'd you have to go'n sleep with her? It makes everything more complicated. Now, afore you know it, Beth's gonna want you to ask her to marry her," Fitch leads Blaze into the livery stables at the end of town, takes the reigns and closes Blaze's gate behind him. Fitch swings his saddle up onto the nearest separating beam between stables and pats Blaze on the star-dusted muzzle.

"Well now, not that that is a bad notion... to marry Beth. She's a looker, put together well, stands on her own two feet, and a business woman to boot. She don't need a man 'round. Got her

140

own spread. Set for a soft life. No plowin' or hoein'. Never have to work a day in the fields runnin' that hotel of hers. She can even probably cook alright, I reckon. Not a bad roll in the hay, either..." Fitch fills Blaze's feeding trough with barley and oats. Tossing the bucket aside, Fitch nods toward the blacksmith tending to the other horses in his care throughout the livery. Fitch turns toward Blaze as he continues to munch on the morning meal. *"What am I talkin' 'bout? Beth was better than any of those burlesque gals in Philly or Boston."* Blaze snorts. "What?" Fitch says aloud, "You were there, too. That mare of yours. You stud!" Blaze snort again.

"I know, I know. I should ask Beth to marry me and settle down. Have a slew of young'uns. Fix up the Woolley Ranch nice 'n proper to raise a family. Start a cattle ranch or even breed horses," Fitch turns toward Blaze. "You'd like that, wouldn't ya?" Blaze looks up a moment from his barley and oats. *"I don't know. What in blazes am I doin' here?"* Fitch rounds the outer stables, lifts his Stetson, running his fingers through his hair… confused and slightly nauseous.

"Fine then!" Fitch declares to Blaze as he leans over the top rail of the stable. "Fine! Alright then! I'll ask Beth to marry me right after-"

"Fitch!" Jay storms into the livery stables clutching onto his pounding head. This is the worse hangover he's had since The Forth of July.

"What it is, Jay?"

"Come quick! The bank's bein' held up!"

BLAM-BLAM. BLAM-BLAM. BLAM. BLAM. BLAM-BLAM…

CHAPTER V

"I told you, Mr. Fuller," Dandy smiles, "I'd be gettin' this back." Dandy reaches into the inside pocket of Mr. Fuller's jacket and retrieves the filled lavender poke with the gold tie string. Dandy clutches onto his Henry rifle in the other hand, shoving Mr. Fuller across the room.

BLAM-BLAM. BLAM. BLAM-BLAM.

Cougar fires several rounds out through the cracked open door of the bank. Chote' scans Main Street to see the slew stagecoaches and pedestrians fleeing for cover. "Where is'e?" Chote' exclaims.

"'E'll be here!" Cougar snaps as he fires again out onto Main Street.

From across the street, Ivan hobbles out through the swinging batwing doors of Bell's, finding cover behind a hitched cargo wagon. Ivan fires several shots at the Wells Fargo Bank across the street. Luke races on foot along the boardwalk heading from the train depot along the same side of the street as Ivan. In a matter of moments, Luke and Ivan are shoulder to shoulder with their guns drawn and ready for battle.

Fitch and Jay draw their revolvers dashing from the sheriff's office and jail, passing by livery. Cory bolts out of the jail as he loads a double barrel shotgun. "Anyone know who it 'tis?" Fitch blurts out in a full gallop along the boardwalk. His heavy boots thundering below him against the wooden planks. *Jingle-jingle-jingle.*

"I'll give ya three guesses 'n you'll only need one!" Jay replies growing out of breath.

"Cougar!"

"Yep!" Jay replies a few steps behind Fitch.

"Well then, let's not keep 'im waiting!"

Across the street, Ivan and Luke have positioned themselves to cover the main entrance of the bank. Cougar leers out through the crack in the door and fires off several more rounds. Using a borrowed pistol from Jesse, Chote' breaks a front window and fires. He spots Fitch, Jay and Cory positioning themselves around the corner of Katy's Boarding house next door, Cougar fires of a few rounds. "Where _is_ that boy?" Dandy blurts out.

"I _said_ 'e'll be here!" Cougar orders.

Thundering hooves rattle the side windows of the bank. Dandy peers out through the window to see Jesse galloping up from behind the backsides of the row of structures and buildings along their side of the street. Jesse rides his own mount with the three others in tow.

BLAM. BLAM. BLAM. BLAM. BLAM.

The front windows of the bank shatter due to Ivan and Luke's continuous gunplay. "Time 't go!" Cougar commands. Taking three filled, Wells Fargo Bank – Purgatory money bags in hand, Cougar thrusts himself through the side window toppling onto the ground just outside the alleyway. The money bags rattle and clank together with the gold and silver coins among the wads of paper money. As Cougar lumbers up onto his saddled beast, Chote' crashes through the window and with more grace, lands center on the bareback of his mount. "You'll 'ave to teach me that sometime," Cougar sneers.

"Don't think now's the time, Cougar," Chote' sarcastically responds with a playful sneer.

KA-BLAM-KA-BLAM. KA-BLAM.

The sounds of Dandy's Henry rifle cut through the air. Dandy clutches onto a pair of filled money bags in one hand and his Henry rifle in the other, leaping out through the window, to the ground, then effortlessly onto his saddled horse. "Now comes the tough part," Cougar quickly loads as fresh cylinder into his revolver. Adjusting his Civil War saber at his hip, Cougar spurs his horse. "Haw!"

Cory and Jay have made their way from Katy's Boarding House to the front of the shattered windows of the bank. With their weapons drawn, they peer inside. At that moment, Cougar, Dandy, Jesse and Chote' thunder into view from around the corner. Jay manages to get one shot off. Chote' draws one of his numerous throwing knives and hurls it toward Cory. The blade is thrust into Cory's chest. He staggers a moment, firing into the air then topples onto the boardwalk in a growing pool of blood.

Jay fires at the fleeing outlaws with bullets flying over their heads. Jesse returns fire winging Jay in the arm who continues to fires, now in pain. With both ivory Colt revolvers drawn, Fitch steps off the boardwalk in front of the bank and fires quickly, in anger at Cougar and his gang.

BLAM. BLAM. BLAM. BLAM. BLAM…

Every shot misses. Seeing Fitch's daring maneuver as he dashes from his cover, Ivan and Luke dart from out behind the cargo wagon across the street, firing as they go. Dandy side saddles his galloping horse.

KA-BLAM. KA-BLAM.

Dandy swings himself about and rides past Bell's heading after the others out of Purgatory. Ivan staggers a moment, raising his wooden limb to his pair of gut-shot wounds. The wooden limb is covered with blood. Ivan struggles to stay on his feet then falls face first onto Main Street. Luke's body already growing cold slouched over the cargo wagon behind. "Jay," Fitch whispers. "I might need some help here…"

Winged, Jay turns to see Fitch struggling to keep on his feet, leaning against a supporting beam. A pair of gunshot wounds spill out blood from Fitch's lower side stomach, another wound in his left shoulder and another on his upper right thigh. Smoke from the ferocious gun battle lingers through the air with cowardly pedestrians creeping out from their cover. Several of the business owners and shopkeepers peer out through their bullet ridden windows to see if the coast is clear. Fitch drops his pair of ivory handled revolvers into the dirt and sand, slouches over and falls limp in Jay's arms. "Fitch! Fitch," Beth screams as she dashes from the Katherine Hotel toward them.

Totting his medical black bag, Doc checks Ivan then Luke for a pulse. Shaking his head, Doc races across the street to examine Cory. He too, is dead. Doc quickly makes his way over toward Jay and Fitch. "You alright, son?" Doc asks.

"Fine, Doc. They just winged me," Jay replies. "Fitch's been shot up pretty good. Look after 'im."

"Let's get 'im inside."

"Fitch!" Beth swoops in toward Fitch with Cleo close behind. Jay holds onto Fitch slouched in his bloody arms. Beth approaches. Jay and Beth stare a long moment into each others eyes. Conflict. Love. Anger. "Fitch..." Beth whispers. Jay slides Fitch from himself allowing Beth and Cleo to support his weight. "Take him to the Katherine. I don't want him in that God awful place you call an operating room, Doc," Beth scolds. Doc approaches Jay to examine his wound as Beth and Cleo drag Fitch across the street toward the Katherine Hotel.

"What's wrong with my operating room?" Doc snidely asks Jay.

"Don'know, Doc. "Women,'" Jay responds.

Ever so slowly, the townspeople, Mayor, laborers, handfuls of wranglers and tourists inch their way out onto Main Street. The festive New Year's decorations now seem tarnished and violated. The lingering smoke of gunplay feels heavy and dark. An ominous cloud of darkness looms overhead. A storm's coming...

Fitch's bullet riddled shirt lays in a bloody pile on the floor next to his soiled trousers, boots and silver spurs. His oversized grey Stetson hat hangs on a hook along side of his holstered pair of ivory handled Colt revolvers across the room. Beth sits on one side of the bed as Fitch lays face up half covered with a blanket. Doc hovers over Fitch cleaning and tending to Fitch's numerous wounds. "I was so worried. How are you doing, Fitch," Beth tearfully replies.

"I'll be just fine. Doc'll fix me up." Fitch turns and looks up at Doc. "I wish <u>you</u> would've shot me, Doc. Then I won't need so much work."

"Be still, Fitch," Doc orders with a chuckle. "I've been tryin' to shoot you fer months." Fitch laughs. Pain wells through his body. "Ya know, Fitch. Patchin' up your family is gettin' to be a lifetime occupation."

"Call it job security," Fitch chuckles.

"That's fine 'till there's none of your family left," Doc replies with a somber tone. Fitch's chuckling manner quickly subsides.

"Fitch! I'm here," Beth slides in closer.

"Elizabeth, you may want to leave now," Doc fatherly suggests.

"I'm staying. I'm staying right <u>here</u> by Fitch's side," Beth declares.

"Suit yerself, dear," Doc says reaching into his black medical bag resting on his side of the bed. Doc first removes a small wooden cylinder bound with a leather strap with odd markings. "Bite down on this, Sheriff. It's gonna hurt a bit." Doc places the mouthpiece into Fitch's jaws who bites down on it. Doc takes an instrument with a wide base to extremely sharp and narrow pointed surgical blade from his bag. Looking down into Fitch's eyes for a split second, Doc thrusts the point of the blade into Fitch's left shoulder wound. Blood spurts out from the wound splattering Beth's cheek.

Beth explodes from the upstairs hotel suite crashing into Jay, Robert and Bell causing them to nearly topple over the railing. Beth pushes them aside and lunges over the railing herself. Beth pukes over the railing with the vile nearly hitting Cleo at the front desk counter by inches. "Sorry, Cleo. I'll tend to that," Beth says while wiping her mouth.

"I should hope so, miss!"

Robert smirks at Beth's response to Doc's attention and care for Fitch. "Well, guess Doc's started then." Bell and Jay

146

come to Beth's side, escorting her down the staircase. Robert pulls up a chair along the hallway mezzanine, props it up against the wall and begins his wait. From inside the suite, Robert can hear the faint cries of pain from Fitch as Doc continues to remove the numerous chunks of metal from his wounds.

With the bullets removed from Fitch's flesh, Doc bounds the last wound and covers Fitch up with a blanket. "You'll need to rest for a few days, Fitch."

"What about The Cougar Gang? What about the bank? I have a job to do."

"Just like you'r Grandpa," Robert replies from the opened doorway. Straining, Fitch turns to see Robert entering with a fresh pair of trousers, shirt and under garments. "Thanks, Doc," Robert pats Doc on the shoulder as he collects his bloody rags, blades and bottles of cleanser.

"If you need me, I'll be at Bell's gettin' corned," Doc snorts wiping Fitch's blood from his hands.

"Just don't go'n get yerself buck-naked, again. I'm in no shape to come after you."

"That's a deal, Sheriff," Doc smiles as he exits with his black medical bag.

"*Sheriff*"," Fitch thinks to himself. *"I'll never get used to that."* Fitch pauses a moment before tossing the blanket off of himself, attempting to rise up. The numerous wounds drive unbearable pain throughout his body. Robert eases Fitch back into bed then pulls up Beth's chair along side.

"Cougar'll be there and so will your job. You need to rest now," Robert orders.

"Whatta ya mean, "just like you'r Grandpa?""

"I knew Theodore very well," Robert pauses to take a flask from his inside vest pocket, taking a swing of whiskey. "Theodore was my brother. Recon that makes you and I related." Fitch becomes pale. Robert hands the flask to Fitch who swallows down a bellyful of rot-gut.

"I don't know what to say," Fitch manages to blurt out. Robert leans over to embrace Fitch.

"Say hello to your Uncle Bob!" Robert carefully hugs Fitch who unassuredly reaches up and pats Robert on the back of the shoulders. Robert slides back into his chair and takes another swig of his whiskey, replacing it back into his inside vest pocket.

"Why didn't anyone tell me I had an uncle? Why was there such a secret?"

"It's a long story, Fitch."

"It seems I've got time. Doc says I'll be laid up for a few days."

"Alright, Fitch... Sometime in '43 when Theodore and I was finished with the one of the many Indian Battles, we took up The Woolley Family, yes, your Ma 'n Pa too, you was nothin' but a spit then. We came out west hearin' word of gold in California. Didn't quite make it that far. The wagon trail took up a few problems and settled in Sattler's Springs for a spell."

"Seemed that we weren't cut out for minin'. The "law" caught Theodore's eye and well, Bell caught my eye. I came to Purgatory in early '46 'n new I was gonna stay. Bell was already the owner 'n operator of Bell's though she hadn't renamed it yet. A few years later, after your Ma 'n Pa had died, Theodore rolled up into Purgatory with you tucked under his arm with the flashy badge on his chest. He was only a deputy at the time."

"Was easy for 'im to get a badge seein's that all he did in the Indian Wars. Only took a few years 'till he became sheriff. Now, this is where it gets "interesting". Theodore was the sheriff and I took a liking to the bar business and took up with Bell. Well, Bell had, shall we say, a "colorful" history. "You can take the girl outta the ill repute but you can't take the ill repute outta the girl". Theodore and I thought it would be in <u>his</u> best interest if no one knew we were related... lawman and barkeep cavorting around with a dancehall girl. So, we kept it a secret," Robert reaches for his flask again taking a swig. "You'r folks would've been very proud of you."

"How well did you know my folks?" Fitch attempts to sit up again.

"Another time, Fitch. That's even a longer story. Now then, get some rest," Robert rises and messes up Fitch's hair… just like Grandpa used to do so many years ago. As Robert approaches the door, Beth peers inside around the corner and enters. "Beth," Robert smiles.

"Robert," Beth returns the gesture. Beth slightly closes the door behind herself and pulls up her chair. Tenderly taking Fitch by the hand, she lifts it, kisses his palm and rests it back down on the bed. "I'll be here for as long as it takes, Fitch," Beth whispers.

Fitch strains a smile, trying to stay awake. His eyes flutter for a moment before slipping into a deep slumber. Beth clings onto his hand, staring lovingly it him. Yet, a curious look dawns her face. A look of wonderment. A look of confusion. A look… a look of love…

"Our Father, who art in Heaven, hollowed be thy name," Doc recites The Lord's Prayer in a low voice as he stands at the head of three fresh graves; Ivan, Cory and Luke. Gathered around Doc, the mass of townspeople of Purgatory in either their Sunday-go-to-meeting clothes, waves of black suits and dresses, with other cowboys and wranglers wearing the best attire they could rustle up. Doc's recital of the prayer seems to drift in and out of Fitch's consciousness.

Fitch stands atop of the fresh graves with Grandpa Theo's unattended headstone a mere few graves over. He wears his grey oversized Stetson, ivory handled Colt revolvers holstered low at his hips and otherwise plain clothing. Grandpa Theo's sheriff's badge, inherited by Ivan, now inherited by Sheriff Fitch Woolley… the badge now seems to sparkle and gleam upon Fitch's chest… finally back in the family.

Wearing a black dress and veil, Beth hovers near Fitch, trying to comfort him, clinging onto his good arm. Fitch glances to the far side of Grandpa's grave, focusing on his parent's headstones. "…and thou I walk through the valley of the shadow of death, I shall fear no evil, for-"

"I'm done buryin' my family 'n friends," Fitch interrupts. All eyes fall upon him. A deathly stillness spreads throughout the gathered assembly of mourners. Fitch looks all around at the gazing stares. "I done buryin' my family 'n friends," Fitch mumbles. Fitch turns and heads past Doc's hertz wagon, pauses a moment and slumps to the supporting windowed sides. Beth rushes to his side keeping Fitch on his feet. Almost reluctantly, Jay appears and collects Fitch from the other side. Fitch strains to look up at the gathered towns people. "I'm gettin' a posse together! Who's with me? I'll pay twenty dollars a week to go after The Cougar Gang?"

Ashamed and cowardice, the people of Purgatory turn away and lower their heads. "I thought as much. And you're the people I'm paid to protect?" Fitch mockingly blurts out with contempt.

Beth and Jay assist Fitch up into Beth's chaise. The funeral ceremonies are over. The assembly lowers their heads for a silent prayer then begins to file away. Doc tosses Bell and Robert an uncertain glance, shaking his head. Jay stands off from the chaise as Beth clicks her mouth coaxing her horse forward. Beth and Fitch gallop away down the sloping lull in the hillside heading down the narrow roadway into Purgatory.

"You need your rest," Beth whispers, sliding Fitch back into bed of his hotel suite. Beth pulls the comforter over his bare chest. Fitch's left shoulder and side wound tended to yet both continues to seep blood from the bandages. Beth kisses Fitch on the forehead then turns to exit.

"You're a good woman, Elizabeth," Fitch strains to respond. Wide eyed and pale, Beth turns at the opened door, staring blankly at Fitch with his head propped up on the pillow yet cocked over to see her. "Why didn't you ever settle down?"

"I was waiting for a young man to return from his travels," Beth says with a twinkle in her eye. "Like in the fairy tales, to return to me, kiss me and sweep me off of my feet."

"Has he?"

"Well..." Beth whispers as she begins to slip out through the doorway, "...two outta three ain't bad." Beth tenderly closes the door behind herself. Fitch slightly chuckles a moment, holding his stomach wound in pain. Gritting his teeth, Fitch holds his side, closes his eyes and tries to drift off to sleep with an odd smirk on his face.

Endless oceans of sand sprawl out across the wasteland of the desert. The dimming sliver of a moon hangs low in the cloudless sky. It is a starry night. Clear and peaceful. In the nearing distance, a small town is seen. The outlaying huts are primitive with shake roofs and dried clay walls. No functioning doors or shutters. The openings of the huts are open to the night, allowing the desert breeze to cool the dark skinned occupants.

Beyond the huts, a town-of-sorts flickers its lit lanterns from inside of the structures. What appears to be a main street, cuts through the no more than a dozen buildings. A pair of general stores, a boarding house or two, a run down hotel with harlots lingering in the shadows, "inviting" all visiting cowboys and ranchers inward for "refreshment" and what would a "thriving" town be without... a saloon?

Several horses appear hitched to the posts directly outside the Dead Horse Saloon. A cargo wagon stands off to the side with four rigged horses standing for their riders to return. A sole figure from inside the saloon flutters his fingers across the strings of a guitar. The sounds are soothing, not up-beat, with a Latin flare. It's drawing close to the end of the night.

Cougar stands at the center of the tattered saloon bar. On opposite sides of him, Dandy, with a Latino dancer at his side and Jesse, finishing his glass of warm beer. On Cougar's other side, Chote' flips and twirls his Bowie knife through his fingers. "Barman! 'Nother round over'ere!" Cougar orders. The plump, filthy and fowl smelling bartender shuffles his way to face Cougar and his gang.

"'Bout to close up for th'night, Señor'" the bartender nervously responds. Cougar looks around the saloon. A trio of caballeros lay passed out over a poker table. A Latina dancer braces her chin sitting at another poker table, fast asleep. "Yeah," Cougar looks directly at the bartender, "looks like you'ad a real good night."

"This round's on me," Dandy chimes in taking Mr. Fuller's lavender poke with the gold tie string from his inside jacket pocket. Dandy tosses several gold coins onto the bar.

CLANK. CLICKITY-CLANK. CLANK.

The sounds of the money dropping on the saloon bar draws attention to the trio of caballeros. Looking about, they smile with their missing teeth, raise a bottle of tequila toward the bar then resume their poker playing like they had been awake all along. Several Latina dancers slink their way from the backroom, sliding in closer toward Cougar and Jesse. "Taking one for the team", one dancer files in along Chote's arm, trying to get in the mood. Cougar turns toward the mariachi player in the corner. "Play sump'thn, greaser!" Cougar tosses a silver coin at the guitar player's feet. The dark skinned man nods and begins a lively instrumental sending music into the air.

As if on cue, wranglers and caballeros begin to file into the Dead Horse. In a matter of moments, the saloon appears as if they were in the middle of a mining town or booming metropolis. The poker tables are filled. So-called dancehall girls appear from nowhere continuing their "trade of solicitation", Cougar, Dandy, Jesse and Chote' are joined at the bar with grinning Mexicans. "Well, why not?!" Dandy blurts out as he tosses Mr. Fuller's lavender poke onto the bar, "Drinks'r on me!" Cheers roar up. Mexicans approach Dandy and pat him on the back. Cougar smiles toward Dandy with a devilish grin.

"You sure got a way with pep'le, Dandy."

"Learned from the best, Cougar," Dandy raises his filled tequila shot glass toward Cougar. Chote', Jesse, Dandy and Cougar all raise their filled shot glasses then slam the liquid down their throats. Cougar quickly takes a Latina dancer up in his arms and spins her about the opened area of the saloon. Cougar's Civil War sword slapping at his thigh. Dandy and Jesse collect up a quartet of dancers, twirling and spinning them about. At the bar, Chote' looks over at his designated dancer. She smiles at him with as many teeth as she has. Chote' takes a bottle of tequila from the bar, powerfully takes the dancer by the hand and leads her into a narrow hallway leading into the back "entertaining" rooms...

The main street of the sleepy Mexican town is still and quiet. The lit lanterns from the surrounding general stores and businesses have been extinguished. Cougar and his gang's horses remained hitched to the posts outside of The Dead Horse Saloon. Numerous other horses appear among the hitched along side. Suddenly, the swinging batwing doors of The Dead Horse explode open. With a dancer on each arm, Cougar stumbles out onto the rickety boardwalk. In Cougar's left hand, he holds a Wells Fargo Bank – Purgatory money bag. In his right hand, a bottle of tequila. Cougar and the dancers laugh and poke at each other toppling along the boardwalk.

Across the street several business down, Sheriff Hiller, a stout man, steps from the sheriff's office strapping on his old style gunbelt. Sporting a single peacemaker, Hiller stretches and yawns. A commotion catches his attention from up the street, lowering his wide brimmed hat over his eyes shielding him from the rising sun.

Cougar and the pair of dancers stumble out onto the dusty street. Hiller instantly notices the "Purgatory" money bag in Cougar's left hand. Taking a deep breath, Hiller places his palm onto the handle of his peacemaker, stepping forward.

"What's goin'on 'ere, mister," Hiller billows out. The pair of Latina dancers see Hiller first. They quickly back away from

Cougar, disappearing back into The Dead Horse. With a money bag in one hand, Cougar is left alone in the street with Hiller continuing to approach. "I ask'd, what you were doin'?!"

"Jest lookin' fer a good time, Sheriff," Cougar snorts. Hiller trembles as he prepares to draw his peacemaker. Cougar arrogantly takes a large swig of tequila then releases the bottle. The glass bottle shatters on the ground soaking into the sand.

"P-put the money bag d-down on the ground 'n r-raise you'r hand-hands in th' air," Hiller commands.

""Hand-hands" Sheriff?" Cougar mocks, "is hand-hands like a can-can or a two-two?"

"P-please, mister. Put th-the money bag down 'n r-raise you'r h-hands up."

From the swinging batwing doors of The Dead Horse, the rest of The Cougar Gang appears. Dandy, with his Henry rifle propped over his shoulder, Jesse, twirling his pair of six-shooters about his fingers and Chote', with his Bowie knife in one hand and another large blade in the other, exit, step out onto the boardwalk then down onto the street fanning out behind Cougar in a migrating flock of birds formation. "P-please, mister..."

The stout bartender, dancers and hung-over Mexican patrons file out of The Dead Horse and stop in their tracks along the rotting boardwalk. Cougar and Hiller are the only souls on the street. Cougar raises the Purgatory money bag high in the air then... releases it. Hiller watches it fall from Cougar's hand. Hiller fumbles to draw his peacemaker. Dandy whips about his Henry rifle as Jesse draws his pair of six-shooters...

KA-BLAM. BLAM-BLAM. KA-BLAM. BLAM-BLAM.

With smoke from the barrel of his Henry, Dandy twirls it, replacing back onto his shoulder. Jesse spins his six-shooter, then holsters it. Cougar, without firing a shot, turns toward Chote'. "Sorry, maybe next time." Chote' slides his Bowie and other large blade back into his sash with a disappointed look on his face. Cougar looks around the street. Gawking eyes focus upon him.

The bartender. Dancers. Locals. Passing through wranglers and caballeros. Cougar picks up the fallen Purgatory money bag and slightly waves it in the air. "Now, where were we…"

Cougar's pair of dancers inch their way from The Dead Horse as the stout bartender enters through the batwing doors. The sole mariachi begins to play a lively guitar instrumental. Laughter fills the air as if nothing had happen. Sheriff Hiller's body left unattended. Laying face down in the center of the street…

A passenger train puffs and billows out steam from the forward locomotive. The train chugs and chugs until eventually moving forward. Locals fill the depot platform waving their good-byes. Jay appears through the crowds making his way toward the opened clerk's office window. "Deputy, this jest came in this 'mornin'," the youthful clerk hands Jay a telegraph. Jay quickly reads over the wire with widening eyes.

"Thanks!" Jay blurts out, turning at full speed heading back along Main Street. Jay manages his way through the incoming stagecoaches and cargo wagons. All of the New Year's decorations and see-saw barricades have been removed and packed away for next year. Businessmen and cowboys cross to and fro through Main Street with Jay dashing along heading toward the Katherine Hotel.

"It's been three days short of a week and Fitch has hardly come out of his room. What's he doing in there? Sleeping? Polishing his guns? What? I've wondered over the past few days if I'd made the right choice to "give myself" to Fitch. The Good Book says you're not to give unto sin until you're married."

"I wasn't giving into sin. I've loved Fitch for as long as I can remember. It's not like we're not going to

155

be wed. It's just a matter of timing and it's not right now. I know Fitch'll ask me... but when? Jay is becoming more of a distraction. He follows me around like a lost puppy when Fitch isn't about. He comes up with excuses like, "Fitch told me to look after you", and," I'll help you with those packages, Fitch asked me to help out," when I know full well Jay's acting on his own accord. Jay... James. What am I to do with –"

"Beth!" Jay charges into the lobby of the Katherine Hotel. As usual... unannounced.

"What is it, Jay?"

"Trouble, The Cougar Gang shot 'n killed a sheriff a few counties over," Jay responds with a concerned expression. Taking the telegraph in hand, Jay bolts from the front desk counter toward the foot of the staircase leading up to the mezzanine. Puzzled, Beth quickly follows behind. At the top of the staircase, Jay nearly collides into Doc exiting Fitch's suite. Beth slowly follows, cocking her head to the side, trying to hear the news... it must be bad.

"Where do you think you're goin', lad?" Doc scolds.

"I've gotta get this't Fitch," Jay waves the telegraph in the air.

"Not t'day!" Doc stands directly in Jay's path preventing him from passing. Doc and Jay shuffle back and forth in a little jig for a moment before Jay sternly pushes Doc aside.

"<u>Please</u>, Doc," Jay urges. With his black medical bag in hand, Doc lowers and shakes his head allowing Jay to pass. Jay bounds up the rickety staircase, rounds the wooden railing, then reaches for the brass door knob and enters the suite without knocking. The door nearly slams shut from behind Jay followed by a long silence. Doc stands at the foot of the staircase with Beth mere inches away from him. The silence is deafening. Not even the sounds of the passing stagecoaches and cargo wagons are heard from Main Street.

Beth quietly opens the suite door and stands motionless. Jay stands off to the side of the room, waiting. Fitch has risen and faces the mirrored vanity across the room. Fitch takes a fresh shirt from a hook and slips it on. Pain wells up from his shoulder and stomach wounds. Fitch's arm is still bandaged from Doc's buck-naked shooting spree. He looks at himself in the mirror as he dresses. While slipping on his trousers, he looks into the mirror to see Beth remaining in the doorway, blankly staring at him. Jay shuffles his weight from side to side. Fitch is nearly dressed. Shiny badge on his vest chest. Holstered ivory handled Colt revolvers hanging low at his hips. The silver spurs clung tight to the heels of his boots. *Jingle-jingle.*

Fitch reaches for his oversized grey Stetson hat and places it upon his head. He turns and pauses for a lingering moment. He reaches for the unmade bed and takes the telegraph in hand. Fitch glares at Jay, not out of anger but of determination. Fitch crumples up the telegraph and tosses it to the floor. He makes his way toward the door and stands inches away from Beth. "I have to go."

"You can't! You need your rest. If you ride now you could open your wounds," Beth pleads.

"Sheriff, let the Marshals take care of this. It's not your fight," Jay chimes in.

"Is that what I'm su'pose to tell the people that live in this town? "It's not my fight?""

"This isn't about the money and you know it," Beth's eyes begin to well up with tears. "It's about Grandpa. I loved him too but going after Cougar won't change anything. What's it gonna matter if you bring Cougar back."

"I'm *not* bringin' 'im back," Fitch growls as he tenderly presses his way past Beth exiting the suite.

"Fitch?" Beth whispers.

"Elizabeth," Fitch replies. Beth smiles, he rarely calls her by her given name. But the moment is lost. With full force, Beth slaps Fitch hard across the face. Fitch is stunned at first and motions to make a more hastened departure. As he turns, Beth grabs him by the arm, presses him tightly against herself and plants a long and wanting kiss. Jay shifts his weight again from side to side. Opening his eyes, Fitch lovingly pushes Beth away, turns and exits. Beth wipes away a tear as Jay carefully approaches her.

"'Ya know, I was thinkin' 'bout goin' with 'im," Jay replies hoping for a kiss. Without a second thought, Beth reaches up and slaps Jay across the face. Nearly breaking down in tears, Beth dashes from the suite. Jay slightly rubs his swelling face, "That's *not* what I had in mind."

Fitch has made his way to the bottom of the staircase standing along side of the front desk counter with Doc sipping on his whiskey flask. The thundering sounds of footsteps echo's overhead. Fitch and Doc look upward to see Beth dashing from the suite, tossing Fitch a hurtful glare then disappearing down the mezzanine hallway. Jay steps out from the suite and saunters his way down toward Fitch and Doc. "Thanks for everything, Doc. Look after Beth for me, will ya'?"

"We will," Doc replies as he and Fitch shake hands.

"Doc," Fitch whispers so is not to allow Jay to hear. "I'm finished. I'll go out 'n take care of Cougar then I'm done," Fitch smiles and exits the lobby.

"That's what I'm afraid of, Sheriff," Doc replies under his breath. Jay quickly passes Doc and follows after Fitch. Doc remains at the front desk counter watching Jay catch up with Fitch, weaving their way though the passing cargo wagons and stagecoaches across Main Street.

Fitch opens a lower drawer to his sheriff's office desk. He retrieves a thin stack of worn and even charred looking fliers or "wanted posters". "Have Mr. Huckaby print more of these up. Have 'im add "wanted for murder and bank robbery", Fitch hands the fliers to Jay. Looking the fliers over, Jay sees the drawn images of Cougar on the first flier. Flipping through the thin stack, Jay sees a variation of drawn fliers with The Cougar Gang as a whole, then of individual images of Jesse, Chote' and Dandy. The last flier in the stack is a group drawn image, "WANTED – DEAD OR ALIVE – MURDER – BANK ROBBERY – STAGECOACH BANDITS - $1000.00 REWARD" then below, "U.S MARSHAL LOGAN – ST. LOUIS, MO." Jay is struck. He looks oddly at Fitch.

"The Cougar Gang fliers? How did you get these?"

"Marshal Logan's been sending 'em to me since I came back to town," Fitch responds with a stern tone. From the nearest jail cell, Spider perks up, stands and presses himself against the steel bars trying to listen. Fitch suddenly whips about and faces Spider. "Where's Cougar?"

"Don' know nuthin'," Spider sneers.

"People saw you come into town with 'im. Where's he goin'?"

"Don'- know – nuthin'."

"Fine, for beatin' Bryson Rockefeller, you can just stay in there for a week."

"A week?" Spider protests.

"How 'bout two?" Fitch bellow as Spider quickly settles down and sits on his meager cot. "Besides, I *know* where they're goin," Fitch turns to Jay. "They're goin' to Diablo Canyon. I'll cut 'em off there."

"Diablo Canyon? That's a rough part of country," Jay replies. "Good-luck, Sheriff." Fitch motions a moment toward the door then turns toward Jay.

"If I'm not back in a month, *you're* the new Sheriff." Fitch and Jay stand awkwardly facing each other at the opened door. "Jay, about Beth. I ah…"

"I know, Fitch. I know," Jay replies as brotherly as he is able to.

"Look after her for me."

"I will, Sheriff," Jay and Fitch shake hands.

" "Sheriff", I still will never get used to that, " Fitch thinks.

"Blaze's all packed up jest like you asked," the humble blacksmith reports, patting Blaze on the mane. Fitch enters the opened stable to find Blaze saddled with Fitch's bedroll and two weeks rations for Blaze as well as two weeks of food-stuff and jerky for Fitch. "It's not too late, Sheriff."

""Too late" for what?"

"Stay here, here in Purgatory. No need to go off 'n git yerself kilt," the blacksmith pauses. "Stay."

"Could you?" Fitch takes a hold of the saddle's horn and heaves himself upward.

"Reckon not..." the blacksmith proudly nods. Tipping the oversized Stetson, Fitch slightly coaxes Blaze from the opened stable then out through the opened doors of the livery. The blacksmith lowers his head not knowing if he's ever to see Fitch again. Well, see him alive, anyway...

Fitch and Blaze slowly make their way from the livery. Jay steps out from the sheriff's office and jail and gives a casual nod. Fitch and Blaze continue down Main Street. One by one, business men, shopkeepers, dancehall girls, the Mayor, saddled cowboys and wranglers cease their daily activities and pause. The entire town of Purgatory simply stops. Every cargo wagon and stagecoach driver seems to pull over to the side of Main Street creating a central area like Moses parting the Red Sea. Fitch and Blaze continue onward. From the shadows of the jail cell, Spider bellows out an evil laugh.

Fitch rides along past Katy's Boarding House then Wells Fargo Bank. Across the street, Fitch looks upon the Katherine Hotel. There are no traces of Beth to be seen. Pedestrians lower their heads and look away. A deathly stillness covers Main Street. One could hear the falling of a strand of hay or straw. Faintly, the tender fingers and hands of Trigger softly are heard, continuing to play at the piano inside the stillness of Bell's. Melodic and soothing, yet the sounds and feelings of "solace". More of a dirge played at a funeral home or wake.

Bell and Robert tiptoe out from the swinging batwing doors of Bell's shielding their eyes from the warming sun. They watch Fitch and Blaze saunter past. Fitch nods with a tip of his hat. Doc appears inside from the shadows, simply looking over the tops of the batwing doors. Doc shakes his head in sadness. "Robert, I need 'nother drink," Doc blurts.

"Hells bells, Doc. Git it yerself," Bell snorts. Robert remains steadfast along side of Bell.

"Fine then," Doc scolds as he returns back inside to the bar.

At the utmost edge of town, Fitch pauses and turns. Every eye is upon him. Fitch scans Main Street and the buildings for Beth. There is no sign of her. *Jingle-jingle.* He slightly kicks his silver spurs into Blaze's side, maneuvering his mount around, turning his back on Purgatory. Ever so slowly, activity returns. Stagecoach drivers and cargo wagons resume their routes. Pedestrians stroll to and fro along the wooden boardwalks as Robert and Bell slip into the shadows of the saloon.

The lobby and parlor of the Katherine is void of patrons. Cleo totes her wash bucket through the parlor approaching the far set of windows. The staircase leading to the second floor is quiet. The upper hallways are still with a single door opened near the far end.

Beth stares blankly out the curtain drawn window. Beth wipes a single tear from her cheek. Looking outside, Beth sees the fading image of Fitch and Blaze strolling out of town. The stroll turns to a gallop then a three quarter run. Dust flies behind them leaving only a faint glimmer of their images. Then, they are gone...

Fitch clutches onto Blazes reigns remaining in his saddle. He pauses as he looks over the rows of grave sites and headstones inside the poorly painted cast iron fence. Grandpa Theo's ghostly image sits in his rocking chair, puffing on his pipe under the gathering of Joshua Trees. Theo smiles and winks at Fitch giving him a playful nod. Fitch reaches out to wave returning the smile.

Grandpa Theo's haunting figure vanishes. Fitch is all but alone as he sadly lowers his extended hand. Taking the reigns, Fitch coaxes Blaze onward and away from the cemetery. A slight breeze blows across the headstones rustling the wild grass all around. In a matter of moments, Fitch and Blaze disappear from sight, heading out into the unknown future that awaits them…

"It's been nearly a week since Fitch has left. There's been no word of his efforts. Has he captured or killed The Cougar Gang? Is he dead himself? These blasted fliers Jay keeps posting all over town is a grim reminder that Fitch may not be coming back. Even if he finds them and kills them, will he come back to Purgatory? Will he come back to me?"

Beth holds her weight on the tall stool behind the front desk counter as she writes. Glancing out through the propped open front door, Beth sees Trigger escorting Bell along the far side of the wooden boardwalk. Trigger carries several packages and bundles of dry goods wearing his usual attire. Bell's French dress flows behind herself as she continues to lead the young lad toward another general store.

"Bell. "Hells Bells" Bell. Quite a woman taking Trigger in like that. After Father died, Doc took me in. I thank him for that but he didn't know how to raise a young'n let a lone a girl. Bell started looking after me and teaching me how to run The Katherine. As time often does, I grew up and sorry to say, out grew Bell's assistance. Bell seemed lost for awhile. First losing her boys in the war, then losing me to age, she seemed out-of-sorts for a spell."

"*Back in '59, a Mormon wagon train of evangelists were passing through about a hundred miles out of Purgatory. That night while making camp, a large band of bandito's attacked them. Stole everything they didn't rape or kill. Only one left barely alive was a nine year old boy. He'd lost his memory or simply blocked it out due to his ordeal. No one really knows for sure. He didn't talk for the longest time. Bell and Robert took him in and cared him back to health. The boy didn't even know his name or chose not to remember.*"

"*So Bell tells me, one night, the boy woke up screaming about the attack. Something triggered in him. That's how he got his name, "Trigger". He seemed to have snapped out of his block and the name stuck. He never spoke of it again. Robert and Bell gave him room and board for helping around the saloon. Robert had a knack for music but with little time running the bar, didn't play much.*"

"*One afternoon with his chores finished, Trigger sat down at the piano and started plunking around. He had an ear for it. A gift. It took a few years afore Blake, the old piano player simply couldn't play any longer due to his hand cramps. That was something else. A Friday night and Bell's saloon without a piano player.*"

"*Trigger sat in to the amazement of the patrons as well as Robert and Bell and has been the piano player ever since. Robert took a liking to him, ordering sheet music from time to time from New York. I'll hate to see the day when Trigger out grows Robert and Bell. Just the same. I'm sure Purgatory will rustle up another orphan for Bell to raise."*

Beth looks up from her worded onion pages. Bell and Trigger exit from a dry goods store greeted by Jay who shuffles across the street. Jay smiles at Bell then focuses his attention toward Trigger. He reaches down and messes up Trigger's hair. Tipping his hat toward Bell, Jay motions and moves along the wooden boardwalk in their opposite directions. Beth returns to her plume and onion paper.

"Jay... He is a sweet man. After Fitch left, Trigger needed to look up to someone. Robert and Doc were always there and I know it's only been a week but a young and impressionable man needs constant care. Trigger looked to Jay who eagerly accepted. Jay even gave Trigger a tin star making him an "honorable deputy". Why didn't Fitch ever do that? What am I to do? Maybe Doc can help me with the answer. I have an appointment to see him this afternoon. I haven't been feeling well in the last few days..."

"Alright, Spider. Times up," Jay moves toward the locked cell with keys in hand.

"Been a week already?" Spider sneers. Jay unlocks the cell allowing Spider to slink outward. Spider smells fowl as he passes. Jay moves toward the desk and hands Spider his older model peacemaker and bull whip. Spider checks the pistol to see if it's ready to fire… it is not.

"You'cn load it <u>after</u> you leave town."

"What about my horse?"

"What do you think you've been eatin' for the last week?"

"Thanks," Spider sarcastically replies.

"Your welcome," Jay gloats. Spider collects his peacemaker and bull whip and quickly exits. Jay turns toward the cluttered desk top and fiddles with a thin stack of fliers. "THE COUGAR GANG – WANTED FOR BANK ROBBERY AND MURDER - $1000.00 REWARD – DEAD OR ALIVE – SHERIFF FITCH WOOLLEY – PURGATORY – NEW MEXICO TERRITORY".

Purgatory has fallen back into its normal routine. Quiet and peaceful. The stilted lamp lighters roam from block to block lighting the well placed torches at each corner. Flickering light casts odd shadows against the straggling pedestrians and sparse arriving and departing stagecoaches. Jay saunters along the far boardwalk to see Cleo manning the front desk of the Katherine. Along the side alleyway, Beth's horse and chaise has already departed. Jay makes his way across the street heading toward the sheriff's office and jail.

The deputy sheriff enters into the quiet room with only a single kerosene lamp on the desk top. Adjusting his gunbelt, Jay settles into his chair and blankly stares at the glimmering flame of the lamp. He begins to nod off, feeling secure with the three jail cells opened and empty behind himself.

Spider sits at the end of the saloon bar of Bell's. Trigger sits at the piano playing a slow and soothing classical arrangement. Bell stands along the cash register counting out the day's returns while Robert continues to clean the last of the glasses. A pair of worn looking gamblers face the dealer at their sole table. Not another soul is in the place. "Drink up!" Robert barks at Spider. "We're 'bout to close.

Spider slams his shot of whiskey down his throat and stands. Without leaving a tip of any kind on the bar, Spider turns and shuffles through the opened central area and exits with the batwing doors swinging behind himself. Spider pauses a moment looking at the pair of gambler's hitched and saddled horses. He pats his hand on the leather handle of his bull whip loosely fastened to his hip. An evil smile crosses Spider's lips.

Ever so quietly, Spider lurks through the shadows of the livery at the far end of town. The snoring blacksmith lies in his primitive cot along the far side of the wall. Spider tiptoes toward the far stall. Diamond snorts as Spider opens the stable gate and quickly saddles him. Taking Diamond by the reigns, he leads Jay's mount out through the opened livery doors. Spider glares through the outside of the barred windows of the sheriff's office and jail next door as he exits.

Spider quietly heaves himself upward into Diamond's saddle and half turns toward the jail cells, '"What do you think you've bin eatin' fer the last week"?' Spider sarcastically snarls. Kicking Diamond in the sides, Spiders bolts out of town, galloping into the darkness.

"What are you doing, Woolley?" Fitch asks himself riding along Blaze. *Jingle-jingle* the silver spurs answer from his heels. The landscape is barren and desolate. The afternoon's sun beating down on his shoulders, the scorching heat seeping through his oversized grey Stetson. Slightly tipping his hat above his brow, Fitch sees the foothills of a medium sized mountain range rolling across the horizon. Fitch lowers the brim of his hat and coaxes Blaze toward the inviting foothills.

"I should be headin' north back to Boston or Philadelphia, not heading after The Cougar Gang. I should let this be. It's not my fight. Let the U.S. Marshals take care of Cougar." Fitch pauses a moment. *"But what about Cougar? He killed Grandpa. Can I let that be?"*

"What about Beth? What would happen to her if I simply took care of The Cougar Gang and jest kept goin'? Goin' north with Purgatory at my back? She'll make out alright. She's got Jay to look after her now. Yeah, Jay to look after her. What was I

thinking allowing him to cut in on the dance? Woolley, you opened that door. Someone was bound to walk through it. No point in whinin' 'bout it now."

The soothing breeze of the nearing foothills welcomes Fitch and Blaze. Gatherings of trees provide shade for the desert creatures of the area. Clusters of boulders are sparse along the rolling terrain with Fitch and Blaze slowing their route. Fitch looks about the area, surveying for the best course to take. Glancing downward, he sees several horse tracks among the mixing of the desert sand and the fresh dirt of the foothills. "Guess they went that'a way, Blaze," Fitch declares with uncertainty. Blaze snorts in agreement. Fitch dismounts, takes Blaze by the reigns and begins to lead him up the most fitting path into the shaded foothills.

The evening air is cool and brisk. Fitch reaches into one of the saddle bags and retrieves a leather scoop of oats. He tosses the oats into a small pile on the ground for Blaze to feed. Reaching into the opposite side of the saddle bags, Fitch pulls out a large strip of jerky. Fitch runs his hand down along Blaze's lowered mane as he munches on his meager supper.

The air is still with woodland creatures keeping silent for some unknown reason. Blaze appears in the far shadows loosely hitched to a tree. Fitch slides along the ground on his stomach nearing a crest in a plateau. Tipping the brim of his Stetson away from his brow, Fitch quietly looks over the crest. Below in a small clearing with trees all about, The Cougar Gang!

Chote' and Jesse continue to stagger around the crackling campfire swapping turns at the tequila bottle. Cougar has propped himself up against a setting of boulders with the Wells Fargo Bank of Purgatory money bags between his straddled legs. Cougar continues to count the paper money as well as the gold and silver coins. Never taking his eyes off of the gang, Fitch lowers his hand and draws one of his ivory handled Colt revolvers. Fitch carefully extends out his revolver in one hand, cups the other and braces it taking careful aim directly at Cougar's head.

From behind Fitch, Blaze snorts out a warning. Fitch pays no heed with his hatred toward Cougar, welling up inside of him. Blaze snorts a second time with more urgency. Fitch remains focused on Cougar.

SNAP!

The breaking twig from behind causes Fitch to instantly roll over from his stomach to his back as he attempts to cock the hammer of his Colt revolver. Too late. With the butt of his Henry rifle, Dandy slams the wooden stock into Fitch's forehead. Fitch is stunned, still trying to get a shot off as he rolls to his side. Dandy slams the butt of the Henry rifle into the side of Fitch's head. Fitch moans as blood begins to flow from the wound.

Dandy reaches down and takes both ivory handled revolvers, tucking them into his belt along side of Mr. Fuller's lavender money poke. Dandy props his rifle in one hand over his shoulder. Dandy powerfully kicks Fitch several times in the side causing tremendous pain in Fitch's bandaged stomach wound. Blood begins to seep from the wound soaking his shirt. Fitch struggles to get to his feet. Dandy laughs as he lunges toward the Sheriff and kicks him in the side. Fitch topples to the ground.

Dandy turns and begins to approach Blaze who nervously whinnies and backs away from the hitched tree. Dandy cocks his Henry rifle and raises toward Blaze's head. The beast bucks and thrashes about. Dandy tries to get a good head shot but cannot. Blaze violently breaks away from the tree and gallops away into the wooded area. Dandy lowers his rifle as he turns refocusing his attention toward Fitch who has now made it to his knees. "Where do ya think you're goin', Sheriff?" Dandy gloats.

"You're… you're under a-arrest," Fitch weakly blurts out.

"Gonna take us all in by yerself?"

"Y-yes… now drop y-you're rifle an-and there'll be no trouble."

"Too late fer that, Sheriff," Dandy grins. "Yer'n a whole heap of it." With that, Dandy takes a few swift steps forward and slams the heel of his boot into Fitch's chest. Fitch is hurled off his knees and topples backward over the crest of the plateau. Dandy smirks as he steps forward to see Fitch flop and flip down the dusty slope like a worn rag doll. With his Henry rifle over his shoulder, Dandy selects his footing, carefully following behind Fitch's tumbling body.

Seeing the wake of dust and commotion, Cougar springs to his feet, drawing his revolver. Jesse draws his pistol along side of Chote' who draws his Bowie knife in one hand and another blood stained throwing knife in the other. End over end, Fitch's body plummets down the slope with Dandy closing in behind. Cougar smiles with a devilish grin, holstering his revolver. Fitch hits hard several feet away from the campfire then rolls to a halt. Jesse and Chote' remain armed as the three approach and circle Fitch.

Dandy hovers over Fitch as he reaches for his belt, handing Cougar each of the ivory handled Colt revolvers. Bloody from the fall and Dandy's abuse, Fitch attempts to get to his feet. He falls to the side, extending out his hand toward Cougar. "Well, Sheriff," Cougar leers, motioning around the camp with one of Fitch's ivory Colt revolvers in each hand, "… if I know'd we was gonna have company, I woudda picked up the place." The Cougar Gang laughs, beginning to circle the campfire and Fitch as if they were starving vultures waiting for their prey to die.

CHAPTER VI

The crackling campfire echo's through the surrounding wooded area of the small clearing at the bottom of the slope. Cougar evilly squats down facing Fitch who again attempts to get to his feet. Fitch's vest and torn clothing is swiftly becoming saturated with blood extending from his numerous wounds. "Sheriff says 'e's all by hisself," Dandy declares still towering over Fitch.

"All by yerself, eh?" Cougar snarls, "that takes big'uns, Sheriff. Real big'uns comin' after The Cougar Gang by yerself." Cougar pauses a moment then stands.

"What'r we gonna do with 'im?" Jesse chimes in. Cougar begins to circle his three amigos tapping his hand of the hilt of his Civil War saber swinging at his hip.

"I shoudda killed you when I had the chance," Fitch strains.

"Oh, you mean at the horse race? Yeah, you shoudda." Cougar playfully leans up against Chote's shoulder. "I'll tell you what Johnny Lawman, I'll give ya 'nother chance. To kill me. Bring us all in't justice'n be the hero," Cougar backs away then motions his head toward the others. Understanding Cougar's silent command, Chote', Jesse and Dandy all back away from Fitch and the campfire, all nearly huddling together in a pack.

Cougar takes the pair of ivory handled Colt revolvers and switches them from hand to hand, checking the loaded cylinders one by one. "Lawman, looks like you got full rounds, that's twelve shots'n there's only four of us. That should be plenty." Cougar pauses a moment before tossing the Colt revolvers into the dirt just out of Fitch's reach. Fitch eyes the four bandits for a long moment before slowly beginning to reach for his weapons. Cougar slightly nods toward Jesse who swiftly draws his pistol from his belt.

BLAM. BLAM.

Fitch screams out in sheer pain. Each of Jesse's rounds had hit the backsides of each of Fitch's hands. Blood gushes from the bullet wounds. Fitch cowers in pain, cupping each of his bloody hands in the other. The Cougar Gang laughs. "Well, help'im up, boys." Cougar orders.

Dandy, Jesse and Chote' rush Fitch, beginning to ruthlessly pound and kick him to the ground. Fitch curls up in a morbid ball of bloody flesh on the ground. His blood beginning to saturate the dirt all around himself. The violent abuse continues for what seems like hours. Smashing fist after fist. Thrusting kick after kick. Fitch can take no more. His embryonic position looses. Fitch falls flat onto the dirt. "That's enough, boys," Cougar barks as he steps forward. Dandy, Jesse and Chote' back away from Fitch with Cougar leaning over, colleting the pair of ivory handled revolvers. "Here, Sheriff. Let me help you."

Cougar holsters the revolvers at Fitch's hips then heaves the bloody figure to his feet. Fitch wobbles from side to side. His face a molten layer of bloody flesh. The bullet wounds from the backsides of his hands and palms gush clotting blood. Fitch can barely see Cougar back away from him as he joins the others. "Lawman! You've got twelve shots! Aim careful like," Cougar mocks. Fitch's hand trembles attempting to draw his right revolver. The Colt shakes in his hand. Fitch raises up his left hand to support his right. Fitch pulls back the hammer of the revolver after each shot.

BLAM. BLAM.

The pair of rounds recklessly whiz into a gathering of trees behind The Cougar Gang. Cougar gloats as Fitch wipes the blood away from his brow taking a few staggering steps forward.

BLAM. BLAM.

Jesse is becoming visually nervous. That pair of rounds came dangerously close to his right ear. Jesse places his hand on his pistol tucked into his belt. Fitch wobbles to the side trying to get a fix on the four raising his Colt again. He slowly cocks back the hammer with his bloody thumb.

BLAM. BLAM.

"That there one's empty, Sheriff." Cougar smiles unharmed by the latest round of gun fire. Fitch takes a few steps forward as he holsters his right Colt. Fitch painfully draws his left revolver supporting it with his right bloody hand. "Make 'em count, lawman. You only got six left!"

BLAM. BLAM.

The pair of rounds hit the dirt mere inches in front of Chote's feet. He nervously clutches onto the hilt of his Bowie knife sheathed at his hip. Fitch sways from side to side taking a few steps forward. "You sonuva-bitch! You killed my grandpa!" Fitch blurts out.

"I've kilt a lot of grandpas... 'n grandmas, 'n mothers, 'n fathers, 'n... Well, the list goes on," Cougar chuckles.

"My grandpa you shot in the back in Purgatory in a saloon."

Cougar's one eye widens with remembrance and a hint of resentment. "Oh yeah, I remember 'im now. He's the one who gave me this," Cougar taps the black patch over his left eye. Fitch staggers a few steps forward supporting his bloody left hand clutching onto his Colt. He painfully cocks back the hammer.

BLAM. BLAM.

The bullets embed themselves into a tree just behind Cougar. He laughs seeing Fitch loose his strength, lowering his Colt to his bloody side. "What's the matter, Sheriff? You got two left in that fancy hog-leg of yours!" Cougar sneers. With all his strength, Fitch attempts to raise his Colt. All to in vain. Fitch's sight becomes blurred. The flowing blood from his numerous wounds causes dizziness. Fitch wobbles to the side. Suddenly finding the will to live, Fitch rapidly raises his revolver toward Cougar.

BLAM. BLAM.

The last two shots. Cougar looks defiantly toward Fitch as Fitch lowers his Colt to his side for the last time. Cougar removes his Civil War wide brimmed hat and looks it over. A pair of smoking bullet holes have been shot mere inches from his scalp. Shaking his head, Cougar replaces his hat upon his head. "I've jest 'bout had enough of you," Cougar snaps as he draws his saber from it's sheath.

Cougar lunges toward Fitch and runs the blade through Fitch along its full extension stopping the hilt at Fitch's stomach. Blood gurgles from Fitch's lips. He slumps over bracing his forehead upon Cougar's shoulder. Cougar twists the blade inside of Fitch, pauses for a split second then swiftly removes it.

Fitch staggers for a moment then topples to the dirt a few feet away from the dying campfire. Almost disgusted that this resilient sheriff won't just die, the foursome turn away a moment then begin to circle again. "This gringo wont' be needing this anymore," Chote' declares as he swiftly moves in toward Fitch and takes the oversized grey Stetson from the dirt. Chote' brushes off the dust from the Stetson, tosses his own worn hat aside and places it upon his head. A perfect fit.

"Reckon you won't be needin' those either," Dandy chimes in making his way toward the silver spurs at Fitch's boot heels. Dandy takes the spurs, props himself along a boulder and slips them onto his own boot heels planting them solidly onto the ground. *Jingle-jingle.*

"I've had my eye one these since I first run 'cross 'ya," Jesse lumbers forward. He effortlessly flips Fitch over onto his back loosening the ivory handled Colt revolver gunbelt. Fitch mumbles out incoherent words in protest. Jesse swings the gunbelt into place around his own hips then triumphantly slides the ivory handled Colts into their holsters. He adjusts the matching pair of leather snap cases with the preloaded replacement cylinders. Jesse pauses a moment before quick drawing the Colts, spins them about around his forefingers a moment then effortlessly slides them back into their holsters.

Cougar saunters toward Fitch, carefully circling him, looking down upon the beaten sheriff. "Well now, 'sides taking your horse which we can't find 'n the clothes off yer back, what else's there?" Cougar nearly whispers. Cougar instantly pauses then abruptly draws his saber and slashes several deep cuts into Fitch's chest. With the point of the blade, Cougar carefully lifts Grandpa Theo's, now Sheriff Fitch Woolley's, badge from his bloody chest. "This'll do jest fine."

Cougar lifts the blade and dangles the badge toward himself, takes it and pins it to his caballero style jacket. Fitch moans tying to get to his feet. Cougar takes his boot heel and slams it into Fitch's skull. Fitch instantly drops to the ground. "Whatta'ya gonna do, lawman? Arrest me?" The Cougar Gang deeply laughs, fanning out away from Fitch. "Oh, where's my manners? The Sheriff here might git cold durin' the night." Cougar approaches Fitch and kicks mounds of dirt onto him. Fitch sputters, attempting to wipe away his face. "'Night, Sheriff," Cougar snarls.

Jesse and Dandy kneel themselves down atop of their laid out bedrolls and settle in. Chote' has found his resting place propped up along a nearby tree with the handle of his Bowie knife in hand like a sadistic teddy bear.

Fitch lays in a bloody pool. His torn and tattered clothing seeping with blood. Pain aches from head to toe. His efforts to stay alive rapidly dwindling from his soul. *Beth? Elizabeth? Can you hear me? Where are you? Help me please. Beth. Grandpa. Oh God, please somebody help me. Please…someone…help…me…*

Cougar chuckles to himself, making his way to his own laid out bedroll. Laying on his back, Cougar looks down, breaths on his newly acquired badge and polishes it a moment. Grinning to himself, Cougar lowers his wide brimmed Civil War hat over his eyes and begins to drift off asleep.

Sleep…

Sleep… sleep…

The smoldering coals softly glow inside the rounded rocks of the campfire. Three pairs of boots surround the fading embers. One particular pair of sportingly handsome boots with silver spurs fastened to their heels. *Jingle-jingle.*

Cougar takes a last swig of his coffee mug then splashes the remaining dark fluid onto the embers of the campfire. Cougar motions his head toward Dandy, Jesse and Chote'. The four fan out and approach their saddled and packed horses. One by one, they hurl themselves up into their saddles clutching tightly onto their reigns. Jesse is the first to gallop away swiftly followed by Chote' then Dandy. Cougar spins his mount to the side and pauses a moment. "Sleep well, Sheriff?" Cougar mockingly retorts.

Fitch lays along side of the smoldering campfire still covered in a layer of dirt. He has been still and motionless for the entire night. Fitch strains a response but falls weak, his face nearly buried in the dirt. "Hey, Sheriff!" Cougar calls out, "Heard this sayin' from a travelin' salesman." Cougar sarcastically tips his hats toward Fitch laying in a muck of drying blood on the ground. ""Ave a nice day"."

Cougar swiftly turns his horse around, powerfully kicks the beast in the sides and gallops off after his gang. The thundering sounds of horse's hooves quickly fade from Fitch's awareness. Fitch struggles to get to his feet. He topples over laying on his side. He is alone and forgotten. The rising sun beginning to burn his wounded frame.

Fitch lays there by the smoldering embers for what seems an eternity, staring blankly at the rocks forming the circle about the campfire. *"Get up, Woolley. Get up, blast you! What? Are you gonna lay here 'n die?"* Fitch strains to lift himself upward. He is too weak. Fitch falls back face down in the dirt. *"Get up, blast you! You gonna let those bastards get away with this? With killin' Grandpa? With... with..."* Fitch blacks out. For how long, he doesn't recall but is awakened by a familiar sent. A familiar sound...

SNORT. SNORT-SNORT.

175

Fitch strains to lift his head, covering his squinting eyes with his blood stained forearm. "Blaze?" Fitch pauses a moment. "Blaze, is that you boy?" Blaze's darkened shadow over powers Fitch, instantly shielding the human from the mid-morning's rising sun. "Blaze, I thought you'd left me t'go 'n find yourself a wild filly." Blaze snorts a welcoming sound, lowering his head and reigns toward his master and best friend.

Blaze nudges his muzzle against Fitch's wounded back, coaxing him upward. "Alright, alright!" Fitch barks. Fitch reaches up and pulls himself upward along the extent of Blaze's reigns as the stallion lifts his head slightly upward to assist the frail man. Fitch stumbles along side of the saddle and attempts to pull himself upward. Blaze snorts. "I know, I know! Gimme a secon'," Fitch grumbles as he finally heaves himself painfully up into the saddle. Fitch lashes the reigns to the horn of the saddle then about his wrists not allowing himself to fall out of the saddle. "Blaze, I'm finished," Fitch mumbles. "Let's go back to Boston. Let the Marshals take care of Cougar." Blaze shakes his head and snorts. "Let's go, boy. Let's go home…" Fitch slumps over the horn of the saddle.

Blaze is still for a long moment. What did he mean, "Let's go home?" Did the stallion's master mean let's go back to Philadelphia or Boston? Let's go back to Elizabeth in Purgatory? Let's go home after The Cougar Gang? Home? Blaze thinks for a moment. "Home… home is where the heart is." That's what Grandpa Theo used to say. So, where is his heart? In Boston? In Philadelphia? With Elizabeth? Where is my master's heart?" Blaze cocks his head to both sides waving his mane in wild directions. Blaze knows where Sheriff Fitch Woolley's heart is… his heart is set on revenge…

Not a single cloud in the endless sky of blue. Waves of heat roll up and across the vastness of the wasteland of sand. A silhouette image is sparsely made out among the scattered gatherings of full sized cacti. Blaze trudges forward… thirsty…

hungry... dying. His hooves leave a wake of weaving tracks in the sand. Blaze pauses a moment then attempts to forge ahead a few steps. Blaze continues on for several moments then pauses again until... toppling to the side.

Although lashed to the horn by the reigns, Fitch is tossed from the saddle, rolling in a flopping manner until flipping to a stillness facing upward to the heavens. Fitch squints his eyes toward the blistering sun, rolls over to see Blaze reluctantly folding to his knees then topples to his side breathing, gasping for his every breath. Fitch fumbles across the burning sand toward his faithful stallion. Fitch fatherly runs his bullet holed palm down Blaze's muzzle. "Don't you die on me. Everyone 'n everything I've ever loved 'as died on me. Don't you die on me, too," Fitch pleads.

SNORT. SNORT-SNORT.

Blaze rears up his head and looks directly into Fitch's eyes. "I'm not gonna die on you, you stupid man! I'm jest tired! Now git off yer ass'n help me up!" Fitch seems to have heard Blaze's thoughts. Fitch strains to get to his feet, rounds Blaze and coaxes him upward. Fitch lowers himself and loosens the saddle, saddle bags and covering blanket upon Blaze's back. Fitch slides the blanket from under the saddle and covers Blaze's head.

"This may not do much but it'll help I think," Fitch runs his dried blood palm along Blaze's muzzle. Blaze snorts. "Yeah, you too," Fitch painfully smiles. Taking the reigns in hand, Fitch leads Blaze further into the vastness of sand, oceans of heat waves and the tormenting sun above.

Fitch has begun to stagger from side to side, still clutching onto the loose reigns trailing behind himself. Blaze has slowed his pace trying to keep up with Fitch, yet tired and slow due to the heat of the setting sun. Then... Blaze snorts as he rears up his head. His activity hastens. He stops in his tracks causing Fitch to be pulled backward a step or two. Angrily, Fitch turns toward Blaze, "What is it, boy?" Fitch questions. Blaze tilts his head from side to side a moment then bolts forward in a full gallop. Fitch is nearly dragged behind until finally releasing his clutch from the reigns, falling flat on his face in a mound of sand.

Blaze gallops off toward the nearside of a small range with sparse trees and clusters of boulders. Fitch raises up, dusts off his face from the sand and painfully strains to his feet. He staggers forward after his mount who leaves a noticeable wake of sand clouds easily for Fitch to follow.

The desert oasis is soothing and inviting. Wild grass grows freely along the edges of a still pond. A narrow brook rolls from along the rocky terrain of the small range seemingly with the water simply coming out from the earth, an underground spring of some sorts. Blaze laps up the refreshing water of the pond as Fitch appears from around the corner of a cluster of boulders. "Sure, start without me," Fitch playfully makes his way toward Blaze.

Fitch throws himself into the water wading first up to his knees, waist then completely submerges himself for a long moment. His torn and blood stained vest, shirt and trousers instantly react to the water, soaking Fitch to the bone. The dried blood seeps from the clothing and spreads out along the surface of the pond. This doesn't seem to bother Blaze as the stallion continues to lap up the refreshing liquid.

Fitch surfaces from the pond, wiping his face from water. His bones ache. His wounds throb but feel slightly better than before. Fitch glances around and notices first the scattered trees and wild shrubs. A valley or small canyon of sort leads deeper into a wooded area the small range boarders. Then, it catches his attention. An opening to an abandoned mine shaft. Trouble? Would The Cougar Gang hide out there? Bandits? *"Blast it all, I wish I had my Colts!"* Fitch thinks.

Fitch quietly makes his way from the pond and takes a fallen branch in hand, carefully stalking the entrance of the mine shaft. What would he find inside? Fitch tiptoes closer and closer, leering inside the damp and dark entrance. "Hello!?" Fitch calls out. *"That was stupid, Woolley! If there'r The Cougar Gang they wouldn't come right out and say, "Sorry for leavin' you fer dead. We give up!" with their hands in the air."*

Fitch inches his way closer toward the mine's entrance. Looking quickly down upon the mixture of dirt and sand, there appears to have been no activity nor footprints for some time. Feeling assured, Fitch tosses the branch aside then turns back toward Blaze, "Guess we shack up here for the night." Blaze raises his head from the pond and lets out a wet snort.

Fitch stands at the entrance of the mine shaft half looking into the darkness and glancing about to his outer surroundings. *"The ridge would be good for an ambush. The canyon would allow a head on attack. The plateaus would give Cougar a sniper's advantage."* Fitch quiets his thoughts a moment. *"Stop it! Cougar is miles away. He thinks you'r dead. Let it be for now. Get some rest. There's always tomorrow..."*

A small crackling campfire flickers its soft glow along the carved out rocks and supporting beams of the entrance of the mine shaft. Blaze munches on a pile of wild grass Fitch had colleted for him from right out side of the entrance. Fitch leans back on a rotting supporting beam nearly fifty feet inside of the mine shaft. He tears a piece of jerky with his teeth, rests the larger portion in his lap and painfully chews on the rest.

Fitch glances out toward Blaze then beyond his faithful mount. The setting sun casts orange and amber rays through the small gatherings of trees leading out to the extended wooded area. A calming sight, the setting sun, after all he's been through the last few days. Fitch gazes upon the lowering sun, admiring it, being warmed by it, watching it set for the last time... Then, it is gone. The sun dips below the trees and horizon, leaving only the fading colors painted across the sky.

Fitch rips another section of jerky from the larger portion and chews on it as he painfully stands and approaches the inner entrance of the mine shaft. He reaches up into one of the saddle bags and removes a worn but clean stretch of cloth. Fitch runs his hands along Blaze's mane and pats him lovingly on the star cluster on his muzzle. "Thanks, boy. G'night." Fitch takes the cloth and enters the mine shaft.

Taking the cloth, Fitch rips it in long sections. Taking each section, Fitch tends to his wounds, Doc's bullet skimming his arm, Jesse's bullet wounds in each of his palms, his other various bullet wounds and yes, Cougar's piercing saber through the side just missing his stomach. Finished with his task, Fitch looks himself over, "I look like one of those mummies in one'f Beth's picture books," Fitch barks out toward Blaze who snorts out a disinterested response.

Fitch slides himself downward along the supporting beam with his worn boots a few feet from the crackling campfire. He looks up for a moment to study the jagged rocks and upper supporting beams of the mine shaft. Taking a deep sign of relief and simple realization that he's still alive, Fitch closes his eyes attempting to fall asleep. He tosses from side to side a few minutes before finding the most comfortable position on his back with the side supporting beam behind himself… right where he started.

…scratch-scratch.

…scratch-scratch.

…scratch-scratch.

Fitch slightly stirs as he opens his eyes to see the fading campfire. The embers are still warming the mine shaft in his little area. Fitch thinks nothing of it, rolling over to his side to try that sleeping position again.

...scratch-scratch.

Just as he closes his eyes a moment, Fitch shots up from his laying position.

…scratch-scratch.

"Oh, hell no," Fitch thinks to himself as he springs to his feet. He instantly reaches for the largest branch burning in the fading campfire, spinning it around in front of himself. He swings the flames toward the entrance toward the mine shaft, then

knowing what he'll find, Fitch waves the burning branch toward the darkness of the unknown depths of the mine.

...scratch-scratch.

Fitch flutters the burning branch in front of himself, trying to focus on the inner regions of the dark mine. He sees nothing. Slowly, Fitch waves the branch from side to side, then pauses still trying to see deeper into the darkness. Still, nothing...

...scratch-scratch.

Ever so faintly at first, a low muffled sound, growing louder. The muffling mutates to a constant growl, then the sounds of a distant waterfall. The soothing and constant sounds of the waterfall swiftly transform to a nearing thundering sound. Louder and louder...

The thundering continues to approach until reaching a nearly deafening roar. Fitch frantically waves the burning branch in all directions in front of himself. Too late! Hundreds of pair of eyes cut through the darkness heading directly toward him. The hundreds become thousands. Evil eyes. Piercing eyes. Flying eyes. The thousands of pairs of flapping wings thunder and roar toward Fitch. He screams. Waving his burning branch futilely at the approaching attack of vampire bats.

The smell of blood overwhelms the carnivorous winged creatures. Fitch's seeping wounds covering his body seems to be an open invitation for a feast. The bats swarm Fitch as he feverishly swings his burning branch in all directions. The bats seem to have built up an immunity to fire and flame. The bats swarm, violently colliding into Fitch, knocking him in all directions. Fitch attempts to fend off the attacking bats, waving the burning branch as he tossed from to side of the rocky mine shaft. Fitch screams...

One bite...

Two bites...

Three bites...

The pairs of flying canine teeth consume him. A blinding chaos of hungered wings surround and swarm the frail human.

Fitch is knocked from his feet. He flips and thrashes about the mine shaft floor frantically trying to beat away the attacking bats. Bite after bite. The bats begin to settle in and latch hold of Fitch's flesh and bloody wrapped wounds. Fitch thrashes about but the bats are too many. In a matter of moments, Fitch is completely consumed and covered with flapping bat wings, bloody canine teeth and the incurable hunger for fresh blood...

Feeding.

Feeding... feeding...

The mass of the colony of night creatures thunder out into the night. Blaze is spooked at first then realizes his life is in danger. The bats swarm Blaze, nipping and scratching their claws into his smoky-blue coat. Blaze whinnies and bucks trying to fend off the flying beasts. Blaze bucks and thrashes about until turning tail and galloping into the nearby canyon. The ocean of bats dart sharply through the sky in a unison manner, flying out into the darkness in search of their next meal.

Fitch is all but consumed by the remaining frenzied creatures. Nor an inch of his body is able to be seen from the flurry of flapping wings. The bats feed on his flesh, on his blood, causing hundreds upon hundreds of bites and torn sections of flesh. In a final fury of rage, Fitch screams as he springs to his feet. Fitch dashes forward for what he thinks is the mine shaft's entrance... he is mistaken.

The swarming bats follow close behind Fitch as he rams into the opposite sides of the mine shaft, colliding into the upward supporting beams, recklessly staggering deeper into the darkness and depths of the mine. Fitch pauses a moment to attempt to get his bearings. The darkness is overwhelming. He can see nothing. Not even an image or outline of the approaching mine shaft or supporting beams. The powerful thrust of swarming bats collides into Fitch's back. The force causes him to step forward, into nothingness. There is no ground to stop his descent.

Fitch freefalls for several moments before splashing into what seems another reservoir of the underground brook and pond's water. The bats continue to swarm. Biting and tearing at his bloody wounds and flesh. Fitch wallows in the muck... it is thicker than water. Oozing through his fingers. The stench is overwhelming of methane fumes. The bats swarm. Fitch begins to lose his human features covered with layer after layer of flesh wounds and bites.

Fitch frantically attempts to climb out of his darkened pit to no avail. The feeding bats are too much for him. He slides down a slight embankment in the darkness face upward half way submerged in the unseen liquid muck.

The bats.

The bats.

The bats continue to feed ruthlessly upon Fitch's bloody wounds and flesh. He attempts to fend and wave them off. The bats are too many. The darkness of the pit is drowned by the muffling sounds of fluttering bat wings. The sounds of carnivorous feeding. The slurping of fresh blood. Then with Fitch's final gasp for life... there is nothing...

...scratch-scratch.

...scratch-scratch.

...scratch-scratch.

In his blackened-out state, Fitch can faintly hear the thousands of bats returning from their night of hunting. He fades in and out of awareness, still slouched from the waist down in the liquid muck, choking from the thick methane fumes. Fitch strains for a moment to see his surroundings. There is nothing but darkness. Fitch slumps lower and deeper into the muck loosing all awareness. *"Mama? Papa? Don't go! Please don't go! Who'll tend to me? I'll be alone!"* Fitch thinks back on his distant past...

Young Fitch Woolley leans over the tossed bed of his Mother and Father. Standing along the far wall, a younger Doc Herring clutches onto his black medical back. Doc's face is kinder and more gentler with less grey facial hair. Grandpa Theodore

Woolley enters the stark room carrying a dampened cloth. Theo wears plain ranchers clothing looking younger and more fit.

Theo hands the damp cloth to young Fitch who tenderly runs it across his Mother's forehead. "I'm so sorry, Fitch," Doc replies from the shadows, "once the pox gits hold'f you, there's nuttin more to do than wait to see what God's planned."

"I don't want to wait," Fitch cries out, "I want them back!"

Mother gasps. Fitch turns to her, wiping the damp cloth on her brow. She smiles in a pleasant way, reaches up to touch Fitch's cheek then slips away into the heavens...

"That's when it happened. I was all set off for Philadelphia. I was there on the wagon with young Blaze hitched to the tailgate. Why did I have to get out of the wagon? Why did I have to kiss her the first time? I could've just left."

A teenaged Fitch Woolley lumbers from his wagon halted along Main Street of Purgatory. He dashes directly toward a teenaged Beth and plants the softest and wettest kiss on her lips. Without a word, Fitch turns, jimmies up into the wagon and rides away. *"Beth. Oh, dearest Elizabeth. What am I to do?"*

Trigger, the suave young gentleman that is, escorts Bell off the boardwalk and joins the gleeful crowd frolicking along Main Street. From behind, Fitch feels a tap on his shoulder. "May I cut in?" Jay nervously asks. Fitch and Beth slightly part. Fitch and Jay awkwardly look each other over.

"I reckon, Jay. I'm not gettin' the hang of this." Fitch tosses Beth a defeated glance, turns, and sulks away. Jay takes up Beth's hand and wraps his other arm around her waist. *"I shouldn't'a let Jay cut in like that. That was... that was..."*

"That was the longest moment of my life. Where was she? Everyone else treated me as if I were a leaper. Where was Beth?" Fitch remains still in the saddle. Blaze slightly tosses his head from side to side waiting for his master's commands. Fitch sports

the silver spurs at his heels, ivory handled Colt revolvers holstered at his hips, polished badge upon his chest and Theo's oversized grey Stetson hat. Where was Beth?

Trigger continues to play the mournful solace tune on the piano deep inside of Bell's with Robert and Bell standing outside of the swinging batwing doors waving an uncertain goodbye. Jay is seen in the far distance outside of the sheriff's office and jail. The entire assembly of wranglers, cowboys, stagecoaches, pedestrians and cargo wagons have stopped in their tracks. With no sign of Beth, Fitch gives a smile and a tip of his hat, turns and gallops out of Purgatory... out of sight.

Fitch wallows in the liquid muck, opens his eyes for a moment reaching out his wrapped and bloody palms. *"Just one more kiss from your tender lips,, Elizabeth. That's all I ask..."* Fitch sees a tender image of Beth, embracing him, kissing him as a wife would... as a wife would.

"No!" Fitch blares out in a determined tone struggling to his feet. The slippery surface below him causes him to slip and slide. He strains to focus. To see his surroundings. Ever so faintly, a soft glow of light appears from above. Fitch's eyes begin to adjust and focus. The cavern is fifty feet deep and over three hundred feet round and wide.

...scratch-scratch.

...scratch-scratch.

...scratch-scratch.

The bats have come home to roost. The thousands of pair of eyes flutter then close, hanging from the jarred pit ceiling above. Fitch appears to have fallen in pit of some sorts. A mining cavern blasted shut after its precious metal had been stripped from the earth. The soft glow becomes brighter and brighter as Fitch's eyes continue to adjust to the darkness.

All about the unseen floor of the cavern lays a murky pool of collected bat guano seeping deep into his numerous wounds and vampire bat bites. The stench of the fumes is horrific. The pain is beginning to become unbearable. Fitch looks up the jagged face of the cavern wall toward the soft glow. Its going to be a tough climb. Seeing a handhold just out of reach above himself, Fitch removes his vest then his tattered shirt. He slides his vest painfully back over his shoulders then loops his tattered shirt around in a loop fashion and tosses it upward clinging onto the bottom sections of rock. The looped shirt grabs the handhold.

Fitch tugs at the shirt and begins to pull himself upward. Just inches away from the handhold, the shirt breaks free causing Fitch to topple backward into the pool of bat guano with a mucky splash. The stale water and guano seeps deeper into Fitch's bat bites and wounds covering his body. He angrily slaps his hand into the water, manages to his feet and loops the shirt a second time. Tossing the shirt upward, Fitch pulls himself upward, straining with all his might. Just as the shirt breaks free from the jagged face, Fitch lunges his weight upward clinging recklessly to the handhold.

Fitch dangles there for a moment before painfully pulling himself upward. Finding a foothold, Fitch searches the rocky face for another upward handhold. The process is painful and time consuming. Minutes seem like hours. Inch by inch. Fitch scales the jagged face until reaching the edge. With his last bit of strength, Fitch heaves himself upward into the mine shaft. The faint and soft glow of the outside light seems to be miles away from the entrance of the mine shaft.

Fitch crawls on all fours toward the increasingly blinding light, daylight. But which day? How long had he been down there? Fitch strains through the brightness of the sun. A friendly snort echo's from just outside the entrance of the mine shaft. *"Well, at least Blaze is alright,"* Fitch thinks as he continues to crawl toward the entrance. More and more light filters into the mine shaft revealing Fitch's extensive wounds.

Cougar's sharp saber blade run through his side near his stomach…

Jesse's bullet wounds through both of his wrapped and bloody hands...

Dandy's Henry rifle butt crushed into his skull...

Chote's Bowie knife slash across his chest...

Doc' buck-naked shooting spree bullet wound along his arm...

The bank robbery's gun battle bullet wounds in his side and arm...

And yes... the hundreds of tearing bites all seeping with guano and the carnivorous saliva of the bats... of the bats. Fitch makes his way to the cold campfire and falls limp. Straining to roll over onto his back, he takes several breaths, pale from the extreme loss of blood. Weak and frail.

Fitch attempts to catch his breath but finds none to gasp. His heart, beating ever so slowly. Slower and slower until the beating of his heart sounds like a roaring locomotive thundering down the tracks. Louder and louder. Slower and slower until... Fitch's heart stops. Eyes burning wide open. Motionless, Fitch painlessly enters the next life that awaits him...

"It's been over three weeks now and no word from Fitch. Did he find The Cougar Gang? It he wounded? Shot? Even worse, is he dead? Did Fitch simply say to blazes with it and return to Philadelphia or Boston? Did he head for California? Oh, God almighty, where are you Fitch?"

Beth sits behind the front desk counter of the Katherine Hotel scribbling on her thinning stack of onion paper. Glancing upward she sees the young lamplighters hobbling along their stilts lighting Purgatory's street lamps. The air is cool and even slightly damp. Darkness continues to fall across Purgatory.

"I went to go see Doc again the other day. He says he has a good idea what I'm ailing from but wants to

wait another week or so to be sure. Doc's not telling me what is it but from his assuring tone, he says it's nothing to fret about. It's just the <u>way</u> he said it with that devilish grin of his."

"Jay… now that's another story. What if Fitch did turn tail and leave us? What then? I can't imagine that he did… but just what if? Do I settle down with Jay? He's come to court me nearly every evening this week. Does he know something that I don't? Has Fitch sent word and Jay's not telling me nor anyone? Is Jay hiding the truth? Is Fitch dead? When's he coming back? <u>Is</u> he coming back?"

"G'evenin', miss," Cleo cheerfully calls out as she enters through the opened front door. Beth quickly tucks away her onion papers and quill.

"Evening, Cleo," Beth attempts a smile.

"Still writin' that letter o' yours?"

"Letter, Cleo?"

"Yes, miss. Those papers you's always writin' on."

"Oh," Beth smiles, "it's not a letter it's my diary."

"Dairy?" Cleo exclaims. "Then you's be getting' to the water room right quick!"

"Water room?"

"Yes, miss. You's not been feelin' well. You's don' wanna mess yours drawers wit diary!"

Beth pauses a moment to take in what Cleo is trying to tell her. "Oh!" Beth nearly chuckles to herself. "You mean the lavatory to "relieve" myself."

"Yes, miss. Diary."

"Thank-you, Cleo but I'm fine in that area." Beth makes her way around the front desk counter as Cleo finds her place. "Have a good night, Cleo."

"And you, miss," Cleo shuffles a stack of register slips and other papers. Beth takes a breath of the cool night air and disappears onto the wooden planked boardwalk. "Can I escort you home?" "Why yes, that would be lovely, Jay." "I've been meanin't talk with you." "What about, Jay?" "Well, it's like this…" Jay continues to pace back and forth across the sheriff's office floor continuing his one-sided conversation with himself. A celled drunkard leans out through the bars of the nearest locked cell in wonderment watching Jay's talk to himself. ""What is it, Jay?" "I'd like to call'a courtin' you more offen." "I think that would be splendid."

"Cm'on, boy," the drunkard barks out, "Jest git on with it!"

Jay turns, realizing that he had been talking out loud. "Git on with what?"

"Reckon you'r in love with 'er. Git! Go court 'er!"

"Think I should?"

"Indeed," the drunkard pauses, "you think you could let me out first?"

Jay grins as he shakes and taunts the cell's keys at the drunkard then tosses them with a clank onto the desk. Jay darts out the opened door onto the boardwalk. "It's worth a lash," the drunkard replies to himself as he settles back down onto his primitive cot in his cell.

Jay scans the forward façade of the Katherine seeing Cleo inside behind the front desk counter. Quickly turning, Jay spies Beth's chaise galloping away into the darkness away from Main Street. Too late. Jay deeply sighs, turns and slips back inside of the sheriff's office and jail. ""Cm'on, boy! Jest git on with it,'" Jay mocks the drunkard closing the door behind himself.

Fitch lays on his back facing up toward the jagged ceiling of the mine shaft. The rows of supporting beams overhead. His burning eyes wide open. His chest is void from any breath. His heart is still and silent. Not a single movement. Fitch is cold as a stone from a river. Then from the darkness of the cavern, Fitch begins to hear the heartbeats of a single bat. Then two. Then eight. Then forty. Then one-hundred. Then the entire assembly of carnivorous night creatures. The heartbeats are nearly deafening.

Thump-thump.

Thump-thump.

Thump-thump.

As swiftly as the racing bat heartbeats had toned into his consciousness, they are gone. Fitch hears the soft imprints of footsteps. Footsteps? Is someone drawing nearer? Is it Doc to come carry him away to his burial place? Has Cougar returned to finish the job? The footsteps continue. Louder and louder.

A desert tarantula slips along the edge of Fitch's boot, up along his pant leg, toward his waist, then effortlessly walks along his wounded bat bitten torso. With each step of its eight legs, the sound of the tarantula's footsteps rattle inside of Fitch's head. Louder and louder until suddenly, vanishing. The tarantula slips off of Fitch's shoulder and continues along the rocky mine shaft floor until disappearing from sight into the blinding afternoon's sunlight.

Thump-thump.

Thump-thump.

Thump-thump.

Blaze's heartbeat fills Fitch's ears. Over and over. Blaze stands no less than fifty yards from Fitch's motionless body. Louder and louder the stallion's heart pounds. Then, the flapping wings of the circling vultures overhead. The sounds. Oh God, the sounds are deafening. Make them stop! Make them stop...

Fitch gasps! He lunges upward frantically scanning his surroundings. The mine shaft. Blaze. Cougar. Beth... beth. Fitch collapses, falling to the side. He flutters his eyes, breaths easy then drifts off into a groggy daze. The afternoon's sun begins to set, casting its amber and orange rays into the entrance of the mine shaft. Blaze snorts becoming uneasy with the setting sun and circling vultures. Fitch slightly stirs and rolls over onto his back… fast asleep.

"Where am I? I feel… I feel as I have no weight. Am I falling? Yes, I'm falling. What is that smell? That foul odor. My God, where am I? That smell, what is it? Faster now. Faster. Darkness all around me. Wait, there's a light below. Growing brighter now. Oh, the smell reminds me of a trip to the Arizona Territory. The smell of…sulfur."

"The light is brighter. I'm still falling but slower now. There! There's the ground. Is it the ground? All I see is…God no! Fire everywhere! Flames. An endless ocean of flames with the stench of sulfur filling my lungs. God help me! I thought I'd never end up here. Help me!"

Fitch free falls for several moments before slowing and landing with a gentle thud along the rocky bay of the ocean of flames. Fitch rises to his feet looking himself over. He's in fair condition with no traces of any wounds nor vampiric bat bits. His bullet riddled palms show no signs of injuries nor scars. Continuing to look himself over, he notices he only wears his long-john bottoms. No vest, no shirt nor boots. Fitch is nearly completely undressed.

Fitch begins to stroll along the fiery shore of the bay with jagged rocks and boulders shooting up from the crashing waves of flames and surf. "Have you been waiting long?" a deep voice asks from the shadows. Clutching his fists, Fitch spins in all directions for the location of the deep voice. He sees no image or figure just the flames of the endless ocean of fire surrounded by the sulfuric landscape.

"Who's out there? Show yourself," Fitch commands.

"I am but you. You who you were. You who you are. You who you are to be," the deep voice draws nearer.

"Show yourself!"

A fury of fists thunder from the shadows powerfully colliding into Fitch knocking him from his feet. Toppling to his knees, Fitch rolls and scans for his attacker. There, just in the faint flickering light of the dancing flames of the bay, the figure, the image of... of himself!

The Demonic Fitch is pale in flesh color wearing no clothing. The creature's sexual organs are absent. Not as if they had been removed but had never been there in the first place. It's feet are smooth like a fish with silky skin and noticeable talons where the toes should be. A mirror image of himself but...

It's lips are red and slightly parted revealing its canine teeth, more of a dog or of a wolf. The creature's facial features are narrow and pointed as if it hadn't eaten a bite in weeks. The Demonic Fitch stands lean in a stalking manner as if it were studying its prey. The thing moves closer toward Fitch. "Where am I," Fitch finally sputters.

"Why, you're fast asleep in the mine shaft. You're condition is quite fine."

"Why are you doing this then?"

"I am doing nothing," the creature responds. "I am here to take you where you belong. With me... with us."

A sudden terrible pain violently rips through Fitch's stomach. He drops to his knees rolling over on the sulfuric ground. Fitch screams as he clutches onto his bare torso. The pain is unbelievable. "So, it has begun," the beast sneers.

With all his might, Fitch lunges upward and collides into the Demonic Fitch. Each man exchanges a flurry of fist blows. The creature hammers his curved talon foot into Fitch's side sending him reeling backward yet Fitch remains on his feet. Fitch suddenly realizes that he is becoming stronger and quicker.

Fitch attacks the beast with fists flying. The Demonic Fitch is slightly tossed backward yet stands its ground delivering an exchange of blows itself. With each powerful blow, the creature becomes more evil and hideous. Fitch is growing stronger and stronger. "What am I? What have you done to me!?" Fitch cries.

"You are one of us for now and always," the Demonic Fitch laughs.

"I'm not the Devil! I'm not the Devil!" Fitch screams. The Demonic Fitch slams its fist powerfully into Fitch's jaw sending him flying back into the fiery bay. Fitch splashes into the flaming water, beginning to drown. The beast lunges into the water bringing the waves up to his waist. The creature scoops up Fitch into his arms, bares his fangs among his canine teeth and sinks them deep into Fitch's neck.

Blood spurts from Fitch's bite as he screams and thrashes about in the blazing water. Blood from Fitch's neck pours into the bay and spreads mixing into the sulpheric stench. Fitch looses strength and slips from the creature's arms, disappearing from the fiery and bloody surface of the water.

"No, you're not the Devil," the Demonic Fitch watches Fitch's transforming corpse slip from his sight beneath the fiery surface, "no, but you will be…"

Fitch gasps for air rolling over onto his side. Panicking, he springs to his feet with fists clutched. The mid-day's sun is blinding, pouring inward from the entrance of the mine shaft. Standing in the coolness of the shadows, Fitch quickly looks down at his fists. They are still wrapped into the blood stained bandages covering Jesse's bullet wounds. Fitch wreaks of bat guano and the murky pool of water from the below cavern.

Taking a few moments to adjust his eyesight from the rays of the sun, Fitch inches his way closer toward the mine shaft's entrance. Good 'ole Blaze. Hovering over the outer pond of water lapping his fill. Fitch takes a sigh of relieve… he's still alive. "Blaze!" Fitch calls out as he continues to approach the mine shaft's entrance. Blaze raises his head and snorts out a "hello". Blaze nearly gallops toward Fitch nearly exiting the shadows of the entrance then slips to a halt.

Blaze snorts again shaking his mousy-blue mane. Blaze has stopped in his tracks. "What is it, boy?" Fitch extends out his hand. The rays of the sun scald Fitch's flesh. He quickly withdraws his hand back into the protection of the shadows. "What in tar nation?" Fitch exclaims. Blaze backs away from the entrance of the mine shaft and watches his master just inside.

Fitch slowly extends out his hand a second time into the sunlight. Pain rips through his hand, arm and body. His flesh smolders, burning the wrapped bandage of his bullet wounds. Fitch retracts his hand and quickly begins to examine it. The charred section of his flesh smolders a moment then miraculously heals itself. "What?"

Fitch swiftly unwraps his hand gazing down upon it. Jesse's bullet wound has completely healed itself. Only a small round scar remains both along the backside and the palm. Fitch unwraps his other hand only to find the same result. Jesse's bullet wound is completely healed leaving only a small scar on opposite sides of his hand.

Fitch begins to breathe heavily in a frantic state of mind. Taking his hands, he runs his palms across his body. The hundreds of carnivorous vampire bat bites have been healed leaving only traces of small scars across his body. Cougar, Dandy, Chote' and even Doc's wounds are completely healed, again only leaving the smallest of scars. Fitch feels stronger yet hungry. A hunger he has never felt before.

Fitch moves to the entrance of the mine shaft to collect Blaze. The hoofed companion snorts and backs away sensing something changed about the man. "Blaze, come 'ere, boy," Fitch commands. Blaze lingers around the warming water of the pond trying to stay as far away from Fitch as possible. Fitch steps forward from the shadows of the entrance of the mine shaft. His boots appear intact. Then, his guano soaked trousers remain cool from the dampness. Fitch extends out his hands into the sunlight.

His pale flesh burns and painfully smolders. Fitch falls to his knees in screaming pain withdrawing his hands. Gazing down upon them, the charred and smoldering only lasts a few moments until healing themselves. Fitch plops down at the edge of the entrance of the mine shaft mere inches from the daunting sunlight. "What's happened to me? Am I cursed? What am I'ta do?" Fitch mumbles to himself.

Slightly looking outward, he sees Blaze in a painful condition. The raging heat and burning sun of the day, *"How many days have I been here,"* Fitch thinks. The endless days of heat has worn on Blaze. His mane is matted. Saliva has collected around his nostrils. His smoky-blue coloring doused with stained sweat and sun blasts. "You're gonna die out there!" Fitch barks. Blaze merely snorts at the changed human. There is something just not right about him. "Blaze!" Fitch shouts with more urgency. "Blaze!"

Blaze cocks his head upward to see the circling vultures. He slowly lowers his head and begins to head toward the cool and inviting shade of the mine shaft. Blaze is reluctant as he approaches. Fitch extends out his hand just to feel the flickering of the sun's rays. The sun's heat burn and scalds his flesh yet Fitch is determined to collect his horse. Blaze saunters closer, smelling Fitch. Smelling the darkness of the mine shaft and beyond cavern. Blaze snorts, mere inches from Fitch's grasp. "That'a boy," Fitch replies with an encouraging tone as he snags Blaze's reigns.

Blaze slightly bucks and thrashes about a moment before Fitch reaches up and sooths his healed palm down and across Blaze's mane. This appears to comfort the stallion as Fitch leads him deeper into the cooling shadows of the mine shaft. "Now, that wasn't too bad, 'eh boy?" Fitch loosely ties Blaze's reigns to an upward supporting beam then swiftly moves to the nearest side saddle bag.

Taking several leather scoopfuls of oats from the bag, Fitch tosses them onto the ground. Blaze shakes his matted mane in thanks and instantly begins to feed. Fitch makes his way to the opposite side of Blaze reaching into the far saddle bag retrieving a large section of beef jerky. Famished, Fitch nearly shoves the entire piece of jerky into his mouth and begins to chew it. He swallows large portions attempting to feed his enormous hunger all at once.

Fitch heaves over with an uncontrollable pain wrenching through his stomach. He violently tosses-up the consumed jerky. The pain appears to have gone. Puzzled, Fitch takes several bites of the jerky, chews and again swallows. In a matter of moments, pain wells up inside of Fitch. He thrusts over, discarding the dried meat from his stomach. "That's just peaches. Can't go'n the sun'n can't eat." Fitch pauses. "What's next?"

Looking extremely exhausted, Fitch gazes out into the burning sun. The heat is overwhelming. Blaze continues to munch on his ration of oats as Fitch turns away from the entrance of the mine shaft, slides his back along the nearest upward supporting beam and stretches out his shoulders. Propping his head along the beam, Fitch closes his eyes, attempting to drift off. In a matter of moments, the cool and darkness of the beyond cavern seems to rock him to sleep...

The campfire is cold and lifeless. Wearing his blood stained vest and what is left of his tattered shirt and trousers, Fitch lays on his side several yards from the mine shaft's darkening entrance.
...scratch-scratch.
...scratch-scratch.
...scratch-scratch.
Blaze stirs, standing just inside of the mine shaft's entrance. The hoofed companion rattles his reigns becoming increasingly uneasy. The vultures overhead have given up for the day, fanning out and flying in odd directions. The sun dips, hovers a moment, then fades below the horizon. A deathly stillness falls across the oasis.
...scratch-scratch.
...scratch-scratch.
...scratch-scratch.

Fitch bolts awake, confused at first by his surroundings. No campfire. No warm bed on The Woolley Ranch. No Beth beside him. No comforts of home. The jagged carved out mine shaft is all that greets him. Fitch staggers to his feet as he adjusts his eyesight to the growing darkness. Unsure of his own sanity, Fitch looks himself over again. *"Sure 'nuff,"* Fitch thinks, *"I wasn't dreamin'."* Jesse's healed bullet wounds leave only small round scars in his palms upon the backs of his hands. The hundreds upon hundreds of carnivorous vampire bat bites have healed leaving only traces of their existence. All of Fitch's wounds have been rejuvenated.

…scratch-scratch.

…scratch-scratch.

…scratch-scratch.

Fitch begins to panic from the familiar sounds of the hordes of bats in the beyond cavern, beginning to awake for their nocturnal feeding. Too late. The soft roar of flapping wings transforms into a thundering barrage of hundreds of pairs of glaring eyes racing toward him. Fitch cries out, turning and spinning in all directions searching for the mine shaft's entrance. He is powerfully overcome by the first wave of departing bats. Fitch cowers, covering his head and face with his crossed arms. Then… there is nothing but the fluttering air about him. The swarm of bats simply fly around him.

Fitch slowly lowers his arms to see the second wave of bats roar out from the depths of the cavern. Again, the bats swoop and swarm around him, his entire self as if to survey their visitor, then flap out into the night. The oddest thing… a small sized bat, the runt of the liters to be certain, flaps and swoops around Fitch's head several times before landing gently on his shoulder.

The tiny creature is hideous. Its jagged fangs seemingly smiling at Fitch as he stares the creature down from the corner of his eye. The bat sits there for a moment with its wings neatly tucked in beside itself. With a playful smile, Fitch cocks his head and blows gently at the small bat. The bat blurts out a low screech, turns its body then flaps away into the night.

Fitch grins to himself feeling an oddness with his changing body and overwhelming hunger. The kind of hunger that won't go away. As he turns and approaches the inner mine shaft's entrance, a third and final wave of bats thunder out from the darkness, swoops and swarms him a moment then flaps out into the cool night's air. Fitch pauses a moment at the entrance then carefully extends both of his hands outward with palms facing upward.

The moon's soothing rays seem to seep into Fitch's flesh. No pain. Nothing. Taking a deep sigh, he steps cautiously forward, exiting the mine shaft with his eyes shut tight waiting for the tormenting pain to return. It does not.

Fitch slowly opens his eyes to see the pond off to one side and Blaze timidly returning to the area, frightened away by the swarms of departing bats. "Blaze," Fitch beckons in a calm voice. Blaze snorts and cautiously approaches him. Fitch reaches up and runs his hand tenderly down Blaze's muzzle. "Guess the trick's to stay outta the sunlight." Fitch pauses. "Well then, we should be gettin' on then."

Fully saddled, Blaze lowers his head and takes a final slurp of the pond's water. Fitch checks the saddle bags and straps then slings himself up into the saddle without using the foot peg. Odd. He's never done that before. Never been able to due to Blaze's girth and height. Fitch settles into the saddle taking the reigns in hand. He neither coaxes nor motions Blaze in any direction. Just sits there in the saddle for a long moment.

Having his fill of the refreshing water, Blaze raises up his head and swings it around to the side looking up at Fitch. "I dunno, boy," Fitch smiles. "Where to? I reckon Cougar's headed to Diablo Canyon. That's due east. Boston and Philadelphia are north-east." Fitch pauses. "I reckon we <u>could</u> settle this with Cougar then head north. Beth <u>would</u> be upset, though." Fitch clutches onto the reigns. "Friend of mine," Fitch calls out to

Blaze, "you decide. South to Mexico or due east to Diablo Canyon."

Blaze snorts, rearing his head around. Without coaxing or commands, Blaze begins to move is mighty hooves forward. Fitch is unsure where his faithful mount will lead him but will enjoy the ride... as long as they can stay out of the sunlight and get him something to eat... something to eat. Fitch attempts to ignore the hunger pains in his stomach however they are growing with intensity with every passing moment.

"What a calming feeling. The drifting moon overhead. The soft sounds of the passing breeze. Blaze's constant "clop-clop" of his hooves along the rocky terrain. Not a care in the world," Fitch thinks to himself as he continues riding along in the saddle. *"I am free from all that haunts me but...but Elizabeth. Blast it, woman! Why do you taunt me so?"*

Fitch gazes up to see the first traces of the rising sun beyond the horizon. His shoulders are becoming warm. His body is becoming uneasy. Below himself, Blaze seems to be quickening his saunter to a slow gallop. "Where we gonin', Blaze?" The stallion continues forward heading swiftly along the edgy parameter of the foothills of a sparse mountain range. Blaze seems to be searching for something although Fitch is uncertain of what.

Blaze gallops into a wooded area with a variety of shrubs, clusters of boulders and trees, several of which have fallen. The sun continues to rise just below the horizon. Fitch is bewildered as Blaze continues onward through the trees. Sunlight beginning to shine throughout the sky. The first ray of sun hits Fitch in the front of the shoulder. He cries out in agony, clutching at the painful area. Blaze continues onward, now at a full gallop. Another ray of sun hits Fitch along the side of his face. He screams out in pain trying to conceal the barrage of sunlight pounding upon him.

Suddenly, Blaze halts dead in his tracks sending Fitch reeling over the saddle horn, over Blaze's lowered head, landing with a thud onto the ground. The oncoming sunlight seeps through the maze of treetops inching their way closer and closer toward Fitch. He scampers to his stomach searching for a hiding place. All that he sees is a fallen and rotted out tree. Fitch crawls on all fours toward the tree trunk and slips inside. The sun has fully risen.

The sparse wooded area is flooded with sunlight bearing down on the shrubs, clusters of boulders and gatherings of trees. Blaze stands fast as he is covered with the warming rays of the sun. Fitch pokes his head out from the end of the rotted out tree trunk looking oddly up toward Blaze. "You'n I're gonna have to work on this," Fitch strains to get comfortable. "If you know sump'thn that I don' know, you need to tell me." Blaze shakes his mane and snorts down toward Fitch cowering inside of the hollowed tree, "Sheriff, you'r gonna have't figure this out fer yerself," Blaze thinks. "Silly man…"

CHAPTER VII

"Elizabeth," Bell smiles with a jovial wink, "How've you been?"

"I'm fine, Bell," Beth attempts a smile from behind the front desk counter of the Katherine Hotel. Beth shuffles some papers trying to look busy as Bell adjusts her corset under her left arm.

"Just lookin' in on ya."

"Thank-you, Bell. I'm just fine." Beth is not convincing.

"Heard any word on Fitch?"

"Not yet but I'm still hopeful."

"Are ya now?" Bell gleams as she turns and exits through the opened front door. Beth remains there for a moment watching Bell cruise along the wooden boardwalk then disappearing from sight. In an instant, Beth grasps her thin onion papers from below the counter and takes a plume in hand.

"Who does she think she is? Yes, she taught me how to run father's business. Yes, she taught me how to take care of myself. Yes, she is like a second mother to me. But, how dare she presume to know and understand my affairs."

Beth angrily declares on her pages of onion papers. She slowly takes a deep breath, fiddles with the plume and continues to write.

"I know. I need to be more like Bell. Taking matters into my own hands. Do I chose Fitch? Do I

chose Jay? Do I say t'blazes with both of them? Bell made up her mind 'long time ago."

"Father and Mother hadn't arrived here as yet. I think it was in '41 when Bell and the City Slicker came to blows. She was a dancehall girl working for a well-off banker from Kansas City who'd come here to make himself even richer. He bought himself a saloon and was running it into the dirt. Robert was much "smaller" than he is now. Put on some weight he has. "

"Somehow, Bell and the banker got into this poker game. Not just another poker game but the kind you take your clothes off kinda game. So, there's the banker standing at the table wearing his long-johns, gun rig, top hat and boots. Bell's looking across the table wearing nothing but her knickers. What a sight I'm sure it was. "

"The hand came down to the last card. The banker was sure he'd 'a won but Bell wasn't gonna give in. The banker shouts, "Bell, if I win, you bed me. If you win, the saloon's yours!" That was a bet Bell couldn't pass up. Even sure, as Doc tells me, Bell stripped down to nothing but her laced boots, standing there in front of God and everyone with her... with her "self" hanging out. She says, "I will see your raise and call. You win, I'm yours. I win, this is all mine,'" Bell motions around the room."

"Now Robert had already had a thing for, or with Bell , I'm not sure, so he was kinda embarrassed to see her in "her glory" out in front of everyone. The last card *was dealt. Bell didn't even have to look at it with a gleam on her face. The banker looked at his cards then cursed a few times and stormed out of the saloon, now Bell's Saloon, never to be seen again. So Doc tells me. He drinks a lot from time to time so I don't know how true the story is."*

"Yes, sir. Bell took things into her own hands. That's for sure. So, Jay'll take me to the Valentine's Gala in two weeks. Jay even told me that Fitch told him that if he wasn't back in four weeks, Jay would be sheriff. Well, it's been over four weeks. I need to look out for myself. Take things into my own hands."

"What if Fitch is still alive? Injured? Dying? I don't think I could live with myself. I've waited this long for young Woolley, what's another week or two? God, Fitch. Come back to me or leave me forever. I can't stand for this for much longer..."

The setting sun lingers along the amber painted skyline. The soft rays of sunlight beam through the gatherings of trees throughout the sparsely cluttered wooded area. Blaze stands about with his reigns dangling to the ground from his mouth piece near a tree, cooled by the growing shadows of the setting sun. Inside the fallen hollowed log, Fitch tosses and turns. A restless days sleep...

"I feel in the oddest way. I'm floating...higher and higher. The night is as pitch. I can see myself ever floating higher. What's that sound? My God! They're returning. The hideous little flying creatures! I...I can't move! God, help me!"

Having assumed his carnivorous bat-like demonic features, smooth and hairless, slightly pointed ears, clawed feet, no sexual organs and a set of growing canine teeth, Fitch floats effortlessly above the below treetops. The sounds of thundering bat wings draws nearer and nearer. Fitch flaps his arms as if to fly but looks ridicules in the process. With legs and arms flapping, the swarms of bats consume him in flight. Whizzing and roaring all about him. Not harming him or even in a threatening manner.

Fitch thinks harder to himself as he straightens out his body, bringing his legs together and tightening his shoulders. His flight increases forward, now catching up with the fluttering little varmint, the runt of the liter. Faster and faster. Fitch begins a game of tag in flight with the little bat. To and fro through the air above the below passing treetops. Within a matter of moments, Fitch and the runt catch up with the swarms of bats racing through the sky.

Fitch gracefully weaves his sleek form in and out of the swarms of bats as they welcome him into their carnivorous flock. As he continues to soar among the creatures, Fitch extends out his hand, gently brushing his scared palms across the fury backs of the flying bats. They squawk and squeal with his every touch, not a sound of harm, but of affection. Fitch and the flurry of bats dance across the sky. The rising moon casting frantic shadows across the ground and treetops below. Faster and faster. Fitch quickly becomes at ease though helplessly floating in midair.

The swarms of bats swoosh about his head, turn and veer, darting off into the night's sky. The runt of the liter remains in a coaxing manner. The little creature squeaks as it flaps its tiny wings beckoning Fitch to follow it. The bat swoops about in circles, showing Fitch how flight is managed. Holding his arms slightly lowered and parted from him smooth sides, Fitch leans forward. He begins to move slowly forward through the air. The little bat squeals in delight darting ahead. The flying swarm becoming close to frenzied. Then, there below, the swarm of bats smell the sent of blood… it's feeding time.

The bats thunder downward toward a sleeping herd of cattle on the open range. Like locus, the bats swarm the cattle, sinking their fangs deep into the beasts. Rivers of blood spill from the cattle as the bats drain their blood, dropping one by one to the ground. Fitch circles above for a moment to see the nearby wranglers springing from their bedrolls around the smoldering campfire near the chuck wagon.

The half dressed wranglers recklessly fire their revolvers, rifles and shotguns into the air attempting to fend of the frenzied bats. Several shots find their mark sending handfuls of bats painfully fluttering to the ground. Rage overwhelms Fitch for his injured family members. Fitch bears down his canine teeth, thundering downward. He swoops over a trio of wranglers instantly knocking them to the ground with swift blows to the head.

Fitch lands with a thud in the center of the confused wranglers. They spin and fire at the evil looking intruder. Fitch swings back his hand sending another wrangler crashing into the chuck wagon. With never before gracefulness, Fitch seems to float above the ground instead of conscience movement of walking. He slams his fists into another pair of wranglers sending them to the ground. The Range Master fumbles to reload his shotgun as Fitch begins to stalk him.

The Range Master flips the barrel of his shotgun into place, cocks the weapon and raises it to fire at Fitch who swiftly approaches him. Fitch powerfully knocks the shotgun barrel upward causing the Range Master to fire into the air harming no one. Fitch knocks away the shotgun from the frightened man then clutches onto his throat. Fitch turns away a moment to see the swarms of bats continue to consume the herd of cattle… drinking the larger beast's blood. Vein after vein. Drop after drop. Fitch turns back toward the Range Master, bears his fanged jaws and thrusts his opened mouth down upon the Range Master's throat. "Nnnnoooooooooooooo!" The Range Master screams out in shear terror…

Fitch bolts awake, slamming his head to the inner top of the fallen hollowed tree. The thinnest streamline of the setting sun's rays have found their way through a knothole along the top of the fallen tree. The faint rays of sun scald Fitch's hand causing it to smolder. Fitch pulls his hand away from the light and begins to panic, forgetting where he is. The rays of setting sunlight quickly fade away, calming Fitch. He looks around a moment as he gathers his senses… trying to remember where he is.

Taking a few moments to make sure that the sun has set completely set, Fitch crawls along his stomach, making his way out from the hollowed tree. Continuing to crawl a moment, Blaze looks down at him and snorts. "Good morning?" Fitch asks. Blaze shakes his bluish mane and snorts again. Fitch stands, dusting himself off from the thin layer of dirt he had gathered inside of the fallen tree.

Fitch looks about his surroundings getting a feeling for the area. "I reckon we're south-east, eh boy?" Blaze fails to answer as he nudges his muzzle into Fitch's tattered and blood stained side. "I know, I'm hungry too." Fitch makes his way along side of Blaze reaching into a side saddle bag. He takes the leather scoop of oats and plops them into a pile onto the ground. Blaze instantly begins to feed.

Fitch rounds Blaze reaching into the opposite saddle bag taking a strip of jerky in hand. *"Might's well give it another lash,"* Fitch thinks putting the jerky into his mouth. He tears off a large section and begins to chew. *"So far so good."* Fitch swallows. For a long moment, he's fine. Suddenly, Fitch heaves over bracing him palms upon his knees, violently discarding the jerky from his stomach. "I reckon I spoke too soon." Fitch tosses the remaining portion of the jerky onto the ground.

Mounted, Fitch slightly coaxes Blaze onward and past the fallen tree through the clusters and sparse rows of timber. The air is brisk and cool with the raising moon teasing the beyond horizon. The moon, nearly three-quarters. *"That's peculiar. When I left, Purgatory the moon's jest a sliver. What day's this?"* Fitch wonders. Fitch and Blaze stroll along for a spell until finally weaving their way out of sight among the gatherings of trees and clusters of woodland boulders.

"Do you hear that, Blaze?" Fitch asks his faithful stallion. Off in the distance, the faint bleating of an injured animal. The surrounding trees have grown denser as Fitch and Blaze have come across a narrow roadway following it to its uncertain destination. The nearing bleating sound of the wounded creature draws closer. Then, a different set of sounds cut through the darkness. The sounds of rabid dogs nipping and growling. Probably over their latest slain victim. The bleating can still be faintly heard as the nipping and growling grows louder.

Fitch and Blaze appear along the roadway at the edge of a spanning treeline. A vast clearing stands before them lined with a new fangled invention... barbwire. The prickly fence surrounds the large clearing with the faint glimmerings of a ranch or homestead in the distance. A medium sized barn stands next to the home with a tall and thickly planked corral close to the far side of the structure.

"My eyes," Fitch thinks. "What's the matter with my eyes? I can see clearly. Clearly in the blessed dark. What's happenin' to me?" Fitch coaxes Blaze slightly forward drawing nearer to the outer areas of the spanning barbwire fence as he locates the source of the ruckus.

A wild pack of timber wolves continue to nip and growl at a large silver and grey backed wolf. The obvious leader of the pack. The silver backed wolf attempts to defend itself from the attacking pack of wolves. The pack leader has stepped into a steel jawed trap tightly secured to a near barbwire fence post. The silver backed wolf is trapped.

The vicious wolf pack rips patches of flesh and fur from the silver backed wolf fighting for control of the pack. The larger wolf is losing its battle. A smaller black wolf catches wind of an approaching enemy. The wolf turns to see Fitch and Blaze strolling closer. Knowing that the silver backed wolf is confined to the steel trap, the rabid wolf pack turns their attention toward Fitch and Blaze, charging at full speed toward them. "Oh, wonderful," Fitch sarcastically mumbles. "Are you ready for this, Blaze?" Fitch's stallion stands his ground not budging an inch from the approaching wolf pack.

The wolf pack are but mere inches away from Fitch and Blaze. The smallest wolf skids to a halt, cowering and whimpering at Fitch's presence. In suit, the wolf pack ceases their attack, skidding to a halt. Timidly, the wolves sniff the air surrounding Fitch. A few whimpers seep out from the pack. Then, as if they were being violently beaten, the wolves cry out in screaming pain. The wolves turn tail whimpering away, forgetting all about the trapped silver back wolf and the booty of slain sleep in the clearing. "This trip's gettin' odder'n odder as we go, Blaze," Fitch shakes his head.

Fitch slings his foot around and leaps onto the ground. Blaze remains steadfast as Fitch approaches the trapped silver backed wolf. The steel trap, cutting away at its right hind leg. Unlike the fleeing wolf pack, the silver back wolf is unafraid of Fitch as he approaches. Fitch extends out his palm for the wolf to sniff. No growl nor snapping. The large wolf was obviously the leader, strong and proud. Unafraid of anything.

Fitch slowly approaches the silver backed wolf and crouches down along side of it. He and the canine look at each other for a long moment before Fitch reaches down toward the steel trap. "That's a fine steel trap you got you're self into." The silver backed wolf looks calmly up at Fitch, seeming to understand the human's kind words. Placing one foot on the constricted lever, Fitch releases the trap. The silver backed wolf is freed from the steel trap. The wolf quickly sniffs and licks his wounded hind leg… it'll heal.

The released silver backed wolf, Steele, sniffs then licks Fitch's hand. Quickly turning, Steele charges full force away from the barbwire fence, dashing into the treeline after his rebellious pack. "You're welcome," Fitch bellows after a moment too late.

Steele has disappeared into the trees. Fitch makes his way back toward Blaze then takes the reigns in his hand. Fitch and Blaze approach the closed wooden planked gate of the barbwire fence, opens it and enters the property.

Leading Blaze by the reigns, Fitch continues along the narrowing roadway cutting through the homestead. Along opposite sides of the roadway, slaughtered sheep with their throats ripped open from the departed wolf pack. The smell of blood lingers through the air. A cowering herd of sheep timidly hover in the far corner of the inner area of the barbwire fence. They are frightened at Fitch's presence. Fitch pays no heed to the flock of sheep, continuing onward toward the house, wooden planked corral and barn.

...bleat-bleat.

...bleat-bleat.

Laying along side of the roadway, a wounded lamb cries out for help. Its hind leg torn and bloody from the wolves' attack. Fitch and Blaze continue onward for a moment but the smell of fresh and <u>live</u> blood of the wounded lamb is overwhelming. A terrible aching wells up inside of Fitch's stomach. Painful. God, so painful Fitch's entire body aches. The smell...the smell of... blood. Fitch can take no more.

Fitch tosses Blaze's reigns to the side and hurls himself toward the bleating lamb. He flings the fragile creature into his arms, bearing his fanged jaws. Fitch lowers his mouth toward the lamb... pausing. *"What am I doing? I am not a beast! Oh! Oh, the pain! I'm so hungry!"* Fitch bears down onto the bleating lamb. His fangs mere inches from its bloody throat.

KA-BLOOM!

The unseen shotgun blast knocks Fitch from his feet. Fitch topples onto his back. The shotgun's bullets, a direct hit into his chest. Fitch lies there beside the bleating lamb... motionless, without life. A shadowy figure reloads his shotgun as he dashes nearer. As the figure approaches and hovers over Fitch, his facial and bodily features are made out through the darkness, Trask Bailey.

Wearing his work boots and full set of long-johns, Trask flings his shotgun over his shoulder, looking down at the damage he had caused to Fitch. The shotgun blast covering Fitch's entire chest. Fitch remains still and breathless. "I thought you were one of them. Blasted wolves," Trask pauses. "Sorry, mister." Trask sets his shotgun down on the ground, yet still in reach, takes Fitch by the underarms and heaves the limp corpse sideways up onto Blaze's saddle. Trask tucks his shotgun under one of Blaze's saddle bags then leans down toward the injured lamb taking it up in one arm.

Trask carries the lamb in one arm taking Blaze's reigns in hand with the other. "Well, might's well get you in side so's the sonsuv-bitches don't tear you a new one. Sure they'll be back," Trask mumbles to Fitch flopping sideways along the saddle. "I'll take you back to town t'morrow." Leading Blaze along, Trask heads for his home in the nearing distance.

Trask opens the barn door and slides the wounded lamb inside. "I'll have to tend to you later." The lamb bleats with Trask closing the barn door behind. He saunters along a pathway along side his house. A lantern has been lit inside casting flickering light out through the well placed windows. Trask approaches Blaze, hitching him along a supporting beam of the primitive porch. The stout man slides Fitch from over the saddle and swings the lifeless body over his shoulders. Turning, Trask carries the unknown stranger toward the opened front door of his home.

Trask carries Fitch inside and plops him face up on the planked dining table. A wall lantern glimmers along the far side of the well furnished dining room. Trask makes his way toward another wall lantern, lighting it then replaces his shotgun over the smoldering fireplace hearth. A pot belly stove stands in one corner. A modest kitchen area leading off to a hallway with two slightly cracked open doors leading into the rest of the primitive house.

Trask pours himself a glass of whiskey, takes a swig, turns and approaches Fitch laying on his back on the table. "Well, lets take a look at you," Trask takes another swig of his whiskey. Setting the glass down on the table top, Trask carefully opens what remains of Fitch's bloodied vest and tattered shirt. There are no open wounds. No shotgun blast. Nothing but thousands of healed bites. Thousands of them. "Where in tar nation you been, mister?" Trask asks his unresponsive guest. Trask looks upward at Fitch's face, studying him. "Hey, mister. I know you. You're that Sheriff from Purgatory," Trask continues talking to himself. "Splendid, I go and shoot me a lawman. Go to hell fer sure now."

Trask curiously resumes his examination of Fitch's lifeless body. Cougar's sword wound. Jesse's bullet wounds through each of his palms. "Looks like you been through a lot, Sheriff."

"More than you'cn imagine," Fitch declares. Trask nearly loses his skin, jumping back across the room. Trask is pale with terror. Fitch flutters his eyes and slightly rolls over onto his side. "Where am I?"

"My home," Trask sputters.

"No. Where am I?" Fitch demands.

"New Mexico Territory. 'Bout four days out of Purgatory, Sheriff.

"You know me?"

Trask eases up a bit slowly inching his way back toward Fitch. "Sure, you're that sheriff from Purgatory. You're Theodore Woolley's kin. Young Fitch Woolley. The prodigal son returns."

"Wouldn't go as that far," Fitch raises up, slinging his legs off the edge of the table sitting up facing Trask who slowly pokes a finger at Fitch, drawing closer.

"You were dead to rights. No pulse. No breathing or such. You were dead to rights."

"Reckon so," Fitch looks himself over. "Well," Fitch smiles. "At least I died with my boots on." Trask circles Fitch sitting up on the table.

211

"I heard about people like you. The walking dead," Trask pauses. "But not around these parts." Trask makes his way around the table to face Fitch. "Don't know where you've been but you smell and look awful." Trask turns and makes his way along the far wall to a steamer trunk. Opening it, Trask removes a handful of mothball smelling clothing. The outfit is of all black in nature. A much smaller fitting preacher's attire, trousers, white undershirt, and a black caballero style jacket. A reverend's collar falls out from the stack. It must have fit many years ago when Trask was much smaller in girth.

"You a preacher?" Fitch asks.

"Among other things." Trask answers as he faces Fitch. "We'll get to that later. Go 'round back. There's a rain barrel you can clean up."

"Thanks…"

"Trask."

"Thank-you, Trask," Fitch hops off the kitchen table heading for the door. Fitch opens the door then slightly cocks his head back. "Trask?" Fitch pauses to continue his thoughts. "I remember hearing 'bout you. You're that school teacher who was run outta town when I was younger. You and Bell had a…"

"Yes, boy!" Trask interrupts. "That was me. Now go'n get you're self cleaned up you're stinkin' up the place!" Trask commands. Fitch keeps his thoughts to himself as he turns and exits out into the night. His newly acquired clothing tucked under his arm.

With his eyes easily adjusted to the darkness, Fitch makes his way around the side of the house passing by the thick planked corral along side of the barn. From the depths of the barn, Fitch hears the faint bleating of the wounded lamb. Fitch deeply inhales the sent. The sent of live blood. Shaking off the temptation, Fitch finds the three quarter filled rain barrel. Hanging the black preachers garb over a wooden railing, Fitch strips off his tattered and blood stained clothing.

Trask appears from one of the backrooms dressing himself. Cautiously looking out through the cracked open front door for any signs of Fitch, he returns to the opened steamer trunk and removes a gold cross necklace. Trask kisses the cross and loops the chain around his neck, tucking the cross under his shirt. Again, Trask reaches into the trunk and removes a flask, a Bible and a small wooden box. Trask places the items onto the dining area table and sits in one of the chairs pouring himself another shot of whiskey. "This'll be interesting…" Trask mumbles.

Trask stokes the warming flames of the pot belly stove with a charred poker. Without Trask's notice, Fitch quietly enters the home and stands mere feet away from behind. Trask turns to be startled. "Sorry, Trask," Fitch humbly replies dressed in Trask's younger day's preacher attire. All in black. Looking quite normal yet with a sense of evil about himself.

"Don't be sneakin' up on people like that," Trask shakes the poker at him. With his bare hand, Fitch opens the pot belly stove's forward facing door. The heat and pain must be unbearable but does not seem to phase him. With his other hand, Fitch tosses in his vest and tattered, blood stained clothing.

"Didn't want't leave 'em out by the wood pile 'case the wolves come back."

"Good thinkin'" Trask nervously replies. "Now then, let's really have a look at you. Up on the table, Sheriff."

" "Sheriff", I'll still never get used to that," Fitch thinks as he hops up on the dining area table. Trask approaches and faces Fitch with the flask in hand. He "crosses" the flask in a Catholic manner then opens it. Trask splashes the blessed Holy Water all over Fitch's chest and shoulders. The blessed Holy Water has no effect on Fitch.

"What was that supposed to do?" Fitch asks as he takes the flask in hand and takes a large gulp of the blessed Holy Water. Fitch swishes the water around in his mouth, careful not to swallow any of it then spits it out onto the pot belly stove. Steam rises up from the evaporating water with Fitch arrogantly handing the flask back to Trask with a cocky smile. Frustrated, Trask sets down the flask next to Fitch and reaches into the neck of his shirt.

"How 'bout <u>this</u>?" Trask exclaims revealing his gold cross mere inches from Fitch's face.

"Very nice, Trask. Did you get that in Purgatory or on one of your many travels I've heard so much about?"

"That'll be enough of that!" Trask pauses a moment before reaching for the small wooden box. Opening it, Trask retrieves a single Holy Wafer from a small stack inside of the box. Trask faces Fitch and gently places the Holy Wafer onto Fitch's forehead. At first, there is no effect. Then, Fitch's head begins twitching from side to side. Pain covers Fitch's face as Trask backs away from Fitch expecting him to explode or something. Fitch's inner demons cause him to lunge from the table and begin thrashing on the wooden planked floor. Trask is in shear terror watching Fitch scream and thrash about. Then suddenly, Fitch's body falls limp and motionless.

Trask pauses a few moments before carefully approaching Fitch, slightly kicking him in the side for any signs of life. There are none. Trask timidly crouches down and shakes Fitch by the shoulder. There is no life nor movement.

"Aaaaahhhhhhh!" Fitch springs to life, bearing his fanged teeth and mimicking a clawing effect with his hands. Trask nearly jumps out of his skin, toppling on his backside onto the floor. Fitch can hardly contain his laughter as he rises. "Was that what you were expecting, Trask? Do you know any other parlor tricks?" Fitch chuckles.

"That was <u>not</u> amusing!" Trask stands as he brushes himself off. Trask circles Fitch for a long moment looking his uninvited guest over from head to toe. "This is puzzling. You should've been effected by the Holy Water, the cross and the wafers." Trask scratches his head. "Come with me." Trask leads Fitch toward and out through the front door.

Trask and Fitch make their way past the far end of the house leading into a large clearing away from the sleeping flock of sheep. Entering through another gate on the far side of the homestead, Trask leads Fitch across a grassy meadow along a narrow path to an uncertain destination. "Sheriff," Trask begins.

"Please, Trask. Call me Fitch. "Sheriff" doesn't quite suit me."

"Just as well... Fitch. Where you been all this time? Purgatory has done given up on you."

""All this time?"" Fitch stops cold in his tracks with Trask taking a few steps forward, realizing that Fitch is no longer following then returns to face him.

"It's February," Trask pauses. "It's February forth. You've been gone around a month."

"Can't be! How long was I in that mine shaft? Over three weeks? That can't be right... I've lost three weeks?!" Fitch argues with himself. Trask motions for Fitch to continue.

"At any rate, I kind of take care of the people 'round here. Teacher. Doctor. Preacher. Jack of all trades if you will. The closest town is Purgatory. Nothing much else for nearly two hundred miles in all directions. A few days back, one of my student's folks came back from town with the news."

"What news?"

"Sheriff James Williams was appointed by the Mayor. He made it all official. When you didn't come back, town needed a Sheriff. Don't have hard feelings for the lad. A week after you left'n didn't come back, he coaxed nearly a dozen men into a posse to go out and look for you," Trask laughs.

"What's so funny?" Fitch asks.

"'Bout a week after you left, he got his horse stolen. The new "Sheriff" had to go out on a posse with someone else's horse."

"Diamond was stolen?"

"Don't know the horse's name but I do know the Sheriff never found'im. They lasted out there for 'bout a week'n a half then came back. If its any consolation to you, I hear young Elizabeth that you'd been courtin' was heart broken."

"Yeah," Fitch sarcastically remarks. "So heart broken she ran to the arms of another man. "The Sheriff."

"Don't know anything 'bout that. But, I reckon if you <u>do</u> love'er, you'd best high-tail it back to town to remind'er." Trask and Fitch continue along the narrow pathway through the darkness. In the nearing distance, an extended rectangular building appears from the shadows.

"My Grandpa Theo used to say…"

"Theo, good man," Trask interrupts.

"Thank-you," Fitch continues, "Grandpa Theo used to say, "If you love something, set it free. If it…"

"If it comes back," Trask interrupts again. Both Fitch and Trask stop in their tracks and grin at it other.

"If it comes back, shoot it!" they say in unison with a chuckle in their voices. The humorous moment has passed followed by an awkward stillness.

Trask takes Fitch by the arm, turning him to face him a few yards from the front of the lifeless school house. "If you want to follow in Theo's footsteps, know this. He never gave up on anything he ever wanted. He shied away from as many fights as he could but when there was no other way, Theo fought. Fitch, don't know too much 'bout you but if you're kin to Theo I know this. If you love that girl, go after her. Fight. If you don't, never mind gonin' back to Purgatory and be on your way. Forget 'bout The Cougar Gang."

"What?" a shocked look crosses Fitch's brow.

"Yes, I know about that, too. I still lived in town when Cougar shot your grandpa. Bastards! Ivan was too much of a coward to go after'im. Grandpa died for nothing. Just donin' his job."

"I don't wanna die for "just donin' my job". I wanna die for something I believe in."

"Sounds like you have more demons that I figured. Come on," Trask motions Fitch toward the closed front door of the near end of the school house. Trask enters into the darkness of the structure and lights a kerosene lantern. The flickering light dances along the inside walls heading toward the far end. Just as Fitch is to step up onto the porch of the schoolhouse, an odd sound catches his attention.

Fitch steps off of the porch and takes a few strides away from the building, staring blankly at the treeline just beyond the grassy meadow. The sounds grow louder. Fitch's hearing is growing in power as his eyesight had. Louder and louder.

The sounds of a wild pack of dogs in a betting saloon fight he had heard so many times. Growling and barking. The sounds are hideous. Pain. Mounds of pain. The whimpering of a beaten puppy. The shredding of flesh and fur. The clamping of canine jaws. Then, all is silent. Fitch cocks his head to the side a moment to hear a singular howl through the trees. The howl, not of remorse nor beckoning the rest of the pack to a slain victim, but the howl of defiance. Of triumph. Then, the howl ceases.

Fitch walks along the central aisle of the opposite rows of children's desks and chairs. The desks are plain and handmade with rickety chairs. The extended walls on opposite sides of the schoolhouse are sported with tall windows allowing as much daylight in as possible. Trask continues to rummage through an extended shelf along the backside of the building behind his cluttered desk at the front of the room. One by one, Trask looks at the titles and covers of books along a dusty section at the bottom corner of the shelves. "What are you looking for, Trask?"

"This!" Trask removes an old looking leather bound book from the shelf. Trask flips through several chapters of the book until locating the section he was searching for. "This is what I was looking for, Fitch," Trask gloats. Fitch rounds the last of the student's desks and approaches the near side of Trask's teacher's desk. Trask flops the opened book onto the desk top and points at the opened page. Fitch glances at the page a moment then reaches down toward the book and slightly closes it to read the cover, "MYTHS AND LEGENDS". Trask flips back through the pages of the book, landing on an illustration. Fitch takes note.

The colored drawing is a trio of rabid wolves surrounding a coffin half buried in the dirt. The fleeing caretakers are covered with blood, scampering from the rows of gravesites and headstones. The wolves. The wolves. The wolves linger in Trask's mind. Fitch returns to the page where Trask had opened the book and begins to read for several moments. In an instant, Fitch quickly looks up and stares blankly at Trask. "You've got to be pulling my leg!" Fitch exclaims.

"That's the only thing I can figure," Trask points to the opened pages. "You have no pulse yet you breathe. I shot you in the chest yet you have no wounds. What you've told me, you are effected by sunlight."

"What about the cross and the Holy Water? See? It's here in the book!"

"I reckon some of the legends are wrong," Trask pauses. "We could see what your reaction is to fire."

"Let's not!" Fitch continues to glance across the pages. "You've read this book, what else does it say?"

"Well, if the other myths are true, a stake through the heart, burning and the removal of your head are 'bout the only things that can kill you."

"True, but that could kill any man. That doesn't sound that special," Fitch mumbles. At that instant, Fitch looks up toward the nearest window. The amber rays of the impending sunrise begin to awaken beyond the horizon.

"Appears you don't have much time," Trask bites his tongue. "I have a cellar you can... can, ah... "rest" in if you'd like."

"Thank-you."

"But then tomorrow you're on your way."

"Yes, sir," Fitch humbly responds. "Thank-you."

Trask and Fitch stand there a moment awkwardly looking at each other. Trask closes the mythical book and hands it to Fitch. "Odd," Trask thinks. "A being. A creature that this man, Fitch is to become or is becoming, wearing the clothing of a "man of the cloth". "Life sure's peculiar," Trask says aloud to Fitch leading him toward the far opened door of the schoolhouse

Trask and Fitch stroll along the narrow pathway leading from the schoolhouse toward the backside of Trask's home. The book, "MYTHS AND LEDENDS", tucked under Fitch's arm. Without another word between them, the two round the front of the house, step up onto the porch and approach the opened front door. Trask instantly enters with Fitch pausing a moment to look over his shoulder.

"I will miss that if what Trask says is true," Fitch thinks as he gazes upon the first glimmerings of amber rays of the rising sun. *"Never to see a sunset or a sunrise again... What have I become? What is to become of me?"* Fitch takes a deep sighing breath, turns and follows behind Trask inside.

"Not much down there. Figured, if Indians ever came I could hide-out for awhile. It's dark and quiet," Trask opens a hidden trap door leading down into the dirt cellar. Fitch approaches Trask, looks over his shoulder then into the darkness of the cellar.

""Dark and quiet". Are you trying to tell me something?" Fitch snorts.

"No! No, not at all. Just your kind…"

"My kind?"

"Blast it, read the book! Git yer backside in there before you fry… or whatever it is that you do!"

Fitch takes each step of the makeshift ladder leading down into the cellar with the "MYTHS AND LEGENDS" tucked neatly under his arm. Lower and lower Fitch sinks into the cellar until he finally disappears from Trask's sight. "Do you need any more dirt or anything?"

"Dirt?!" Fitch exclaims from below. "Why would I need dirt?"

"Read the book!" Trask slams the hidden cellar door closed and stomps away. Trask paces for several moments across his wooden planked floor. Below, Fitch is already annoyed at the noise from above but settles in. He rests his back against the tight quarters of the supporting beams of the house above. The lower planks of the floor are no more than three feet from top to bottom. Across from him along the far side, a small rectangular window is seen covered with a think layer of dirty glass.

Fitch sits there for a moment looking about the piles of stored items; the dark colored horse blankets, pots and pans, mounds of rusted tools and a worn saddle. Seeing perfectly well in the dark, Fitch opens the book of "MYTHS AND LEGENDS" and flips through the pages. "Oh, well," Fitch mumbles to himself. "Might's well start at the beginning. I've got all day." As he turns to the front page to begin reading, the faintest rays of daylight appear through the far window. Fitch struggles a moment to adjust his sight from the darkness and growing light in the cramped area...

Trask tosses on his tweed jacket and heads for the door. Placing his spectacles on the bridge of his nose, he exits his home. Trask stops dead in his tracks between the door jam. Steele lays in an upward position looking outward from the porch at first. The silver backed wolf calmly turns its head to see Trask gawking down at him. Trask remains motionless for several moments as Steele sniffs the air around him then turns his head, returning to his watchful post. "It figures. I reckon some of the myths are true," Trask snorts.

Carefully closing the front door behind himself, Trask tiptoes around Steele so is not to disturb him. Slinking off the porch, Trask never lets Steele out of his sight, making his way around the side of the house. Steele remains laying in an upright position, listening and watching for any intruders who may cause harm to his new master.

The wide meadow is surrounded by the treeline on three sides with the central area filled with playing and frolicking children of an array of ages. The sun is warming as it continues to rise over the horizon.

Trask scurries along the narrow path heading toward the near end of the schoolhouse. The children smile and greet him with a playful wave then return to their games. Trask disappears inside of the schoolhouse a moment then reappears along side the front opened door. Taking a worn rope in hand, he tugs on it several times causing the school bell to ring.

Ding-ding.

Ding-ding.

Ding-ding.

The children turn tail and dash toward the opened front door filing inward slightly shoving and pushing at each other in a playful manner.

The school bell echoes with a slight ringing as Trask makes his way along side of the building and follows the last child inward, leaving the front door open for what little air circulation that part of the country has to offer. "Good-morning," Trask calls out.

"Good-morning, Mr. Bailey," the classroom of children respond in unison with different pitches and tones. Trask makes his way along the central aisle separating the opposite sides of filled rows of desks and chairs. At the front of the class, Trask turns in front of his desk and surveys his students. Yep, all the chairs and desks are filled. Every child is accounted for and present.

The eldest of the students sit along the back rows of the schoolhouse with the next of age toward the center and the youngest nearing the front closest to Trask and his desk.

Trask motions over his desk top toward a stack of large pieces of blank paper and primitive crayons. "We're going to do something different today, class. I want you each to come up and take a piece of paper and some crayons. I want you to draw a picture of your *favorite* holiday. *Remember,* Valentine's Day is coming and I want you to give these pictures to your folks," Trask informs the children.

In an orderly fashion, the youngest children stand and file along the front of the class collecting the sheets of paper and crayons from the edge of Trask's desk. After returning to their desks, the middle area of students stand and likewise approach the desk and collect sheets of paper and crayons.

The midday's sun warms the schoolhouse casting soft light through the far wall of windows. The students continue to draw and color their favorite holiday pictures with Trask slowly walking in and out of the desks and chairs looking over the children's shoulders. The pictures are very colorful and some even quite good.

Christmas…

Thanksgiving…

Saint Patrick's Day…

The Forth of July… even a handful of Valentine's Day pictures filled with hearts and red colors… mostly by the younger children. Trask glances down over the shoulder of a girl probably ten or eleven. Vicki has rolling blonde curls, a dimple in her chin, wearing a light colored frilly dress. Trask studies her holiday picture for a long moment. It's not like any of the other students. "Vicki," Trask fatherly asks. "Why did you chose Halloween?"

"Mr. Bailey, you said to draw a picture of our favorite holiday. Halloween is my favorite," Vicki gleams. Trask reaches down and takes the picture in hand to study it further. Vicki has drawn a pair of witches flying through the air on their broom sticks over a dark and dim cemetery. Numerous black cats and flying bats fill the rest of the sheet of paper. A very grim image for a farm girl so young. "Mr. Bailey, do _you_ believe in witches?"

Vicki asks. Every head turns throughout the classroom for every student waits to listen to Trask's answer.

Seeing he has all of his students unwanted attention, Trask pauses a moment to think for a proper response. "Well, class," Trask reluctantly begins. "I've seen a lot of odd things in my travels and have read a number of books." Trask pauses. "Yes, I believe that there <u>were</u> and <u>could be</u> witches and werewolves and vamp..." He almost said it! The "V" word. "But not around in these parts," Trask's exact words to Fitch haunt him as they slip out of his mouth. Quickly, Trask responds, "Play time! Everyone outside!"

The children cheer as they scamper from their chairs and desks as they shove their way out into the sunlight. Vicki tosses Trask a playful smile as she too follows the students outside. Seeing that all the children have vacated, Trask looks downward, staring blankly at Vicki's Halloween drawing in hand, studying it for a long moment.

Steele remains laying in an upright manner looking outward and away from Trask's house. The air is still. There are no sounds of woodland creatures nor birds. The feeling is still and deathly.

Fitch continues to read from the book nearly three-quarters through. From the far window, the sunlight creeps closer and closer toward Fitch's boot until shining upon it. There is no effect. The sunlight draws higher along his leg then waist. Fitch continues to read from the book. The sunlight tips the cover of the book then touches Fitch's hand. It instantly burns and smolders.

Fitch drops the book and frantically scoots away from the nearing sunlight. Looking upon his hand now out of the light, it heals itself returning to its scared form. The sunlight daunts Fitch, beginning to fill the cellar. There is nowhere to hide to avoid the sunlight. Fitch is trapped. Thinking quickly on what he has read from the book, Fitch begins to cover himself with handfuls of dirt from the cellar. The dirt is not enough as the sunlight continues to beam inward.

Fitch panics as he scans the area for some sort of cover or protection. He lunges forward, snagging the top dark colored horse blanket from the pile. Sliding as far as he can into the mounds of dirt, Fitch tosses the horse blanket over himself as the sunlight cascades into his corner, consuming himself. Fitch cowers under the shield of the horse blanket, feeling the heat of the sunlight upon his back and shoulders. *"I guess more dirt wouldn't've been a bad idea,"* Fitch thinks of Trask's last words as he left for school. Feeling slightly at ease, Fitch flutters his eyes, drifting off to sleep. The horse blanket and layer of dirt protecting him from the burning sunlight filling the cellar.

Ding-ding.
Ding-ding.
Ding-ding.

Trask walks along the side of the schoolhouse then steps up onto the front porch along side of the front opened door. The bell echoes for a moment with the school children scampering from inside dashing outward with their school books tucked under their arms. "Thank-you, ladies and gentlemen. I'll see you all on Monday," Trask bellows out after the fleeing students.

The children dart off in all direction toward their scattered homes. In what seems a heart beat, Trask is left all alone in silence standing on the front porch of the schoolhouse. "Well then," Trask states to himself. "Home… home to see what our nocturnal guest has been up to." Trask closes the front door of the schoolhouse and begins his lonely trek along the narrow path leading home. The sun begins to dip lower into the sky, dashing behind a layer of clouds. The cool air sooths Trask yet, the impending conversation with the visitor in his cellar, disturbs him as he slows his walk home.

"There-there," Trask whispers hovering over the injured lamb in the barn. Trask tightens the fresh wrap around the lamb's neck and hind leg. The thankful creature bleats out then skips away heading toward a lowered trough of wheat. Trask wipes the lamb's blood from his hands onto his work trousers as he stands and heads for the opened barn door. Exiting, Trask closes the barn door behind himself. He looks up to see Steele remaining on post, laying across the porch of his house.

Trask cautiously approaches his porch and steps up onto it. Steele sniffs the air that surrounds Trask then looks away, disinterested. Trask slightly turns to see the sun continuing to set beyond the horizon. "It won't be more than an hour or less," Trask says to himself. Steele blurts out a low growl, not at Trask himself but at his attempt of communication with him. Unsure of what the silver backed wolf will do next, Trask slowly sidesteps the hulking canine, opens his front door and enters.

Placing his spectacles on the kitchen area table, Trask pauses a moment, staring blankly at the closed cellar door. Ever so quietly, Trask moves forward and timidly opens the door looking in and downward. "Sheriff?" Trask whispers. "Fitch, are you still down there?" There is no reply. Only the faint sounds of Fitch's snoring. "Reckon so," Trask quietly closes the cellar door. Trask moves across the planked floor toward the opened front door and gazes outward upon the setting sun for several minutes.

Darkness fills the Bailey home with Trask moving about the kitchen area lighting kerosene lanterns. The soft flickering of the flames casts shadows throughout the room as Trask approaches the central table cutting fresh vegetables with a large bladed knife. There... the sun has set. What is the night to hold for him?

Steele springs to his feet catching Trask off guard. Trask whips the large knife toward Steele who stands in the opened doorway. Steele looks toward Trask, slightly growls, more of a low bark, lips his chops then scampers away into the night. Steele gallops passed Blaze and Trask's horse freely grazing along the inner areas of the barbwire fence of the property. Trask lowers his knife from the door, turns and resumes chopping at the vegetables on the table.

The lumpy horse blanket on the dirt floor of the cellar moves with sudden twitches and jarring actions. Fitch is asleep underneath the horse blanket but... what dreams torment him? Cougar? His own death? Elizabeth? Grandpa Theo? The last shades of the setting sun disappear from the window. Darkness fills the cellar. Fitch tosses and turns under the layers of dirt and the covering of the dark colored horse blanket.

"I can feel the air around me. I'm not flying but yet moving ever so swiftly. The trees are spinning past me. What's that behind the ridge? Friend or foe?" Demonic Fitch crouches down behind a gathering of bushes. The wooded area is dark and dim, easily seen through with Fitch's newly found sight. Steele lumbers around the corner of a series of fallen trees.

Steele approaches Fitch, sniffs then licks his face. Fitch reaches up and runs his scared palm down along Steele's silvery back. The fur is warm and soft to the touch. Steele slightly growls toward Fitch. Not in a threatening manner but more of an invitation to follow. The silver backed wolf turns away from Fitch and begins a slow gallop through the wooded area. Fitch stands and quickly begins to follow his daytime guardian.

"I feel alive. My senses are reeling. Where is this wolf leading me?" Fitch's trot turns to a gallop. Steele's four paws seem to lightly thunder across the wooded floor. Faster and faster. With little effort, Fitch catches up with Steele beginning to play a canine form of "tag". Steele playfully barks out several times as Fitch reaches down and playfully tugs at his flopping tail. Fitch and Steele increase their speed to a full run now. The trees whizzing past. Not a woodland creature to be heard from for miles. The pair's treading seems to be gliding instead of running. Steele suddenly breaks away from Fitch darting into a small grove. Fitch stops dead in his tracks.

Steele hurdles himself through the air, violently colliding into two small wolves of his former pack. The pack of wolves are stunned as they are disturbed from their slain deer. Steele rips his powerful jaws through one of the smaller wolves then turns to attack the other four. The beasts claw and bite at Steele's silvery fun. He is no match for the remaining four wolves. A pair of the wolves snap their jaws into Steele's throat pinning him to the ground. All looks lost for Steele.

Fitch thrusts himself toward the nearest pair of wolves. He takes hold of one wolf and ruthlessly snaps its back, tossing it aside like a worn rag doll. Another wolf lunges upward attacking Fitch who in turn counter attacks. The two crash into each other in midair, colliding to the ground. Steele fends off the other pair of wolves, tearing one's throat out, yet sparing the last, pinning it to the ground. Fitch bares his fanged jaws and shreds the last wolf's jugular. Fitch tosses the slain wolf to the ground.

The entire area is covered with bloody fur and mangled wolf corpses. Fitch turns to see Steele continuing to pin the last surviving wolf to the ground. The smell of live blood overwhelms him. Fitch turns away from the kill. Steele growls with urgency. With his stomach turning and spinning with severe hunger and the disgust and distaste of what he has become, Fitch slowly approaches Steele and the confined wolf.

Mere inches away, Steele releases the wolf, frantically attempting to flee. Fitch grasps onto the wolf, clutching it tightly in his arms. The beast whines as it tries to escape. Fitch bares his fangs, opens his jaw and slams his mouth down onto the wolf's throat. Steele sits off to the side calmly liking his wounds as if this were all normal, just another night in the life of a nocturnal creature…

Fitch starts awake abruptly sitting upward, knocking his head on the lower support beams of the wooden planked floor above. His eyes are blood red. His skin more pale. His canine teeth and fingernails, slightly grown and extended. He scans his surroundings, the dark colored horse blanket had been covering him long with the mounds of collected dirt. The folded blankets and worn saddle across from him. The small window casting in the last fading traces of the setting sun. Fitch crouches over and dusts himself off then tosses the horse blanket onto the top of the pile. Remaining hunched over, Fitch makes his way toward the closed upward cellar door.

Trask hums a ditty to himself as he continues to chop and slice the meager assortment of vegetables on the dinning area table. The only sounds are of Trask's out-of-tune melody. Trask tosses the cut vegetables into a pot then slides a large portion of bloody beef in front of himself. He takes his large knife and begins slicing the beef into stew sized chunks. One by one, Trask tosses the chunks into the pot of vegetables, his hands growing more and more bloody from the beef. "Smells great. Wish I could have some," Fitch nearly whispers coming up from behind Trask from the opened cellar door.

Trask spins around, slicing his finger with the large knife. "I… I didn't hear you come up," Trask fumbles as he backs away from Fitch. There's something different about his uninvited guest. His eyes. His skin. His manner. His teeth! Defiantly, Fitch's teeth. Fitch rounds the table and inhales the freshly made stew nearly ready for simmering. The aroma of the vegetables, broth and bloody beef. Fitch catches a different scent. A scent of live blood.

Fitch glances down, noticing Trask's sliced finger. Trask fumbles with a worn rag to conceal the injury. Too late. Fitch moves toward Trask with slyful grace. Hovering across the floor instead of purposely walking or moving. Face to face, Fitch and Trask stare at each other. The smell of Trask's live blood seeping into Fitch's veins, down to the very depths of his transforming soul.

Fitch makes a suddenly movement as if to attack Trask with Trask waving his bloody knife toward him as if it would really fend him off. In terrible pain, Fitch cries out, grasping onto his head and face. He turns and thunders out through the opened front door. Clutching onto his bloody knife, Trask quickly follows outward, stopping short along the edge of his porch.

Fitch hurls himself through the air, completely clearing the wooden planked corral between the side of the house and the barn. Fitch glides through the air, not as a leap, but as of flight. Fitch lands hard on the opposite side of the corral not loosing a step. He thunders through the barn's closed front doors nearly smashing them to bits. Inside, the faint bleating sounds of the wounded lamb. Trask stares blankly into the darkness trying to focus his sight on the barn. Then, there is no need to.

The small lamb screams out in horrific pain. Kicking and bleating. The screams slide down Trask's spine, the sounds of an animal being harmed or tortured. Silence. Deathly stillness. Trask strains to see into the barn. What is to appear from the shadows? A Sheriff? Fitch? A creature? Trask clutches onto his large knife as a figure appears from the barn. Fitch is covered with the lamb's blood. His hands, face, neck and front of his black preacher's jacket. Sadly, Trask lowers his blade as Fitch approaches, attempting to wipe away some of the lamb's blood. "I'm sorry, Trask," Fitch steps up onto the porch standing side by side with Trask. "I'll gather my things'n be on my way."

Fitch pauses for a long moment, searching for the right words for an apology. There are none to be found. Humbly, Fitch pats Trask on the shoulder, nearly lowers his head and enters the house in silence...

CHAPTER VIII

Main Street of Purgatory bustles along. Stagecoaches roll to a halt in front of their various destinations either the Katherine Hotel, Katy's Boarding house or of course the Stardust Saloon or Bell's Saloon. The wooden planked boardwalks are becoming scarce of pedestrians with the setting sun dipping over the horizon. The young lamplighters hobble along on their stilts lighting the well placed street lamps at the corners of town.

Cleo saunters her way past City Hall along the boardwalk making her way toward the Katherine Hotel for her night shift. The air is cool with a light breeze sending the fragrant smells of horse drawn cargo wagons out into the night. Cleo is politely greeted by a pair of local wranglers as she smiles with a nod and turns into the opened door of the Katherine.

"Evenin', miss," Cleo cheerfully calls out toward Beth remaining behind the front desk counter. Beth smiles as she quickly tucks away her growing stack of faded onion papers.

"Good evening, Cleo. Have a good few days off," Beth asks as she tidies up the counter.

"Yes, miss. My brother came out t' see me from Kansas City."

"That's marvelous. Does he have a place to stay? He can always take up a room here… at no charge."

"Thank-you, miss. He's set'lin' in fine'n my room. We've shar'd smaller livin' room. Only be stayin' a few days."

"Well, I look forward to meeting him," Beth slides the hotel's guest registrar across the front desk counter toward Cleo who stands along side of her employer. "A handful of miners passing through, few gamblers headed for California and Doc's upstairs sleeping it off…"

230

"Again!" Cleo and Beth say in unison as they giggle like gitty school girls. The thumping of boot steps quiets the pair of ladies as Jay strolls inward through the opened front door of the hotel. Jay swaggers forward, leaning his elbow in an arrogant manner on the front desk counter facing Beth and Cleo.

"Cleo," Jay grins. "G'evening, Beth."

"Evenin', Sheriff," Cleo shifts her weight from side to side.

"Good-evening, Jay," Beth smiles with a beaming aura.

"I noticed from the street you were gettin' off shift. Could I escort you home?" Jay slyly asks Beth."

"That'll be the third time this week," Cleo interrupts.

"*Thank-you,* Cleo," Beth gently slaps Cleo in the thigh from behind the front desk counter so is Jay is not to see. Beth runs her hands down the sides of her dress straightening out the wrinkles, as if there were any. "That would be fine, Sheriff." Jay and Beth make their way toward the front opened door. Just exiting, Beth turns over her shoulder, "Have a good night, Cleo."

"'N'you, miss," Cleo responds toward Beth with a cockeyed look about her expression. Cleo shakes her head, "Foolish, love's wasted on the young'uns," she thinks as she straightens the already tidied counter top of papers and guest registrar.

With Jay's borrowed and homely looking horse in tow behind Beth chaise, the carriage bobbles along the narrow two lane dirt roadway leading out of town. Jay clutches onto the reigns of Beth's horse with Beth sitting quietly along side of Jay, close beside Jay along the narrow two-seater. Beth begins to look around the surrounding landscape and the three-quarter moon hanging low overhead. Jay steers the chaise to the left of a fork in the road. "Jay, you're going the wrong way."

"Am I?" Jay playfully sneers. Beth becomes uncertain, yet trusts Jay with all her heart. Well, the rest of her heart that doesn't belong to Fitch. The roadway narrows a bit following a primitive wagon trail leading along and following a slow moving river. The soothing sounds of the rolling water comfort Beth, rocking back and forth in the narrow seat of the chaise, closer and closer to Jay.

The wagon trail continues along the furthest outskirts of the Williams Ranch, Jay's folk's ranch. Herds of cattle roam freely across the vast property. Some grazing on the tall wild grass with other cattle asleep in their upright positions. A sprawling ranch house, liveries, a pair of well built barns and a horse corral are dimly seen in the distance with a single lit lantern casting its light from the main house. "You're taking me to meet your folks at this hour?" Beth asks.

"Not 'xactly," Jay grins leading Beth's horse and chaise along the river heading toward the treeline of a densely wooden area.

"Where are you taking me, Jay?" Beth whispers with a tremble in her voice.

"You'll see," Jay pauses. "You'll see…"

Beth turns herself around in the narrow seat looking over her shoulder. The wagon trail has disappeared from behind. The wooden area appears to be closing in on them as they continue forward through the dense wooded area. The soothing sounds of the calm river has dissipated. Beth becomes visually nervous, turning back forward in her seat. Darkness surrounds them. The three-quarter moon's rays have all but disappeared. "Jay?"

"…there it is," Jay whispers as he points forward. Beth strains at first to see the flickering lights in front of them. The lights are not of a homestead lantern nor a campfire. The flickering lights appears to dance and frolic through the air. Closer and closer, the random lights begin to grow brighter.

"Fireflies!" Beth exclaims. "I haven't seen fireflies in years." Jay smiles continuing to lead Beth's horse and chaise deeper into the thickening wooded area. The fireflies grow in numbers. At first, a dozen. Then, scores of the glowing insects. Then, hundreds upon hundreds flutter and dance through the air completely surrounding Beth. She reaches out toward them like a queen of the fairies calling out toward her subjects. Beth giggles with several of the fireflies fluttering in front of her, brushing their tiny wings across her cheek.

"We're home," Jay confidently states beginning to slow the chaise. Beth has been distracted by the aluminous fireflies to see the rustic, one room cabin drawing nearer. A kerosene lantern has already been lit inside, casting its inviting amber shades outward. Jay slows the chaise to a halt and hops off. Turning like a gentleman should, he extends out his arms to assist Beth from the narrow seat. Beth moves across the seat, extends out her hands and slides down into Jay's arms. They face each other for a long awkward moment. "Let me show you around," Jay takes Beth by the hand.

Jay leads Beth around the near and far side of the one room cabin, motioning and pointing toward the various structures as he goes. "Pa'n a few neighbors help't me build the barn'n corrals last spring. Don't have any cattle yet but come auction time, Pa says he'll give me a herd'f my own."

"That's wonderful, Jay," Beth smiles. Jay leads Beth from the back of the cabin toward the front, approaching a well built porch and awning. Jay leaps up onto the porch and opens the front door of his meager home for Beth. She politely smiles with a nod and enters. Jay follows closely behind leaving the front door open.

"Not much't look at, but its home."

"That's for sure," Beth thinks to herself looking about. A modest kitchen table stands off to the left with four hand carved chairs surrounding it. A wood stove appears next to the table with half filled shelves of canned goods, sugar and coffee. All that a single man would need. A makeshift closet appears in the far corner next to a lopsided dresser. A medium sized bed stands along the far wall under the pained window.

"All it needs in a woman's touch," Jay hints.

"That and a stick of dynamite," Beth giggles to herself.

"'Ave one more thing to show you, Beth," Jay leans in and whispers nearly touching his lips to her ear. Goose bumps run up and down Beth's arms as Jay tenderly takes her by the hand and leads her outside. Jay nearly tugs at Beth's arm as they dash across the small field deep into the treeline of the wooded area.

Beth follows blindly through the darkness clutching tighter and tighter to Jay's hand. "Blind faith," Beth thinks. Jay's cabin is lost from her sight from behind. Faster and faster Jay and Beth dash through the narrowing trees. Beth has nearly lost her breath when Jay abruptly stops, nearly tossing Beth forward into a small clearing. She stands there for a moment to take the sight all in.

The treeline spans for ten or so yards in a curved manner around the clearing. A crackling campfire has already been built and stoked. The slow moving river lays near the campfire with the sprawling countryside just beyond.

A calming lagoon is seen just this side of the river, a quick but brisk walk to the campfire. A few yards inward from the warming campfire, a makeshift lean-to with a set of laced pillows and a handmade comforter covered with hand picked rose peddles sprinkled on top. The mood is warm and romantic. Jay turns toward Beth and takes both her hands in his. "Will you marry me, Elizabeth?" Beth quickly looks up, deep into Jay's hazel eyes.

"I'm going to marry Fitch," Beth nervously responds.

"Does he know that? Has he even asked you?"

"… no."

"Fitch isn't coming back," Jay states as it was a matter of fact. "Make me the happiest man in the world… marry me, Elizabeth."

"Oh, James…" Beth and Jay tightly embrace and kiss. A warm and loving kiss full of love and emotion. Jay's hands run all up and down Beth's backside, small of her back, her hips and clutch tightly on her shoulders, pressing her closer toward him.

Beth slightly presses Jay away yet still facing him. With a devilish gleam in her eye, Beth reaches down and unfastens Jay's gunbelt, tossing it to the ground between the cracking campfire and the edge of the calm lagoon boarding the river. Tenderly, Jay reaches up and begins to unfasten the front buttons of Beth's dress down to her navel. Jay slips the shoulders of the dress off of Beth as she reaches up and begins to unfasten the buttons of Jay's shirt.

Two piles of clothing are lumped together along the shore of the lagoon with Jay's gunbelt and revolver buried under the attire. Jay and Beth slide into the chilly water of the calm river, playfully spinning and turning around each other like love struck otters.

Jay lunges forward grasping onto Beth, clinging her close to him. His warm body seems to take the chill off the water. Beth snuggles in close toward Jay's embrace. They tenderly kiss. The three-quarter moon beaming brightly down on their shivering and naked bodies. Jay and Beth embrace and kiss again.

SNAP!

Wading through the pool of water waist high, Jay spins about scanning the shore, campfire and lean-to for any signs of trespassers. A lurking shadow appears from behind the campfire making the image difficult to make out. Then, Steele strolls from the thick treeline into view. Steele circles the campfire several times before focusing on Jay and Beth shivering in the lagoon along the river.

Jay slides his body away from Beth then approaches the shore line and the piles of his and Beth's clothing. Jay's gunbelt and revolver remain buried under the clothing. Steele sits back on his hind quarters calmly licking one of his fore paws. Jay slowly wades out of the lagoon and squats over the pile of clothing, searching for his revolver. Jay draws his weapon from its holster and prepares to fire upon the canine visitor. "If you shoot him, Jay. You'll have to shoot me as well," a familiar voice echoes out from the darkened treeline.

Jay draws his attention form the silver backed wolf staring back at him, spanning his drawn revolver in haphazard directions. With a great deal of arrogance, Fitch steps out from the darkness, approaches Steele and fatherly pats his companion on the head. Steele returns the affection with a lick on the hand. Fitch stands facing Jay, stunned at his friend's reappearance, wearing his former sheriff's attire.

Theo's oversized grey Stetson, polished badge pinned to his vest, ivory handled Colt revolvers holstered low on his hips and the silver spurs at his heels. Fitch steps closer toward the shore. *Jingle-jingle.*

"I reckon I caught you with your pants down, Jay," Fitch smirks.

"This ain't what it looks like, Fitch."

"Sure is," Fitch stares blankly down toward Jay then turns his attention toward Beth a few yards behind Jay shivering in the pool of river water. "I never expected <u>this</u> from you, Elizabeth." Beth covers herself the best she is able... naked and ashamed. Fitch looks back toward Jay. "My deputy. My friend. Stealing <u>my</u> girl," Fitch continues with sternness in his voice.

"<u>Your</u> girl?" Jay responds with a sarcastic tone. "She's <u>not</u> your girl... never was." Jay attempts to slowly maneuver his revolver upward so is not for Fitch to notice... but Fitch does.

"The only sensible thing to do as far as I'm concerned," Fitch glares a moment at Beth still covering herself the best she can, then stares deathly at Jay. "If I can't have her, neither can you..." Jay whips his revolver upward and fires off a shot. Fitch quick draws and cocks both of his ivory handled revolvers and levels them downward toward Jay.

BLAM. BLAM. BLAM. BLAM. BLAM. BLAM. BLAM. BLAM. BLAM...

"Miss," Cleo whispers at first. "Miss, wake up. Its time'ta go home." Cleo motherly shakes Beth's shoulder. Beth bolts awake from her nightmare having fallen asleep on her small stack of onion papers littering the top of the Katherine Hotel's front desk counter. Beth briskly wipes her tussled hair from her face as she quickly looks about her surroundings.

Realizing that she is fine and unharmed, Beth stands from behind the front desk counter, shuffles her onion papers into a stack and neatly files them under the counter. "Good evening, Cleo. Have a few good days off?" Beth manages to mumble out.

"Yes, miss. My brother came out to see me from Kansas City."

"That's marvelous. Does he have a place to stay? He can always take up a room here…at no charge."

"Thank-you, miss. He's set'lin' in fine'n my room. We've shar'd smaller livin' room. Only be stayin' a few days."

"Well, I look forward to meeting him," Beth slides the hotel's guest registrar across the front desk counter toward Cleo who stands along side of her employer. "A handful of miners passing through, few gamblers headed for California and Doc's upstairs sleeping it off…"

"Again!" Cleo and Beth say in unison as they giggle like gitty school girls. The thumping of boot steps quiets the pair of ladies as Jay strolls inward through the opened front door of the hotel. Jay swaggers forward, leaning his elbow in an arrogant manner on the front desk counter facing Beth and Cleo.

"Cleo," Jay grins. "G'evening, Beth."

"Evenin', Sheriff," Cleo shifts her weight from side to side. Beth's eyes bulge from their sockets. She turns pale with terror and fright. Beth's nightmare is coming true! Without a word, Beth bolts from behind the front desk counter, slams into the corner of a wall, dashing down the hallway of the first floor away from Cleo and Jay.

Beth frantically glances behind her shoulder as she crashes into a vacant hotel suite at the end of the hall. She pauses a brief moment to stare at Jay then hurls herself in through the suite, slamming and locking the door behind herself. Cleo and Jay exchange odd looks, "All I said was "g'evening, Beth."

"I'll check in on'er in a bit," Cleo muffles her laughter slightly amused at the two lovebirds in denial.

"Thank-you, Cleo," Jay turns and heads toward the opened front door. "G'night."

"Night, Sheriff," Cleo shuffles some papers across the front desk top, still hiding her amusement and laughter.

Jay steps off the wooden planked boardwalk in front of the Katherine Hotel and makes his way slightly onto Main Street. Scattered cowboys and wranglers lead their horses on foot along the well worn street. The corner lampposts flicker their light downward casting shadows over the few strolling pedestrians. Jay turns with a nod and a wave toward the sheriff's office and jail down the street.

The newly appointed deputy, Morris Allen, is a young buck, no more than twenty-two years old. Full of confidence and sure-firedness. Morris smiles with a wave back toward Jay indicating everything's under control at the ole' jailhouse. Jay turns and follows Trigger's up-beat ragtime melody seeping out into the street from Bell's just down the way. Jay nods and smiles toward a rancher leading his cargo wagon out of town with the covered wagon brimming with supplies.

Jay calmly swings the batwing doors open and enters. Bell's saloon is moderately filled with numerous tables surrounded by dealers, wranglers and gamblers. The pitcher tosses the trio of dice off in the far corner of the chuck-a-luck table with a pair of gamblers facing him. Across the central walkway, pairs of businessmen and hustlers hover around the billiard tables. Trigger pounds out his repertoire of tunes on the piano at the foot of the staircase leading up the upper mezzanine and rooms.

Dancehall girls mill their way in and out of the establishment, trying to temp their "men" to take them upstairs before they loose all their money. Jay's manner is smooth and polite. Making his way along the central opened area toward the bar along the far wall. Robert continues to scamper along the backside of the bar, pouring drinks, cutting off the heads of frothy beers and taking a shot or two for himself from time to time.

Bell gives Jay a playful wink merely standing at the end of the bar looking out toward Trigger, the billiard tables, poker tables, chuck-a-luck dice game in the far corner and the girls wheeling their trade. Jay plops down on a stool next to Mr. Fuller at the end of the bar. "Evenin', Mr. Fuller."

"Sheriff," Mr. Fuller replies with an obvious slur.

"'Nother round here, Robert," Jay calls out in a tone so is not to annoy Robert too much with his order.

"So, 'ows the 'lil misses this evening?" Mr. Fuller swings his head in Jay's general direction. Jay has no clue what Mr. Fuller is talking about, with the "deer in wagon trail" look on his face.

"What's that, Mr. Fuller?" Jay asks. Robert slides the pair of flat beers and shots of whiskey in front of them, pauses with a concerned look then returns to his other patrons sitting across from the bar.

"Said, 'ows the 'lil lady feeling?"

"Reckon she's alright," Jay takes a swig of beer. "Why, Mr. Fuller? Is there sump'thn I should know?" Mr. Fuller slams the whiskey shot down his throat and chases it with a gulp of beer.

"If ya don't know now, ya will," Mr. Fuller laughs.

"What're you talkin' 'bout, Mr. Fuller?"

"Hells bells, Lewis," Bell quickly interrupts facing the two from the opposite side of the bar. "Think you've said quite enuff. Now, finish your beer'n be on your way!" Nearly sulking, Mr. Fuller slides the rest of the stale beer down his throat, staggers to a stance placing his black hat upon his head, attempts to tip his hat toward Bell then turns and sways toward the swinging batwing doors.

"What was Mr. Fuller talkin' 'bout, Bell?" Jay asks sipping on his beer.

"You never mind'im. He's corned as usual," Bell tries to shift Jay's thoughts to another matter.

"Prob'ly right," Jay pauses. "One more round then I'll be off."

"Comin' right up, Sheriff," Bell smiles turning to pour Jay another shot of whiskey.

"'Sheriff'. That's right. I'm the Sheriff," Jay gloats to himself. He slightly turns about on his stool glancing around the brisk activity filling Bell's. "Wonder if I'll ever get used't bein' called that…"

Fitch steps up from Trask's cellar totting his bedroll under one arm. In his other hand, the book of "MYTHS AND LEGENDS". He glances down at the book in his hand with a slight smile, then tenderly places it onto the dinning area table top. "Fitch!" Trask bellows out from below in the cellar. Fitch turns to see Trask appearing from below with several black and dark colored horse blankets in hand. Stepping up onto the main wooden planked floor, Trask and Fitch face each other. "Here, you might need these."

"For what?"

"Never know. Shade's mighty hard to find in some parts 'round here." Fitch fidgets a moment searching for something to say.

"I'll pay you back for the lamb'n the barn door."

"The door and the lamb can be replaced… my hospitality cannot," Trask solemnly responds. "You'll keep changin', Fitch. Once you've had human blood, there'll be no turnin' back. I don't need a book to tell me that," Trask shows Fitch the door. "Don't worry 'bout the lamb or the barn door. Don't come back here. If you do, I'll have'ta kill you."

"From what that book says, you'cn try," Fitch says trying to ease the moment.

"Yes, I'll have'ta try," Trask extends out his hand.

"Thank-you, Mr. Bailey," Fitch respectfully takes Trask's hand and gentlemanly shakes it. Taking his bedroll and graciously given horse blankets, Fitch turns and exits. Trask slowly follows behind remaining at the door jam looking outward into the night.

Already saddled, Blaze waits patiently along the foot of the porch. Fitch ties down the bedroll and blankets toward the rear of the saddle then swoops himself upward into the saddle without

240

using the foot pegs. Without another word, Fitch coaxes Blaze onward, away from the Trask home, out... out into the darkness.

With Blaze at a mere stroll, Fitch looks over his shoulder. Trask is nowhere to be seen along his property, around the corral or barn or even any area along his porch. From inside the log home, the last kerosene lantern is blown out. Emptiness with no shadows covering the home. All is quiet and still. Fitch turns forward in the saddle and coaxes Blaze onward leading toward the treeline in front of them and away from the homestead and schoolhouse.

Fitch seems at ease with the soothing blanket of night. Blaze trots along the fading pathway through the wooded area with cascading light beaming down from the nearing full moon overhead. A slight motion draws Fitch's attention from behind them. Looking over his shoulder, Steele walks at a quick pace to catch up with them. Fitch rears back on the reigns causing Blaze to halt. Likewise, Steele halts in his tracks waiting for Fitch to continue forward.

Fitch coaxes Blaze forward with Steele following suit, closing the gap between them. Again, Fitch pulls back on the reigns halting Blaze. Steele pauses looking up at Fitch wondering what the foolish man is doing. Fitch coaxes Blaze forward along the narrowing trail. Steele moves along, swiftly catching up with Fitch and Blaze, now walking exactly along side of them. Fitch glances down toward Steele then runs his fingers through Blaze's smoky mane. "Looks like we've got a travelin' companion, Blaze." Fitch glances down toward Steele following along side, "I reckon you come along with the package, eh? Night sight. Hearin'. 'Lergic't sun. Wolf," Fitch pauses a moment. "Reckon every Dead Man Walkin' needs a Hound of Hell." Steele obediently barks up toward Fitch then suddenly stops in his tracks. "What?" Steele barks again as Fitch draws Blaze to a stop along the outskirts of a small clearing.

Fitch looks into the clearing to see the outlines of figures or images scattered along the bloody ground. Blaze slightly becomes uneasy at first, then settles down. Fitch gazes into the clearing, seeing the ruthless carnage of the barbarically slaughtered wolf pack... Steele's wolf pack.

The wolf carcasses are recklessly scattered throughout the bloody area, with heads ripped off of their torsos, front and hind limbs scattered about, maimed hind ends several yards away from their forefronts. Fitch looks down at his newly acquired guardian, "What a pair we make." Blaze snorts. "Sorry, what a trio..." Fitch coaxes Blaze forward with Steele walking along side of them as a Hound of Hell would to his nocturnal master.

The wooded area and treeline has far but passed behind them. The outstretching desert is all that faces them. Fitch looks up beyond the horizon to see the first traces of the daunting sunrise. Nervous now, Fitch looks about the surrounding landscape for any cover from the sun. "Reckon this's what Trask meant," Fitch halts Blaze. Steele looks up at Fitch and Blaze then obediently and heals.

Fitch loosely fastens Blaze's reigns to a tumbleweed, like that'll keep Blaze from running off if he really wanted to. Fitch unties the bedroll and horse blankets from the rear end of the saddle. He tosses all but one of the horse blankets over Blaze's head, shoulders and hind section leaving only the bedroll and one dark colored horse blanket for himself.

Fitch plops down onto the soft sand and scoops several piles off to the side making a slight grave for himself. Sliding into the hole and laying halfway down, Fitch covers his bedroll over himself. Reaching over to the side, Fitch gathers the small mounds of sand over his legs, waist then torso. Laying fully backward, he tosses the rest of his bedroll over his chest and head area still with his arms and hands outward.

Unable to see what he is doing, but merely feeling the earth, Fitch pulls the last of the small sand mounds over his chest and head area, tucking his arms in afterward. Blaze snorts under his camouflage of dark blankets protecting him from the oncoming furry of the desert sun. Steele paces several times around Blaze's legs then settles in directly underneath Blaze, hoping his larger companion will cause shade from his under belly.

The late afternoon sun is merciless. Blaze has lowered his head with his body heated from the earlier day. Steele pants heavily, under Blaze's under belly shielded by a sliver of shade. The sun dips lower and lower toward the horizon. Soft clouds float effortlessly through the sky. A cooling desert breeze begins to cool Blaze and Steele yet still no sign of Fitch emerging from his burial of sand.

A desert rattlesnake slithers along the cooling sand. Steele cocks his head upward looking at the vile creature as it approaches. Blaze remains still and calm under the covered horse blankets. The rattlesnake senses something ahead... Blaze and Steele. A threat? A meal? What does the rattlesnake sense. The scaly rattler flicks its tongue mere feet from Steele and Blaze's left hind legs. Steele growls.

The rattlesnake rears up its head, feverishly shakes its tail and lunges forward to strike at Blaze and Steele in defense. With lightening speed, Fitch thrusts his hand out from below his makeshift burial sight and grasps the snake just below the head. Slowly... slowly... the sun dips past the horizon leaving only amber and orange colored clouds in its wake. Fitch leans upward from his waist tossing his covering bedroll and mounds of sand off of himself. Looking at the wiggling rattlesnake in his hand, he looks up toward Blaze then toward Steele. "Hungry? I sure am!" Fitch exclaims.

Fitch is slightly amused at the rattlesnake, flipping and flopping to escape from his grasp. Fitch bares his fangs and buries them deep into the snake's undercarriage. Blood easily flows from the snake into Fitch's mouth... oozing down his throat. *Ah, that feels better,* Fitch thinks. "Here!" Fitch tosses the dead reptile onto the sand toward Steele. "Not much, but it'll do for now."

Steele circles the dead rattlesnake and sniffs it a moment. Steele crouches down and begins to devour the reptile making sure not to consume any of the poisonous areas. Fitch stands, taking his sandy bedroll in hand and shakes it off. He makes his way toward Blaze and fatherly runs his hand down his side, removing the covering horse blankets. "How you doin', boy?" Blaze snorts.

Fitch rounds the saddles bags, reaches in and takes two leather scoops of the depleting oats. He tosses them down into a pile in the sand. Odd, Blaze and Steele, a pair of unalike creatures, eating their meals side by side. Fitch strolls along side of Blaze picking up the bedroll and horse blankets, rolling them tightly then fastening them to the rear of Blaze's saddle.

"Whatta ya' think?" Fitch declares somewhat to himself but still wanting a reaction of response from Blaze and Steele. Deep inside of the valley below, a flickering town is seen. Its singular main street cuts through the central of facing rows of buildings and facades. Not much to look at. Like Purgatory was some fifteen years ago. Blaze shakes his mane up and down, he could use some fresh rations and feed. Fitch looks down toward Steele looking forward to the town below. Not much to offer for a silver backed wolf. "Stay close," Fitch orders his daylight guardian. Fitch flaps the reigns causing Blaze to move forward and down the slight slope of the hillside heading toward the town below.

Culver City… a growing mining town. Rumors of silver deposits around the area have spawn a flux of population. Not one the local law enforcement would want. Looters and road bandits. Stagecoach robbers and cattle wrestlers. Horse thieves and gambling hustlers. Fitch will fit right in.

The sun has yet to make an appearance. Fitch swings his leg over the horn of the saddle and dismounts. His heavy boots sound up along the slopping ramp of the train depot. *Jingle-jingle.*

The wooden platform is barren of all life forms. Well stacked trunks, crates and various luggage bags are lined up against the wall of the extended building running the length of the train platform. Fitch strolls to the caged and barred ticket window to see a young man wearing a small brimmed hat, coat and matching trousers, slouched back in his chair... fast asleep.

Fitch knocks his fist on the narrow ticket table spanning his side and the inner room of the asleep teller. There is no response from the young teller. Fitch knocks his fist again with more urgency seeing the faint glimmer of the rising sun in the distance. The teller starts awake, wipes his eyes and yawns at Fitch. "Not open yet," the teller fumbles his speech. "Closed 'till seven."

"I need to send a telegram."

"Said we're closed, mister," the teller responds with a snotty tone. "Waitin' on the train. It's due in at seven."

"What's keeping you from sending a telegram until then?" Fitch stares blankly at the teller. The young man sits up in his chair and gazes back into Fitch's deep reddening eyes. Almost in a hypnotic way.

"N-nothin', mister."

""Nothin'"," Fitch glares. In an instant, the teller springs to his feet and faces Fitch from the inner area of the barred window. The teller takes a piece of paper from a small stack and pen in hand.

"Who'd ya want this to go to?"

"Sheriff's office in Purgatory, New Mexico Territory. "I'm doing well and will be back to town once business is settled. Sheriff Fitch Woolley"," Fitch instructs the teller as he writes down the message.

"Will that be all, Sheriff?" the teller finishes writing and looks upward. All the young man sees is the silver backed wolf's tail flopping from side to side in the darkness heading down along the dim train platform. No sheriff. No horse. Just the wagging tail of the departing silver backed wolf. The teller takes the message toward the telegraph machine and begins tapping and clicking the information across the wire... from Culver City to Purgatory. "Only take a few hours to get there," the teller says to himself.

245

Fitch appears from the opened doors of the local livery nearing the end of town, like most liveries are. Steele trots along side of Fitch as they make their way down along the center of the main street cutting through town. The shops and business are locked and closed. Faint haunting piano music seeps from the innards of the sole watering hole, "SIDNEY'S BAR AND GRILLS". Sparse cowboys ride in groups from the saloon heading out back onto the range. There are no stagecoaches nor cargo wagons along the main street. Culver City has yet to awake from the night.

Fitch steps up onto the wooden boardwalk of Sidney's Bar and Grills, pauses a moment to listen to the soft piano playing. Reminds Fitch of Trigger. *"Wonder how that boy's doing?"* Fitch thinks as he swings open the rotting batwing doors and enters. Steele looks about a moment, circles himself then sits in a statuesque manner directly outside of the doorway of the saloon. Looking onward and outward. Never swaying.

"Come back later!" Sidney, the stout barkeep lets out from behind the extended bar at the far end of the saloon. "Not open 'till nine!" Fitch tosses his attention to the elderly black man sitting at the piano plunking out the soft melody. He's dressed in a worn black and white suit, still probably paying for it from years of toiling at the black and white keys.

"Train arrives at seven. Saloon don't open 'till nine. Reckon Purgatory's a boomin' city compared to this place!" Fitch thinks to himself as he continues to walk through the haphazardly placed poker tables filling the inner opened area of the saloon. "Do you have a room for the night?"

""The night", mister? Sun's 'bout to come up," Sidney pauses seeing that Fitch is not amused as he continues to approach. "Room's us'llay comes with a girl. Come back at nine like I said. I can set you up with both," Sidney barks at Fitch still approaching the near side of the extended bar.

"I don't <u>have</u> until nine," Fitch steps up to the bar and faces Sidney. The fowl smelling bartender begins to become nervous at first, then seems to slip into a slight trance.

"Think I'cn make 'ception from time't time," Sidney motions to the staircase leading up to the second floor around the wooden railing lining the overlooking mezzanine. "Third door on the left. Need anything, let me know," Sidney humbly replies. Fitch nods with a polite manner as he approaches the foot of the rickety staircase.

"Bartender, 'bout your sign outside. I've seen the "bar" but where are the "grills"?", Fitch asks as he begins to climb the stairs.

"Hired me a stupid sign maker a few years back. Couldn't spell worth a spit. Sign shoudda said "Bar and Girls". Fool was run outta town afore he could fix it. The place'n sign kinda stuck," Sidney angrily answers.

Laughing to himself, Fitch reaches the platform of the mezzanine then looks over the railing, "Much obliged, barman." Fitch strolls down the hallway cluttered with worn and tired looking dancehall girls heading for the third door on the left. The ragged ladies of the night smile and wink at Fitch attempting to draw his attention. Fitch politely motions away, finds his room and quietly slips inside.

Fitch closes the door behind himself and looks around the plain and drab room. A dresser stands along the far wall with a wash basin and pitcher atop. The single bed stands along the opposite wall made up with rustic blankets. A cracked open door leads to a small closet across from the main door. At the far wall along the dresser, a glass paned window with lace curtains.

Fitch moves across the wooden planked floor toward the window and peers outside onto the lower central street. Bustling cargo wagons and sparse stagecoaches begin to roll into town with the activity beginning to quicken. Over the façade tops of the facing buildings on the far side of the street, the sun's amber rays brighten. Sunrise is mere minutes away. Fitch draws the lace curtains allowing the impending sunlight inward. *"This won't do,"* Fitch thinks to himself.

Quickly, Fitch shuffles across the floor toward the bed, rips the blankets from it then slides under the bed covering himself with the blanket. *"Blast it!"* Fitch wallows on the hard floor. The sun has risen. Rays of sunlight begin to pour into the room. Closer and closer toward Fitch. The rays cover the dresser and wash basin, across the floor and touches the heel of Fitch's boot…

Entering wranglers, gamblers and cowboys take note of the silver backed wolf standing post at the rotting swinging batwing doors of Sidney's Bar and Grills. Steele glances upward at the passing humans as they toss concerned looks in the canine's direction. Steele remains steadfast at his post with the midday's sun sprawling across the saloon.

Sidney storms up the staircase, turns the corner and shoves his way past a small flock of working dancehall girls. He briskly knocks on Fitch's door and allows himself inward, "Hey, mister! Mister." Sidney enters and stops several feet inside of the room. "You've gotta do sump'thn 'bout that dog'f yours," Sidney commands.

The bed is unmade with the primitive blankets tossed across the lumpy mattress. The sunlight beams throughout the room in every corner and even under the bed. There is no sign of Fitch. As if he were disturbing the dead, Sidney quietly tiptoes backward out the door, closing it gently. As he makes his way down the hallway, Sidney motions toward the scattered dancehall girls. "Did ya see this feller leave?" One by one, the girls shake their heads "no". Sidney scratches his head and makes his way across the mezzanine then down the rickety staircase.

"I'll be hogtied," Jay whispers to himself.

"Everythin' alright, Sheriff," the train depot teller asks Jay.

"Yeah, kid," Jay responds with a seemingly disappointed tone. "Everything's just fine." Jay stares blankly at the received telegraph. The teller returns to his stack of papers and train tickets behind the barred window as Jay turns and strolls in a slight daze along the train depot platform.

Main Street is filled with cargo wagons and stagecoaches with swarms of pedestrians criss-crossing from boardwalk to boardwalk.

"G'afternoon," Beth looks up from her plume and sheet of onion paper on the front desk counter. Jay enters further into the lobby with the telegraph in his hand lowered to his side. Ever so slowly, Beth's cheerful greeting turns to concern with a slight scowl across her brow. "Jay, what is it?"

"Fitch's alive," Jay whispers.

"What!" Beth exclaims at first with joy and enthusiasm. Jay slowly hands Beth the telegraph. She grabs it from his hand and quickly reads. Her facial expression is all Jay needs to see. The scowl transforms to enlightenment. Nearly with tears of joy welling up in her eyes, Beth looks up from the telegraph toward Jay. He is quiet and solemn. "Oh, James," Beth responds with an apologetic tone. "I...I...," the smile from her face is gone. Without another word, Jay turns and slithers outside, swiftly disappearing into the commotion of Main Street.

Jay angrily flings the sheriff's office door open and stomps inside. The three jail cells are vacant of prisoners. The room is still and quiet. The filled shotgun and rifle rack invites him to take one and... Jay plops himself into the wheeled chair behind the main desk and opens the bottom drawer. Taking a bottle of whiskey from inside, Jay leaves the large shot glass in the bottom of the drawer.

Jay raises the bottle to his lips and chugs more than half of the intoxicating liquid down his throat. Resting the bottle in his lap, Jay stares angrily at the shotgun rack, "Why did Fitch have to be alive?" Jay mumbles before taking another drink.

"What're you doin' in here, doll?" Bell asks as Beth approaches the far end of the bar. Robert makes his way back and forth from behind the bar pouring and serving up drinks to the scattered patrons. The poker tables are sparsely occupied with only one of the three billiard tables in use. Trigger remains at the piano, plunking out a soft melody along the black and white keys. Beth hands Bell the telegraph.

"Hell's bells!" she exclaims reading aloud. ""Sheriff's office, Purgatory, New Mexico Territory. I'm doin' well and will be back as soon as business is finished. Sheriff Fitch Woolley.""" Bell turns toward Robert, the surrounding patrons and Trigger across the room. "Fitch's alive!" Bell declares.

"Next round's on me!" Robert shouts with cheers rising up from the saloon. Bell looks around the room to see proud slaps on the shoulders, handshakes and general celebration. Fitch is very much loved and missed… although no one wanted to participate in the posse to go out and find him. Bell's smile focuses on Beth. A concerned look. An expression of regret? Of… of confusion.

"Elizabeth," Bell leans in toward Beth, motherly touching her shoulder. "I know exactly what you're going through.

"How could you, Bell?" Robert grins from ear to ear sliding a pair of filled whiskey shot glasses in front of the two ladies. Robert winks at Bell then returns to his patrons, pouring them their free round of drinks. Bell takes her shot and raises it toward Beth.

"Bottom's up," Bell smiles. Beth slightly pushes the shot of whiskey away from herself.

"I can't, Bell."

"One's not gonna kill ya."

Beth reluctantly takes the glass and respectfully raises it toward Bell. The ladies tap their glasses together then slide their shots down their throats. After placing her glass onto the top of the bar, Bell takes a hold of Beth's arm and moves her to the side slightly under the dual staircase leading upstairs to the "entertaining" rooms. Bell leans even closer in toward Beth speaking under the ongoing piano playing of Trigger.

"'While back, I was a few years older than you are now. I found myself in love with a good man. Was a school teacher. He courted me for a spell when another man came to town."

"Robert?"

"Yes. I was twixed. I had me a good man but I wanted the other. Hell's bells, I wanted'em both... and I did. This went on for awhile 'till the Mayor's wife found out 'bout it. Bitch! So's't keep it quiet, the good man left town. Wasn't run out like the stories tell. He left cuz' he loved me so."

"Mr. Bailey."

Bell responds with a quiet nod. "It's not that I don't love Robert, I do. You have't make up your own mind, dear. Can't tell you what't do. Fitch <u>and</u> Jay both love you. Be honest with'em both. You might hurt one of 'em now but its better in the end."

"Bell?" Beth timidly asks. "You ever wish you'd stayed with Mr. Bailey?" Bell reaches across the bar and takes the nearest patron's double filled shot glass and slams it down her throat. Bell stares Beth dead in the eye.

"Every damn day..."

"He's'a mighty fine horse, mister," the blacksmith snorts making his way around the glowing furnace and beaten anvil. Fitch strolls through the central walkway of the livery stables making his way toward Blaze feeding from a trough of fresh oats. Fitch reaches across the stable gate and runs his fingers through Blaze's mane.

"Thank-you. He's not just a horse... he's my friend," Fitch corrects the humbled blacksmith. Steele barks at the opened door of the livery as he wags his tail. "Go on," Fitch orders. Steele cocks his head upward a moment, turns then disappears into the fading sunset.

"Neat trick, mister," the blacksmith chuckles taking a worn horseshoe in hand.

"Wanna see another?" Fitch mockingly asks. The blacksmith backs away from the opened furnace as Fitch approaches and glares at the stout man. Fitch thrusts his bare hand into the furnace allowing the intense flames to burn and boil his flesh. The blacksmith cowers from the obvious pain and foul stench of the smoldering flesh.

Fitch removes his hand from the flames and holds up his charred limb in front of the blacksmith. The blacksmith's eyes widen in terror and fear more than in amazement. Fitch's burned flesh molds and cover's his hand. Miraculously and swiftly healing itself. In a matter of moments, Fitch's charred hand is as it was, a simple scar in the center from Jesse's bullet wound. "Take care of my horse," Fitch commands.

"Yes, sir," the blacksmith fumbles as he backs away ever further. Fitch politely nods, turns and exits through the opened livery doors out into the growing darkness. Fitch stands there a moment, taking a deep breath. The street is thinning out, less and less pedestrians cluttering the wooden boardwalks.

Fitch seems to uncontrollably close his eyes. Blurred images fill his head, swooning his thoughts. He suddenly opens his eyes, focusing on Sidney's Bar and Grills. *"That's the place,"* Fitch thinks. "'Bout time for a drink," he says aloud to himself as his feet begin to carry him forward without his knowing. Sidney's draws close with wranglers and gamblers making a path toward the swinging batwing doors for him like the parting Red Sea.

"Whiskey! Leave the bottle," Fitch orders Sidney who nervously obeys. The saloon bar is filled with wranglers and well dressed business men. The poker tables are half filled with gamblers as the dealers toss out the various cards of the ongoing hands. Sidney, wearing a stained white shirt, tan trousers and an apron, asks for no money nor form of payment as he slides the filled whiskey bottle and filled whiskey shot glass in front of Fitch.

Fitch takes the filled whiskey glass to his lips and pauses. He raises the glass to his nostrils and inhales deeply. The whiskey… the whiskey. The smell haunts Fitch as he takes the filled glass and bottle from the bar, turns and scans the active saloon. The far table in the dimly lit corner is surrounded by three extremely large wranglers, each with a six-shooter holstered low on their hips. Fitch cuts through the room heading toward the three hulking men. "I believe you're sitting at my table."

The wranglers look up at Fitch and laugh. "Mister, think you might wanna sit somewhere's else," sneers the first.

"Think he's bin nippin' 'lil too much," says the second.

"Give'em the table," grumbles the third.

"Whatta ya talkin' 'bout?"

"Give'em... the... table," the third motions his hand below the table. The other pair of wranglers slowly lean over and look under the table. Steele has his jaws opened and locked on the third wrangler's crotch. His hands tremble at his sides. The pair of wranglers rise up from below the table and quickly stand. "Table's yours, mister," the first pulls out his chair for Fitch.

Steele releases his jaws from the third wrangler as the second wrangler slides in closer to his companion. The three wranglers shuffle to the side never taking their eyes off of Fitch and the silver backed wolf as they swiftly exit.

Fitch sets the filled shot glass and bottle of whiskey onto the table top and sits. Steele appears from under the table and sits along Fitch, at his side, awaiting another opportunity to assist his master. Fitch raises the filled shot glass of whiskey to his nose and deeply inhales again. The aroma is refreshing, although he will never be able to taste the liquor again.

"What am I to do? Fitch is alive and he'll be coming home soon. Will he still want me? What am I to do about Jay? I've promised myself to him for the Valentine's Dance. Am I a harlot? Should I have waited longer after Fitch had not returned? It's only been a month's time. Did I rush into courting with Jay? I feel so... lost."

Beth reaches the bottom of the page of onion paper and draws another from the bottom of the stack. Taking her plume in hand, she sighs, gazing at the well dressed couples and pedestrians passing along the wooden planked boardwalk in front of the Katherine Hotel. Taking a sip of her coffee, Beth sets down the mug and resumes writing.

"I had another dream last night. I should say it was more of a nightmare. The same nightmare only it was worse. The campfire was warming along the shore of the river. Jay and I were... "bathing" in the water when a hideous grey wolf invaded the camp. "

"Jay went for his gun when Fitch appeared from the shadows. Something was different about him. He looked the same however I felt something had changed inside of him. He turned in to a terrible creature. Ruthless and vile. The creature, Fitch, sneered as he drew both of his guns and opened fire on Jay and myself. But that wasn't the last of it."

"This foul thing hovered over our naked bodies on the shoreline of the river, feeding on us. Devouring our flesh while we were still alive. The grey wolf seemed to merely laugh at us as the beast sat awaiting for Fitch, the creature, to finish us off. I cannot speak of these things to anyone for they would think me mad."

"Are these dreams, dare I say nightmares, a curse or a cause for my encouraging Jay to pursue infidelity? I have waited so long for Fitch to ask for my hand and

now I feel I have foiled the opportunity with my own reckless lust for Jay."

"I have to tell him. "Him". Which one? If I were to tell Fitch he may leave without notice. If I tell Jay, I would be deceptive for my lust and my actions are two entirely different matters. What am I to do? I'm so lost..."

Light footsteps enter the opened front door of the Katherine Hotel's lobby. "G'evenin', miss," Cleo cheerfully calls out as she rounds the end of the front desk counter.

"Good evening, Cleo," Beth attempts a smile as she stacks her onion papers and stuffs them under the counter. "The usual's going on," Beth slides the opened hotel guest registrar across the counter toward Cleo.

"Feelin' alright, miss?"

"A little under the weather, that's all," Beth gently presses her opened palm against the side of her stomach.

"There's a cure fer that, miss," Cleo stands on the far side of the front desk counter as Beth collects her bag and begins to head for the front door to leave.

"Cure for what, Cleo?"

"You're tummy pains."

"What's that?"

"Aspirin."

"I've taken all the pills and potions that Doc's given me."

"No, miss," Cleo responds with a playful smirk. "Don' take the aspirin. You put it 'tween yer knees." Beth stands at the doorway wondering what in tar nation Cleo is talking about. With a polite smile, Beth waves her hand behind herself as she exits.

"Good-night, Cleo."

"G'night, miss."

Beth steps out onto the boardwalk. The corner lampposts have already been lit with apposing up-beat music echoing from opposite ends of Main Street from the Stardust Saloon and of Bell's. Beth makes her way around the corner toward the alley where her horse and chaise await. As she nearly passes into the darkness, Beth spies Jay leaning against the upward supporting beam of the sheriff's office and jail down the street.

Jay eagerly smiles with a tip of his hat. Beth reluctantly returns the smile with a gaunt wave of her hand. She's unsure as if to encourage Jay along or not. Beth quickly turns the corner and darts into the alley. Jay folds his arms and scans Main Street for any trouble. Only sparse pedestrians and a sole stagecoach are seen. From the backsides of the facing row of façade buildings across the street, Jay watches Beth steer her chaise out of town, avoiding any contact or conversation with him.

Bustling activity fills Sidney's Bar and Grills. Every poker table is filled with gamblers and cowboys as the dealers toss out the probably marked playing cards. Up-beat piano playing soars through the cigar smoke filled air. Dancehall girls make their rounds throughout the filled tables attempting to coax a little business for themselves.

Sidney shuffles behind the extended bar tending to his facing row of patrons consuming the bar in front of himself. Causally looking upward from a pouring bottle of rum, Sidney spots Fitch sitting toward the back of the bar in the dim corner. Still, the bottle of whiskey and filled shot whiskey glass remain on the table in front of him. The odd sight of the silver backed wolf healing at his side. A dancehall girl mingles her way through the maze of tables toward Fitch.

Over the noise of the ongoing poker tables and uproar of the piano music, Sidney can't make out the conversation. Fitch merely smiles up at the dancehall girl and declines her company. The dancehall girl turns, making her way back onto the main floor, searching for another prospect. Fitch raises the filled whiskey shot glass to his lips and sniffs the alcohol... never tasting it.

From his side, Steele lets out a deep and low growl. Fitch takes a last whiff of the whiskey and sets the glass down onto the table top. Sidney glances upward a moment to see Fitch and the silver backed wolf in the dimly lit far corner. The swinging batwing doors fly open drawing Sidney's attention.

The tall, dark haired Indian wears a wide brimmed, grey Stetson hat. Dust rolls off his shoulders from his caballero jacket with countless knives and bladed weapons sheathed and sticking out of his leather belt. The handle of an extremely large Bowie knife is seen tucked in the front of the faded leather belt of the Indian as he saunters toward the middle of the bar. Sidney looks away from the native toward the dimly lit far corner just for a moment. Fitch and the silver backed wolf are gone. "What kin I git ya, mister?" Sidney asks the tall Indian.

"I'd like a room with a view," Chote' raises his eyebrow toward Sidney.

"This here's Culver City. Ain't no views."

Chote' slightly turns away from the bar and motions toward a trio of dancehall girls milling around the nearest occupied poker table. "They'll do." Sidney gives a slight whistle across the room causing the dancehall girls to turn and begin to approach. Chote' opens his arms widely, wrapping them around the three ladies of the night. The four turn and face Sidney. "Give the ladies whatever they want," Chote' orders. The dancehall girls giggle as Sidney quickly begins to pour their drinks.

"Excuse me," Fitch growls in a low voice coming up from behind Chote' at the bar. "Is that a knife handle stickin' outta yer pants or're you just glad to see me?" Chote' quickly grasps the handle of his Bowie knife tucked in his leather belt and turns around to stand face to face with Fitch, the sheriff he and the rest of The Cougar Gang had left for dead.

257

CHAPTER IX

"I see you've healed up well, Sheriff," Chote' nearly whispers as he backs away from the bar, drawing the front flaps of his jacket back revealing his numerous bladed weapons and Bowie knife. "Sheriff?" the filled saloon thinks. The trio of dancehall girls quickly shuffle away from Chote' leaving him and Fitch standing face to face nearly twenty feet apart. "Don't know quite what to think about yer new getup though." Chote' pauses, "Preacher?"

"Just a loan 'till I get my belongings back," Fitch stares blankly into Chote's eyes. "You're wearing my hat."

"Don't think a grey Stetson'll go with black."

"I'll make do," Fitch pauses a moment. "I'd like my hat back… please."

"Needs blocking."

"I know. Was waitin' to git'ta that."

"You'll have'ta wait a'lil longer then," Chote' replies with a sneer. One could hear a pin drop. Sidney makes his way along the back side of the bar standing at a distance from the pair of confronting men. Chote' looks over Fitch. He is unarmed with no bladed weapons nor any revolvers or pistols. With lightening speed, Chote' draws a medium sized knife from his belt and hurls it toward Fitch.

Effortlessly, Fitch whips his hands upward and clasps his scarred palms together against the flinging blade, catching it in midair. Fitch takes the knife and sticks the blade deep into the top of the bar. Chote' draws a pair of larger knives from his belt and throws them at Fitch who, without taking his eyes off of Chote's glare, bats the knives away from himself, leaving them rattling to the wooden planked floor.

258

Chote' begins to nervously backing away from Fitch along the near side of the bar. Step by step, Fitch follows, beginning to close the gap between them. With fists of fury, Chote' draws all the remaining blades but the Bowie knife from his belt, frantically throwing them at Fitch. One by one as Fitch continues to approach Chote', the thrown knives are batted away from harm, clinking and rattling to the floor.

With the last quartette of flying knives heading toward Fitch, Chote' draws his Bowie knife and with all his might, throws it toward Fitch. The extended blade of the large knife powerfully imbeds itself deep into Fitch's upper left chest all the way to the hilt. Fitch calmly stands there facing Chote'. All eyes of the saloon bulge. Jaws drop. Fitch, the sheriff-preacher, should be growing cold, dead on the floor.

Chote' has backed his way against the far wall. Fitch continues to slowly approach him, pausing a mere ten feet away. Fitch carefully reaches up his right hand, defiantly pulling the Bowie knife from his chest by the handle. Oddly, there is very little blood along the extended blade. A mere incision is left behind from the knife cutting through the fabric of the black jacket. Fitch flips the Bowie knife in the air, catching it by the blade then hurls it toward Chote'.

K-THWAP.

The Bowie knife is thrust through Chote's chest and imbeds itself deep into the wall behind him, pinning Chote' to the wall. Chote' gasps for air. His life quickly slipping away from himself. Fitch defiantly walks toward Chote, standing inches away... face to face. "I did say, _please_." Fitch reaches up to Chote's chest and twists the blade several times. Chote' cries out in pain. The cowering saloon shutters.

Fitch rips the Bowie knife from Chote's chest. The tall Indian staggers a moment before falling forward against Fitch's shoulder. The sheriff-preacher remains steadfast for a moment then moves his shoulder to the side. Chote' blurts out one last breath of air then topples to the floor. Fitch turns to see the gaping mouths of the saloon. Sidney takes a large gulp of whiskey from the nearest bottle.

Fitch takes the toe of his boot and rolls Chote over. He leans over the slain Indian clutching onto the bloody Bowie knife. The overwhelming smell of fresh blood consumes him. Fitch trembles. He hasn't eaten since he fed on a wayward rattlesnake. Fitch takes the Bowie knife and wipes Chote's blood on the leg on the native's pant leg. Fitch moves the knife about himself and tucks it into the small of his back inside of his black preacher trousers.

Fitch turns, startling Sidney, the dancehall girls and the gamblers. Fitch strolls a moment toward the door then pauses, slightly leaning over. He takes the oversized grey Stetson hat in hand then stands upright. As he scans the terrified faces of the saloon, Fitch places the wide brimmed Stetson hat upon is head. "He was right," Fitch continues his route toward the swinging batwing doors. "The hat does need blocking…"

Steele waits patiently along the wooden planked boardwalk just outside of Sidney's Bar and Grills. Fitch slightly looks down at the befriended wolf and nods. Without a word, Fitch and Steele step off the boardwalk and begin making their way down the center of the central street toward the livery. Loud murmurs and muffled whispers of terror seep out from the saloon.

Fitch disappears into the darkness for a moment. Sidney is accompanied by a slew of gamblers, cowboys and dancehall girls exiting the saloon. They look in all directions for any trace of the mysterious sheriff-preacher. The soft sounds of an approaching horse draws their attention toward the far end of town.

Fitch rides high and proud with Blaze strutting past the saloon. Steele trots along side, growling at the foolish people peering out from the saloon. "For the great day of his wrath has come, and who is able to stand?"

Fitch nods and smiles, tipping his reacquired Stetson hat toward the frightened dancehall girls. Fitch eases back on the reigns, slightly maneuvering Blaze about so is to face the stunned onlookers. Sidney reluctantly waves as Fitch turns forward in the saddle, slightly slapping his reigns then turns Blaze, riding off into the darkness with his sliver backed wolf trotting along at his side.

The weather in Culver City in the early spring is mild. A cool breeze blows through the air with a brisk chill. Not much to do. Scattered cargo wagons file inward through the central street with their drivers halting in front of various general stores and supply shops. A sole rider gallops into town from the near side of the facing rows of façade buildings.

Spider maneuvers Diamond along the far side of the boardwalk, glancing about as he goes. Trying to be neat in appearance and manner, Spider slicks back his hair with spit in his hand. He suddenly heaves back on the reigns, stopping his stolen mount. Chote' has been placed in a pine coffin, propped up against the outside of Sidney's Bar and Grills.

Spider storms into the saloon with scattered gamblers sitting around sparse poker tables. The handful of dealers wearily toss out the poker cards with worn and tired looking dancehall girls milling about the nonprofitable tables. Spider slams himself against the near side of the bar facing Sidney, still working on his first pot of coffee. "What happen'?"

"Ta'what?" Sidney snorts back.

"Ta'the Indian outside!"

"El' Diablo Blanco," replies a large and sweaty Latino poker dealer. Spider whips around to the dealer for a glance, then back toward Sidney.

"What's'e sayin'!" Spider barks out.

""El' Diablo Blanco", means "The White Devil"," Sidney resumes cleaning his piles of shot glasses. "Sheriff came in yesterday. Dressed in black. Not much was said. That preacher fella-"

"Thought you said he was'a sheriff," Spider interrupts.

"No, dressed like a preacher but that Indian kept callin'im "Sheriff". They had few words. Indian tried killin' the preacher'r

261

sheriff then he took a knife in the chest all the way up'ta the hilt. *No* man shoudda walked away from that. But he did without a scratch on'im. As you'cn see, the Indian didn' fair so well. All that stranger said was'e wanted'is hat back."

"His hat?"

"Yeah. That Indian feller kept callin' the stranger "Sheriff". Really liked that hat. Kilt'em fer it," Sidney looks up from his soiled shot glasses. All he sees is a vacant spot where Spider had stood at the bar and the swinging batwing doors. A few moments later, Sidney hears the thundering hoof sounds of a horse… quickly departing town.

Miles of sand dunes cover the landscape. Sparse desert trees pop up from time to time with the blazing heat beating downward. The light winds toss waves of sand over and around the dunes leading out toward a shallow and narrow valley. A flickering image appears off in the distance, remaining motionless and quiet.

Blaze stands with head lowered and covered with the layered horse blankets about his head, shoulders, midsection and backside. Steele lays under his larger quadruped companion, panting in the shade from above. There is no trace of Fitch. No mine shaft to hide in. No fallen hollowed tree to sleep in. Nothing but miles of soft sand and rolling sand dunes.

Off along the horizon, a galloping figure is faintly seen through the waves of heat flowing across the surface of the sand. Spider trudges along Diamond over and around a series of sand dunes, focused on his trek. Blaze and Steele slightly look upward in Spider and Diamond's direction a moment then return to their daytime slumber. In an instant, Diamond's thundering hooves disappear over the last sand dune…

"Is it time to come out yet? Is this the price for immortality? If it is, I don't want it. I don't want to have anything'ta do with it." Fitch pauses in his head. *"Yet…the*

powers inside of me are growing. Chote' shoudda killed me with that knife of his but yet, I live."

"Was the book right? What _can_ kill me? Kill one of my kind? Are there any others like me or am I alone? Alone...gettin' kinda used't that. Instead of sleeping comfortably in my bed with Beth at my side, I'm napping in the middle of nowhere with my horse and a wolf to watch over me. What kinda life is that? Is this "thing" I've become a blessing or a curse? Visions of death keep burnin' through my head. Am I still a peace keeper, a lawman or have I passed on through to the other side? Revenge. Why is killing Cougar so important now?"

"This "thing" I've become seems to be leading me without control. I _have_ to kill Cougar now. But why? He is but a mere insect to me now. I can return to Purgatory, ask Beth for her hand and live out the rest of my life quietly keeping the peace. I can live a normal life..."

The desert sun dips beyond the horizon casting amber colors throughout the light blue sky. Steele instantly rises up from below Blaze's shading undercarriage and begins to feverishly bark and growl. Blaze tries to keep calm as the desert sidewinder rattles its angry tail, slithering toward them.

The sidewinder raises and cocks back its head, baring its fangs. Steele barks at the reptile. The sidewinder leans its head slightly backward then thrusts itself forward, lunging toward Blaze's front left ankle. Fitch's hand explodes upward from below the sand near Blaze's hoof then grasps onto the sidewinder's throat.

The snake violently flip-flops around trying to free itself from Fitch's handhold. At the waist, Fitch raises up from underneath Blaze. A thick layer of soft sand flows from his shoulders and torso covered by the last of the horse blankets. Steele growls and steps off to the side as Fitch leans over, supports himself with his free hand and comes up from under Blaze. The sidewinder hisses and bares its teeth at the human. "Is that all you've got, friend," Fitch mockingly asks the snake.

Fitch gazes into the cold and blank eyes of the reptile a moment before swiftly raising the creature to his mouth, baring his own fangs and sinks them into it. The live and fresh blood seems to ease Fitch's pain. Even if only for a moment. The blood flows from the reptile into Fitch's mouth, down his throat, seeping into his nocturnal veins. The sidewinder struggles from Fitch's grasp then falls limp and dead in his hand. "Here ya' go," Fitch tosses the slain reptile to the sand.

Steele pads his way over to the snake and begins to devour it. Fitch faces Blaze, removes and rolls back the horse blankets. "I didn't forget about you, boy," Fitch runs his hand down along Blaze's mane. Fitch takes his grey Stetson from the horn of the saddle hidden under the layer of horse blankets and flips it over. Reaching into one of the saddle bags, Fitch takes the leather scoop with the dwindling oats then pours them into the hat. Setting the Stetson on the sand for Blaze to feed, Fitch turns to look out over the horizon… the last fading rays of the setting sun.

The booming mining town is filled with, of course, miners. Silverton rests on the outskirts of the desert just opposite to a rolling range of hills filled with inviting silver. The main street has facing buildings, mostly consumed with lively saloons and boarding houses. Scruffy looking miners, a handful of cowboys and wranglers make their way from side to side street, clomping their heavy boots onto the wooden planked boardwalks.

With a slight trot, Spider maneuvers Diamond along the far entrance of the central street. Glancing about, Spider recognizes a familiar structure at the far end of town, "BUCKLEY'S SALOON". Spider slows and halts Diamond, quickly dismounting and hitches the hoofed one to the post. Dusting off himself from the layers of sand, Spider steps up onto the boardwalk and enters Buckley's, overwhelmed by the cigar smoke and lively piano music.

Poker tables are filled with dealers tossing out their cards. Ladies of the evening mill about the tables prying for their next meal. The piano player glances over his shoulder and winks toward Spider who slightly tips his hat back. Old friends. Well, old ridding partners at least. Spider makes his way toward the filled saloon bar along the near wall and hovers at the end. The bartender, Huck, a large fellow with a snowy beard and mustache, turns and shrugs his shoulders as he totes a glass of warm ale toward a patron. "Whiskey, leave the bottle," Spider orders.

"How ya been, Spider?" Huck sarcastically snorts taking a bottle of whiskey from the below rack and slides it toward Spider.

"Fine," Spider quickly pauses. "Where's Dandy?"

"Upstairs." Huck motions toward the bottle of whiskey as Spider takes it in hand and moves toward the foot of the staircase. "How you gonna pay fer that?"

"Dandy'll take care of it," Spider calls out half way up the staircase.

"He's got company!" Huck shouts as Spider bounds the top of the stairs and disappears down the upper hallway.

The unmade bed is cluttered with legs and arms sticking out from every which way under the tossed sheets. Dandy wallows over the three ladies wearing nothing but their unmentionables. Dandy chuckles a moment, flipping himself upward and on top of a pair of gals pinning them to the bed. A sudden commotion of foot steps clomping to the door causes Dandy to lunge across the bed, off the gals, reaching for his Henry rifle propped up along side of the nightstand.

Dandy cocks the Henry rifle, levels it and aims at the door as it bursts open. The three ladies of the night scamper for cover, dashing off the sides of the bed, covering themselves as best at they can with the soiled sheets. Spider bursts into the room without knocking and stands in fear with Dandy readying himself to fire. "Sure, Spider," Dandy lowers his rifle. "Come on in, I wasn't busy. Would you like'ta join us?"

"We'ave'ta talk," Spider approaches the side of the bed trying not to step on a pair of ladies cowering on the floor.

"Anything you'ave'ta say. You'cn say in front of them," Dandy motions toward the three half naked gals. The girls timidly smile as they slowly raise up and face toward Spider then toward Dandy.

"He's back!" Spider nervously sits on the edge of the bed.

"Who's back?"

"That sheriff from Purgatory!"

"Out! Git out!" Dandy commands the trio of girls. They scamper to the door collecting their clothing as they go. The one last slams the door shut as Dandy whips his legs over the far side of the bed, sliding into his trousers.

"Chote's dead. Saw'im fer myself. All duded up in a coffin in Culver City. The sheriff'r preacher, that's what'es dressed like, run Chote' through with'is own knife. The sheriff'r preacher sounded pretty pissed off'ta me."

"Wouldn't you be pissed off if someone killed you?" Dandy snaps as he slips into his boots with Theo's silver spurs attached to the heels of his polished boots. *Jingle-jingle.*

"Reckon so," Spider timidly answers.

"Go'n find Jesse!" Dandy throws his overcoat onto his shoulders. Let'em know what's goin' on."

"Then what?" Spider slinks his way toward the door.

"I'll meet up with ya in a few days," fully dressed, Dandy takes hold of his Henry rifle and follows Spider toward the door. Nearly shoving him outward, Dandy closes the door behind himself following Spider down the rickety staircase of Buckley's.

Spider and Dandy quickly exit the saloon. Spider leaps off the boardwalk and unhitches Diamond then springs up into the saddle. Spider spins Diamond around and gallops out of town. Dandy lifts his Henry rifle upward and rests it on his shoulder. Pausing a moment, Dandy steps off the boardwalk, weaving his way through the hectic traffic of stagecoaches and cargo wagons of the growing mining town.

Stepping up onto the train depot platform, Dandy politely nods and tips his hat toward the departing passengers of the

266

awaiting train. He makes his way through the crowds and approaches the telegraph office. A lanky young man faces him from the opposite side of the bared window. "I'd like to send a telegram, please," Dandy smiles as he reaches for Mr. Fuller's coin filled lavender poke with the gold string hanging from his belt.

A rumbling stagecoach appears from the end of town and roars to a halt along front of a three story hotel. The driver secures the brake and reigns, leaps off from the upper seat and flings the side door open for the well dressed passengers. A cool desert breeze blows through the late afternoon sky as the setting sun continues to dip closer to the beyond horizon.

The boardwalks are littered with banks and mining assessors. Handfuls of worn and dirty miners, badly in need of a bath and a shave, mill across the street back and forth, politely nodding and greeting each other, searching for a bank assessor to give them a fair price for their newly acquired poke.

As the stagecoach driver escorts the couple through the opened hotel front door, Dandy turns a corner and strolls past them. He totes his Henry rifle over his shoulder looking damper and well put together. *Jingle-jingle.* Theo's silver spurs echoes from the heels of his boots, continuing along the wooden planked boardwalk.

Nearing the end of town, Dandy pauses a moment to admire his stylish attire and scruffy facial hair through the front window of a barber's shop. Mr. Fuller's lavender purse hanging from his belt with his revolver holstered at his right hip. The façade is dreary and damp looking yet, a quartette of lit kerosene lanterns seems inviting. Dandy runs his free hand over his gruff beard as he moves forward to enter. Dandy nearly trips over the silver backed wolf, sitting patiently at the doorway, not growling nor giving any offence to any who enter or exit. Just sitting there, looking about at the passing activity and wagons along the central street.

"That's a neat trick," Dandy bellows out as he approaches one of the three upright barber's chairs.

"What's that, mister?" the tall and thin barber answers as he makes his way from the back room. The barber sports a white shirt, dark trousers and an off white apron tied around the back of himself.

"Neat trick, the wolf I mean," Dandy rests the Henry rifle against the facing counter with the butt to the floor and the barrel upward.

"Not mine," the barber answers as Dandy sits in a vacant barber chair closest to the door. "It's his." The barber motions his head toward the second barber's chair occupied by a lumpy figure. The man, Dandy reckons, is covered entirely from the front with a barber's wrap cloth. He leans backward in the reclined chair with layers of steaming towels concealing his face. Resting on the forward facing counter cluttered with jars of cleansing scissors and combs and a wide brimmed grey Stetson hat. "That feller came in early this 'mornin', afore the sun came up afore I was even open. Said'ed pay me in gold if'in I let'im rest fer the day."

"Takes all kinds."

"Reckon so," the barber flips a drop cloth around Dandy's front, tying it about the back of his neck. "Now, sir," the barber looks at Dandy's reflection standing behind him. "What'cn I do fer you t'day?"

"A shave and a trim."

"Very well, sir," the barber maneuvers from around Dandy taking a cleansed pair of scissors from a jar of blue cleaning fluid. Dandy reaches up, removes his hat and places it on the counter in front of himself. Settling back into the barber's chair, Dandy glances around the room. Nothing seems out of order. His Henry rifle nearly a foot away from his grasp. "Gettin' all gussied up fer a lady friend, are ya?"

Dandy looks upward, deep into the barber's reflection standing behind him beginning to trim small locks of his hair, "Gonna kill me a sheriff! Gotta problem with that, clipper?"

"No, sir," the barber fumbles trying to keep his hands still, trimming at Dandy's wool hair. Looking slightly to the side, Dandy sees that his comment of killing a sheriff has had no effect on the stranger sitting next to him. Dandy slightly faces forward, looking at the barber's reflection in the facing wall mirror.

"That fella hasn't moved a spec since I got here," Dandy glares. "You sure'e ain't dead?"

"Dead as a doornail," the stranger responds from under the layer of cooled towels covering his face. The stranger slowly, even defiantly reaches up and removes one layer at a time from his face. Fully standing upright facing the forward wall mirror, Fitch looks into Dandy's reflection as he removes and tosses aside the barber's drop cloth. "Like my spurs back."

Dandy lowers his boots from the barber's chair foot rest, plopping them onto the wooden floor. *Jingle-jingle.* "I never killed the same man twice," Dandy slowly turns the barber's chair to face Fitch. The frightened barber backs away, cornering himself by the door.

BLAM. BLAM. BLAM. BLAM. BLAM...

Fitch is hurled backward off of his feet, toppling to the wooden floor on his back. Motionless and still. Slight clouds of revolver's gunfire seep out from under Dandy's drop cloth that covers him. The sounds of an empty revolver being holstered from under the drop cloth. Dandy calmly turns the barber's chair back forward, looking at the terrified barber cowering in the corner.

"Well, reckon I'm already in the chair. I'll take that cut'n shave anyway," Dandy smirks. The barber timidly inches his way across the floor with trembling hands, still clutching onto a comb and a pair of scissors. Trying to remain calm, the barber resumes trimming at the back of Dandy's head. The barber slips, nicking at Dandy's ear. "Clipper!" Dandy snorts. "Do that again'n you'll be layin' next to'im!"

"Sorry, sir," the barber trembles taking a small cloth, wiping the blood from Dandy's ear. The smell of blood floats through the air filling the barber shop. Fitch remains motionless on his back on the wooden floor. His nose twitches. The bullet wounds appear scattered upon his chest. Fitch's fiery eyes open. His flesh is pale. The tips of his fangs part his reddening lips.

""'Never killed the same man twice?'"" Fitch mockingly whispers as he stands to his feet. "You still haven't." The barber nearly soils himself backing away from Dandy who cocks his head to the side, looking at Fitch's unharmed self, standing before him. Dandy pauses a long hard moment, staring blankly into Fitch's flaming eyes.

Dandy springs to his feet, ripping the barber's drop cloth from himself, flinging it at Fitch. As Fitch bats the drop cloth away from himself, Dandy turns and reaches for his Henry rifle, cocking it and leveling it at the sheriff dressed like a preacher. Dandy effortlessly cocks the brass level down and back after every shot.

KA-BLAM. KA-BLAM. KA-BLAM-KA-BLAM. KA-BLAM. KA-BLAM. KA-BLAM-KA-BLAM. KA-BLAM-KA-BLAM. KA-BLAM-KA- BLAM…

Dandy's onslaught of rifle fire rips through Fitch, impaling the bullets along the far wall behind him. Unharmed, Fitch remains upright, slightly wrenching from the pain. No trickles nor trances of blood seep out from the numerous bullet wounds. Stunned, Dandy backs away from Fitch as he approaches.

Face to face, Fitch and Dandy stare at each other. Fitch calmly reaches for Dandy's Henry rifle then toward Dandy's gunbelt. One by one, Fitch takes a round from Dandy's gunbelt and reloads the rifle. Finished with the task, Fitch forcefully thrusts the Henry rifle back into Dandy's grasp. "Here," Fitch commands. "Try it again."

Never taking his eyes off of Dandy, Fitch steps backward, halting nearly twenty feet away. Dandy's eyes are wide and bugged. He glances over to the barber cowering into the corner by the door, quickly turns, aims and levels his rifle toward Fitch. Dandy furiously cocks the lever down and back with more intensity than before.

KA-BLAM-KA-BLAM.
KA-BLAM-KA-BLAM.
KA-BLAM-KA-BLAM.
KA-BLAM-KA-BLAM.
KA-BLAM-KA-BLAM.
KA-BLAM-KA-BLAM.
KA-BLAM-KA-BLAM-KA-BLAM.
CLICK-CLICK-CLICK...
Rifle smoke pours out from the end of the barrel of the Henry rifle. Dandy strains to peer through the smoke. As the smoke slowly lifts, he sees Fitch unharmed, storming toward him with an angry and terrifying glare on his face. Fangs barred. Eyes blazing. A sheer sight of horror and terror.

"To arms! To arms!" the barber screams as he frantically races out of the barber shop, nearly tripping over Steele along the wooden boardwalk, then toppling to the street. Several miners swiftly approach the barber collecting him to his feet. The barber wildly waves his hands at his shop. "There's a man, not a man! He's in there! He's in there! Have'ta kill'im 'fore he kills us all!" The miners surround the barber keeping him on his feet. A small crowd of cargo wagon drivers, stagecoach drivers, wranglers and gamblers swiftly surround the barber and miners.

CRASH!

The front window of the barber shop is shattered. Dandy's limp and lifeless body is hurled outward, entirely clearing the wooden boardwalk, landing with a violent thud in the middle of the street. Every bone in Dandy's body has been broken... snapped in two. Dandy's corpse lays their as a forgotten rag doll, discarded and tossed aside.

From the flickering shadows of the lit lanterns inside of the barber shop, Fitch steps forward to the opened door. His appearance is dark and evil. Not a scratch on him. He glances down at Steele waiting in the doorway. The sun hasn't fully set. The amber and orange rays flood over the awning spanning over the boardwalk, barber shop and surrounding shops and general

271

stores. Fitch is trapped. The barber screams, "That's'im! Kill'im! Kill'im!"

"...time to leave," Steele thinks to himself. Letting out a series of growls and barks, Steele bolts from the boardwalk, disappearing into the growing darkness of the impending night. The miners and wranglers quickly draw their pistols and revolvers, opening fire onto the barber shop. The echo of gunfire is deafening.

Windows shatter. Wood beams splinter. The front door is completely destroyed, falling off its hinges, landing to the boardwalk with a series of thuds. The gunfire stops. The street is filled with smoke seeping out from the countless gun barrels. The barber looks upon his shop. It is nearly destroyed yet, there is no trace of Fitch.

The miners, wrangler and gamblers slowly enter the remains of the barber shop. The wall of mirrors, the barber's chairs, the bottles and jars of cleansing scissors and combs... all but destroyed. The wriggly men wave their drawn weapons in all directions for any sign of the demonic creature. The "thing" that terrified the barber so. Nothing...

As the barber timidly enters and follows behind the small army of men, he pauses to assess the damage... all is lost. But, at least the creature is dead. "Where is'e?" the barber whispers to the nearest miner. A single drop of blood splatters on the shoulder of the barber. He looks up to see Fitch hanging from his bent knees from an above supporting ceiling beam. Fitch is outraged, releasing himself from the beam, landing on the wooden floor with a powerful thud. "My God! Help us!" the barber frantically scampers for the door.

The miners, wranglers and gamblers open fire at Fitch as he stalks them. One by one. Singling them out for the kill. The panicked men topple over each other, continuing to fire their weapons, fleeing for the door. The rays of sunlight burst inward, confining Fitch to the back area of the barber shop. Again... still, he is trapped.

A mob has formed around Dandy's corpse in the middle of the street. Silverton's sheriff, a stout man wearing a tarnished badge, mills around the center of the semicircle formed around Dandy. The dark shadows of the barber shop grow more dim. The fading sunset has nearly reached its crescendo. "Let's go'in after'im," one miner shouts.

"I'm not goin'in there," a scruffy wrangler replies. "You go'in after'im!"

"Let's burn'im out," a second unshaved miner declares. The barber shoves his way toward the front of the angry mob.

"No! No, please don' burn my place!" the barber waves his arms about. "It's all I'ave!" The miners, wranglers and gamblers all are silent as they look each other over. Not a single shaved chin nor trimmed head in the bunch. They have no need for a barber.

"Right!" the untamed third miner answers. "We'll burn'im out!" Cheers roar out from the mob. The Sheriff is merely shoved behind the crowds of angry town folk to watch the enviable burning of the barber shop. Wranglers and miners quickly gather up torches with the gamblers lighting the ends of the kerosene doused cloths with their small boxes of matches.

"*Great,*" Fitch sarcastically murmurs to himself seeing the approaching mob of wranglers, miners and gamblers making their way to the front of the barber shop with lit torches. Fitch scans the barber shop for another way out. There is none. No other windows. No back door. "Who built this place, the post office?"

The bottom of the setting sun crests to the top of the beyond horizon. It'll only be minutes now before the sun will set. Yet, Fitch is running out of time. The gathered mob of wranglers and miners swiftly approach the front of the barber shop, hurling the lit torches inward through the destroyed front windows and unhinged door. Glass jars of cleansing fluid shatter sending their flammable liquid across the wooden planked floor.

Flames quickly spread throughout the barber shop, cornering Fitch in the far back. The roaring flames grow with intense heat, consuming the barber chairs, counters and shattered mirrored walls. Fitch is surrounded by approaching flames. From outside, he can hear the cheers of the wranglers, miners, and gamblers. In the faint distance, the sobs of the barber.

Fitch leaps upward, balancing himself on one of the ceiling supports, resting Dandy's Henry rifle across a pair of the beams. The thin wooden planked roof is his only way out. Taking Chote's Bowie knife from the small of his back, Fitch slams the large blade into the bottom planks of the roof. Below, the flames continue to grow. Inching their way upward along the walls and surrounding supporting beams.

A long plank is jarred loose from the roof. Then another. Then another. Fitch hammers away at the opening. Thick black smoke begins to fill the charring barber shop below. In an instant, the flames leap upward along the walls, spreading across the ceiling supporting beams, engulfing Fitch. With a final thrust of the Bowie knife, Fitch slams the roof opening wider. Taking the Henry rifle in hand, he tosses it through the opening in the roof. Fitch leaps upward, disappearing from the attacking flames and smoke below.

A trio of miners surround the barber, weeping at the loss of his business. The gathered mob stands blankly at the roaring flames, now spitting its heat and torment out through the unhinged door and shattered front windows. An occasional gambler tosses a glance at Dandy's broken and lifeless body piled in the center of the street.

"Do not be afraid, I am the first and the last!" Fitch roars with laughter from the top of the blazing barber shop. He leers downward over the forward facing façade, down toward the sniveling townspeople of Silverton. The mob gasps as Fitch rests Dandy's Henry rifle over his shoulder then tucks Chote's Bowie knife in the small of his back.

Fitch steps forward from the edge of the barber shop roof and leaps into the air. The dark creature of the night appears to soar a moment, even fly and hover before gracefully landing with a heavy thud in the center of the gathered mob. The only sound is the crackling and charring of the barber shop behind him. An eerie sight. The shadows of the thick smoke and the awesome flames of the fire seem to silhouette the creature, stepping slowly forward.

The mob backs away as Fitch approaches Dandy's corpse and pauses a moment. He squats down and one by one, removes his silver spurs from Dandy's boots. Still in the downward position, Fitch slides the silver spurs into place along the heels of his own boots. Making sure the spurs are secured and in place, he stomps at the dirt street several times. *Jingle-jingle. Jingle-jingle.*

From the far end of town, a hulking image appears through the growing dark smoke of the flames, filtering out across the mining town. The mob turns to see Steele strutting toward them with Blaze's reigns in his canine jowls. The hoofed companion follows the silver back's lead as the oddly paired duo approach Fitch. Obedient to their nocturnal master, Blaze and Steele halt in front of him.

Without a word to the mob, Fitch slides Dandy's Henry rifle along the saddle bags and saddle along side of Blaze. The barber continues to weep, but covers his mouth in fear of what else might happen from Fitch's anger. Fitch slightly glances at the terrified mob then toward the anguished barber.

Fitch turns away from Blaze and Steele, returning to Dandy's lifeless body. He reaches down and rips Mr. Fuller's lavender poke with the gold tie string from Dandy's belt. Fitch gently tosses the purse in his scarred palm several times feeling the weight. As he returns to Blaze, Fitch tosses the lavender poke to the barber. "Recall I said I'd pay you in gold," Fitch pauses a moment before swinging himself upward into the saddle without using the foot peg. "Sorry 'bout your place. That'll be more'n enough to rebuild."

With that, Fitch tips his oversized grey Stetson hat to the frightened mob, turns Blaze about and coaxes his stallion onward. Steele licks his chops, glaring at the townspeople and miners, wags his tail and follows behind. The crackling flames of the crumbling barber shop casts evil shadows on their backs as they slip out into the night leaving the people of Silverton wondering, "What in tar nation just happened here?"…

"I can feel him drawing nearer. Closer with every passing day. I can feel it as if I can even sense him coming to me. I often dream of our night together. New Year's Eve. Fitch was so gentle and tender. I was a nervous wreak. I'd never been with a man before. Would I measure up to his expectations? Would I be as good as the others he had had? Yes, I know about Boston and Philadelphia. Bell told me about his "adventures". How she found out, God only knows."

"How do I confront the man that I love? The boy who has grown to a man? The man that I have grown to love over these many years? Blazes! Either way I am to be the bride of a sheriff. Fitch. James. No woman should be as perplexed as I. Is this what Bell had to go through in her younger years with Robert and Trask?"

"There's that feeling again. Deep inside of my stomach like a turning or kicking. I can feel Fitch coming to me. Yet, something's wrong. He is not the same man he was when he left. He's changed somehow. Different. Something's happened to him. Is he wounded? Something dreadful I fear. How can I bear to tell him… How can I not? How can I tell him that…"

"Good afternoon, Beth," Jay swaggers in through the front lobby door of the Katherine Hotel. Beth fumbles to stack and file away the growing collection of faded onion papers.

"Afternoon, Jay."

"When're you ever gonna let me read those letters you write," Jay smiles as he leans against the far side of the front desk counter. Beth slides the stack of papers under the counter and faces him with an arrogant smirk.

"When you're a-hundred and fifty-two."

"I'cn wait," Jay grins as he scans the rest of the front desk counter top. Several versions of wanted posters or fliers rest toward the end of the counter. Jay reaches for one, staring at Cougar's sketched face. He studies it for a moment before replacing it back onto the stack of newspapers and newspaper clippings.

"Have you heard anything from Fitch yet?"

"No," Jay nearly whispers. "Not yet." The glimmer in Beth's eye is gone. Jay fidgets a moment, shifting his weight from one boot to the other. "Whatta ya gonna tell'im?"

"About what?"

"'Bout us."

"There is no "us", Jay," Beth abruptly declares. Jay is hurt, shaking his head, leaning away from the front desk counter as if to leave.

"Jay!" Robert and Bell storm into the lobby. "Saw you comin' in from across the street. Any word from Fitch," Robert faces the newly appointed Sheriff. Bell and Beth exchange awkward glances. Bell can see that Beth was nearly crying when they had barged in on them.

"Not yet. Haven't heard nothin'," Jay responds with a nod toward Robert, beginning to feel the awkwardness filling the lobby.

"Alrighty, well then," Robert takes Bell lovingly by the arm. "If there's no news, we'll be on our way."

"But, Robert," Bell slightly pulls away from him trying to stay and speak with Beth a moment.

"Come on, dear," Robert tenderly squeezes Bell's arm.

"I'll check in on you 'nother time," Bell attempts a smile at Beth.

"Thank-you, Bell."

"Sheriff," Robert nods to Jay.

"Sheriff," Bell winks at Jay who tips his hat as Robert and Bell shuffle out the front lobby door. Jay turns and leans back on the front desk counter. Beth and Jay stare blankly at one another. Nothing to say, but so much to talk about.

"Fine then," Jay snorts turning for the door. "I reckon I'll check in on you later's well." Beth tries to blurt out a comforting tone or a word, nothing comes out. Jay stomps out into the afternoon sun, instantly hopping off of the planked boardwalk, mixing in and disappearing into the passing traffic of cargo wagons and stagecoaches. Beth is left alone with her feelings. Her thoughts. Her growing stacks of written words on sheets onion papers and The Cougar Gang's wanted fliers scattered about the front desk counter.

A roving band of musicians dressed in an Arabian fashion play their lutes and horns along the outskirts of the laid three rings. The Ringmaster tips his hat and smiles to the locals with swarms of tourists and out-of-towners taking in the oddities around them. In one ring, the trainer leads the zebras around the inner area. Maneuvering a zebra one at a time, they perform jumping tricks and balancing acts.

Arm in arm, Jay and Beth stroll away from the first ring of galloping zebras and pause at the nearby second ring. Although wearing his Sunday best attire, a sheriff's badge sparkles, pinned to Jay's vest. Beth is covered in light yellow lace, a lavish French dress, keeping her bosom and grasp close to Jay. Another trainer holds the reigns of a camel while four monkeys flip and perform tricks along the camel's pair of humps. "Want some cotton candy," Trigger bellows out as he frolics toward Jay and Beth.

"Thanks, "deputy"," Jay fatherly ruffles Trigger's hair then takes a finger full of cotton candy from Trigger's hand.

"Want some Beth?" Trigger politely asks.

"No thank-you, Trigger. Doc says I have to watch what I eat," Beth replies patting her nearly nine month along belly. The unborn baby will be due any day now.

Off to the side, the third ring houses an elephant along side of a platform. The trainer leads gleeful children atop the custom saddle of the elephant. The trainer leads the elephant and children around the inner area of the third ring three times. The children's parents smile and wave at their offspring from the outer area of the ring. Jay motions to the riding children and passing elephant. "Wanna go for a ride?"

"Gracious, no! I'm not getting up on that beast!" Beth protests clutching onto Jay's hand.

"I'll go! I'll ride it!" Trigger leaps up and down.

"Fine then," Jay smiles as he reaches into his trouser pocket for a few coins. The trainer leads the children and elephant back around to the platform. The trainer assists the children from the saddle motioning the next batch of riders up the platform. Trigger nearly topples over the smaller children making his way along side of the trainer, handing him the coins for the ride.

With the custom saddle filled, the trainer makes his way down from the platform, takes the makes shift reigns in hand and begins leading the elephant, Trigger and the other children around the inner ring. Trigger grins from ear to ear, waving and nearly falling off the saddle several times as he passes by Jay and Beth waiting for him.

A carnie worker sits at his stool with the inner areas of the adjoined boxcars of the visiting carnival train shielded by a positional barrier. "Three bits a piece, folks," the carnie worker barks as Jay, Beth and Trigger appear from the line of entering tourists and locals. Jay reaches into his trouser pocket and retrieves nine bits. "Thank-you folks. Enjoy!" Taking Beth by the hand, Jay leads her and Trigger up the slight ramp making their way into the first compartment as a visiting well dressed couple files in behind them. "Three bits a piece, folks!"

Beth nearly looses her breath. The "wolf boy" is the first attraction, sitting in his "cage", "growling" at the passing on-lookers. Next to the "wolf boy", the obese bearded lady weighting in at nearly eight hundred pounds. Her full length beard and mustache covers her entire face, covering her massive chest and stomach, drooping down to where Jay thinks her knees should be. Jay, Beth and Trigger mill along the narrow pathway inside of the darkly lit enclosed boxcar leading toward the next attraction.

The Siamese Twin brothers are connected at the midriff. The pair share the same heart, lungs and liver. Each brother has one arm having to work as a team, a single functioning unit. Oddly, the Siamese Twins have three legs making it assuredly difficult to get around.

Jay, Beth and Trigger continue along, exiting the first boxcar, entering the second by a well placed ramp leading between the two boxcars. A thinly shaped tattooed man with bulging eyes, swoops his sword in wild directions. Cocking his head back, the tattooed man lifts the sword and swallows it whole. Retracting the sword, he appears unharmed and repeats the stunt for the following tourists. The boxcar becomes unusually cold in temperature as Jay, Beth and Trigger round the next corner.

Sparsely lit kerosene wall lanterns cast eerie glows and flickering shadows across the last attraction of the boxcar. The rattling sounds of silver coated chains sends shivers up and down Beth's spine. The area is dark and damp. Jay, Beth and Trigger stop cold in their tracks. What a hideous creature this is!

Fitch, in his demonic form, no facial nor bodily hair. Smooth, almost leathery skin. No sexual organs, not as if they had been removed, the organs have never existed. The evil bat creature's ears are tall and pointy. Its flesh is pale from the lack of sunlight. Red flaming eyes burning into all that look upon him. Fangs. Yes, the fangs barred from the jaws of a carnivorous mouth. This thing. This man-bat, a freak of nature. This unnatural hideous abomination of God should be destroyed. "Elizabeth..." the hideous beast whispers.

Jay maneuvers his body in front of Beth, blocking her from the grasp of the Demonic Fitch. The creature lunges outward toward her attempting to grab hold. The rattling silver chains knock Trigger to the boxcar floor. He scampers away, now cornered along the near wall of the boxcar. Entering tourists scream to see the naked bat creature thrusting itself away from its confined wall, lusting and feverishly wanting Beth. The demonic beast continues to tug and pull at the chains, the restraining bolts in the far wall begin to loosen and give way. Jay swiftly draws his revolver and levels it at the evil creature. Jay fans his opened palm over the revolver's hammer after every deadly shot.

BLAM-BLAM. BLAM-BLAM. BLAM-BLAM.

Jay has emptied his weapon into the furious man-bat, still lunging at Beth, trying to escape. The Demonic Fitch breaks free from the silver chains. It takes a hold of Jay, snaps his spine in two then violently hurls his slain body along side of Trigger cowering in the corner.

Turning with a blood thirsty glare, the Demonic Fitch takes several heavy steps forward, inching its way closer to Beth. She lets out a blood curdling scream as the evil nocturnal creature thrusts her into its arms, bares its fangs and thrusts them deep into Beth's neck. She kicks and screams trying to flee but quickly feels her strength leave herself. Beth's blood flows freely from her neck running down Demonic Fitch's throat. With mouth and bared fangs covered in Beth's blood, the creature rears back its head and bellows out a thunderous roar...

Fitch screams out in terror, hammering his confined boots and fists along the damp surface of darkness. He tosses himself around, realizing it was only a bad dream. A very bad dream. A daymare. Blackness surrounds him in his upright position. With his keen eyesight, Fitch reaches up in front of himself, taking hold of the handle of Chote's Bowie knife. With little effort, Fitch shoves at the handle of the knife swaying his weight forward.

The tip of Chote's Bowie knife sticks out from inside of the tall free standing cactus. The trunk is thick and wide with a pair of curved extended arms reaching out from the torso of the desert scarecrow. Fitch kicks out the carved opening from the trunk, just large enough to creep inside, protected from the daylight.

Fitch solidly lands onto the hard surface of the sand. *Jingle-jingle.* The ground was too ridged to dig himself a temporary grave for shelter. He retrieves the large blade from the carved face of the cactus and tosses the prickly panel to the side, sliding the large knife in the small of his back.

The air is cool and damp with lingering storm clouds gathering above. Fitch makes his way around the trunk of the towering cactus, running his hand along Blaze's smoky mane, beginning to remove the covering horse blankets from his saddle, hind end, shoulders and head. Blaze snorts out a welcome with Steele sitting up from below the hoofed companion, looking up at Fitch for orders.

Reaching into one side of the saddle bags, Fitch removes a handful of jerky, tossing it to the hard sand for Steele to consume. Rounding the other side of the saddle, Fitch removes his grey Stetson from the horn, turns it upside and pours a leather scoop of stale oats into it. Placing the hat onto the ground, Blaze begins to feed while Fitch resumes rolling and securing the horse blankets behind Blaze's saddle…

The terrain has changed, transformed into the vastness of the desert to molding ridges and low laying ranges. The towering cactuses have vanished replaced by clusters of desert trees gathered among boulders and clusters of shrubs. Fitch rides along Blaze at a moderate pace, not a gallop but more than a trot. Steele frolics along side taking in the cooling air of the night.

"I'd like to have one of those calves, mister," Fitch settles into Blaze's saddle coming to a halt. Obedient, Steele heals along side. The trio of dark skinned wranglers look oddly toward Fitch, uneasy in their saddles. The small herd of cattle bump into one another along the narrowing walls of the rocky canyon, confined within.

"Not fer sale, Señor," the first Caballero sneers. The other pair of Mexican cowboys slightly chuckle toward one another. Fitch quickly looks over the herd, nearly a half dozen brands appear scorched along the beef's hind ends. Clearly, stolen cattle.

"I would <u>like</u> to <u>have</u> one of those calves... *please*," Fitch commands. The first Caballero seems awe struck. Gazing deeply into Fitch's flaming red eyes.

"Si! Si, Señor," the third Caballero quickly motions his head toward the end of the herd. "Take that one." A small and weakening calf blurts out, worn from the travel. The other pair of dark skinned wranglers glare at the first who shoots them back a deathly stare. "El' Diablo Blanco," the Caballero whispers. The other pair are instantly silenced.

"Thank-you, Señor," Fitch tips his grey Stetson, maneuvers Blaze through the cattle and leads the calf away from the herd. Steele barks up at the three Caballero's, startling them. The three quickly move their probably stolen horses around the remaining herd, leading them out of the narrowing canyon.

Steele lumbers ahead, keeping the calf from straying away as Fitch and Blaze continue to bring up the rear. Slightly glancing behind himself, Fitch sees that the wrangled herd and Caballero's are far from his sight. Without a warning or word, Fitch leaps from the saddle, soaring a moment, colliding into the calf from behind. Blaze halts and awaits Fitch's return with Steele trotting ahead to guard the next bend in the narrowing canyon.

The calf struggles to flee. Fitch powerfully grasps onto the calf, pining the frail creature to the ground. The calf cries out and futilely kicks. Rearing up his head, Fitch bares his fangs, eyes flaming red and buriers his face deep into the calf's throat. The calf's blood flows freely from the wound. Fitch feeds with an overwhelming hunger welling up in his stomach.

The life force from within the calf swiftly fades leaving it limp and motionless. Fitch's face and hands are covered with the calf's blood. He slowly rises up, wiping the blood away with the sleeve of his black preacher's jacket. Steele rounds the corner wagging his tail, barking with urgency.

Fitch looks about the narrowing walls of the rocky canyon, wiping away the last of the calf's blood from his face. Steele barks again as Fitch takes the reigns of Blaze's bridle. Fitch leads Blaze for several moments before approaching Steele, lovingly scratching his silver fur between his ears. "That's right," Fitch smiles down toward his canine guardian. "We're here... Diablo Canyon."

CHAPTER X

The narrowing passageway weaves its way along a series of turns and corners. Jagged rocks poke out from the darkness of the opposite facing canyon walls leading deeper and deeper into the unknown. Scattered along the rock faces, lit torches begin to light the way casting eerie shadows, dancing along the flickering stone walls.

Fitch continues to lead Blaze by the reigns with Steele close to his heels. *Jingle-jingle.* Unbathed and unkept harlots with dark skin, long matted hair, worn and tattered dresses similar to what a respectable dancehall girl would wear and overly painted rouge, begin filtering in along the canyon walls. The harlots pretend to laugh and giggle at the pathetic humor of the assortment of pale faced bandits and dark skinned caballeros.

The shadowy image of Fitch's entrance into the canyon causes low murmurs and whispers. The harlots, bandits and caballeros back away from Fitch, Blaze and the silver backed wolf as they pass. Frightened of what they see. Terrified of what they feel and sense deep inside. This man. This beast dressed like a preacher, is the furthest thing from a man of the cloth.

Fitch strolls his way along the narrowing canyon faces. *Jingle-jingle.* That haunting rattle of his silver spurs causes the canyon to become vacant with every soul darting for their lives in opposite directions. Rounding a turn in the canyon, Fitch pauses a moment and ties Blaze's reigns loosely to a rickety hitching post.

A glimpse back in time. The approaching walls of the canyon are lined with dwellings carved inside of the rocky faced walls. As if an ancient tribe of Native Americans or even the Aztecs or Mayans had built this city of stone and rock, deep into the canyon walls. The flickering lights of the lit torches create a

285

glow about the widening area, the central section of the decaying city.

Along opposite side of the facing walls, carved windows and doorways lead deep into the stone. Torches line the walls casting light into the sporadic openings. In front of the various doorways and windows, rotting hitching posts with saddled horses tied to them. At the nearing end of the wide area of dwellings, a pair of saddled horses. One, surely stolen and the other horse belonging to Fitch's deputy, Jay… Diamond.

"Looks like we're'n the right place," Fitch glances down toward Steele, still at his feet. Looking dead ahead, Fitch defiantly moves forward heading toward the flickering doorway along side of the stolen horse and Diamond. Approaching the horse, Fitch runs his hand along Diamond's mane. Jay's horse is still warm from a hard ride. The thief must have very recently arrived.

The mount recognizes him and snorts, then whinnies. There is something changed about the Sheriff. Fitch turns from the pair of hitched horses and enters through the dimly lit doorway.

"Hello?" Spider calls out timidly into the darkness. Spider clutches onto his drawn pistol in one hand, waving it wildly in all directions, his black bull whip flopping at his hip. The narrow carved hallway leads deep into the larger cavern area with a domed ceiling. Lit torches line the inner walls as Spider enters the main living area of the cavern.

BLAM. BLAM. BLAM. BLAM. BLAM. BLAM.

Spider dives for cover behind a wooden planked table, turning it up on its side providing a little cover. The several tequila bottles and glasses rattle to the hard sandy floor. "Hey! What're you doin'?" Spider yells out. "It's me, Spider!"

"Spider?" Jesse barks out from one of the dark open doorways deeper into the larger area of the domed cavern. "Is that really you, Spider?"

"Yeah! Now go'n put yer gun away!" Spider carefully raises up from behind the sided table. From the darkness of the first doorway, Jesse inches his way outward clutching onto an ivory handled Colt revolver in each hand. His own more primitive revolver still holstered in his belt.

"You scared the b-Jesus outta me, Spider!" Jesse holsters the Colt revolvers at his hips as he continues to approach his lanky fellow outlaw.

"You!?" Spider snorts making his way from around the sided table. "Yer not the one bein' shot at!"

"Sorry 'bout that, partner," Jesse and Spider begin to calm themselves as they face each other nearing the center of the domed cavern. "How bout's a drink?"

"After all I'd seen'n heard, drink sounds fine." Spider follows Jesse over the sided table and both outlaws heave it back onto its rickety legs. Jesse scans the floor for the glasses and tequila bottles, taking a nearly full one in hand, pouring them both a tall shot. They each take the dirty glass and slam the shots down their throats. In an instant, Jesse pours them both another round of tequila. "Kinda jumpy aren't ya, Jesse?" Spider wipes his mouth from the second shot awaiting Jesse to pour a third. "Who'd ya think I was?"

"I already heard 'bout Dandy'n Chote'," Jesse wipes his mouth and pours the two another round. "Thought you might be that sheriff comin' fer me."

"Reckon he is," Spider slides the third shot of tequila down his throat. "Might's well keep those fancy six-shooters in them holsters. That preacher-sheriff can't be shot'r least kilt with a gun."

"How we s'posed to kill'im then?" Jesse finishes his shot and pours them both a forth glass of tequila.

"Don' know. Don' care. I came to warn ya that he's comin' here fer ya."

"Sure Jesse here 'appreciates the warning," Fitch steps out of the darkness of the main entrance hallway. "Reckon I'm already here." Fitch steps soundly onto the hard sandy surface of the floor in the direct center of the carved doorway. *Jingle-jingle.* Jesse and

Spider spin about to face their pursuer. Fitch tosses a glance at Jesse's hips. The holstered ivory handled Colt revolvers.

"S'pose you want these back, sheriff'r preacher, whatever yer are," Jesse sneers. "Well then, 'ere they come!" Jesse draws the pair of ivory handled revolvers with lightening speed. His pair of thumbs cock back the revolvers hammers after each shot.

BLAM. BLAM. BLAM. BLAM. BLAM. BLAM. BLAM. BLAM. BLAM.

Spider simply shakes his head as the smoke begins to clear from the fired rounds of the pair of revolvers. Jesse's eyes widen as his jaw drops in sheer terror. Fitch remains standing in the carved doorway, unharmed by the onslaught of Jesse's gunfire. "I told ya that wasn't gonna work, didn' I?" Spider blurts out to Jesse. Fitch slowly crosses the floor and stands face to face with Jesse.

Fitch reaches up and slaps Jesse across the face. Jesse is stunned. At that same instant, Fitch reaches down and snags both of his ivory handled revolvers from Jesse's hands, tucking them into the front of his black trousers. Jesse clutches his fists and strikes Fitch several times in the jaw and face. This has no effect on the nocturnal creature.

Fitch reaches up and slaps Jesse twice in the face. Before Jesse even knows what had hit him, Fitch has reached down, unfastened his gunbelt and secured it around his own waist with both ivory revolvers holstered. Jesse's own meager pistol taunting inside of Fitch's waistband. Spider cowers in the corner with Jesse slowly backing away from Fitch who turns his back and begins heading for the doorway. With his back turned, Fitch pulls back the loading lever of Jesse's revolver, removes the empty cylinder then reloads the weapon.

Several feet inside of the carved doorway, Fitch turns and tosses Jesse his loaded pistol. Jesse fumbles a moment getting the proper grip on the handle. He has the advantage having the weapon already in his hand. Jesse swiftly raises the pistol to fire at Fitch, this bringer of death.

BLAM-BLAM. BLAM-BLAM. BLAM-BLAM.

Smoke streams out from Fitch's drawn revolver. Jesse never got a shot off. He slumps along the nearest wall, his wounds beginning to smear blood over the rocky surface. The smell of blood... the smell of living blood, wells up inside of Fitch. Jesse staggers a moment attempting to get the drop on Fitch who draws his left revolver, calmly raises both of the ivory handled Colts and levels them at Jesse.

BLAM. BLAM. BLAM. BLAM. BLAM.

The piercing bullets rip through Jesse's palms sending his sole pistol rattling to the floor. Jesse topples to the hard sandy floor, gasping for air as Fitch approaches and levels his right revolver directly at Jesse's head. Jesse screams out in terror. His blood continuing to torment Fitch.

BLAM.

The revolvers are empty. The bullet has grazed Jesse's left ear. He his pale with fright. Jesse gasps for air, then falls slain on the floor. Not of the bullet wounds through his palms, but of terror what would happen to him if he would survive.

CRACK. CRACK.

Spider's bull whip echo's throughout the larger cavern. Fitch turns to face Spider forcing himself out from the far corner. "Git away from me! Git away!" Spider pleads.

CRACK. CRACK.

Spider attempts to maneuver himself around the inner wall heading toward the main doorway leading outside. Fitch is slightly amused at Spider's escape attempt and humors him for a spell. Fitch smirks as he holsters his revolvers, slightly raises his hands in the air and allows Spider to continue to inch his way along the inner wall.

CRACK. CRACK.

Spider's whip had found its mark. A pair of whip marks cut deep into the right side of Fitch's face. Slight trails of blood begin to trickle down along his cheek. Then the blood appears to simply evaporate. The pair of deep whip marks instantly heal themselves leaving no more than traces of faded scars. Spider's eyes gawk open. He turns pale from fear. He cocks back the bull whip for another lashing as he draws closer toward the opened doorway.

CRACK. CRAA-

Fitch reaches up and snags the tip of the bull whip in mid strike. He wraps the tip around his wrist then powerfully heaves back, ripping the handle of the whip from Spider's hand. Spider panics, still trying to make it toward the opened doorway. He lunges forward, inches away. Fitch clutches onto the bull whip's handle and cocks back his hand.

CRACK-CRACK. CRACK-CRACK.

Spider's back and shoulders are torn to pieces. Blood instantly flows from the bull whip wounds. He falls on his hands and knees trying to crawl out of the opened doorway. "Mercy!" Spider pleads. "Please, mercy!" Fitch lowers the bull whip allowing the tip to fall to the hard sandy floor.

"Where's Cougar?" Fitch commands.

"Don' you know?" Spider tries to laugh. Fitch cocks back the bull whip preparing to strike. "He's headed back't Purgatory. Lookin' fer you," Spider cowers. Fitch lowers the bull whip and glares directly into Spider's soul.

"Tell Cougar I'm comin' for'im," Fitch nearly whispers as Spider hurls himself out through the opened doorway. As Fitch slowly follows behind, he pauses a moment, retrieves Jesse's pistol and tucks it into the front waist of his trousers.

Spider frantically bounces back and forth along the opposite walls of the dimly lit tunnel leading to the outside. His back and shoulders bleeding, seeping through the shredded sections of his sweat stained shirt. Spider glances over his shoulder to see the shadowy image of Fitch following behind. *Jingle-jingle.*

Spider thrusts himself through the outer carved doorway leading out of the deep hideout. Spider reaches out for help. The harlots, caballeros and bandits surround him from their nearby dwellings. They stare horror. Who could have done such a thing to a member of The Cougar Gang? "On second thought," Fitch steps out from the darkened opened doorway, cocking back Spider's bull whip. "I'll tell'im myself." Spider reaches up for Diamond's reigns to unhitch them.

KA-WHAP! CRACK!

The tip of Spider's bull whip powerfully whips around Spider's throat and neck. Fitch heaves back on the handle of the whip. The whip tightens between them. Spider falls backward on the ground, gasping for air. He struggles a moment, then falls still and lifeless. Fitch approaches and hovers over the lifeless corpse a moment. The terrified mob of undesirables back away. Fitch loosens his wrist and unwraps the whip from around Spider's throat. He fastens the whip to his hip as he makes his way toward Blaze patiently waiting hitched to a post. Steele continues licking himself, cleaning his paws. Fitch approaches his daytime stallion and his nighttime guardian. *Jingle-jingle.*

Grandpa's over sized grey Stetson upon his head-

Dandy's Henry rifle tucked in under his saddle-

His holstered ivory handled Colt revolvers hanging low at his hips-

Chote's large Bowie knife tucked into the small of his back-

Spider's bull whip fastened to his gunbelt-

Jesse's pistol tucked inside of the front of his black trousers-

Steele wags his tail as Fitch approaches and unhitches Blaze's reigns. Steels hops to his feet and begins to stroll along the canyon walls heading out of the wide central area. The harlots, bandits and caballeros cower in the flickering shadows as Fitch unhitches Diamond from the nearby post and fastens his reigns to his own saddle horn. Fitch smirks toward the terrified onlookers as he swings himself upward into Blaze's saddle.

Politely tipping his Stetson hat toward the ladies of the night, Fitch takes the reigns and coaxes Blaze and Diamond along the narrowing canyon walls with Steele loping ahead, leading the way out of Diablo Canyon...

A light fog lingers through the moonlit sky of the sleepy one horse town consisting of nearly a dozen structures. A worn hotel, a general store, a bank and post office and of course... a saloon. There is no train depot nor sheriff's office. At the end of the assortment of other shops and closed businesses, a livery with a smoldering fire glowing from within.

Cougar appears seated in the padded seat of a cargo wagon from the darkness along the far end of town. An oddly shaped object is covered by a tarp along the rear area of the rolling wagon. His saddled horse tied off and follows behind. The straggling dark skinned locals pay him no heed for they too wish to remain anonymous. The haven for outlaws and cutthroats is dark and dreary with no lit lampposts to light the central street.

Cougar bounces along, glancing at first to Dandy's telegram in his hand. Slightly smiling to himself, Cougar crumples the telegram and stuffs it in his pocket.

Cougar steers the cargo wagon along the damp street heading for the sole saloon. He swings himself off the padded seat near a row of hitched horses outside. Hitching the harnessed horse, Cougar reaches for his saddlebags, slings it over his shoulder and steps up onto the rotting wooden boardwalk of the saloon. Light piano music seeps outward, inviting him inside. Glancing over his shoulder, Cougar turns and enters the saloon.

The ladies of the night are quite gammy, smelling of three day old perfume and a thick layer of sweat. The scattered poker tables are cluttered with card games, with each undesirable player taking little notice of Cougar as he makes his way through the tables heading for the bar, keeping the saddlebags close to him slung over his shoulder.

"Tequila. Leave the bottle," Cougar orders the stout, unkept bartender. The dark skinned barkeep gives Cougar a hint of a smile, sliding a bottle of tequila across the bar. Cougar reaches into the flap of one side of the saddlebags and tosses a small handful of silver coins onto the bar. The sounds of tinkling coinage draws the scattered poker players attention toward him.

"What's the name of this town?" Cougar asks before taking a swig of his bottle.

"Town?" the bartender nearly laughs with a thick Spanish accent. "You call this a town?"

"What's its name, mister?" Cougar abruptly asks a second time.

"'As no name. Its just here," the bartender nervously responds. "Folks who come 'ere don' care if it 'ad one either."

"Fine then," Cougar takes another swig of his bottle of tequila, turning his back toward the bartender, facing the haphazard poker tables. "Does "'as no name" have a metal worker?" Cougar bellows out for all to hear. The saloon falls still. Even the greasy piano player stops playing on the few missing black and white keys. No one answers.

Cougar takes the bottle in hand and saddle bags over his shoulder and begins strolling his way in and out of the poker tables. One by one, Cougar lingers a moment on the card holding hands of the players. The hands of a caballero. The hands of a rancher. The hands of a banker. The hands of a gunfighter, Cougar smirks at the well dressed young fellow. Then, Cougar comes upon a pair of callused hands with soot charred under the fingernails. "You!" Cougar pauses a moment. "You a blacksmith?"

"Si'," the older dark skinned man responds with a tremble in his voice. "I am Jose."

"Well, Jose. Looking at your hand, yer 'bout to fold," Cougar whips around his saddlebags and thunderously tosses them onto the poker table scattering the cards and coins in the pot. Eyes widen to see handfuls of silver coins from the Purgatory's Wells Fargo Bank spill out onto the table. "Got a job fer ya'…"

Jose leads Cougar along the wooden planks of the uneven boardwalk running along the far side of the street. Cougar follows closely behind with the saddlebags again draped over his shoulder. "What you ask will take days, Señor," Jose nervously walks ahead. Cougar powerfully reaches out and grasps onto Jose's shoulder, spinning him around to face him. In his lowered hand, Cougar has drawn his revolver, sticking it into Jose's belly.

"You 'ave until dawn."

"Si! Si, Señor," Jose nearly wets himself. Cougar releases Jose's shoulder, spinning him back around. Jose toddles along the boardwalk with Cougar following close behind. Jose nearly trips off the end of the boardwalk, turning and entering his livery. Cougar pauses a moment to glance around the single street, barren from all souls. Cougar steps off the boardwalk and follows Jose inside of the soft glowing of the smoldering fire.

Cougar sits in a rickety chair leaning back against the outer wall of the livery. His horse, hitched to a nearby post. The cargo wagon is seen along side of Cougar's horse. The rear cargo area of the wagon is tarpped, concealing the hidden object. As Cougar consumes a plate of cornbread and beans, the once smoldering fire from inside is now ablaze. The sounds of a pumping billow casts growing flames outward from within. The billows stop for a moment followed by the hammering sounds of an anvil.

"Señor," Jose calls out from the dwindling flames of the billows deep inside of the livery. Cougar rubs his tired eyes, standing from the rickety chair just outside. Gazing along the near side of the street, he sees the amber colors of the rising sun over the horizon. Slightly stretching, Cougar adjusts his saddlebags over his shoulder and enters the livery.

Jose is covered with soot. His charred hands tremble as he hands Cougar a large leathered poke tied at the top with a leather strap. "Just like you said, before dawn."

"Yes," Cougar smirks, taking the poke from Jose. "Just like I said." Cougar tucks the leather poke into the nearest facing saddlebag. Without a word and a scowl, Cougar crosses the sawdust floor to a primitive work table, slinging the saddlebags from his shoulder. Reaching inside of the opposite flap of the saddlebags, Cougar retrieves two handfuls of Purgatory's silver coins, tossing them onto the table.

Cougar closes the flap of the saddlebags, flings it over his shoulder turns and heads for the opened livery doors. "How many days ride till Purgatory?" Cougar asks over his shoulder walking away from Jose.

"Two days ride, Señor," Jose reluctantly answers. With the sun beginning to rise, Jose looks over his shoulder to see Cougar disappearing outside into the growing sunlight. Jose pauses a long moment, hearing Cougar's cargo wagon and horse gallop away, the hooves swiftly fading out into the desert.

Jose remains steadfast, straining to hear the final departure of his uninvited guest. The hooves have gone. Jose turns and approaches the work table. The shiny silver coins lay scattered about. Jose begins to count them, "Two... three... sixteen... seventeen... eighteen... twenty-eight... twenty-nine..." Jose lifts all the silver coins in his cupped and char stained hands, staring blankly down at them. "Thirty," Jose pauses a moment. "Thirty pieces of silver..."

"It's less than a week afore the Valentine's Day dance. Is Fitch truly going to return? What has happened to him? I feel something is amiss. What is it? I dread something awful is going to happen. What will happen when he does return? Am I to confront him about my feelings that he has never asked me to marry him?"

Beth leans over the front desk counter of the Katherine Hotel, scribbling on her growing stacks of onion papers. She reaches over a takes and whisk of a small bottle of dark liquid. Replacing the small cork in the bottle, Beth reaches for her quill with the rays of the setting sun beaming in through the front windows of the hotel lobby.

"I do love Fitch... with all of my heart. As I do Jay. I don't want them shooting it out over me. Who am I to talk? I'm not worth shooting for. Worth dying for. I have a bastard child in my belly and..."

"Good afternoon, Beth," Deputy Morris clomps in through the opened front door of the lobby. Beth quickly files away her onion papers, running her fingers upward to straighten her loose locks of hair as Morris approaches.

"Afternoon, Deputy. What can I do for you?"

"Nothin', ma'am," Morris leans up against the far side of the front desk counter. "Jest here to check in on ya."

"Where's Jay? What's the matter?" Beth becomes concerned.

"Nothin'. He'ad some other business to 'tend to," Morris eases back his wide brimmed hat off from his brow. "Asked me'ta look in on ya."

"Oh," Beth whispers. "Well, tell'im I'm fine," Beth appears flustered.

"Will do," Morris settles his hat back onto his head. "Will do." Morris turns and stomps out of the opened front door of the Katherine. Beth stands in silence... in shock. It's been over a week and Jay hasn't stopped in to look in after her every day...

"I'm so <u>sick</u> of snakes'n, rabbits'n, birds'n such. I'd like a steak! Like Mrs. Elder used to fix up at that spoon of hers in Boston," Fitch mumbles to himself. *"Bloody'n rare. Still mooin' on the plate with a potato'n fixin's on the side."*

Fitch tosses the blood drained fowl to the soft sandy surface of the outlaying desert. Steele approaches the slain bird, sniffs it, lays on his stomach with his fore paws outward, lowers his head and begins to devourer the fowl. Wiping the side of his mouth from the small bird's blood, Fitch opens the side of his saddle bag and scoops several handfuls of oats into his grey Stetson hat.

Placing it down onto the sand, Blaze and Diamond lowers their heads, taking turns, beginning to feed.

The three quarter full, pale moonlight glows across the desert. Fitch continues to roll and tie the horse blankets to the rear of Blaze and Diamond's saddles, preparing for another night crossing the desert. Steele moves his paw across his muzzle relieving himself of the bird's feathers' from his jaws. Fitch finds this momentarily amusing while securing the last of the horse blankets.

The horse ride is slow and monotonous through the ocean of soft sand and rolling dunes. Fitch sways back and forth in his saddle with Diamond closely following behind Blaze. Steele trots along the soft sand of the desert floor, casually glancing up toward his master from time to time. Suddenly, Steele halts in his tracks, staring straight ahead into the horizon.

Fitch rides along for several moments before realizing that his daytime guardian has stopped. Fitch halts Blaze and Diamond, turning half way around in his saddle. "What is it?" Fitch asks the canine. Steele simply continues to stare over the horizon. Fitch turns forward in his saddle to gaze upon the horizon then slightly turns himself backward toward Steele. "We've got nearly two hours afore the sun rise. Come on!" Fitch commands.

Fitch coaxes Blaze and Diamond forward with Steele reluctantly following behind. Traveling along for almost an hour, Steele begins to feverishly growl and bark. Again, Fitch halts Blaze and Diamond, looking over his shoulder toward the hound. "What is it?" Fitch orders. Steele barks and growls at the unseen foe.

Fitch spins around in his saddle, scanning the forward horizon. There are no traces of enemies, outlaws, nor any other being. Steele continues to bark then turns tail and scampers away.

The soft sand instantly gives way under Diamond's hooves. Jay's horse begins to sink and struggle, attempting to escape the growing sink hole. Fitch is nearly bucked off of Blaze as his horse scampers to hoof its way to solid ground. The sink hole expands causing Diamond to fall deeper into its grasp.

Fitch strains to keep hold of his saddle's horn with Diamond and Blaze beginning to drag him lower and deeper into the sink hole. Steele barks along the edge of the growing hole seemingly knowing its dangerous boundaries. Fitch hurls himself from his saddle landing firmly on the soft sand. He takes hold of Blaze's reigns trying to coax his horse upward from the sinking sand.

Diamond gasps for air and is nearly devoured into the sink hole. Front hooves clomping to a grab onto solid sand. Blaze, beginning to loose his foothold. Fitch, tugging at Blaze's reigns. Steele, aimlessly circling the entire event, barking and growling. With all his might and newly acquired strength, Fitch heaves back on Blaze's reigns, lifting and pulling both horses from the devouring sink hole.

The thrust of power causes Fitch to topple onto his back. Both, Blaze and Diamond find their foothold, standing on solid sand. Fitch rolls over onto his side, takes his hat and begins to dust himself off as Steele reluctantly approaches.

A second sink hole instantly appears and begins to swallow Fitch. He grasps onto Blaze's reigns as the sand continues to suck him downward. Blaze lowers his head, straining to keep Fitch above the sinking surface of the sand. Diamond, not familiar with either Fitch nor Blaze, likewise pulls back on his reigns fastened to Blaze's saddle horn, trying to save Fitch. Too late.

Fitch grasps for air, sinking deep into the sink hole. Waist. Torso. Shoulders. Neck. Blaze and Diamond pull back on the reigns, futilely trying to pull Fitch upward from the swallowing sink hole. The tied reigns to Blaze's saddle horn unravel, releasing Diamond. Jay's ignorant horse stares at the panicked situation for a moment, then turns and wonders off. Steele barks and growls at the growing sink hole with Fitch sinking deeper and deeper. "Blaze! Blaze!" Fitch screams out.

Blaze timidly stomps his fore hooves into the soft sand, lowering his head and loose reins down toward Fitch. He strains to reach upward. The sink hole continuing to consume him. "Lower! Lower, blast you!" Fitch reaches up for the last time.

With one final gasp, Fitch's head is consumed by the ruthless sink hole. All that remains is the oversized, Stetson hat, in the middle of a pool of now solid sand. Blaze backs away from the hat. Looking down on it, shaking his head with a snort, wondering what to do next.

Steele. Faithful Steele, wanders around the outskirts, sniffing, growling for his master's return. There is no trace nor sign of Fitch. He has been consumed by the sink hole, only leaving behind his oversized grey Stetson carefully "placed" on the surface of the now solid layer of sand covering the sink hole. The sun, the warming sun continues to slowly rise over the horizon...

Blaze, uncovered by horse blankets Fitch usually assisted in, are unseen with the dark blankets and Fitch's bedroll still in place along the rear of the saddle. Blaze has lowered his head, burning from the midday sun. Sweating from all areas. Yet, dry from thirst. Steele continues to circle the solid layer of sand, once the sink hole. The silver backed wolf whines and paws from time to time at the grey Stetson hat, wanting his master to return. There is no trace of Fitch.

The vultures overhead have sensed a meal to come. The foul fowl circle above. Waiting. Wanting for something to die below. Blaze blurts out a pathetic whinny, beginning to lose strength. Steele, the canine, is out of his element. Thick coat of silver fur with no cover from the sun for Blaze won't stand still long enough for the wolf to draw shade from below. The pair of beasts, the horse and the wolf, an odd pair, meander about the sink hole. The sun burning down upon them. The vultures continuing to circle above...

Blaze has nearly no strength left. He stands motionless with lowered head, staring blankly down toward the sink hole. Steele remains below the stallion, finally has some shade, laying upward with his forepaws outward, looking into the sink hole. Steele's tongue, cracked and dry, panting.

The vultures are becoming more daring. A few have landed, hopping along the burning surface of the sand, pecking at it. Searching for something decaying and dead. The tall horse and wolf, the carnivorous birds think, will be next on the menu. It's just a matter time...

"I shoudda killed you when I had the chance," Fitch strains looking up at The Cougar Gang swiftly surrounding himself.

"Oh, you mean at the horse race? Yeah, you shoudda," Cougar playfully leans up against Chote's shoulder. "I'll tell you what Johnny Lawman, I'll give ya 'nother chance. To kill me. Bring us all in't justice'n be the hero," Cougar backs away from Fitch and motions his head toward his gang. Checking the ammo in Fitch's ivory handled Colts drawn from his belt, Cougar turns and tosses the pair of revolvers onto the dirt, just out of Fitch's reach. "Lawman, you've got twelve rounds, there's four of us. That should be plenty." Fitch slowly crawls along the dirt, reaching for his revolvers.

BLAM. BLAM.

Fitch screams out in sheer pain. Each of Jesse's rounds had hit the backsides of each of his hands. Blood gushes from the bullet wounds. Dandy rushes in and slams the butt of his Henry rifle numerous times in the back of Fitch's skull. Fitch is stunned, bewildered, continuing to reach for his revolvers.

Staggering to his knees, Fitch flops onto the revolvers attempting to grasp them in is bloody and wounded hands. Chote' springs forward and stabs Fitch several times in the sides with his large Bowie knife, like he was ruthlessly gutting a pig. Fitch falters to the ground. He grasps onto his revolvers, trying to place his fingers along the bloody triggers.

Cougar draws his Civil War saber and thrusts it sideways entirely through Fitch. The tip of the blade explodes from Fitch's opposite side of his torso. Fitch screams out in terror. Cougar twists the blade several times before quickly withdrawing it. Fitch falls to his knees, still grasping onto his pair of revolvers. "Well, help'im up, boys," Cougar orders...

"Sonuva-bitch! You killed my grandpa!" Fitch blurts out.

"I've kilt a lot of grandpas...'n grandmas'n, mothers'n, fathers'n... Well, the list goes on," Cougar smiles.

"<u>My</u> grandpa, you shot in the back in Purgatory in a saloon."

Cougar's one eye widens with a recalling and a hint of hatred. "Oh, yeah, I remember'im now. He's the one who gave me this," Cougar taps the black patch over his left eye. Fitch staggers a few steps forward, supporting his bloody left hand clutching onto his Colt revolver.

BLAM. BLAM.

The bullets embed themselves into a tree just behind Cougar. He laughs. Seeing Fitch quickly losing his strength, lowering his bloody ivory handled Colt to his side. Fitch becomes wobbly, swaying from side to side. He raises his Colt again toward Cougar.

BLAM. BLAM.

The last two shots. Cougar looks defiantly toward the lawman as Fitch lowers his Colt to his side for the last time. Cougar removes his Civil War wide brimmed hat and looks it over. A pair of smoking bullet holes have been shot mere inches from his scalp. "I've jest 'bout had enough of you, Sheriff," Cougar snaps as he draws his Civil War saber from it's sheath.

Cougar lunges toward Fitch and runs the blade through Fitch along its full extension, stopping the hilt at Fitch's stomach. Blood gurgles from Fitch's lips. He slumps over, bracing his forehead upon Cougar's shoulder.

Cougar twists the blade of the saber inside of Fitch, pauses a moment then swiftly removes it. "This gringo won't be needin' this anymore," Chote' declares as he swiftly moves in toward Fitch and takes the oversized grey Stetson hat from the dirt. Chote' brushes off the dust from the wide brimmed hat, tosses his own worn hat to the side and places Fitch's hat upon his head. A perfect fit.

"Reckon you won't be needin' those either," Dandy chimes in making his way toward the silver spurs at Fitch's boot heels. Dandy takes the spurs, props himself along a boulder and slips them onto his own boot heels, planting them solidly onto the ground. *Jingle-jingle.*

"I've 'ad my eyes one these since I first run 'cross 'ya," Jesse lumbers forward He effortlessly flips Fitch onto his back, loosening the gunbelt. Jesse wraps the gunbelt around his waist and fastens it. He pulls the empty Colt revolvers from Fitch's bloody hands then quick-draws both of them. Jesse twirls and spins them around his hands and fingers getting the feel for them. He smirks as he holsters the revolvers and stands to the side.

"What else is there?" Cougar surveys Fitch's wallowing body in a growing pool of blood. "This'll do jest fine," Cougar raises the tip of his Civil War saber a moment, then lowers it toward Fitch's chest. With the saber, Cougar rips Grandpa Theo's sheriff's badge from Fitch's chest.

Cougar lifts the blade and dangles the badge in front of himself, takes it then pins it to his dusty caballero style jacket. Fitch moans, trying to get to his feet. Cougar takes his boot heel and slams it into Fitch's skull. Fitch instantly drops to the ground. "Whatta 'ya gonna do, lawman? Arrest me?" The Cougar Gang roars with laughter, fanning out away from Fitch. "G-night, Sheriff," Cougar snarls.

Fitch lays in a bloody pool. Torn and tattered clothing seeping with blood. Pain aches from head to toe. His efforts to stay alive rapidly dwindling from his soul. *"Beth? Elizabeth? Can you hear me? Where are you? Help me, please. Beth... Elizabeth. Grandpa. God, somebody help. Please, someone help me..."*

The flock of starving vultures hop and skip across the burning sand in the distance. The afternoon sun, scorching everything it touches. The blacken scavengers peck at the sand, loping their way closer toward Blaze. Uncovered by the horse blankets, still secured and rolled along the backside of his saddle, Blaze slowly tromps about, trying to keep moving. His mane and exposed fore and hind quarters are drenched with sweat, scalding from the day's sun. Steele pants. Never wavering from the sight of Fitch's grey Stetson remaining in a dip in the sand where the sink hole had consumed him. Steele lets out a faint whine between feverish pants of his drying tongue. The vultures, hopping closer and closer to them. Waiting for either the horse or wolf to die. Waiting for something to die…

Louder and louder the thundering sounds approach until reaching a nearly deafening roar. Fitch frantically waves the burning branch in all directions in front of himself. Too late! Hundreds of pairs of eyes cut through the darkness heading directly toward him. The hundreds of pair of eyes become thousands. Evil eyes. Piercing eyes. Flying eyes. The thousands of pairs of flapping wings thunder and roar toward Fitch. He screams. Waving his burning branch futilely at the approaching attack of vampire bats.
One bite…
Two bites…
Three bites…
The thousands of pairs of flying canine teeth consume Fitch. A blinding chaos of hungered wings surround and swarm the helpless human. Fitch is knocked off his feet. He flips and thrashes about the mine shaft floor frantically trying to beat away the attacking bats. Bite after bite. The bats begin to settle in and latch hold of Fitch's flesh and bloody wrapped wounds. Fitch thrashes about but the bats are too many. In a matter of moments, Fitch is completely consumed and covered with flapping vampire bat wings, bloody canine teeth and the incurable hunger for blood.
In a final fury of rage, Fitch screams as he springs to his feet. He dashes forward to what he thinks is the mine shaft's

entrance, he is mistaken. The swarming bats follow close behind Fitch as he rams into opposite sides of the mine shaft, colliding into several upward supporting beams, recklessly staggering deeper into the darkness of the unknown.

Fitch pauses a moment to attempt to get his bearings. The darkness is blinding. He can see nothing. Not even an image or outline of the approaching mine shaft. The powerful thrust of swarming bats collides into Fitch's back. The force causes him to step forward, into nothingness. There is no ground to stop his descent as Fitch freefalls into the cavern pit, splashing into the pool of bat guano, with the confined air filled with methane gas.

Fitch gasps for air, clawing and reaching for the smooth surface of the pit, trying to climb up and outward. The frenzied bats swarm and consume him. The hundreds upon hundreds of bat bites, the loss of blood, no food, the methane fumes... Fitch faces the wall, reaching upward, futilely attempting to claw his way out. The pain and feeding bats are too much for him. He slides down the slight embankment in the darkness, facing upward, halfway submerged in the unseen pool of liquid muck...

"No!" Fitch blurts out in a determined tone struggling to his feet. The sloping side of the embankment nearly has no hand or foot holds. He strains to focus to see his surroundings. Ever so faintly, the soft glow of light appears from above. Fitch's eyes begin to adjust and focus. The cavern pit is nearly fifty feet deep and over three hundred feet round and wide. *"It's going to be a tough climb,"* Fitch thinks.

Seeing the only handhold just out of his reach, Fitch removes his tattered shirt, flips it around in a loop fashion and tosses it upward clinging onto the bottom sections. The looped shirt grabs the handhold. Fitch painfully begins to pull and strain his way up the smooth face of the cavern pit. Climbing inch by inch. Higher and higher...

The desert sun continues to set over the amber horizon. The flock of vultures remain, hopping closer and closer toward Blaze and Steele. The stallion is weak and frail from the day's sun. Head lowered. Ready to give into death. Steele remains steadfast, laying on his belly with forepaws forward, staring at the grey Stetson resting in the dip in the sand. The vultures hop closer to find Steele is not that far gone with a growl and a snap of his canine jaws.

Fending off the vultures for the moment, Steele returns to his blank stare at the wide brimmed hat on the sand. Then, the silver backed wolf's ear twitches. Steele sniffs the air. There is nothing at first. The wolf's ear twitches again. Hearing something... something faint. Steele raises up on all fours, staring down at the grey hat. His ear twitches again.

Steele barks at the Stetson hat. There is no movement. The vultures continue to hop across the cooling sand drawing closer. Blaze is too tired to fend them off, lowering his worn mane and head downward. Steele's ear twitches again. Steele blurts out a series of growls and barks at the hat. From several dozen yards away, Fitch's scared hand explodes from below the surface of the sand, clutching onto an unwary vulture. The hideous bird flaps and screeches for help as the rest of the flock quickly flap away.

Fitch's second hand erupts from below the surface of the sand, grasping onto the vulture. Steele joyfully barks as he gallops across the sand toward Fitch. Blaze slowly turns his weak head in their direction and attempts a trot toward them. Fitch pulls himself upward from below the sand, taking the vulture into is grasp. Shaking the sand from his face, he buries his barred fangs deep into the flapping vultures throat.

The bird flaps its wings for several moments before falling limp in Fitch's hands. He tosses the slain bird aside as Steele lopes toward him, sniffing him and licking his face. Fitch glances around to see his Stetson hat dozens of yards away. "Well, not what I had in mind. Reckon it'll do," Fitch reaches up and scratches the fur between Steele's ears.

Pressing himself completely upward from the grave of desert sand, Fitch brushes himself off. Steele circles Fitch's legs several times then dives toward the slain vulture. The first fresh meat in days. Fitch glances toward the setting sun over the horizon as Blaze approaches. Fitch runs his hands through Blaze's sweaty mane. "Sorry 'bout that, Blaze," Fitch fatherly whispers.

Fitch takes Blaze's reigns and leads him back toward his resting hat. Taking it, Fitch flips it over, scoops handfuls of drying oats from one of the saddle bags and pours them into his hat. Resting it down onto the sand, Fitch turns and begins to unfasten the saddle and horse blankets.

Fitch tosses the saddle to the ground, relieving Blaze from some of the heat and pressure. Several yards away, Steele feeds on the remains of the vulture. Blaze feeds on the oats in Fitch's overturned hat. Fitch, the man, or what's left of the man, turns to watch the last rays of the setting sun. The sky filled with orange and amber colors. *"Will I ever see a sunset or a sunrise again? What will be come of me? Am I to walk the earth in eternal darkness and damnation?"* Fitch wonders as he runs his hand down along Blaze's drying mane.

Steele trots along leading the way through the cooling desert sand. The rising three quarter full moon lingers among clustering billows of clouds growing dark and luminous. A burst of energy overcomes Steele as he begins to frolic and rolls in the fading sand dunes ahead. Fitch smiles at his daylight guardian. The first smile to cross Fitch's mug in weeks.

Fitch rides along with Blaze keeping a moderate yet not swift pace. His hooves leaving a narrow wake behind themselves. Steele bounds over the last rise in a row of low sloping sand dunes. He barks several times over the dune, cocking his head back as if to warn Fitch that something was ahead. Pulling back Dandy's Henry rifle, Fitch coaxes Blaze forward, closer toward Steele and over the dune.

"So this's where you run off to," Fitch shakes his head, replacing the cocked Henry rifle back between the saddle bags and saddle. Diamond turns his head and looks blankly, stupidly at the trio approaching him. Jay's foolish horse has lost his way.

306

Stopping cold in his tracks. Staring at the growing treeline ahead. "It's a wonder you made it this far."

Diamond is skittish at first as Fitch dismounts Blaze and cautiously makes his way closer. Raising up and out his arms showing the pale stallion no harm, Fitch approaches and carefully takes Diamond's reigns. He pats the horse on the shoulders and mane, turns and tightly fastens the reigns to Blaze's saddle horn. "Can we go now?" Fitch sarcastically replies to Diamond. Jay's horse snorts with a shake of his head. "There may jest be hope for you."

Fitch swings his weight and leg up and over Blaze's saddle without using the foot peg. Glancing over his shoulder to see Steele continuing to roll and frolic in the sand, Fitch coaxes Blaze and Diamond forward, heading directly toward the spanning treeline.

It's nearly midnight when the caravan of oddities make their way through the weaving path of the wooded area. The desert sand has past and gone. The hanging moon casts shadows through the thickening tree tops. Fitch cocks his head, noticing Steele becoming uneasy, sticking close to Blaze from below. A low growl echoes up from Steele tossing a glace to the side, a small clearing.

The rotting carcasses for his former wolf pack lay in ruin and decay along the clearing floor. Other predators have visited this sight. Large patches of fur and scattered canine teeth, jaws and torso bones lay in haphazard mounds. Their flesh and meat, all but devoured and picked clean.

Reaching the far end of the wooded area, Fitch gently pulls back on the reigns, halting Blaze and Diamond. Steele sniffs the air. The sent is familiar. Fitch leans forward on his saddle horn gazing upon the homestead and ranch ahead of him. A flock of sheep cower in the far corner of the barbwire parameter having sensed the approaching silver backed wolf.

Trask's meager home looks abandoned. The nearby barn and corrals vacant of all movement. The house, dark and cold. No lit lanterns. No activity. Yet, it is still early in the morning, *"...or late,"* Fitch thinks as he pats Blaze on the mane. "Should we stop in and say "hello"?" Fitch asks his mount. There is no reply from Blaze. Fitch eases his Stetson back off his forehead and thinks a moment.

"You'll keep changing, Sheriff. Once you've had human blood, there'll be no turning back. I don't need a book to tell me that," Trask pauses his monologue running through Fitch's head. "Don't worry 'bout the lamb or the barn door. Don't come back here. If you do, I'll have'ta kill you."

"From what that book says, you can try," Fitch says trying to ease the moment.

"Yes, I'll have'ta try…" Trask sadly responds extending out his hand.

Fitch adjusts his wide brimmed hat lower onto his head. Taking the reigns in hand, he coaxes Blaze and Diamond forward. Steele, keeping close to them loping along. "We'll go around," Fitch states to Blaze and Steele. Rounding the edge of the barbwire fence outlaying the property, Fitch steers Blaze along the outskirts, never taking his eye off of Trask's home.

The flock of sheep bleat out, nervous of Steele's approach. The silver backed wolf licks his chops. *"A late night snack wouldn't be so bad 'bout now,"* Steele thinks. "Yeah, it would be nice," Fitch says a loud to the wolf. "I'm hungry, too. But not here. Not now. I don't want to intrude on Mr. Bailey's hospitality again."

Fitch maneuvers Steele and Diamond around the far end of the barbwire fence. The flock of sheep have scattered in a bleating manner. Steele pauses a moment to take a last glimpse of the woolly meal then turns and follows behind his master disappearing into the treeline.

Not bothering to look over is shoulder, Fitch focuses forward, heading deep into the dark wooded area. Behind him, Trask's ranch and homestead. The flock of sheep helplessly continue to bleat in a gathering along the inner side of the barbwire fence. The house's front door stands wide open. Still, dark and silent inside. Several pools of drying blood lay about the wooden planks of the front porch. The pools of blood thin, leading toward a trail of drying blood heading in through the opened front door...

CHAPTER XI

"I took note that you'n Beth been spendin' a lot of time courtin' each other while Fitch was out rustlin' up Cougar and his gang," Robert fatherly replies as he continues to puff on his pipe. Robert strolls through the tall grassy lull along Beth's property with Jay a few steps behind.

Jay saunters his feet through the grass sporting his deputy's vest, pair of six-shooters at his hips and his dim and smudged deputy's badge upon his chest. The moon is high and full, lighting their route around the outskirts of Beth's log home in the near distance. Along side of the house, Diamond, Robert and Bell's horse drawn carriage, as well as Beth's chaise with her stallion, all loosely hitched to the lean-to and wood pile.

The house is lit from within by numerous kerosene lanterns flickering their soft glow outward through the forward facing windows. "Whatta you tryin' to say, Robert?" Jay finally responds.

"None of my business," Robert puffs on his pipe, pauses and turns allowing Jay to catch up with him. "Jest gonna be interesting to see the kid's blood-line when the runt gets older," Robert smirks, pipe smoke billowing out from his lips. Jay moves forward and opens his mouth to respond when a blood curdling scream echoes out from the log home behind them.

Robert and Jay turn and dash through the tall grass toward the front porch as Bell explodes from the front door nearly knocking down the hanging horseshoe above the door jam. "Any sign of Doc yet?" Bell gasps.

"Fitch went'ta fetch'im. Should be back anytime…" Robert's statement is cut short by the faint galloping sounds of approaching hooves. Robert and Jay turn over their shoulders to see Fitch clutching onto the reigns of Doc's one seated carriage. Doc frantically bobbles along the narrow seat with Fitch nearly standing, coaxing the pair of drawn horses faster and faster. "Here they come!" Robert waves his hand in the air toward them.

Fitch nearly crashes the raging carriage into the front porch, skidding the horses to a halt mere inches away from Robert and Jay. Fitch, wearing his full sheriff's attire, grey Stetson hat, shiny sheriff's badge upon his chest, ivory handled Colt revolvers hanging at his hips and silver spurs, leaps front the narrow seat and lands with a thud on the wooden planked porch. *Jingle-jingle.*

Fitch tosses the reigns to Jay in an insulting manner like a magnificent knight to a lowly squire. Fitch turns and assists Doc from the seat totting his black medical bag. Jay slinks off to the side, hitching Doc's horses to a supporting beam from the porch. From inside the house, Beth screams out in pain.

Bell frantically waves Doc inward. "'Bout to have the baby without 'ya, Doc," she takes him by the arm leading him in through the opened front door. Robert quickly follows behind with Fitch bringing up the rear. At the opened doorway, Doc slightly motions Robert back. "Sorry, Robert," Doc replies nearly out of breath. "You'll have to stay out here," turning... "with Jay and Bell."

"What?" Bell exclaims as Doc motions her out the door along side of Robert standing on the front porch. "You've done all you can do. It's all up to Beth now," Doc waves Fitch inward. Beth screams from her bedroom. Doc and Fitch enter, closing the front door behind themselves.

"Reckon we wait," Robert puffs on his pipe as Bell begins to fiddle with her loose locks of hair, drawing them back and away from her face. Having secured Doc's horses and carriage, Jay sulks his way back onto view. He leans up against a lower supporting beam. Beth screams again. Jay spins his head toward the closed front door, glancing at the hanging horseshoe above the upper door jam.

Robert and Bell toss a glance toward each other seeing the worry and concern in Jay's expression. The odd companions shake their heads at one another as Bell rests her backside in the rickety rocking chair along the end of the porch. About the shorter area of grass, Jay begins to pace back and forth. Eager and anxious. Pacing... like an expecting father.

Beth lays propped up by a stack of down pillows in the center of her bed. Her nightshirt, soaking wet from the hours of intense labor. Several lit kerosene lanterns have been placed on the dresser, the table along the far wall under the window and a pair of lit lanterns along the side of the bed resting on top of the Saratoga chest.

Fitch stands at Beth's side, gripping her hand as the contractions continue. Doc places his black medical bag on top of the dresser, takes a sheet and cleansed drying cloths in hand and places them around Beth's propped up feet and legs. "Are you ready, my dear?" Doc attempts a calming tone. Beth scrams again, turning to look up toward Fitch, still at her side clutching onto her tightening grip.

Doc lifts up the soaked blankets that cover Beth's lower areas, adjusts her propped up legs then covers the bottom of the bed with the sheet and cleansed cloths. Beth frantically looks down between her propped up legs at Doc who calmly looks up at her then turns to look up toward Fitch. He smiles down at her, leans in and kisses her on her sweaty forehead.

From inside, Beth screams. Nearly in a trance, Jay makes his way up the steps of the porch, staring blankly through the front window. Flickering light dances across his face from the lit lanterns inside. Robert continues to puff on his pipe as Bell nervously moves back and forth in the rocking chair.

"Push!" Doc exclaims, waiting for the baby's arrival. Beth leans upward and strains with all her might. Fitch looks down at Beth in awe, then stares down at her propped up legs, then up at Doc. Beth screams. "Push, Elizabeth!" Doc blurts out. "I can see the head!" Doc reaches down to Beth's lower area, preparing to welcome the baby into the world. Blood begins to cover the well placed sheet and cleansed cloths.

Beth grips onto Fitch's hand, nearly crushing it. She heaves herself upward. Pushing. Straining. The pain. The pain. "Ah! The baby's head is out!" Doc declares overjoyed as he removes the bloody child's shoulders, torso then legs, taking the child in his trembling hands. Beth leans upward to see her baby. Fitch smiles down with pride at Beth, then also looks toward Doc and the newborn. There is no sound from the child. No whimpering. No crying. A terrified look has consumed Doc's face aging.

Holding the bloody and silent baby, Doc backs away from the end of the bed. Away from Beth. Away from Fitch. Doc holds the child away from himself as if it were a disease in fear of contagion. Fitch smiles as he kisses Beth on the forehead again, releases her white knuckled hand then approaches Doc and the baby. "Truly, this is my child," Fitch reaches out to take the still baby from Doc's bloody and frightened hands.

Doc nearly falls backward over himself, trying to get as far as possible away from Fitch and the silent baby. Beth thrusts herself upward in bed, her view blocked by Fitch's turned back clutching onto the infant. "I want to see my baby!" Beth demands. "I want to see my baby!" With his newborn in his arms, Fitch turns toward her. Beth turns pale with terror, clutching onto herself, feeling unclean. Foul and disgusting. She couldn't have given birth to that!

The newborn, bald with not a trace of hair upon its body, lays still and lifeless in Fitch's arms. There are no sexual organs, not as if they had been removed, but have never existed. Neither boy or a girl. The tiny feet appear as if to be claws, the claws of a rodent or a bat. A pair of small pointed ears are seen from the goo and blood still layering the child.

Fitch proudly begins to wipe off the blood and goo from the motionless baby. Doc reaches into his black medical bag, retrieves a brass flask of whiskey and slams the liquid down his throat. In sheer terror, Beth screams, awaking the child. As the baby cries for the first time, it reveals a pair of canine teeth with a sharp pair of bloody fangs along the forefront of the infant creature's opened mouth.

Its eyes are flaming red, opening for the first time. The cries of this thing are ear piercing. Not of a human baby but that of a mutated, half-breed, infant bat-child. Beth nearly passes out, letting out one final scream of terror.

Jay crashes through the closed front door, storming in through the forward dining area, heading down the narrow hallway leading toward the pair of doors at the back of the house. Jay slams his shoulder through Beth's bedroom door. He stops cold in his tracks. Robert and Bell follow close behind, approaching Jay from the back, pushing and shoving their way to get a better look at Beth's baby. Jay quickly draws his revolvers from his hips, aims and levels the weapons into the room.

Sheriff Fitch Woolley has shed all his earthly appearances. The smoothed skinned, Demonic Fitch, stands in the center of the lantern lit room clutching, cradling his newborn son. The beast smiles down and fiddles his finger at the newborn. The bloody infant responds by reaching up toward his father, clutching onto the larger finger. The evil father and son quickly bond. Alike in every way. Like father… like son.

Beth presses her body as far back onto the bed, pushing herself into the headboard. Fitch sneers with the bat-like child in his arms, turns and heads toward the opened bedroom door. Bell and Robert back away from him and the child as Doc takes another swig from his flask. Fitch exits the room passing by Jay with trembling hands clutching onto his revolvers. "Don't take my baby!" Beth screams in anguish. "Don't take my baby!"

Fitch strolls into the kitchen area with the infant coming more to life, moving around in his arms. At the front opened door, Fitch turns and cocks his head back at Jay, arrogantly smiling with a wink. As Fitch turns to exit, Jay opens fire, emptying one of his revolvers into Fitch's turned back. The bullets embed themselves into the smooth skin of the beast, with no injuries and small trickles of blood. The wounds instantly heal. Jay levels and aims at the departing creature again. Beth strains, heaving herself into the bedroom doorway, clutching onto her belly. As Jay empties his second revolver into Demonic Fitch's back, Beth screams in aguish...

Sheriff Fitch Woolley dashes in through the front door of Beth's house. Lit lanterns cast dancing shadows across the log walls. A simmering pot of stew rests on the wood burning stove. Beth strains to support herself along the doorway of their bedroom. She clutches onto her expanded belly, nearly nine months pregnant. "Elizabeth," Fitch tosses his grey Stetson hat onto the kitchen area table, "Are you alright?"

Beth nearly falls over as Fitch catches her. She lovingly looks up into his eyes as she clings onto his shoulders. "I'm fine," she whispers. "Lil' Sarah will be along anytime now." Fitch helps Beth to a chair along the wooden planked table in the center of the room.

"'Lil' Sarah'," Fitch smiles as he leans down and kisses Beth on the forehead. "Don't you mean Lil' Theodore?" Fitch fatherly places his hand onto Beth's large belly, rubbing it gently.

"'Theodore'?" Beth snickers. "That'll be an odd name for a little girl."

"My son's not gonna be named Sarah," Fitch smiles as he continues to tenderly rub Beth's belly. The baby inside kicks. Fitch and Beth look lovingly at each other. "We'll let the baby decide what to name it." Fitch leans down and kisses Beth on the forehead again.

Beth reaches up and wraps her arms around Fitch's neck, kissing him back on the cheek. Fitch kisses Beth's cheek several times. Beth's breathing turns to a near pant, kissing Fitch feverishly on the mouth. Fitch returns the passionate kiss, slides his lips across her cheek, then begins kissing her neck.

315

Beth closes her eyes, losing herself in the moment, the passion. Fitch's kisses up and down her neck are warm and welcoming. Beth slightly opens her eyes. The loving kisses turn to playful nibbles. His clutch on her shoulders become tighter, more powerful. Beth squeezes her arms around his neck. The nibbles becoming more intense, more painful. "Fitch!" Beth exclaims pushing Fitch away from herself.

The Demonic Fitch hovers over her. Naked and smoothed skinned. His flaming eyes burn deep into her soul. Pointed bat-like ears, pale skin and canine teeth barring his forward fangs. Beth kicks and screams as the nocturnal creature thrusts is powerful hands into her shoulders, drawing his fangs quickly down toward her neck. The blood thirsty beast thrusts its fangs deep into Beth's throat. She gurgles out a scream...

Beth bolts awake, disoriented. She quickly looks around to see Cleo hovering over her, facing her from the far side of the front desk counter. The lit wall lanterns light the lobby of the Katherine. Scattered onion papers litter the top of the front desk counter. "Are you l'right, miss," Cleo finally blurts out. "I heard you'a screamin' from down the hall!"

"Yes, Cleo," Beth brushes a lose strand of red hair away from her sweaty brow, "I'm fine. Thank-you."

"Must'a been an awful dream you was havin', ta' scare you like that."

"It was just a dream," Beth struggles for a smile, not even convincing herself. "Just a dream."

"Go'on home now. You need to git some rest."

"It's late. I think I'll stay here for the night."

"Yes, miss," Cleo turns and heads down the side hallway leading out of the lobby. "I'll make up yer room fer ya'."

"Thank-you, Cleo," Beth strains a smile as she begins shuffling her loose pages of onion papers. A pair of heavy footsteps enters through the front door lobby. Sliding the onion papers below the front desk counter, Beth looks up to see Jay

316

approaching, placing his hat onto the counter. From outside, a second pair of footsteps are heard along the wooden planked boardwalk, then quickly diminish. "Beth," Jay smiles in a warm manner facing her.

"What are you doing here?" Beth straightens the hips of her dress trying to look presentable. "Shouldn't you be out doing sheriff business?"

"I am," Jay pauses with a smile. "I'm lookin' in after you."

"You know Fitch wouldn't care for it too much if he new you were tending to me so."

"Fitch ain't here," Jay arrogantly answers. "'Sides, what he don't know won't hurt'im."

"Yes," Beth whispers. "It will." Beth turns away from Jay's intoxicating stare, shuffling her guest registrar and paperwork across the top of the front desk counter. "I've got a lot to do Jay," Beth abruptly continues. Seeing the change in her tone and manner, Jay takes his hat from the counter.

"I was gonna see you home."

"I'm staying here tonight," Beth becomes cold and ridged. "Thank-you."

"Yeah, well," Jay fumbles. "Reckon I need'ta get back doin' "sheriff business". "G'night, Beth," Jay places his hat upon his head, quickly turns and heads for the door. Before she can even get out a word edgewise, Jay has exited.

"While the rooster's away, the hen's'll play," Cleo replies in a low voice coming up the hallway. Beth snaps her head around to see Cleo standing along the corner of the lobby.

"What was that, Cleo?" Beth demands.

"Said room's ready, miss," Cleo conceals her humor. Beth makes her way from around the counter, slightly turning her head toward Cleo.

"Thank-you. Goodnight, Cleo."

"G'night, miss," Cleo makes her way around the back of the front desk counter. Beth saunters down the hallway, turning toward a far door, pauses a moment then enters into the single lit lantern suite. Glancing over her shoulder, Cleo confirms Beth has retired for the evening. Slyly, Cleo reaches under the front desk counter, retrieves the growing stack of onion papers and begins to secretly read the pages of entries.

Jay remains standing on the wooden planked boardwalk outside of the Katherine Hotel. Sighing deeply, he glances around Main Street. The last of the lamplighters wobble along on their stilts, disappearing into the night. Scattered cowboys and wranglers stroll along the opposite facing boardwalk with no stagecoaches nor cargo wagons rattling along the street. A pretty quiet night.

As Jay steps off the boardwalk heading along the central area of Main Street, a shadowy figure lowers his hat, leaning up against the outer door jam of the Katherine. Feeling an odd sense, Jay looks back to the figure, turning and heading in the opposite direction of the boardwalk.

"Fitch?" Jay thinks to himself. No, not Fitch. The walk. The strut is different. Besides, if Fitch were back in town, he'd let Jay know... wouldn't he? Jay shrugs his shoulders, adjusts his revolvers holstered at his hips and continues down along Main street. The shadowy figure swiftly continues his route until coming to the middle cross street of town. The figure slightly raises his hat, noticing a flier hanging from an upward supporting post.

Cougar nearly laughs at the wanted flier clutched in his hand. The sketched images of himself and the rest of The Cougar Gang. He tosses the flier to the ground, glances over his shoulder, seeing Cleo fiddling with Beth's onion papers. Turning in the opposite direction, he sees Jay approaching Bell's at the far end of town.

Cougar steps off the boardwalk, stepping directly in the center of the tossed aside flier, leaving his heavy boot print onto it. Cautiously looking about himself, Cougar keeps to the shadows, heading toward the far end of town. Light and up-beat piano music seeps out from the Stardust Saloon across the street.

Cougar leans back against a supporting post of a general store, keeping a close eye on the saloon. Through the front windows, he sees scattered tables of poker players and gamblers, dancehall girls strolling around the filled tables and the bartender swiftly moving about the backside of the bar pouring drinks.

Along the outer porch and mezzanine of the second floor, flickering lit lanterns cast their glowing light outward onto the street. From inside the forward facing windows, Cougar sees several dancehall girls "entertaining" their "companions". From the far corner window, one dancehall girl, Sophie, escorts a robust man to the closed door of her room. The round man smiles and pats her on the backside before curiously opening the door, looking out into the hallway and slips out of the room.

Cougar smiles to himself, making his way across Main Street. He passes by a trio of wranglers, making his way up onto the opposite facing boardwalk. Trotting his way down the dark passageway between the Stardust Saloon and the next door general store, Cougar makes his way to the bottom to the outside staircase. He quietly tromps up the staircase, bounds over the outer railing and moves across the porch and mezzanine.

Glancing at the closed window to one side, Cougar turns to study Main Street below. The livery stands at the far end of the street directly below and in front of himself. Next to the stables, the jail and sheriff's office. Deputy Morris leans along a supporting post along the boardwalk, tossing careless glances from the opened door of the sheriff's office behind himself. Cougar decides that this entertaining room will be a perfect location to keep an eye on things. Cougar turns toward the closed window and peers inside.

Sophie sits on a small stool in front of her mirrored vanity. Her long dark hair hanging loose over her shoulders and back. Her worn, black and red undergarments hang low over her tanned shoulders. From behind, Cougar opens the window with one hand, waving his drawn pistol in the other, allowing himself inward.

319

Unafraid, Sophie looks into the facing mirror over her shoulder as Cougar closes the window behind himself. "Sorry, mister," Sophie pats some powder on her cheeks. "I've got others waitin' on me. Have'ta git in line."

"The line starts here," Cougar approaches her from behind, then whips her around on her stool. She looks him up and down. The raggedy man with a black patch over his eye. "Hey, fella," Sophie exclaims. "You're that man on the wanted fliers!"

"Yes, ma'am," Cougar thrusts the end of his pistol barrel under Sophie's raised chin and cocks the hammer. "Are we gonna have a tiff?"

Sophie calmly raises her hand, lowering the weapon from her chin. In a seductive manner, she tenderly takes Cougar's hand, holstering the pistol at his hip. "Not'it all," Sophie licks her lips as she stands toe to toe with him. "These fellas lately bin kinda limp," Sophie smiles. "Change'll be good," she whispers as she playfully pushes Cougar at the shoulders, forcing him backward onto her unmade bed…

Steele sits under the overhanging branches of a somber looking tree. The wooded area is damp with the light rain continuing to splatter along the ground. Blaze and Diamond appear loosely tied to a tree stump under another cluster of trees near the fallen and hollowed tree trunk. Thick clouds slowly roll along the skyline concealing the setting sun. The fallen hollowed trunk stirs and slightly rocks.

Fitch wiggles his way out from the tree trunk, slightly brushes himself off and sports a slight smile as he looks about the area. His faithful mount, Jay's horse and daylight guardian remain where he had left them the dusk before. Looking up into the sky, the light rain mists his wide brimmed hat. The cool rain feels good upon his face. At least he hasn't lost all of his human senses.

Fitch approaches Blaze and runs his cold fingers down along his smoky mane. Blaze snorts out a welcoming sound. Steele raises up, wagging his tail for some kind of affection. Fitch leans over and scratches Steele between the ears. In an instant, Steele lets out a playful bark, turns tail and dashes into the wooded area in search for a meal...

Fitch remains saddled holding onto the reigns. He cautiously looks ahead beyond the edge of the treeline around himself. Steele lopes into view from the side and heals at Blaze's hooves with Diamond in tow. Along the horizon, the lingering rain clouds slowly roll along. A slight drizzle persists hiding the impending sunrise. "Well, boys," Fitch says aloud. "Whatta 'ya think?" Steele curiously looks up at his master.

Fitch swings his leg over the saddle and dismounts. He moves to the hind end of Blaze and begins to unfasten the rolled dark colored horse blankets. "We have a couple days to make up," Fitch informs his trio, unsure of what he is about to do. He removes his Stetson and rests it on the saddle horn. One by one, he wraps the horse blankets around himself, covering his entire body.

Lastly, Fitch takes the grey hat and places it upon his head. Finally, with the dark horse blanket drooped over his head and shoulders, the oversized Stetson fits. Fitch is completely covered and wrapped in horse blankets. The wide brim of his hat shielding his face. With little effort, he swings himself up into the saddle. He stares blankly forward. The dark lingering rain clouds. The rising sun peeking up just over the horizon.

The soft glow of the sun beams through the rain clouds. But merely, just a soft glow. The rays seem not to penetrate the rain clouds, protecting the nocturnal creature. "Reckon we get goin' then," Fitch orders. Slightly coaxing Blaze and Diamond forward, Fitch rides out and away from the treeline, heading out into the desert. The drizzle. The constant drizzle annoys Steele. Soaking his sliver coat of fur. Drops of rain collecting then dripping off his muzzle. This is going to be a long day...

"Whatta 'ya think, my dear," Robert lovingly asks Bell as he puffs on his pipe. Bell looks out from under the extended awning of her saloon standing just outside the closed swinging batwing doors. The approaching rain clouds look ominous overhead. A storm in coming. Trigger's constant tinkering at the black and white keys from inside seem to sooth Bell a tad, but not enough.

"Bell," the Mayor grins as he stomps up along the wooden planks of the boardwalk. "Robert."

"Mayor," Robert nods. Bell, Robert and the Mayor look out onto Main Street. Scattered cargo wagons and stagecoaches roll past at a slow pace. The town is nearly vacant of pedestrians. The storm is coming.

"Looks's if we'll have to call off the dance this year," the Mayor looks about.

"Disappoint a lot of folks, Mayor."

"Well, it's not like its New Year's or The Forth."

"Still," Bell whispers. "Disappoint a lot of folks, Mayor," she mimics Robert. Bell and Robert toss each other a tender smile.

"We could lay saw dust down. That'll cover the mud," Robert motions his smoldering pipe toward Main Street.

"Could have the dance at my place," Bell whispers. "Move out the billiards and card tables. There'd be plenty of room."

"Room for the whole town, Bell?" Robert curiously asks.

"Why not? It's mid February. Purgatory's nearly sparse. Miner's away. Cattle drive's already passed through," she smiles. "Think I'cn fit a few hundred people inside." The Mayor glances toward Robert for approval. Robert merely shrugs his shoulders and tilts his head toward Bell.

"Fine, then," the Mayor declares. "I'll have a few boys sent over to help move things around."

"I want them out of the rain," Bell motions. "Put everything 'round the walk... an' I want Morris an' his boys to stand watch. Makin' sure no one steals anything!"

"Done!" the Mayor nods. "Robert. Bell," the Mayor tips his hat, turns and heads down the planked boardwalk. Robert takes a few puffs of his pipe and glances toward Bell who continues to look forward into Main Street then upward toward the approaching rain clouds.

"That takes care of the dance," Robert quietly moves in closer toward Bell. "Whatta we gonna do 'bout Beth... and Jay. Fitch's due back anytime."

"We haven't heard a thing in quite a spell," Bell sternly looks into Robert's eyes. "Who knows if he's comin' back."

"What if'e does?"

"It's Beth's cross. She'll have to bare it," Bell responds in a cold and distant tone. "I've had to..." Bell abruptly turns and forces her way through the batwing doors. Robert removes the pipe from his lips to respond after her, yet already knows what cross she has bore.

"Trask, you sonuva-bitch," Robert heads along the side of the saloon, away from the entrance and the tinkling music of the piano inside. "Why can't she just let you go? Hell's bells, I wish you were dead!"

"Come'ta bed," Sophie whispers, snuggling under the blankets of her worn-in bed. Wearing his one piece long-johns covered with moth holes, Cougar remains staring out the window. Soft rain drops sprinkle across the thin pane. "He's not comin' t'day. Come'ta bed."

Cougar lingers at the window for a moment before turning and approaches the side of the bed. He tosses back his side of the blankets and slides in beside Sophie. He leans up, glancing about the room. His gunbelt and saddlebags just in reach along the side dresser. His clothes and sheathed Civil War saber laying on the floor next to him. "You will take me with you, won't you?" Sophie pauses. "If I do what you ask?"

"Yes," Cougar pauses a moment. "If you do what I ask," Cougar rolls over and forcefully kisses her.

Steele is miserable. Sand and mud have collected between his paws as he continues to trudge along side of Blaze and

Diamond. Fitch sways from side to side in the saddle. The drizzling rain continues to splatter along this wide brimmed Stetson hat. The hanging sun stretches through the lingering dark clouds, unable to penetrate them. Fitch is protected by his coverings of dark horse blankets and layers of clouds, asleep in the saddle.

"Sophie?" Ned, the bartender of the Stardust Saloon bellows out from the hallway. He is a tall and lanky fellow. His soiled apron tied behind himself, scruffy face whiskers and greased back hair. Ned knocks at her door again.

"Yes," Sophie shouts out from inside of her room. "What 'tis it?"

"Haven't seen you downstairs fer a day or two. Makin' sure yer alright."

"I'm fine, Ned!" Sophie gasps with Cougar wallowing on top of her. "Jest fine! Bin feelin' under the weather's all. I'll be up'n 'round in a few days." Cougar rolls out of bed and makes his way across the room pulling his long-johns from his backside. He reaches into one side of the hanging saddlebags and removes a handful of coins. "Ned?!" Sophie springs from her bed covering herself with her sheet.

"Yeah, Soph?" Ned responds at the door.

"I could use sump'thn'ta eat," Cougar hands Sophie the coins, raises his pistol and slides behind the door as Sophie opens it. Ned noses his way onto the room as Sophie hands him the coins. He spies the unmade bed and Cougar's hanging clothes on the rack along side of the saddle bags.

"Not holdin' out on me are 'ya, Soph?" Ned rattles the coins in his hand.

"Now, Ned. Why would I do that to you?" Sophie winks.

"Bin done afore." Sophie leans out the doorway and kisses Ned on the cheek.

"Maybe," Sophie slips back into her room beginning to close the door. "But not by me." Sophie closes the door. Cougar raises the barrel of his drawn pistol to his lips, "shhhh…" Ned pauses at the closed door, leaning his ear inward. From inside Sophie's room, all Ned can hear is the pitter patter of her feet, climbing back into bed. Satisfied, Ned turns and heads down the mezzanine railing.

Cougar shuffles across the wooden planked floor toward the lace draped window. Keeping out of sight from the window, Cougar looks down toward Main Street. The light drizzle continues creating large puddles of water along the muddy surface. Vague stagecoaches roll along the street, stopping at The Katherine Hotel, dropping off well dressed passengers.

Jay sways back and forth in a rocking chair along the porch under the awning of the sheriff's office and jail. The blacksmith pounds away at his anvil inside the opened doors of the livery next door. The forward facing boardwalk is sparse of pedestrians, strolling in and out of the general stores and shops. There is no sign of Sheriff Fitch Woolley nor anything else out of the ordinary.

Cougar lowers his pistol, turns and crosses the floor. He holsters his weapon then opens the flap of the other saddlebag. He lifts the small leather tied poke Jose had given him days earlier. He flops the poke in his hand creating low rattling sounds. Replacing the poke back into his saddle bag, Cougar tenderly runs his hand along the sheathed Civil War saber. "Now," Cougar turns with a playful leer toward Sophie already in bed. "Where were we?"

"This is mighty fine of you, Bell," the Mayor blurts out leaning on the edge of the bar. Several small wooden boxes cluttering at his feet covered with worn gunnysacks. Robert pours the Mayor another shot of whiskey. The entire saloon is nearly vacant of poker tables, the chuck-a-luck table off in the far corner and two of the three billiard tables. Bell shuffles her way across the floor followed by six local wranglers.

"It's the least I could do, Mayor," Bell motions the wranglers toward the last billiard table. Each of the six men round the last billiard table, one at each corner, with the other pair taking opposite sides near the middle. The wranglers heave up the table and carry it toward the swinging batwing doors. As Bell and Trigger hold the doors open, the wranglers carry the billiard table outside onto the surrounding boardwalk.

The removed poker tables are sparsely cluttered with gamblers and local cowboys. The dealers toss out their cards continuing the various games with a handful of Bell's dancehall girls milling about the tables working their trade. Along the far end of the boardwalk along Bell's, the chuck-a-luck dealer tosses the dice across the table with a trio of players continuing to bet.

The six wranglers move and position the last billiard table along the opposite side of Bell's end to end with the others. A pair of local businessmen play a friendly game of billiards around the last table, protected by the overhanging awning from the constant drizzle of rain. "You boys alright?" Bell smiles toward the local businessmen.

"Fine, Bell," the first answers.

"Bell, this is a fine idea you got. Playin' outside. Might'ave to do this more offen."

"We'll see," Bell tenderly pats the second businessman on the shoulder. "We'll see." She turns and heads past the six wranglers. "Thanks fer yer help, fellas. Drinks're on me." Trigger leads the way back into the saloon with the six wranglers letting out a low cheer. Bell holds the swinging batwing door open as they file inside.

Several dancehall girls hover over the gunnysack boxes and reach inside, removing handfuls of primitive decorations, hearts, garland, red and pink tassels. The dancehall girls begin placing the decorations in well placed locations about the saloon as Trigger finds his seat at the piano across the room and begins playing a light classical melody. The six wranglers bound to the near side of the bar as Robert willingly pours them all a tall glass of warm beer and a shot of whiskey. "Ta' Bell," the wranglers all seem to announce in unison, lifting their glasses, slamming their shots down their throats.

From behind, the batwing doors swing open followed by the soft footsteps of entering boots. "Bell," Jay tips his hat making his way across the floor. Trigger's piano playing pauses a moment then reluctantly continues. The wranglers draw silent as Jay approaches the bar and nods toward Robert. "Thought I'd just check in on 'ya'all."

"Jest like you checked in on Miss O'Donnell," one wrangler replies under his breath. Jay cocks his head and curiously looks at the wrangler.

"What's that supposed to mean, friend," Jay responds. The wrangler leans on the bar as he turns to face Jay.

"I ain't yer friend, "Sheriff"", the wrangler huffs. The second wrangler turns toward Jay, finishing his warm beer.

"Know yer from back east. Must'ave different ways back there," the second wrangler wipes his mouth.

"Whatta 'ya rattlin' on about?"

"Out here, a man doesn't court his best friend's miss. Jest ain't right," the third wrangler chimes in. "Don't matter if'es dead or not. Jest ain't right." The first wrangler, apparently the most opinionated and somewhat the leader, quickly finishes his warm beer and looks Jay dead in the eye.

"The real sheriff will be back soon," he motions the others to follow. "When'e does, there'll be hell to pay." The wrangler leads the other five away from the bar toward the batwing doors. The first pauses at the door as the others exit. He tips his hat toward Bell, "Thanks fer the drinks Bell. Don't reckon we care for the company." With that, the wrangler turns and exits behind his fellow wranglers. In the background, Trigger stammers at the piano, trying to continue the classical melody.

"Whatta'e mean by that," Jay turns toward Bell and Robert.

"Been alotta talk, Jay," Robert pours Jay a warm beer and slides it across the bar toward him. The dancehall girls continue to decorate the saloon with the Mayor keeping to himself at the end of the bar, staying out of the conversation, nothing to do with politics... well, kinda.

"Talk 'bout what, Robert?" Jay sips on his beer.

"Jake's gotta point. Ain't right fer a man to be courtin' his best friend's lady," Robert begins cleaning a stack of glasses. "Listen, I know 'bout these things." Robert tosses an apologetic glance toward Bell. She attempts a smile, realizing Robert is trying to make amends. For what, he doesn't know but Bell does. That's all that matters.

"Gonna help the girls a bit," Bell kisses Robert on the cheek, turns and rounds the end of the bar, approaching the boxes along the Mayor's feet. She reaches in and retrieves a heart garland, droops it in front of herself and hands it to one of the dancehall girls.

"Well, then," the Mayor snorts. "I'll be gettin' on now. Bell," the Mayor tips his hat, shuffling across the room, quickly exiting through the batwing doors. Trigger continues to play at the piano in the background at a louder level, trying to drown out Robert and Jay's conversation. Robert sets down his drying rag and glass, pouring himself a glass of warm beer. He leans over the bar facing Jay, takes a sip of his beer and settles in for the tale.

"'Ya see, son," Robert begins, "Awhile back, I had a best friend and I began courtin' his miss while he wasn't away. He got run outta town fer sump'thn' I did," Robert pauses to take another sip of warm beer, "I got the girl but lost my best friend..."

"You know me, mister?" I don' know you," Cougar cautiously steps back a few feet. Theo slams the last of his whiskey shot down his throat. Theo rises to his feet. His boots land hard onto the wooden planked floor. *Jingle-jingle.*

"I reckon I know you. Last spring you robbed my bank."

"*Your* bank? Sounds'ta me like you think this's *your* town," Cougar laughs with his posse closing in behind him along the bar. Theo fully turns to face Cougar, his sheriff's badge glimmering in Cougar's face. "I'll be skinned!" This's *your* town,

"Sheriff","" Cougar replies with a chuckle. His low laughter fades with an evil and stern glare crossing his face. "But not fer long..."

At that instant, gun fire explodes throughout the saloon. Cougar ducks and covers as Theo draws his pair of ivory handled Colt revolvers returning gunfire. Cougar's pack fans out drawing their weapons, wildly firing at Theo. Ivan and the four deputies charge inward opening fire upon Cougar and his gang. Billows of smoke fill the saloon. Bell cowers in Robert's arm behind the cover of the bar.

A gathering of Purgatory's townspeople carefully approach along Main Street. Blazing gunfire continues for several moments from inside of Bell's. Then... a moment of silence.

BLAM. BLAM!

The riders thunder forward. Fitch and Cougar bolt their mounts, taking up the middle of the pack. Cheers and applaud fill the air as the crowd closes the gap where the riders had just been. "Go, boy! Go!" Ivan yells waving his wooden arm.

"Be careful, Fitch," Beth whispers.

"He'll be alright," a familiar voice is heard from behind Beth. Turning, Jay stands facing her with a wanting look on his face. "He'll be just fine."

"I hope so, Jay," Beth replies unconvinced.

Most of the thundering herd has fallen back. Only a dozen riders remain. Fitch and Cougar are nearing the forward middle. Thundering hooves. Wild dust in their wake. There! A few more riders fall out of the race. Fitch and Cougar are neck and neck. Blaze thunders forward at a full gallop, heaving forward. Fitch looks ahead to see the finish line. A span of cargo wagons on opposite sides with cheering locals and tourists. Fitch and Cougar charge onward.

One...

Three...

Six...

Nine riders fall back. It's only Fitch, Cougar and one last racer. The finish line draws nearer. The gathered crowd cheers. Fitch and Cougar exchange determined looks. The last rider can't make it as his horse slows to a panting halt. All that remains is Fitch and Cougar. Cougar and Fitch. Fitch and Cougar. Cougar and Fitch... the finish line! A TIE! Fitch and Cougar thunder forward out into the desert. Fitch leads for a spell then Cougar catches up. Neck and neck. Shoulder to shoulder. No man giving up...

"Not so fast, Johnny Lawman," Cougar snarls. Cougar has already drawn his revolver and has it dead to rights aimed for Fitch's head. "What's with you, lawman? I've been out-range a long time. All I wanted was a few days'n town with me'n the fellas. No need fer all this ruckus," Cougar slowly holsters his pistol. His horse trots over to him.

Cougar leaps up into the saddle and tip his hat in a sarcastic manner, "'Sheriff'." Motioning his horse away, Cougar gallops off back into town. Snort! Fitch turns and looks up at Blaze looking oddly down at his dusty master.

"What?" Cougar snarls. "Whatta 'ya gonna do lawman? Arrest me?" The Cougar Gang deeply laughs, fanning out away from Fitch. "Oh, where's my manners? The Sheriff here might git cold durin' the night." Cougar approaches Fitch and kicks mounds of dirt onto him. Fitch sputters, attempting to wipe away his face. "'Night, sheriff," Cougar sneers...

The smoldering embers softly glow inside the rounded rocks of the campfire. Four pairs of boots surround the fading embers. One particular pair of sportingly handsome boots with silver spurs fastened to their heels. *Jingle-jingle.* The Cougar Gang, all fast asleep.

Cougar tosses and turns over the hard surface of his laid out bedroll and ground. The flickering flames of the dwindling campfire cast shadows across his face. Cougar hears a stir in the surrounding trees. Pretending he is still asleep, Cougar quietly moves his hand downward and draws one of his revolvers. The stirring and fluttering in the trees continues, becoming louder. Cougar springs over to his side and sits up, wildly waving his cocked pistol in all directions. Cougar's eyes widen. His jaw drops.

A flurry of vampire bats swarm over Chote' and Jesse. Feeding on their struggling and bloody bodies. The flapping wings are nearly deafening under the feeding frenzy. The bats consume the pair of limp bodies, continuing to feed upon their fresh and live blood. Cougar waves his revolver in another direction to find Steele with his bloody muzzle buried deep into Dandy's opened chest.

Steele feeds upon Dandy's flesh and internal organs, liver, heart and lungs. Steele licks his chops, slightly glancing up toward Cougar then returns to his meal of Dandy's corpse. Cougar hears a motion from another direction. He whips his revolver about to see a hideous shadowy image swooping down from the surrounding tree tops.

"Shoudda killed me when you had the chance," Fitch powerfully straddles Cougar, knocking his revolver from his hand. Fitch, wearing his sheriff's attire, without his badge upon his chest, slams Cougar's head back onto the ground several times. Shaking Cougar as if her were a child's plaything or rag doll.

Cougar struggles for his second revolver holstered at his hip. He frantically draws the pistol and buries it deep into Fitch's chest as the demonic beast continues to thrash the frail human across the campsite.

BLAM. BLAM. BLAM.

Smoke slips out from the end of the barrel of Cougar's revolver. Fitch, or whatever this thing is, is unharmed, knocking the second weapon away from Cougar's grasp. "Now," the smoothed skinned Demonic Fitch breaths. "It's my turn..."

The nocturnal creature cocks back its head and bares its fanged teeth among its carnivorous jaws. Cougar screams out in terror, trying to kick and pound his way of escape. The beast bares down, thrusting its fangs upon Cougar's throat. Cougar futilely kicks and screams, pushing himself away from the attacking creature…

"What'id I do?!" Sophie screams as Cougar powerfully shoves her from her bed, out onto the wooden planked floor. Sophie lands with a thud, rolls and covers herself with her stained sheet. Sophie springs to her feet and cowers in the far corner.

Cougar leaps from Sophie's bed, lunges for his holstered revolver and waves the weapon in all directions, not sure of his surroundings or even his own reality. His brow covered with sweat. Confused and dazed. "He's comin'…"

"Who? who's comin'?" Sophie carefully approaches Cougar, slightly lowering his drawn revolver aimed at herself. "Who's comin'?"

"That blasted sheriff!" Cougar reluctantly lowers his pistol. "He's comin' an' I'm ready fer'im…" Cougar turns and makes his way toward the lace drawn windows. The afternoon sun, hanging low over the horizon. Main Street below, filtering out the stagecoaches and cargo wagons. A sense of… a sense on impending danger. A sense of something to come.

The lingering rain clouds overhead continuing to drizzle, beginning to clear up, clear out. The rain is moving onward leaving a muddy trail along Main Street. Pattering along the roofs of Purgatory. Cougar rests himself along the window… clutching onto his revolver… ready for anything. Ready for… something…

"Welcome, all!" Bell exclaims standing along the wooden planked boardwalk just outside of the swinging batwing doors of her saloon. Bell's dressed in a lavish pink Victorian full length dress accented with lace and shiny toggles. Her full figure is commanding and full of confidence. Bell smiles and motions local businessmen inward following the loud, up-beat ragtime music Trigger continues to thunder away.

Various conversations and laughter echoes from inside with a handful of local couples, wearing their Sunday best, filter past Bell, entering the saloon, joining the celebration inside. The well placed poker tables along the far side of the boardwalk outside sport sparse games of cards with the dealers tossing out the cards to awaiting gamblers and cowboys.

Bell winks at her few dancehall girls along the poker tables then turns to the opposite direction drawing her attention to the billiard tables resting along the opposite side of the saloon's boardwalk. Pairs of well dressed locals and tourists continue their polite conversations, taking turns at their billiard shots. Bell glances toward the billiard tables then turns about the corner toward the poker tables. "Now, not to long everyone. Party's 'bout to get started."

Bell quickly gazes up and down Main Street. The general stores, shops and other businesses stand still and quiet, closed for the day. The light drizzle continues in sporadic intervals, keeping the central street scattered with pools of rain water. A large cluster of rolling rain clouds darken the sky, preventing the ray's of the afternoon sun from warming the nearly deserted town.

The guests and tourists as well as the majority of the locals mill about inside of Bell's. The only activity is seen far down the street. A few stragglers and cowboys have assembled down at the Stardust Saloon for one reason or another. Maybe not interested in the dance. Maybe no lady friend to accompany them. For whatever reason, the Stardust Saloon has colleted the remaining population of Purgatory. The damp wooden boardwalks and Main Street, barren and vacant of life.

Bell makes her way into her saloon, greeting locals and tourists with a smile and a friendly pat on the shoulder as she passes. Standing room only. The cleared out central area of the saloon is hosted by couples dancing to Trigger's invigorating music from the corner near under the staircase leading up to the railed mezzanine and second floor.

Robert shuffles back and forth from behind the extended bar, pouring drinks and greeting his patrons. The walls are lined with the outer windows with cluttered wranglers, cowboys, locals and tourists. Bell makes her way to the far end of the bar and lovingly nods her head toward Robert. He smiles as he finishes pouring another round of chilled beer for his forward facing customers. Wiping his hands on his soiled apron, Robert approaches Bell as if he had been summoned. "Yes, my dear?" Robert affectionately grins with a hint of sarcasm.

"Have you seen Beth or Jay?" Bell's tone changes.

"Haven' seen'em all day. Why?"

"Neither'ave I," Bell shakes her head.

"Not to worry," Robert attempts to assure Bell. "Prob'ly out somewhere's gettin' into the Valentine spirit."

"That's what I'm afraid of," Bell lovingly slaps Robert on the shoulder. Bell turns and begins to stroll along the dancing couples filling the opened central area of the saloon. She passes by Trigger plunking away at the piano. Not missing a key, he glances up at her with a smile and continues playing the up-beat ragtime melody.

The feeling of the Valentine Day celebration is light and comforting. All walks of life mingling in with the other, not caring of wealth or stature. An assembly of gathered folk, preparing to welcome in the spring.

Blaze and Diamond appear loosely hitched to the sole Joshua Tree along the outskirts of the outer area of the surrounding cast iron fence. The drizzle continues, wetting their manes and saddles. The hoofed creatures remain still and silent, patiently waiting. Steele lays nearly upright on his belly under the far side of the tree, sheltered from the light rain, yet with musty and damp silver fur. The large wolf seems content, chewing and gnawing at a bone resembling a human's thigh or forearm from an unseen cadaver.

Fitch remains steadfast. His head lowered, still wrapped and covered with the dark colored horse blankets, shielded from the sun attempting to peer through the overcast clouds lingering in the sky. The afternoon light, quickly fading. The drizzle collects and runs off the wide brim of his Stetson hat upon his head. The wetness covers his back and shoulders of the protecting horse blankets. He stands in silence, staring down at Grandpa Theo's grave, now worn in, blending in with the surrounding graves and headstones.

Fitch looks to the side seeing his father and mother's headstones. The graves nearly overrun with wild, unkept weeds and desert grass. The etchings in the headstones, worn and nearly unreadable. No matter... Fitch returns his thoughts and attention to Theo's grave and headstone, listening for a reply of an unasked question...

"When he broke open the forth seal, I heard a cry of the forth living creature call out, "Come forward." I looked, and there was a pale horse. Its rider was named Death and Hell followed with him..."

CHAPTER XII

It's darker than usual in Purgatory for this time of year. The persistent rain clouds continuing to linger. The drizzle has stopped, allowing the young lamplighters to hobble along their slits, lighting the well placed lampposts at the corners of Main Street. The flickering lampposts cast dancing shadows over the unusually dark town with opposite facing closed shops and general stores. Unusually dark...

At the far end of town, faint piano music seeps out from the Stardust Saloon. Sparse activity from within with the lit lanterns casting their light outward onto the slightly muddy street. The last of the lamplighters round the far corner of the Stardust Saloon to one side as a pair of others light the lampposts along the end livery, sheriff's office and jail.

As the young men stomp through the damp course of Main Street, they draw nearer to Bell's at the opposite end of town. Lively up-beat piano music roars outward, inviting them inward. The lamplighters support each other, helping each to the damp wooden planked boardwalk outside of Bell's.

The poker tables to one side and the billiard tables to the opposite side, stand vacant. All players of their various games have left, joining the Valentine's Day celebration inside. The young men lean their stilts along a hitching post cluttered with tied horses, as if their artificial wooden legs were horses themselves. Although underdressed, the young lamplighters playfully shove at each other as they enter Bell's.

The lamplighters are greeted by a swarm of dancing couples and free hoofing wranglers as Trigger whips his fingers across the black and white keys of his piano. The young men filter into the crowds along the bar with Doc Herring bracing himself up on the far end. The lamplighters politely nod toward Doc as he polishes off his mug of warm beer. Trigger's fingers abruptly stop at the end of the melody. The assembly applauds. "Cleo!" Bell exclaims. "Cleo! Sing us a song!"

Cleo shutters in the corner under the upward staircase along side of Trigger and the piano, trying to keep hidden in the shadows. She blushes as Bell swiftly moves toward her, taking her by the arm, forcing her out from the shadows for all to see. "I could'n', Ma'am," Cleo pulls away.

"Fine, then!" Bell turns and wildly waves her hand in the air toward her saloon. "Alright, git out!" Moans and grumbles fill the main floor. "No, I mean it! If Cleo ain't gonna sing, the party's over!"

"Sing!" one man yells out.

"Com'on," a wrangler bellows. In a matter of moments, the entire saloon is filled with cheers and encouraging tones coaxing Cleo to sing. She brushes her hand across her face and slowly approaches Trigger sitting in front of the piano. Her plain dress and commonly looks seem out of place among the hordes of well dressed locals and tourists. Cleo timidly nods toward Trigger as the cheers become quiet. All eyes are upon her.

Trigger slams his fingers down onto the keys in a single cord, startling most of the tourist women and a few of the dancehall girls. Trigger rolls his fingers across the keys leading into a sultry and almost grinding blues tune he had learned on New Year's Eve. Bodies begin to sway. Couples embrace each other.

Lonely cowboys and wranglers begin to dance by themselves or take up with any willing dancehall girl who'll join them. Cleo belts out a growling low voice accompanied by Trigger. The tune, soulful and suggestive. The central area of Bell's saloon becomes instantly cluttered with slow dancing bodies, moving back and forth to Cleo and Trigger's hypnotic melody.

Robert pours a round of whiskey shots for his few remaining forward facing patrons, unties and tosses his apron onto the bar relieving his stout shape then rounds the end of the bar. Coming up from behind, Robert takes Bell into his arms. She seems pleasantly surprised at his embrace. Robert twirls Bell around the floor among the scads of other dancing couples, free flowing cowboys and paired cowboys and dancehall girls as Cleo and Trigger's music fills the air, picking up in tempo and intensity.

The full moon hangs low over the horizon. Departing rain clouds allow the moon's rays to seep downward, soaking up the town of Purgatory. A sole image is seen at the near end of town. The image, resting, sitting in the saddle of a smoky blue horse. Music fills the air as the image remains still and steadfast in a stalking position.

The lit lampposts flicker along the corners of Main Street. Not a soul to be seen nor heard from the closed general stores, shops and damp wooden planked boardwalks. Except for the opposing music of Bell's and the Stardust Saloon at opposite ends of town, there is no life to be seen. The image coaxes his stallion forward, slipping out from the shadows followed by a large silver backed wolf.

"My goodness, Robert," Bell fans herself as she bursts out from the swinging batwing doors, pausing to catch her breath along the boardwalk of her saloon. "We haven't danced like that in years." Robert quickly follows behind, swiftly taking her by the waist, spinning her around. Bell breathes heavily, facing Robert as he leans in and lovingly kisses her on the lips.

"Kinda gettin' into the Valentine spirit myself," Robert tenderly holds her closer. Bell smiles deep into his dark eyes for a moment before leaning inward, wrapping her arms around his stout midsection. Looking over Robert's shoulder, Bell sees the image on horseback appearing from the shadows. Turning pale with fear, Bell pushes Robert away. He quickly turns.

"Hell's bells..." Bell whispers as the image completely emerges from the shadows into the flickering light of the lit lampposts. Robert, a man of the world, has never seen such a sight. A rider. A rider of Death. The Grim Reaper himself.

Here... in Purgatory. This is no man, but... Fitch! Sheriff Fitch Woolley!

Fitch slows and pulls back on the reigns, stopping Blaze and Diamond at the corner of the street in front of Bell's at the corner. He defiantly swings his leg over and dismounts the saddle, still clutching onto Blaze's reigns as Steele sits awaiting his next command. Fitch steps up a few stairs of the boardwalk leading up to Bell's. *Jingle-jingle.* Robert embraces Bell, slightly backing away from the man they once knew approaching them, wrapped from head to toe in dark colored horse blankets.

Fitch slowly removes his grey Stetson, placing it upon the damp boardwalk, then purposely begins to remove the dark horse blankets, draping them over the nearest cross section of a hitching post along side of the stilts. Fitch's attire, the black trousers and short cut caballero jacket looks more of a preacher than a sheriff.

Robert looks Fitch up and down... Fitch reaches down for the oversized Stetson from the boardwalk and places it upon his head. A pair of holstered ivory handled Colt revolvers at his hips. A fastened black bull whip loosely tied to his waist, a primitive revolver tucked into the front of his gunbelt, the Henry rifle tucked into his saddle behind him and the silver spurs at the heels of his boots. *Jingle-jingle.*

"Where's Elizabeth?" Fitch orders. He has never called her "Elizabeth" in public. Robert and Bell cower, backing their way closer to the closed swinging batwing doors behind them. Something has changed inside of Fitch... something not right.

"Haven't seen her all day," Bell sputters.

"And my "Deputy", Jay?" Robert timidly shakes his head. Fitch looks over their shoulders, inside of the saloon, seeing the dancing and celebration. Without a word, Fitch turns back from the boardwalk, slightly tugging at Blaze's reigns. Leading them along, Fitch leads Blaze and Diamond along the damp central course of Main Street with Steele trotting close behind. *Jingle-jingle. Jingle-jingle.*

339

Bell and Robert turn and dash inside, crashing through the batwing doors. "Quiet!" Bell interrupts Trigger and Cleo's second melody. "Quiet, everyone! Fitch's back'n town!" Trigger and Cleo's duet falls silent. The frolicking and dancing ceases. All eyes turn upon Bell and Robert. Some of the faces are overjoyed, the return of their beloved Sheriff.

Other faces appear concerned, knowing the gallivanting and fraternizing of Jay and Beth that most of the local town's people know about. A cold thing to do... taking a man's woman. Rumors will be rumors... in any town. The gathered assembly quickly push and shove their way toward the batwing doors, forcing Bell and Robert back out onto the boardwalk, lunging out toward Main Street.

"Elizabeth!" Fitch calls out in a low voice. He loosely wraps Blaze's reigns along the hitching post outside the Katherine Hotel. He pauses a moment before climbing the wooden stairs leading up to the cracked open front door. "Elizabeth!" Fitch calls out again as he fearlessly makes his way up onto the damp boardwalk.

"Cougar!" Sophie exclaims as she dashes from the lace covered window toward the bed. Cougar lays napping atop the stained sheets of the unmade bed. Sophie lunges for him, shaking him wildly. He quickly sits up in bed with Sophie's hands upon his shoulders, draws one of his revolvers from under the pillow and shoves it into her ribs. Cougar suddenly realizes where his is.

"Sophie?"

"I seen'im from the window!"

"Who?"

"Sheriff Woolley! He's here!"

"Where?" Cougar exclaims as he bolts from the bed, dashes across the wooden floor toward the lace covered window, clutching onto his cocked revolver. Keeping out of sight from the window, Cougar scans Main Street, seeing Fitch glancing over his shoulder turns then disappears under the awning of the Katherine

Hotel. "Remember what'ta do, Sophie?" Cougar darts from the window grabbing his hanging gunbelt from the far hook.

"You promised to take me with you!" Sophie slides into her worn dress. A frantic look covers her face.

"Yeah, yeah," Cougar pulls his jacket over his shoulder, Fitch's shiny Sheriff's badge upon his chest, reaches for his saddlebags and slings them over his shoulder. "I'll take you with me," he replies in an unconvincing tone. "Jest remember what'ta do!"

"I will," Sophie slips a leather garter around her thigh with a loaded and holstered double barreled derringer. Cougar wraps his gunbelt around his waist with his Civil War saber hanging at his hip. He tosses Sophie a kiss on the cheek and flings the door open.

Cougar and Sophie quietly make their way along the dimly lit hallway toward the back of the building. Slipping out through a second floor backdoor, Cougar and Sophie shuffle down the back steps of the Stardust Saloon. The light piano music fills the air from inside. Cougar and Sophie are undetected as they slip around the corner of the Stardust Saloon heading down the narrow alleyway between saloon and the train depot.

Cougar and Sophie pause a moment along side of a cargo wagon. A pair of harnesses dangle from the front of the wagon with no horses to be seen. Along the central area of the wagon, a covered object is faintly made out from the shadows. Cougar and Sophie continue onward a moment until approaching the end of the alleyway, peering out onto the vacant Main Street.

"Elizabeth?" Fitch cautiously strolls into the lobby of The Katherine. The lit lanterns cast flickering light upon the front counter desk. Fitch approaches the desk and takes a hand written note in hand, *'GONE TO DANCE'*. Fitch tosses the note back onto the counter, turns and begins to head out from the lobby, leaving the door opened behind himself as he exits.

Fitch makes his way down from the boardwalk, unties Blaze from the hitching post and leads his stallion and Diamond along the street. Steele trots along side, sniffing the air, sensing something. The silver backed wolf lets out a low growl. "I know," Fitch glances down toward Steele, "I smell'im, too." Fitch continues to lead Blaze and Diamond down Main Street heading toward the far end of town.

"What's gonna happ'n," Trigger clings onto Bell's arm.

"Don't know, hon." Bell motherly replies. The entire assembly of Purgatory fans out all around Bell's saloon along the street below the various poker tables and billiard tables along Bell's boardwalk, trying to keep to this far end of town as possible, yet not wanting to miss any of the impending events to come. Robert slowly makes his way from the swinging batwing doors coming up along side of Bell. He gives her an assuring look, reaches across and messes up Trigger's hair.

Fitch leads Blaze and Diamond toward the livery. *Jingle-jingle.* There is no sign of the blacksmith. The furnace is cold and lifeless. The stables are dark and intimidating. Fitch rounds Blaze and Diamond into their own stables, leaving their saddles in place. Loosely closing each of the stable gates, Fitch turns and heads out of the livery with Steele trotting along side.

Fitch appears from the darkness, standing firm outside the livery. He stares blankly forward, the Stardust Saloon. Sparse activity is seen from within. The light piano music continues with scattered poker tables cluttered with various card games inside. Fitch looks down at Steele and gives his companion a stern glare. Steele understands and obeys, sitting, standing post in front of the livery. Fitch turns and slowly makes his way toward the last building along this side of Main Street... the sheriff's office and jail.

Fitch slowly steps up onto the wooden boardwalk, takes a few steps and slightly pushes open the door. Lit lanterns light up the main area as he enters. Cougar sits at the desk with his feet propped up on a medium sized black powder keg. His saddlebags still draped over his shoulder. He shuffles several pieces of Beth's onion paper journal in his hand among a few of his own wanted fliers. Fitch continues a few feet and pauses, facing Cougar from across the room. "Business is kinda slow, Sheriff," Cougar snarls. "Only got two prisoners in'ere."

Looking over Cougar's shoulder, two of the three jail cells have occupants. Jay in one cell and Morris in the next. Jay and Morris have been badly beaten, faces puffy and bloody, bound at the wrists, hanging from the forward bars of the cells. A deep sword wound pours out blood from Jay's side, bleeding to death. His deputy's badge, smeared with his own blood.

"Looks like yer boy here been kinda busy whiles you been away," Cougar grins as he lifts one of Beth's pages and begins to read aloud in a melodramatic tone. ""Fitch's been gone for nearly a month now. Is he ever to return? Will he want to be with me when he does? And what of James? What am I to tell him? He's been there for me all these years even when Fitch was away to school in Philadelphia,'" Cougar tosses the top page to the desk, shuffles through the stack, nearly reaching the last page and sarcastically looks up at Fitch a moment, "This's where it really gets good."

"Go on," Fitch orders in a low voice.

""...and the baby,'" Cougar continues to read aloud. ""What of the baby?'" Cougar tosses the remaining onion papers onto the desk top then adjusts his boots on the black powder keg. "Looks like yer gonna be a papa, Sheriff," Cougar grins then quickly glances over his shoulder toward Jay hanging in the behind cell. "Oh, well reckon <u>one</u> of 'ya're gonna be a papa."

Fitch looks up away from Cougar. Jay strains to look into his eyes, ashamed of himself. Fitch slightly cocks his head then nods in a forgiving manner. This seems to slightly comfort Jay, slouching his head downward, the loss of blood draining his strength. "Where's Elizabeth?" Fitch orders. The arrogant outlaw smirks as he takes notice that Fitch has reacquired his grey Stetson hat and his pair of ivory handled Colt revolvers holstered at his hips. Cougar looks Fitch up and down seeing his added accessories.

"So, I see you met up with Spider," motioning at the black bull whip hanging from Fitch's hip.

"Reckon he was all choked up to see me," Fitch murmurs. "He won't be joining us anytime soon."

"Too bad," Cougar continues to look over Fitch seeing Jesse's revolver tucked into the front of his gunbelt. "Did'ya take out all of my boys?" Fitch reaches for Jesse's revolver and throws it to the desk top. It lands with a thud and a spin. He reaches into the small of his back, retrieves Chote's Bowie knife and hurls it into the side wall. It sticks with a loud thud. Reaching for Spider's bull whip, Fitch tosses it to the desk top along side of Jesse's revolver.

"I can go fetch the Henry rifle if you'd like," Fitch stares at Cougar.

"Not necessary, Sheriff," Cougar readjusts his boots on the black powder keg. "I'll gather it up later."

"Where's Elizabeth?" Fitch commands for the second time.

"Oh, that fiery redhead?" Cougar sneers as he reaches for a match, striking it across the side of the desk. He lets the match burn for a few moments as he plops a hand rolled cigar in his mouth. Cougar lights the cigar and puffs on it. Still lit, Cougar tosses the match toward his boots, landing on the top of the black powder keg. "Guests check in but they don't check out," Cougar laughs.

"I'll be out front," Fitch turns his back on Cougar and heads toward the door. Cougar breaths on the cuff of his jacket and polishes the badge pinned to his chest, slightly glancing over his shoulder toward Jay.

"That sheriff of yers, I'll give'im one thing," Cougar gloats. "He's got big'uns... real big'uns." The match on the top of the powder keg smolders itself out. Cougar raises up and adjusts the saddle bags along his shoulder. He reaches out and takes Chote's Bowie knife from the wall. Taking the rattling keys, Cougar moves toward the first cell, opening the barred door, approaching Morris. "Not gonna'ave any trouble with you am I?"

344

Morris stammers out a mumbled response. Cougar reaches upward, cutting Morris' ropes from the bars, still keeping him bound at the wrists. Morris staggers to the side causing his chained ankles to rattle. Taking Morris by his bound wrists, Cougar leads him out of the cell, approaching the next cell. Cougar leers in through the bars, ""Ow 'bout you? Gonna'ave any trouble?" Jay strains to raise his head. Large pools of his drying blood have collected around his chained ankles.

Fitch passes the livery. Steele remains at his post standing guard of the stables. Fitch continues along the side of the street, making his way up onto the boardwalk. *Jingle-jingle.* The music has stopped from within the Stardust Saloon. Ned, card dealers, the piano player, worn dancehall girls, as well as the lot of gamblers and wranglers have filed outside, spanning out all along the damp boardwalk. Something's about to happen.

Fitch stomps into the lobby of the Katherine Hotel. He pauses looking into the side parlor then past the side of the front desk counter down along the near hallway. There is no sound. He raises his head and listens. There, upstairs he hears a slight muffling. Taking three leaping strides, Fitch bounds up the entire staircase, standing firm at the top mezzanine. He pauses and listens again. The faint muffling is coming from down along the forward hallway. Fitch runs his powerful hand along the side railing as he moves across the second floor mezzanine toward the last hallway facing Main Street.

"Sheriff!" Sophie blurts out as Fitch rounds the corner stopping in his tracks at the near end of the hallway. She clutches onto a lit kerosene lantern. Along the floor in front of herself, the head of ten fastened fuses. The fuses branch off along the floor like the arms of an octopus, each leading under a separate closed doors along the hallway on opposite sides of herself.

"Sophie?" Fitch calmly asks. "What're you doing?"

"He told me if I did what he said, he'd take me with'im!"

"He won't, Sophie."

"He will!" Sophie exclaims. "Cougar loves me!"

345

"He doesn't," Fitch calmly begins to move forward, entering the hallway.

"He will and he does!" Sophie yells with a tremble in her voice.

"Sophie…" Fitch's tone remains calm yet stern.

"No!" Sophie screams as she cocks back her arm and hurls the lit lantern to the floor. The lantern shatters sending kerosene in all directions. The instant flame ignites the head of the ten fastened fuses. In the blink of an eye, the fuses all begin to burn in ten directions. The seeping kerosene douses Sophie's dress. Flames swiftly creep upward. Sophie frantically spins about trying to flee the growing blaze. "NOOOOooooooo!" The flames consume the surrounding walls, eating their way up and along the ceiling.

Fitch slams through the first closed door as the fuses continue to burn. There is no sign of Beth. The burning fuse along the floor leads to a black powder key on the floor in the middle of the room. Fitch darts from the doorway into the hallway. Roaring flames all around filling the hallway. Fitch crashes in through the second door, scanning the room. Sophie screams out is sheer pain at the end of the hallway, completely engulfed with flames, her dress, her hair, her flesh, smoldering and charring. Blurting out a final scream of terror, Sophie wildly thrashes about, crashing out through the second story window at the end of the hallway in a fiery blaze.

Fitch leaps through the flames filling the hallway and crashes through the sixth closed door and scans the room. There is no trace of Beth. The burning fuse leads to yet another black powder keg on the floor in the middle of the room. Fitch turns and dashes across the inferno of the hallway, smashing into the next room as the fuses continue to burn along the floor.

Beth lays flat on her back, straddled with her wrists and ankles tightly fastened to the four corners of the bed. Her mouth is bound and gagged. The fuse continues to burn along the floor leading to another black powder keg in the middle of the room.

Beth wears her light blue Victorian dress. Her locket loosely drooped along her neck. Fitch races to the side of the bed and unfastens her wrists. Beth swiftly sits up in bed and removes the gag from her mouth. As Fitch leans downward to unfasten her ankles, Beth lunges forward, taking Fitch's head in her hands, forcing his mouth upon hers. The kiss is wet and powerful. Full of intensity. Beth suddenly pushes Fitch away from herself, looks him dead in the eye then hauls off and slaps him in the face.

"How <u>dare</u> you go'n die on me!" she blurts out in anguish. Fitch is stunned for a moment. A single tear wells up in Beth's eye as she reaches for Fitch again and plants another kiss on his welcoming lips. As their lips part, she feels something different. Something has changed. Beth can see it in his eyes.

"We have no time for this right now, Elizabeth," Fitch unfastens her ankles. "We have to get out of here." The growing flames from the hallway leap inward along the doorway and ceiling. Their only route of escape has been cut off. Terror wells up inside of Beth. Fitch scans the room. The fuse burning ever so close to the black powder keg. Fitch powerfully grabs Beth into his arms, sweeping her off of her feet. "Hold on," Fitch whispers in a calm tone. Beth wraps her arms around Fitch's neck, burying her face deep into his chest. Fitch thunders toward the window and leaps into the air.

KA-BOOM! KA-BOOM! KA-BOOM!

One by one, the ten black powder kegs explode. Large fragments of debris are hurled through the air. The entire second story of the Katherine Hotel, demolished in flames. Through a billowing cloud of thick black smoke and a roaring wall of flames, Fitch flies through the air from the burning second story window. Beth, held tightly in his arms. Fitch seems to hover and soar a moment before gracefully gliding downward toward Main Street. The burning Katherine Hotel in their wake.

Fitch lands with a thud. *Jingle-jingle.* He tenderly lowers Beth to the ground. She clutches onto his neck for a long moment, looking deep into his eyes. Reluctantly, Fitch pushes her away, brushing his hand to the side toward Steele. The wolf lets out a low bark, taking his place by Beth's side.

The second story of the Katherine continues to smolder and slowly begins to burn itself out. Smoke billows through the air releasing cinders across Main Street and the roof tops of the nearby buildings. Inside the lobby, Beth's scattered stacks of onion papers lay about the floor behind the front desk counter. Several with charred and burned edges.

Fitch motions Beth and Steele away from himself as he turns to face the far end of town. Slowly, he begins to make his way toward Cougar. Jay and Morris appear hitched and harnessed in front of Cougar's covered cargo wagon in the middle of the street. Jay is weak and pale from the numerous bloody wounds. The harnesses and reigns are heavy upon his shoulders. Jay and Morris remain shackled and the ankles and bound at the wrists.

Cougar, with his saddlebags still hung around his shoulder, arrogantly stands along side of the covered object in the back of the cargo wagon, propping his boot up onto the side panel as Fitch slows to a halt several dozen yards away. "You have something of mine," Fitch calls out in a calm tone. "I want it back."

"Oh," Cougar chuckles. "You mean this badge?" Cougar mockingly polishes the badge pinned to his chest with the cuff of his jacket. "Come'n git it, "Sheriff"." Cougar slyly makes his way around the covered object in the back of the cargo wagon, standing nearly chest high now. "Like'ta show you 'lil sump'thn I picked up during the war!"

Cougar tears off the large tarp covering the object revealing a cocked and loaded Gatling gun. With an evil grin, Cougar opens fire upon Fitch.

CLACKITY- CLACKITY- CLACKITY- CLACKITY- CLACKITY...

The countless rounds of bullets scream through the air, imploding into Fitch's chest. The force of the onslaught of bullets causes Fitch to stammer backwards. His chest riddled with bullets. Beth screams and covers her face. Bell and Robert cling together

348

among the horrified on-looking townspeople and tourists. Ned, dancehall girls and patrons of the Stardust Saloon cower.

CLACKITY- CLACKITY- CLACKITY- CLACKITY- CLACKITY...

Cougar roars out in evil laughter, continuing to fire the Gatling gun upon Fitch. The rounds of the gun seem endless. Fitch is powerfully hurled backward through the air onto the damp ground covered with bullet holes. His smoking chest heaves up with one final breath. Fitch lays in the middle of Main Street, still and motionless.

CLACKITY- CLACKITY- CLICK- CLICK- CLICK...

The Gatling gun is finally empty. Grey smoke seeps out from the ends of the numerous barrels rolling and spinning to a deathly halt. Cougar gloats, making his way from behind the Gatling gun, hopping down to the ground, remaining close to the side of the cargo wagon. Jay and Morris can barely stand. Jay strains to look over to the side, Fitch is dead in the middle of the street. Women weep. Men lower their heads. Beth muffles her crying in her hands, burying her face.

"Cougar!" a shrieking voice echoes out from along side of the smoldering Katherine Hotel. All eyes turn. Cougar carefully places his hand upon the handle of his sheathed Civil War saber at his side. "Cougar, I did what you said!" From the smoky shadows, Sophie appears. Her dress, sooted black and charred. Her once beautiful hair, smoldering revealing her badly burned head and face. Severe burns cover her exposed flesh.

"Git away from me, woman!" Cougar blurts out.

"I did what you said," Sophie tearfully pleads. "You said you'd take me with you!" Sophie continues to stagger toward him.

"Git away!" Cougar begins to draw his sword. Sophie continues toward him, raising the front end of her charred dress, revealing her holstered double barreled derringer from her thigh.

"You said you'd take me with you!"

"Git away, woman!" Cougar commands with his sword drawn. Sophie staggers and slightly sidesteps, raising the derringer.

Cougar lunges behind Jay, using the bloody deputy to block Sophie's attack.

BLAM-BLAM.

The pair of rounds burst into Jay's chest. He slumps to his knees, then falls forward onto the ground with the harnesses suspending him from his shoulders. Weeping, Sophie hurls herself toward Cougar with her arms wide open, wishing for a welcoming embrace. Cougar thrusts his sword deep into Sophie's chest, running her completely through. A shocked and hurtful look covers her charred and bloody face, slouching in Cougar's arm. With a final gasp, Sophie slumps and falls dead to the ground along side of Jay who continues to struggle for life.

"I am He who lives, and was dead, and behold, I am alive forevermore. And I have the keys of Hell and Death!" a low grumbling voice is heard from the darkness.

Cougar turns toward the far end of Main Street. Fitch calmly stands facing him. He pauses a moment, leans down and picks up his oversized grey Stetson hat, defiantly placing it back onto his head. Gasps of terror and shock fill the air. Beth turns pale with fright. Cougar arrogantly steps away from the side of the cargo wagon, facing Fitch several dozen yards away. "I heard that 'bout you."

"What's that?" Fitch responds.

"You can't be stabbed. Can't be shot," Cougar pauses a moment. "Can't be shot?" Cougar slowly raises his hand, reaching into the forward facing flap of the saddlebag hung about his shoulder. Cougar retrieves a book. A book. "MYTHS AND LEGENDS". Cougar mocking flips through the pages, glances upward and grins at Fitch. He tosses the book to the ground next to Jay, gasping for air.

"What did you do to him?" Fitch orders.

"The old man? He didn't suffer," Cougar chuckles, "...much." A tear wells up in Bell's eye. Trying to be understanding, Robert wraps his arm around her. Cougar smirks as he reaches into the forward facing flap of the saddlebag for the second time. He retrieves a small leather poke. Cougar tosses the saddlebags to the ground, the last of the Wells Fargo Bank of Purgatory's paper money and silver coins spill out into the mud.

Cougar opens Jose's poke with one hand and reaches in and pulls out a single round handmade silver bullet. With a cocky smile, Cougar throws the round toward Fitch. The sheriff catches the silver round and examines it in the palm of his scarred hand. At the opposite end of Main Street, Cougar defiantly draws one of his revolvers.

Cougar pulls back the loading lever of his first revolver. He removes the loaded cylinder from the weapon and secures it into an empty leather snap case at his hip. Cougar slides his hand across his gunbelt and unfastens another leather snap case, removing a cylinder loaded with Jose's handmade silver bullets. "Ya' know, Sheriff," Cougar smiles, "We're not so different you'n I. You'd be surprised," Cougar continues to load the cylinder into the revolver. "Ya' see, I know a 'lill sump'thn 'bout silver, too." Fitch cocks his head to the side, wondering what Cougar is up to. Smiling, Cougar holsters his first revolver and calmly draws his second. He repeats his meticulous actions, loading the second revolver with a secondary cylinder, also loaded with Jose's handmade silver bullets. Securing the loading leaver of the second revolver, Cougar glances up toward Fitch. "Oh, I reckon you didn't git to that chapter yet!" Cougar laughs, holstering his loaded revolver.

Cougar takes a few steps forward, halts and steadies his feet onto the ground. Fitch faces him from several dozen yards away. The crackling sounds of the smoldering flames of the Katherine Hotel echo through the air. Beth holds her breath. Steele at her side, tail wagging. Purgatory is deathly still and quiet. It is unusually dark for this time of year. Unusually dark...

"While Doc was lookin' me over t'day, I saw you practicin'."

"Yes, Grandpa?"

"Never showboat or at least try to showboat. That's what gets people kilt. Never draw outta anger or drunkenness. Always

keep focused and in control. Chances are, whoever you'r confronted with is's scarred out of their wits as you'r. Knowin' this and keepin' yer wits about you, you'll live a might longer time'n I have."

"Yes, Grandpa..."

Cougar draws.

Fitch draws.

BLAM-BLAM-BLAM.

Cougar grins at Fitch with a drawn revolver in each hand. Fitch clutches onto his right drawn ivory handled Colt revolver. The scar of his opened left palm hovering over the cocked back hammer. Grey smoke seeps from the end of the barrel. The carefree expression on Cougar's mug slips away. He looks down to his chest, three bullet holes. In shock, Cougar looks up toward Fitch who slowly continues to walk toward him. Cougar lowers his drawn revolvers and drops them to the ground. He falls to his knees, then slumps over Sophie next to him... dying.

Fitch holsters his Colt revolver as he approaches and hovers over Cougar. With his boot, he rolls Cougar over onto his back. *Jingle-jingle.* Cougar looks blankly up into the dark sky. The lingering rain clouds departing. The full moon hanging high overhead. With a final gasp, Cougar's eyes close for the last time.

Fitch steps over Cougar's body and unfastens Morris from the cargo wagon's harnesses. Morris rubs his worn shoulders and steps to the side, unfastening his shackled ankles. Fitch swiftly moves to Jay's side, unfastening him from the cargo wagon's harnesses. His body growing stiff and cold, shivering. Fitch unties Jay's bound wrists and shackled ankles then crouches down holding Jay in his arms. His wounds beyond repair. "Nice shootin'," Jay struggles for a smile. "I reckon I'm not the sheriff anymore..." Fitch holds Jay in his arms, attempting to comfort his dying deputy... his dying friend.

Doc scurries across the street totting his black medical bag, approaching Fitch and Jay. He crouches over, nearly face to face with Fitch. There is something different about the man he spent so many years looking after. Something very different. Doc looks over Jay's wounds then sadly looks up toward Fitch, "I'm truly sorry, Sheriff. There's nothing to be done." Doc shakes his head and rises, reaching into his medical bag for his whiskey flask. As Doc downs a gulp, Bell and Robert slowly approach.

"Is there anything <u>you</u> can do for him, Fitch?" Beth timidly asks, flipping through the pages of the muddy book. Beth hovers over Fitch and Jay looking upon the pages. She pauses at an illustration, The Hounds of Hell. Steele trots over and heals next to Fitch with Jay still cradled in his arms.

"I'm sorry, James," Fitch whispers looking deep into Jay's fading eyes. Cougar's numerous wounds as well as Sophie's fatal gunshots, the smell of blood is overwhelming. Jay's blood covers Fitch's hands, covering his jacket, filling up deep into his soul. Blood... live blood. Fitch rears back his head, barring his fangs among his canine teeth. His eyes boiling red. His bat-like features seemingly rising to the surface. Fitch thrusts his fangs deep into Jay's neck, piercing his cold flesh. A slight gurgle is heard from Jay's throat. Clutching onto the book, Beth watches and backs away in terror.

Jay's breathing becomes erratic, slowing. He gasps for air. Fitch continues to feed upon Jay's warm blood, sealing Jay's fate... as well as his own. His first taste of live human blood. Pumping through his veins. Feeding... feeding... feeding. Fitch powerfully embraces Jay, nearly crushing his ribs, sinking his fangs deeper into his throat. Jay gasps! Then, falls limp in Fitch's arms. Fitch continues to hold Jay for a long moment. The town is quiet.

Fitch raises his head from Jay's throat. His barred fangs dripping with Jay's warm blood. Deep bite marks are seen in Jay's throat with oozing blood dripping down his neck. "For they have shed the blood of Saints and of Prophets, and you have given them blood to drink, for it is their just due," Fitch tenderly whispers to Jay, his deputy...his best friend.

Jay gasps and opens his eyes, looking around in bewilderment. Fitch fatherly lifts Jay upward in his arms, "We have a lot to talk about…" Fitch raises up and helps Jay to his feet. The sheriff and the deputy. Side by side. Both, should be dead.

Clutching to the muddy book in her arms, Beth begins to move toward the pair, toward Fitch then toward Jay. Jay and then Fitch. Beth looks deep into Fitch's eyes for support and comfort… there is none. Beth slowly backs away, standing next to Doc, Robert, Bell and Trigger.

The locals, dancehall girls and visitors slowly creep their way closer, surrounding Fitch and Jay. Cougar and Sophie's slain bodies laying in the mud along side of the cargo wagon and Gatling gun. Fitch turns and approaches Cougar. Crouching down, Fitch reaches out and tears off the sheriff's badge from Cougar's chest. "…and yes, I <u>did</u> git to that chapter…" Standing, Fitch gazes down at Grandpa Theo's shiny badge in the palm of his scarred hand. He looks up for approval.

The Mayor turns his head. Doc looks away. Robert and Bell cling to each other keeping Trigger close. Beth backs away. The townspeople and tourists cower. Jay's blood still covering Fitch's mouth and chin. Fitch chuckles to himself as he turns, tossing his sheriff's badge to Morris, catching it, fumbling it in his hands. Fitch glances toward Beth in a loving manner then motions for Steele.

Fitch and Steele turn away, strolling toward the end of town, heading for the sheriff's office and jail. "Let's get that fire out!" the Mayor bellows. In an instant, the men of Purgatory dash to action. Collecting up buckets, the men form a fire chain from any and all horse troughs. Douses of water are tossed and poured upon The Katherine Hotel, attempting to save her. Fitch and Steele continue toward the end of town drawing nearer to the sheriff's office and jail.

Jay turns to follow. He pauses and turns, looking deep into Beth's eyes, still clutching to the mysterious book. Jay wants to stay. Beth wants him to stay. Yet, Jay is drawn… drawn to follow

Fitch. With an apologetic smile and nod, Jay turns and trots after his Sheriff... his friend.

Beth lingers along the middle of Main Street. The valiant local men and tourists continuing to douse the flames of her hotel trying to salvage the structure. The street is clearing of onlookers. The constant water chain of buckets. Robert escorts Bell and Trigger back to Bell's. Doc wonders off totting his flask in one hand and his black bag in the other. Beth clutches onto the book... the book.

Slightly turning, Beth looks over her shoulder. Steele playfully chases his tail in front of the sheriff's office and jail. Jay has caught up with Fitch. In a commanding manner, Fitch steps up onto the damp wooden planked boardwalk then heads toward the front door with the flickering lights of the inside lanterns of the building casting shadows across his face. Fitch pauses to look over his shoulder, Beth gazing back at him. With a painful smile, Fitch turns and enters. *Jingle-jingle...*

"I don't know if this's such a good idea, Beth," Bell replies in a low motherly voice. Beth continues to scurry around her dinning area with platters of cooked eggs and bacon. Bell and Robert sit plainly about the see-saw legged table in the center of the room. Lit kerosene lanterns flicker, casting dancing shadows across the log walls.

"They said they'd come for breakfast," Beth cheerfully answers. "Oh, I haven't shown you this yet," Beth tosses Bell a smiling glance. Beth darts down the narrow hallway and disappears into the first opened door of her bedroom. Bell and Robert look oddly toward each other from across the table. Beth scampers back into the main room holding up a small one piece outfit. Handmade... to fit a baby.

"It's lovely, dear," Bell responds with an uncertain tone. Beth sets the outfit onto the table and returns to the cooking meat in the simmering skillets on the pot belly stove across the room. Beth hums to herself, preparing the meals for all. Robert reaches across the table, tenderly taking Bell's hand in his. They exchange looks… regretful and sad.

Fitch and Jay stand outside facing the closed front door. The horseshoe hanging atop the doorway. Beth's light humming is heard from inside. The flickering kerosene lanterns reflecting their light outward through the windows. Fitch clutches his fist as if to knock on the door. He pauses. Jay looks puzzled at him. Taking a deep breath, Fitch unclasps his fist, turns and quietly steps off the porch. Looking confused, Jay turns to follow. He reaches out and takes Fitch by the arm, spinning him about. "Why don't we tell'er?"

"Tell'er what, James?" Fitch snorts under his breath. "How would you like me to put it?" he pauses a moment. "The two men that you love are leaving… forever!?" Jay's eyes widen. "Yes, James. I've known you've loved Elizabeth for some time now."

"But, we're both leaving her."

"It's for the best."

"For who?.. You?... Me?... Elizabeth?" Jay whispers. "For who?" Fitch turns and heads away from Beth's house, angrily strolling through the tall wild grass slightly swaying in the wind. The flickering light of the lit lanterns reflection upon his back as he slips into the darkness. He approaches Blaze and swings himself up into the saddle. Taking the reigns in hand, Fitch looks toward Jay, remaining mere feet away from the front porch.

Jay looks up toward Fitch then back to the inviting closed door with the hanging horseshoe. Beth's sweet humming continues to fill his head. Jay slowly reaches up toward his chest, removing his blood smeared deputy's badge. He lifts it to his lips, kisses it and tenderly places it upon the wooden planks of the front porch. Jay makes his way through the tall grass, coming up along side of Diamond and likewise, with little effort, swings himself up into the saddle.

Steele trots up along side as Fitch coaxes Blaze forward. Jay turns to look over his shoulder, hearing Beth's soothing humming, seeing her shadows and outline through the windows.

Jay coaxes Diamond forward, coming up along side of Fitch and Blaze. The setting full moon hangs low over the horizon, beaming its inviting rays through the departing rain clouds.

...screech-screech.

...screech-screech.

Steele wiggles his ears to hear the faint sound. Looking about, the silver backed wolf spies a bat, a runt of the liter, wilding flapping its wings, heading toward them. The little carnivorous creature circles Fitch and Jay several times before flapping and landing on Jay's shoulder.

The odd little beast looks at Jay. The human looks back. Content, the bat turns its head and focuses forward, perched along Jay's shoulder. Jay looks over toward Fitch who returns a puzzled look.

"Reckon this makes you some kinda batman," Fitch smiles.

"Sump'thn like that..." Jay answers with an unsure tone.

Fitch settles into his saddle, riding slowly along Blaze. Steele, the silver backed daytime guardian, trotting along side. Jay chuckles to himself, settling in on Diamond's saddle. His new nocturnal companion, resting easily on his shoulder. Approaching the lull in the slopping hillside, the troop of misfits ride toward the setting full moon, silhouetted images, fading into the night...

"So much has happened lately, I haven't had the time to write. The town has been wonderful to me, all pitching in to help rebuild the Katherine. A little work here, a little work there, everyone seems to be eager to help. Mr. Fuller from the bank, has been quite supportive. He let me keep the last of the money in Cougar's saddlebags from the robbery in January. Turns out, Mr. Fuller filed a hefty insurance policy with the government, some kinda new federal law or something.

From what I hear about town, the bank got more money back than The Cougar Gang had stolen in the first place."

"The Katherine should be reopened for business late in the summer. At least I can stay open using the lower floor, as long as my guests don't mind all the sawing and hammering away."

"Doc's been giving me more of his potions and cures. I truly think he's only doing experiments on me. The liquors' taste foul and don't do anything for me at all. At least they don't seem to be hurting the baby. Sarah Elizabeth. How do I tell her about her father? <u>What</u> do I tell her about her father? Or do I say nothing and let her to believe that Morris is her father?"

"I've decided to marry Morris this April. He's a good man. Still getting the hang of being sheriff of Purgatory. What is it with me and lawmen? Why couldn't I have found a rancher or a banker? Morris has a steady job and a spread outside of town. He's even talking about running for Mayor one day. We don't talk about Fitch or Jay much. Kinda skip over that subject. I know he'll be a good father to Sarah Elizabeth. We were planning on having children of our own... someday."

"I'm keeping the homestead. I figure I won't have much to give Sarah Elizabeth but the hotel and a place to live. I hope that will be enough. I'd like to see the house and hotel stay in the family."

"Fitch came in to town to look in after me last night. We... I don't see him to often anymore. He only comes to Purgatory at night. Always at night. I even see less of James these days. He usually stays only for a few minutes. They both look like they're not eating well. I shudder at that thought, what are they eating or I should say, "who" are they eating. Lost a bit of weight the both of them. They looked like they haven't bathed in months. A foul odor lingers about them."

"From time to time I wonder what is happening to them. What are they doing? How they're fairing? Where do they live? Do they live together or just ride together every once in awhile? Do they live in a home or a... or a cave? That night Fitch returned, changed everything."

"I wonder how my life would have turned out if I had stayed with Fitch or rather, if Fitch would have stayed with me. Then there's Jay. Dear, James. Fitch shoudda let him die that night instead of turning him into a dreadful creature. I've been reading through the book when I find the time. Odd book it is. I still really don't understand what happened to them. Why they turned and changed. Both cursed to walk the earth in eternal darkness..."

Bell frantically waves Doc inward. "'Bout'ta have the baby without 'ya, Doc," she takes him by the arm leading him through the opened door. The hanging horseshoe dangling above the upper door jam. The night, cool and crisp. The quarter moon hanging high in the early autumn sky. Robert douses his pipe and follows Bell and Doc inside. Beth screams out in pain from her back bedroom.

Trigger hovers over the wood burning potbelly stove continuing to tend to boiling pots of water. Robert finds a chair along he central wood planked table with a pair of flickering lit lanterns. Beth screams out again as Bell leads Doc down the short hallway to Beth's bedroom. Trigger takes hold of a pot of boiling water and scampers across the planked floor, following Doc and Bell.

Morris hovers along side the bed with Beth propped up along the headboard with a stack of down pillows. Bell rounds the far side of the bed looking anxiously down at Beth, covered in a layer of sweat, soaking her nightshirt. Trigger enters and begins to place the boiling pot of water on top of the Saratoga chest. "Not there!" Beth growls tightly gripping onto Morris' white knuckled hand.

Trigger scans the kerosene lit lantern room, scampers across and places the boiling pot onto the dresser. "Thank-you, Trigger," Doc smiles as he approaches him and leads him to the door. "You, too, Bell."

"What?" Bell exclaims as Doc motions her out of the room behind Trigger. "You've done all you can do. It's up to Beth now." Doc nearly shoves Bell out of the room and closes the door behind her. Almost sulking, Bell pulls up a chair opposite to Robert, fiddling with his smoldering pipe.

Morris stands at Beth's side, gripping onto her hand as the contractions continue. Doc places his black medical bag on top of the dresser next to the cooling pot of boiling water. Steam has begun to fill the air, slightly fogging up the windows. Doc takes a sheet and cleansed drying cloths in hand and places them around Beth's propped up feet and legs. "Are you ready, my dear?" Doc attempts a calming tone. Beth screams again, turning to look up toward Morris, still at her side clutching onto her tightening grip.

Doc lifts up the soaked blankets that cover Beth's lower areas, adjusts her propped up legs then covers the bottom of the bed with the sheet and cleansed cloths. Beth frantically looks down between her propped up legs down at Doc, looking calmly up at her then turns to look up at Morris. He smiles down at her, leans in and kisses her on the forehead. Beth lunges upward, another painful contraction. She screams, clutching onto Morris' hand, nearly crushing it.

"Push!" Doc exclaims, waiting for the baby's arrival. Beth leans upward and strains with all of her might. Morris looks down at Beth with awe then stares down at her covered and propped up legs then up toward Doc. Beth screams. "Push, Elizabeth!" Doc blurts out. "I can see the head!" Doc reaches down to Beth's lower area, preparing to welcome the baby into the world. Blood begins to cover the well placed sheet and cleansed cloths.

Beth grips onto Morris' hand, nearly breaking it. She heaves herself upward. Pushing. Straining. The pain. The pain. "The baby's head is out!" Doc declares, overjoyed as he removes the bloody child's shoulder, torso then legs, taking the infant in his trembling hands. Beth leans upward to see her baby. Morris smiles down with pride at Beth then also looks toward Doc who quickly wraps the newborn in the cleansed cloths. There is no sound from the child. No whimpering. No crying. Terror covers Beth's face. She begins to weep. Then… the baby begins to cry.

Beth nearly explodes with joy. Doc is beaming from ear to ear, cradling the baby in his arms, rounding the side of the bed. Beth reaches out, taking the baby in her arms, nestling it against her chest. Holding the infant close to her heart.

Doc smiles as Morris hovers over Beth and the baby. Doc moves across the room, wipes his bloody hands off on the last of the cleansed cloths then reaches into his black medical bag taking a large gulp of his flask of whiskey. The baby continues to cry in Beth's arms. A joyful and melodic sound.

Bell, Robert and Trigger explode into the room. Morris, the proud papa, smiles and motions them in. Lingering near the corner, Doc takes another swig of his whiskey flask. Standing arm in arm, Robert and Bell gaze down upon Beth and the wrapped baby who continues to cry. "Are they supos'd'ta do that?" Trigger asks.

"Yes," Beth tearfully smiles. "They're supposed to do that."

"Well, then," Robert leans inward. "What is it?"

"It's a baby," Trigger innocently answers.

"No, I mean "what is it?"" Robert repeats himself...

"It's a girl," Fitch answers as he walks through the tall wild grass about Beth's homestead. The home, warm and inviting behind him. He strolls up to Blaze and swings himself up into the saddle. Jay rests over his saddle horn atop Diamond, the little runt bat perched on his shoulder. Steele laying in the tall grass, wagging his tail. Jay glances over toward Fitch, looking oddly at his discontented expression.

"Congratulations, Fitch," Jay replies in a calming tone. Fitch tosses Jay a look. "No, really. Congratulations, you're a papa."

"Thank-you, James," Fitch pauses with a reluctant smile. "Thank-you. Reckon that makes you an uncle."

"Uncle Batman," Jay chuckles. "Kinda gotta ring to it."

"Let's get goin'. It's gettin' late."

"You mean early," Jay smiles. "Still haven't quite got used to the nighttime thing, yet."

"You will," Fitch fatherly responds. "You will..." Fitch maneuvers Blaze about. Steele springs to his feet and trots along side. Jay takes a final glance at Beth's home. Warm and inviting. Taking the reigns in hand, he turns Diamond about, coming up along side of Fitch and Blaze. The runt bat, still perched on his shoulder.

"I'm hungry," Jay announces to Fitch as they come up over the lull in the grassy hillside, heading away from Beth's homestead.

"Me, too..."

"Eternal damnation is what I would call it. Fitch and Jay. Forced to walk the night forever. I wonder what will become of them. Jay, the Deputy, the friend, will always be at his side. And Fitch. Fearless yet wanting. I hope he finds what he is searching for. Fitch didn't find it in Purgatory."

"Maybe one day, Fitch, my true love, will return to me and we will live as we should have. A family. Father and mother. Husband and wife. For richer or poorer. For sickness and in health. Till death do us part..."

CHAPTER XIII

"Good-morning, ladies and gentlemen," the captain of the 747 politely announces over the aircraft's intercom. The opposite facing rows of passengers begin to unbuckle their seatbelts, rise and collect their carry-on luggage from the upper storage areas. "It's about five minutes till noon. We've arrived in Albuquerque just in time for lunch. The current temperature is a cool seventy-eight degrees," the captain pauses a moment. "Thank-you for flying with Eastern Air and on behalf of myself and the rest of our friendly staff, we wish you a pleasant day and hope to see you soon."

Caroline Moores, Sarah's mother and Madelyn Buffet, Sarah's grandmother, shuffle along with the rest of the departing passengers through the tunneled gangway. Totting their sparse carry-on luggage in hand, the attractive pair of women look tossed and worn from the extended cross country flight.

Caroline is middle aged, appearing in her mid to late fifties, wears a soft textured dress, light colored and comfortable for the journey. Her hair is cut short about her neck line with teased bangs. Strands of fiery red locks attempt to hide the impending gray. Her mother, Madelyn, is well preserved for nearly eighty years old. Quite spry in her step, keeping up with her only surviving child. Gray has taken over Madelyn's strawberry blonde hair, loosely tied with a bow along the shoulders of her outdated attire. "Mother! Gran'ma! Over here!" Sarah's welcoming voice blurts out from the nearing end of the gangway.

"Sarah, my dear. You look marvelous!" Madelyn reaches out her arms. Sarah kisses Gran'ma on the cheek and gives her a warm embrace. The departing passengers file passed them entering the terminal of the airport. Sarah sports a dress t-shirt, jeans and cowboy boots. Her fiery locks of hair flowing freely behind herself. Sarah and Madelyn tenderly part, drawing Sarah's attention to Caroline.

"Mother…"

"Sarah…" Caroline and Sarah almost reluctantly move in toward each other, timidly embracing. The greeting is not as warm nor welcoming as Sarah and Gran'ma's. Seeing the tension of the past years still lingering between the two, Madelyn cheerfully bolts forward with her carry-on in hand.

"Well, then. We're off! Not looking toward the drive ahead." Madelyn tromps off ahead beginning to weave her way in and out of the arriving and departing passengers filling the terminal. Without a word, Sarah reaches down and collects one of her mother's carry-ons, leading her into the maze of herding people.

"I put the top up for you, Gran'ma," Sarah smiles piling the last of Madelyn's luggage into the opened trunk of her convertible.

"Thank-you, my dear. Though I reckon the wind might do this 'ole mop of mine some good," Madelyn tosses her fingers through her grey and strawberry blonde hair. Sarah politely chuckles, taking her mother's luggage in hand, plopping it along side in the trunk. Caroline slides into the opened passenger's side of the convertible, riding shotgun as Sarah leads Gran'ma along the driver's side, assisting her into the backseat.

"You'll be more comfortable in the back. Figured you might need a nap on the way."

"I'm old but not that old, dear," Madelyn playfully snorts. Sarah laughs, bringing her driver's seat upward with Gran'ma settling into the back. Sarah slides in behind the wheel, starting up the engine. Looking back into the rearview mirror, Gran'ma Madelyn has already passed out, fallen asleep with her head propped up on the top of the backseat, cocked to the side.

"Right, mother," Caroline sarcastically whispers. Sarah tosses Caroline a glare, then rests her dark sunglasses on her freckled nose. It's going to be a long drive…

The inviting rays of the early afternoon sun warm the top of Sarah's convertible as it continues down the narrow two lane highway at a moderate speed. The vast wasteland of the desert spans out all around them. Sparse clusters of Joshua Trees and rolling tumbleweeds provide the only scenery. The convertible, quiet with no conversation.

Sarah leans to the side of the rolled down window driving with her other hand. She stares blankly forward along the never ending stretch of road. Her hair flopping through the wind along her shoulders. Caroline sits plainly in silence, tossing a glance over to her daughter from time to time. In the backseat, Madelyn continues to snore and nap. "So," Caroline finally attempts a conversation after nearly two hours in the car. "How's the writing coming along?"

"Fine, mother," Sarah almost snarls.

""Mother"," Caroline thinks to herself. *"I don't like the way that sounded."* Caroline shifts her weight in the seat, pausing a moment, preparing to try again at a civil conversation. "Working on anything new?"

"I'm always working on something new," Sarah adjusts her sunglasses higher on the bridge of her nose as if she were trying to hide from her mother merely two feet away.

"I phoned ahead," Caroline reluctantly changes the subject. "I had three dozen roses sent to the funeral home."

"Do you think three dozen are enough?" Sarah quietly snaps.

"Sarah…" Caroline changes her tone, motherly, at least an attempt of motherly.

"The services will be held on Tuesday. I've taken care of everything, mother."

""Mother", she said it again!" Caroline fumes to herself.

"There wasn't much left after the fire," Sarah glances out the opened window. Caroline is silent, tossing her daughter a look. "All that was left a few gun barrels, part of the rocking chair, the firemen pretty much totaled the Persian rug," Sarah pauses a moment. "Oh... and the chest."

"The chest?" Madelyn chimes in from the backseat. Caroline looks back over her shoulder. Madelyn is fully awake, sitting up and forward.

"Yeah, the chest made it through. It was pretty scorched," Sarah suddenly becomes excited with her tone. "You wouldn't believe what was inside!"

"Was there a blue dress inside?" Gran'ma asks in a low voice.

"Yes!" Sarah exclaims. "How did you know about the blue dress?" Sarah lowers her sunglasses and looks at Madelyn through the rearview mirror. Gran'ma has an odd and puzzling look on her face as she leans back into the backseat.

"I was married in that dress..." Madelyn sighs.

The convertible stands parked a few dozen yards away from the charred remains of the house on the hill. The rolling wild desert grass sways back and forth to the light breeze with the setting sun casting amber and orange colors across the sky. Sarah strolls along the tall grass below the blackened porch. The charred rocking chair, slightly moving to the breeze.

Caroline stands along side of the remaining portion of the hearth and chimney. She carefully runs her hands across the tops of the cindered picture frames and burned trinkets along top the hearth. Madelyn slowly moves across the central floor. The soaked rug squishes under her feet. There is nothing left in the house. Nothing but fading memories of her youth.

Sarah strolls along the side of the porch, glances toward the old, run down log cabin and lean-to in the distance. The amber colors of the setting sun, beaming through the opened windows and door. The desert grass surrounding the wooden planked porch, dancing in the wind. The rusting horseshoe, hanging above the opened front door. "We should be going," Caroline carefully steps off the charred porch, heading toward the parked convertible.

Madelyn stands motionless in the center of the burned remains of the house, her home, so many years ago. What would have changed if she had of stayed? Would Great, Great, Great, Great Grandma Meme still be alive? Would she have burned in the fire as well? So many questions, never to be answered. Madelyn tenderly raises her opened palm to her hand, presses her lips to her fingertips and blows a kiss into the air. With a single tear rolling down her cheek, Gran'ma turns and slowly makes her way toward the convertible.

Standing along side of Sarah, Madelyn smiles at her granddaughter, patting her lovingly on the shoulder. Sarah pushes the driver's seat forward, allowing Madelyn into the backseat. A shadow catches Madelyn's eye. Moving inside and through the rotting log cabin in the distance. Madelyn pauses a moment, transfixed to the cabin. The setting sun playing games with her vision. The shadow inside moves again, then vanishes. "I know, Gran'ma," Sarah smiles. "I've seen it, too." Sarah returns the pat of affection on Madelyn's shoulder.

Caroline quickly turns toward the distant decaying log cabin. She stares at it a long moment. Looking deep into each window. One by one. Then into the opened door with the rusting horseshoe hanging from above. There is nothing there. Caroline sees nothing... she never has.

"Gracious, me," Madelyn exclaims from the backseat. She leans up and forward, clinging onto the top backs of Sarah and Caroline's forward seats. Madelyn is in awe, looking about herself. "Things haven't changed a bit!"

"How long has it been since you've been back, Gran'ma?" Sarah asks as she slows the convertible into the city limits of Purgatory. Madelyn pauses for a long moment, adding the years in her head.

"Its eleven summers, this May," Madelyn responds, looking about herself. Caroline remains still in the front passenger's seat for a moment.

"Nine for me," Caroline turns toward her daughter. "Reckon you know that already." Sarah and Caroline exchange painful looks. Nine years. Nine years... Caroline's husband, Sarah's father, was lost to them. They haven't spoken for about nine long years. Funny... how one death can separate a family and another death can bring them back together. Funny... no, not really.

"Hell's Bells!" Madelyn blurts out as the convertible slowly continues to roll along. The busty, period era dressed actress strolls along the wrap around porch of Bell's. Tourists linger in and out of the swinging batwing doors carrying bags of bought trinkets and souvenirs. The modern facilities are a far cry from when Madelyn used to wander about Main Street.

City Hall. The bank, now having changed several times of name and ownership, no longer the Wells Fargo of days gone past. Miss Katy's Boarding house stands solid and firm. The facing rows of general stores and shops, now transformed into tourists traps, salons and hotels. Hotels... The Katherine Hotel stands firm and inviting. It's opened door along the wooden planked boardwalk where Madelyn used to play.

Sarah slows the convertible to the sole stoplight in the center of town with the opposing street cutting across Main Street. Young men, actors dressed in period attire, hobble along their stilts, mimicking lighting the corner lampposts. With current electricity, there is no need for them, just a part of the show. Attracting more tourists to Purgatory, more and more every year. More and more to hear the blazing story of the Valentine's Day Massacre of 1866. If they only knew the truth...

"The Stardust Saloon," Madelyn finally leans back in the backseat. "Hadn't changed much. Still full of riff-raff." True, out of all the accomplished businesses and current upgrades of Purgatory, the Stardust Saloon is where most of the younger generation resides, partying, getting soused, continuing their lewd behavior. Madelyn's attention focuses on the last building on the left side of Main Street, the train depot then the railroad tracks. She takes a deep breath for she knows what's to her right…

Purgatory's sheriff's office and jail along side of the livery at the end of Main Street. The handsome actor, dressed in a tall, wide brimmed, Stetson hat, ivory handled Colt revolvers holstered at his hips, shiny sheriff's badge pinned to his chest and the pair of silver spurs at his boot heels. *Jangle-jangle.* The sounds of the spurs are different than before. More muffled. Dim and wanting. *Jangle-jangle.*

The young sheriff actor waves his hands in the air, motioning toward a gathering of tourists, hanging on his every word. The monologue rambles, fleeting, not making sense. "It's all rubbish," Madelyn barks out.

"How would you know, Gran'ma?" Sarah asks as she slightly accelerates the convertible.

"I told you, dear. I was *married* in that dress." Not paying attention to her driving, Sarah nearly swerves and hits a row of parked cars along the wooden boardwalk. Staring blankly into the rearview mirror, Sarah tosses off her sunglasses as the convertible crosses over the railroad tracks. The fading sun dips deep over the horizon. The full moon, slowly rising into the cloudless sky. The light of the lampposts about the corners of Main Street, glowing on her cheeks.

"And yes, dear," Madelyn affectionately smiles. "I've read them, too…"

Sarah's convertible stands parked in her driveway. The garage door is closed. A faint light seeps from under the door with shadows of activity inside. Sarah's house, lit up along the lower floor, table lamps and lit lanterns. A few clouds float across the night's sky. The full moon seems to hang in place. Not rising nor setting. Just resting in the sky… watching.

Sarah bursts in through the side door of the garage leading in from the side of the house. The straggly ivy branches and leaves tossing through her hair. In each hand, she carries a cup of steaming coffee. Pausing a moment, Sarah kicks the side garage door closed with her foot, then continues onward toward her mother and Gran'ma. "I hope I remembered how you like it," Sarah replies as she hands them their coffee.

"I'm sure it'll be fine," Madelyn smiles as she takes a sip. Caroline is not so pleased, looking down into the straight black coffee. At least some creamer would have been nice. Sarah's expression and enthusiasm is overwhelming. A kid in a candy store. A child going to the circus for the first time. A daughter discovering a long lost treasure of her family.

"You wouldn't believe what I found!" Sarah exclaims darting across the floor. Caroline and Madelyn set their steaming coffee mugs on the wagon wheel coffee table, sitting each on opposite facing leather bound couches. The wagon wheel coffee table, cluttered with stacks upon stacks of newspapers, all with yellow post-its stuck to their front pages. Scribbled with notes in Sarah's handwriting. "Look, Gran'ma!" Sarah faces a wall of shelved books on the far side of the garage.

Sarah quickly lifts up a makeshift covering of plastic trash bags from a hanging object... the blue dress. Covered with lace and tassels. Sarah takes the dress from the hanger and places it against herself as if to try out the size and fit. Madelyn raises up and slowly makes her way across the floor, facing her granddaughter. "It's just like I remember it," Madelyn tenderly takes the dress in hand and presses it up against herself. She can almost hear the wedding march in her head. Seeing her beloved late husband taking her hands, placing her ring on her finger.

"Gran'ma?" Sarah whispers with a smile, bringing Madelyn out of her near trance. She lovingly takes the dress and returns it to the hanger. Madelyn strolls her way back to the leather couch, sits and sips at her coffee, quietly facing her daughter. "...and look," Sarah dashes across the floor heading toward her cluttered work area. Her computer dark at the moment but with a push of a button, the screen comes to life.

Thousands of typed and printed words. Using the mouse, Sarah scrolls to the top of the article, the story. "I've been reading and writing all weekend. The story of Grandma Meme and of Sheriff Fitch Woolley, my great, great, great, great, grandfather. I think that was enough "greats"". Sarah scrolls to the cover page... "*SLINGER*".

The opposite sides of her computer and keyboard, cluttered with stacks of Beth's onion paper diaries. Sarah looks proud of herself in an almost astounded way. "I've been working on the piece all weekend." Caroline leans to the side of the couch, timidly reaching for the top stack of newspapers covered with post-its. "Oh," Sarah exclaims. "Here's yours, mother."

""Mother"? The way she said it that time nearly sounded...sincere," Caroline thinks as Sarah plops down on the couch next to her. She reaches for the top newspaper then to the fading page of their family tree, Sarah compares the two.

"Here you are on the family tree," Sarah points to the faded page, "...and here's your newspaper on the day you were born." Sarah lunges forward, taking Madelyn's newspaper in hand, moving the post-it to the side. "...and here's yours, Gran'ma." Sarah hands the newspaper to Madelyn and motions to her name on the faded family tree. Taking a more current looking newspaper from the stack, Sarah motions toward the date then toward the family tree. "Here's mine. The paper was on my birthday. The family tree goes all the way back to Theodore Woolley's death in 1852. That's the first one." Sarah reaches into the opened Saratoga trunk at the end of the couch.

In hand, Sarah places a small stack of aging dime novels, Jay's blood stained deputy's badge, several of The Cougar Gang's charred wanted fliers, the book of "MYTHS AND LEGENDS", the several tin types, the one of Fitch and Beth at the carnival as well as the one with Beth holding onto baby Sarah Elizabeth in her arms, Morris, Cleo and the workers in front of the restored Katherine Hotel and several stacks of additional onion paper diaries. "I haven't quite got to all of them yet, I figure I've got at least fifteen or so years to go," Sarah replies. Madelyn places her newspaper onto the wagon wheel coffee table, sadly reaching for the current weekend's edition newspaper. "Oh, that one's Meme's." A deathly stillness falls across the room. "I picked it up Friday. Seems there was no one else to do it. Somebody has to keep up with the family tree and newspapers."

"...and that somebody is you, my dear," Madelyn tenderly whispers. Sarah looks up toward her with a puzzled look as Madelyn reaches up from behind her neck. She unclasps and removes Beth's locket she had received from Jay for her birthday. Madelyn reaches across the table, loops and clasps the locket around Sarah's neck. "My mother, Stephanie Evens, gave it to me. Sarah Elizabeth O'Donnell gave it to her. Sarah Elizabeth O'Donnell was not the daughter of Morris Allen and Elizabeth O'Donnell," Madelyn pauses to take a sip of her coffee. "Sarah Elizabeth was the daughter of Elizabeth O'Donnell and Fitch Woolley." Madelyn pauses a moment, "... but you knew that already."

"Oh, Gran'ma!" Sarah looks loving down at the locket. "Speaking of Fitch, there's one thing that's really puzzling me." Madelyn and Caroline toss each other a concerned glance. Knowing what questions are to come. Sarah takes the faded family tree in hand, sliding her finger across the fragile page. "Here's Fitch's name," she sets the page onto the table. "Here's the newspaper when Fitch was born. I got it from the public records back East." Sarah leans forward and digs through the older stacks of newspapers covered with post-its. She reaches down to the bottom, lifting a pair of worn and tattered papers.

"Here's where Elizabeth died, about when the diaries stopped," she shuffles the papers, "...and here's where Meme, Meme Sarah I'm guessing who I was named after, was born and here's the one I picked up on Friday," Sarah continues to shuffle through the stacks of newspapers.

"What's puzzling you then, dear," Madelyn asks in a reluctant tone.

"Where's Fitch Woolley's newspaper with his obituary in it?" Sarah looks blankly toward her mother then toward Gran'ma. "I mean, I couldn't find it here," Sarah stands and crosses the garage, facing her keyboard and computer screen. She half turns around to face Madelyn and Caroline, fiddling with the keys of the computer as she speaks. "I surfed the net for coroner reports, family trees and histories. I went down to the newspaper and looked through their archives on microfilm. I even went to city hall and the hall of records. It's simply not there."

"Maybe Great Meme had lost it," Caroline responds.

"Or maybe it was never picked up or bought," Madelyn chimes in.

"No!" Sarah insists as she crosses the room heading back toward the leather bound couches and wagon wheeled coffee table. She plops down on the couch next to Caroline, feverishly looking through the stacks of old and worn newspapers. "It <u>has</u> to be here."

KNOCK-KNOCK.

It came from the closed side door leading out of the garage into the side of the house. Madelyn turns pale with fright with her coffee mug trembling in her cupped hands. "Were you expecting anyone, dear," Gran'ma whispers to Sarah.

KNOCK-KNOCK-KNOCK.

"Not at this hour," Sarah rises from the couch along side of Caroline, strolls across the floor and heads toward the closed side door of the garage.

Jingle-jingle...